A TOUCH OF DANGER

He was really very fast. One second he was standing in front of me, the next he had danced in, delivered me a kick in the groin and danced back out.

I was not just furious. I was crazy mad. The pain in my groin was already enough, but I was thinking of the lovely sexy Marie, of Girgis, of the hippies with their violence and their drugs . . .

There was a kind of crazy joy in it. I didn't care if he killed me. If he did, I'd kill him along with me . . .

Available in Fontana by the same author

From Here to Eternity
The Thin Red Line
Go to the Widow-Maker
The Merry Month of May

JAMES JONES

A Touch of
Danger

FONTANA/Collins

First published in 1973 by William Collins Sons & Co Ltd
First issued in Fontana Books 1975

Made and printed in Great Britain by
William Collins Sons & Co Ltd Glasgow

'I wish that strife would vanish away from among gods and mortals, and gall, which makes a man grow angry for all his great mind, that gall of anger that swarms like smoke inside of a man's heart and becomes a thing sweeter to him by far than the dripping of honey.'

Achilles, in *The Iliad of Homer*
Lattimore Translation

GLORIA
Old Trooper
Young Beauty

CHAPTER ONE

The taxi taking me from the Athens Hilton to the Piraeus ferry dock roared around the last cloverleaf of new road and slid in against the high kerb like a scared baserunner with his cleats bared. My neck was jerked. The already dented hubcaps grated and clashed against the badly poured Greek concrete. Before it was stopped, the paunchy moustachioed driver was out of it waving his arms and running for the ferry where a cluster of ship's officers stood together in white uniforms being important.

I had made the mistake of telling him to step on it, that I was running a little late. Now – to buy himself a big tip – he was going to pretend he had personally held the ship's sailing in order to get me aboard.

After a moment to straighten my neck, I gathered my old trenchcoat and hat and briefcase and got out and went over to what had to be the ticket booth. When I said, 'Tsatsos,' the old man in the hotbox made out a pink ticket form and counted on his fingers for me how much I owed him in drachmas.

Around us heat shimmered on the Athens plain. Back from the cleared area for the new road, the buildings seemed to gasp in it. At my feet a square of feverish ill-looking lawn set in the concrete was dusted with it. Athens itself, the Athens of Socrates and Aristophanes and Jackie Kennedy, was not visible from here.

The cab driver came back. 'All A-okay,' he grinned. 'All fine, boss. All fixed up now.'

'My suitcase is still in your trunk,' I said.

His eyes widened. He had forgotten it. He came back with it striding importantly, and handed it grandiloquently to a tottery ancient in a long blue smock and cap who was supposed to fool people like me that he was a porter.

I paid the driver. I gave him his big tip. I have never known how to deal with phonies who pretend they've done more for you than they actually have. You'd think a hard-nosed private detective with fire in his eye would learn how to handle that, but I never have. One of the minor reasons I remained so broke, probably.

I followed the ancient with my suitcase to the ship, hoping he would not collapse with it. The ship was moored stern-on to the quay and connected by a rickety gangplank made of old boards that bowed with every step of every passenger. The ship's officers were herding across it a small mob of Greek citizens carrying paper sacks and cardboard cartons tied with rope. One officer took my ticket and looked at it and passed it to another one. The second one looked at it, tore off the perforated end, which he handed to a slave behind him, and gave it to a third one. The third looked at it as if inspecting it for signs of contraband and handed it back to me with a hard stare. Thus they created work for three men out of a job one guy would have found it hard to spend all his time at. I stared just as hard back at them. They weren't used to that.

I followed the ancient across the swaying plank, matching my steps to the motion and taking the swing with my knees. I was worried about him. I had lived on the edge of collapse myself, in too many different places and too long. But he was good. He was shaky, but he conserved his meagre energy. He deposited my suitcase by the rail in a gangway already crowded with the belongings of other people. Paper sacks oozing juice of squashed fruit; boxes dripping melted sugar at the low corner in the heat. I gave him a big tip, too. I've always been a sucker for over-tipping. The theory is they will remember you if you ever pass that way again. I have never found that it ever got me any extra service or smiles.

The tiny dining-room, when I finally found it amongst all the bellowing adults, screaming kids and barking animals, was nice. But it had been taken over by a bunch of English boys in wild clothes who looked like fag set designers. I found myself a rusting folding chair up forward on the main deck under the tarpaulin and put my feet up on the rail. After a while the ship's horn hooted twice and we departed. Astern, the port and the plain got misty and dim in the heat haze.

So was beginning my month's free, paid vacation. I was already feeling it was a bad mistake, even before I got on board. It was a six hours' trip, to the island of Tsatsos.

'You'll love it down there,' Freddy Tarkoff had told me

on the phone, at the end of my New York call. Freddy Tarkoff was my client. My rich client. My only rich client. Freddy was pleased with the job I had done for him in Europe.

'Just sit in the tavernas, and swim a little, and toast yourself on the beach. Nothing to do but loaf and scratch. You're a spearfisherman, aren't you?'

'I used to be,' I said.

'It's my present to you. I appreciate what you've done, Lobo. It's all laid on. There's a lady friend of mine down there who's setting everything up, and will look after you personally while you're there. Her name is the Countess Chantal von Anders. Got the name?'

Something in his tone of voice stated delicately that he knew her a good bit better than as just a friend.

'I've instructed her to apply herself to your every wish. She's renting a house for you. And a boat with an expert spearfisherman.'

'Okay, I'll go.' I choked on it a little, and it came out too flat, because it was hard for me to say it. I'm inclined to be over-proud.

'You'll love it down there,' he said again.

So here I was. There was a gang of hippie kids under the big tarpaulin, most of them American, a few English. As soon as we were at sea they got out their guitars and about fifty bottles of cheap red wine, and sang folk songs and got drunk and effectively elbowed away from them all the people who were nearby. They made me feel very old. I heard one of them say they were going to Tsatsos, too. I looked ahead bleakly to six hours of their scintillating company.

Six hours' trip to Tsatsos. Well, I had plenty to think about. There was my job for Freddy. There was my life. There was my recent divorce. I didn't want to think about any of them.

I wasn't half as pleased with my job for Tarkoff as he was; for different reasons. My life I wasn't pleased with either, but I didn't know what to do about it. As for my divorce I didn't know whether I was pleased with that or not.

Tarkoff was a good friend. Tarkoff knew a lot about my personal life. That was probably why he organized this junket. I didn't like anybody knowing that much about my personal life.

I gave myself up to the sea. There was a grubby juice and booze bar at the back of the main lounge, run by two short-tempered Greeks who resembled Dean Martin and Jerry Lewis. I got the biggest Scotch they could pour into the biggest smeared glass they had, and brought it back with me and put my feet back up. Like most men from the great middle part of the American continent I had an unreasonable passion for the sea. I took my feet back down and allowed myself to be rudely elbowed farther forward by the expanding rim of the hippie circle without saying anything, then put my feet back up.

The overweight sun beyond the tarpaulin glinted off the wavelets and hammered the sea's face into hundreds of silver collages. Moisture rose from the surface so heavily it gave an opal haze to the air and pinkened the passing ships and islands. The ship's engines rumbled pleasantly in the sea quiet. I sipped my Scotch. There was plenty of time to think about the unpleasant things later. Things like my life.

I listened to the rumbling ship's engines carrying me along, and relaxed. I shouldn't have. I should have grabbed a buoy and jumped overboard; and flagged down a passing tramp to carry me straight back to the Athens Hilton and the airport.

CHAPTER TWO

In the six hours we passed about twenty islands, and stopped at seven of them. All around us tall blue headlands stood up out of the sea. If you didn't know the chart, you could not tell which were islands and which were hills on the mainland. I went back twice for refills of my big smeary Scotch glass. I figured the whisky would antiseptisize the glass.

Finally, the ship headed in for a black humpback whale of a headland straight in front of us, and the hippie kids behind me began putting their guitars away and throwing their sandwich wrappers and empty wine bottles over the side. I watched them. I had just been listening to them talk about pollution.

The distinctive thing about Tsatsos was that it was green. The rest of the land we passed was as dry as a Boy Scout's fire kit. I was assured by every Greek I met that it was not the Greeks who cut off all the timber in Greece, but the Turks. Whoever it was, they certainly did a superior job of it. But somehow they missed Tsatsos.

As it floated closer to us, its single town showed white-white along the sea edge. The green rising behind it accentuated the white. A crusty old Colonel Blimp of an Englishman told me the white dots spotted here and there on the hills were Greek Orthodox chapels. Each one was built on the site of an ancient pagan temple.

A pretty little lighthouse made a white and black checkered spindle at one end of the town. At the other, west end was another landmark not so prepossessing. On a large headland somebody with the taste of an ape had started a big construction of modern apartment units and never finished it. Abandoned in mid-job – in mid-trowel stroke it seemed. Straight-line construction units of four and six apartments, on spindly pre-poured concrete stilts, covered most of the headland and loomed over the town below. Most of them were still uncovered red construction brick, without even door or window frames. It made a real eyesore.

Below it beside the sea in the gathering dusk was what looked like a modern luxury tourist hotel, complete with lush gardens and clients.

Next to me two of the American hippie girls were pointing at the construction site and giggling. Apparently that was where they were going. 'That's the Construction,' one of them whispered to the other.

Behind us the ship's horn high up on the mast gave one long hoot and the engines started churning in reverse, preparing to land us at the big concrete jetty which also served as breakwater for the tiny port.

Nobody met me at the ferry. If the Countess Chantal von Anders was supposed to be looking after me, she wasn't doing her job. The Countess had flunked out on the very first stage. I began to feel depressed again. I picked up my suitcase and went to look for a taxi.

No private cars were allowed on the island, it turned out, and the taxis were two-wheeled horsecabs, of the type that in the 19th century were called cabriolets. In fact, that is where the word cab originally comes from. There was a gang of them in a little square not far from the jetty.

The centre of town was as lit up as a night rocket launching, and had a carnival air about it. Like all resorts in season. Tourists, and a great number of hippies, strolled up and down. Up a little rise from the jetty and the small boat moorings of the Port itself, there was a high wall on the land side with a tree-shaded terrace of cafés on its top. Strings of coloured lights swayed just under the tree branches.

Fortunately for me, I knew the name of my new landlady. I found a cabman who spoke a little English. When I said, 'The Mrs Georgina Taylor house,' he nodded, then laughed a malicious laugh, but he did not explain why. I did not like the laugh.

The town darkened quickly, outside the Port area. We headed east, toward the pretty little lighthouse. We clop-clopped along the seawall road where more hippie groups were strolling. Most of the houses here were built up, at the top of two stories of slanting wall designed to baffle big winter seas. We came around a point and had in front of us suddenly the little lighthouse, the yacht harbour, and the lights of a taverna.

The lighthouse was built out at the end of a long curving arm of land. Directly across from it on the land side were the taverna lights. In between, and reaching almost to our point, small boats and five sailing yachts rocked tranquilly in the lap and chop, protected from the sea's swell outside. The driver stopped at the very last house before the taverna. Between them was a sloping vacant lot. The house was built up the slope and had a wall around it. In the wall was a faded blue-painted door.

'Georgina Taylor Haus,' the driver said.

I held out my palm and let him take what change he wanted, thinking putting him on his honour would make him honest. I found out later he cheated and overcharged me anyway.

When I opened the garden door, it was darker inside, because of two or three scraggly trees. A stone walk led up the slope to the house, and to another blue garden door on the upper street with a brass ship's bell above it. The house had no light in it. But a sort of basement apartment under it built out from the slope of the hill had lights on, and a kerosene lantern burned smokily in the yard. Four figures, two men and two women, sat in its poor light on some outdoor furniture. One of them, a man, got up. He came over to me across the gravel.

He was Con Taylor, he told me, the house's owner and Georgina's husband. They had been waiting on me. Since they heard the ferry come in. They had begun to think I wasn't on it. I said something about having to find myself a cab, and he smiled.

'Chantal didn't meet you? Oh, well. She's inclined to be absent-minded.'

He was a medical scientist, he told me, in a big Athens physics research lab, and had to take the same ferry back tonight. He spoke almost perfect English. The name Taylor sounded English or American, but this guy was pure Greek. I found out later the name came from some romantic ancestor who came to Greece to fight with Byron, and married into an all-Greek family.

He introduced me to the others. Georgina Taylor, clearly English, was a tall woman with her long hair skinned back and tied at the neck. She had enormous eyes, and two small wens on her face. She looked like the salt air and gravity together were slowly drying her up and shrinking her. I couldn't see anything about her that would make the cabman laugh like that.

The other couple were called Sonny and Jane Duval. Americans. Sonny Duval was a big shaggy man, with long hair and an Elliot Gould moustache. He looked forty-four or -five, too old to be the hippie he was dressed as. Jane Duval was more than twenty years his junior, but other than that I couldn't get any fix on her. She was just sullen. She seemed negligent of the three-year-old daughter it turned out that they had with them. I hadn't seen the tiny girl in the bad light.

It was clear that the Taylors were fighting, but trying to hide it in front of me. Tension stretched the air. I had dropped right into the middle of a domestic crisis. The Duvals were apparently witnesses. There seemed to be an odd disquiet between the two couples, covered up in front of me, as if they had all stopped arguing when I opened the garden door.

15

In my trade, you learned early on how to assess situations of this sort very quickly. Well, it wasn't any of my business. But what a hell of a way to start off my free month.

'This is Mr Frank Davies,' Con Taylor said, 'who will be taking the house. I understand they also call you Lobo. That's a timber wolf, isn't it, in the United States?'

'It means that,' I said. 'It also means loner, out in the West where I come from. A solitary.'

'Delightful. Do you mind if we call you that? Lobo?' Con Taylor asked, 'I like that.'

'Not if it makes you feel good,' I said.

'Sonny here is going to be your boat man,' Georgina Taylor cried, too brightly, and emitted a kind of high despairing giggle. 'So in a way we're all your employees. I hope you don't mind our keeping the basement apartment for ourselves.'

'No. I don't mind,' I said. I looked again at the big over-age hippie.

As if aware he was being inspected, the big man got to his feet, and seemed to keep unfolding more and more of himself as he stood up. He was at least six-two because he was at least three inches taller than me. He smiled cheerfully behind his moustache. But his mind seemed a million miles away. A huge peace medallion dangled from his neck. His wife simply sat, sullenly. 'Yeah, I'm going to be working for you.' He put out a meaty hand. 'Chantal von Anders hired me and my boat for the month you'll be here. Be available to you from nine in the morning till six at night.' He sat back down, and seemed to lapse into a kind of tongueless gloom.

'Come on,' Con Taylor said. 'I'll take you up and show you the house and how everything works.' He smiled in a smug way.

I followed him up the walk. It was nice to get out of that tension.

The house was very nice, though much too big for a lone man. Inside the front door three steps on the right led up to a long living-room with a fireplace, french windows and tile floor. One huge long beam supported the ceiling of the room. At the other end a fine porch showed the harbour beyond thick stone arches that gave it a pleasant cave-like feeling. Everything was made of wood and chintz and materials that would stand up against mould in the wet sea air. The bedrooms were on a second floor. It was the kind of place where you expected James Mason and the Flying Dutchman might walk in and pour themselves a brandy at any moment.

Taylor showed me where the electric fuses and the circuit breaker were, and how to turn on and off the French-style hot water heater for the bathtub. There was no shower. I also inherited from the Taylors a Greek woman who sniffed at my one bag as if it had dead rats in it, as she took it upstairs to unpack it.

'I'm sorry I have to leave tonight,' Con Taylor said before he left. 'But I'll be back in two weeks. And then I'll be here two weeks for my summer vacation.'

I said that was just wonderful. We shook hands.

A little later, after I had looked at the bedrooms and was standing on my new porch with a drink in my hand, I heard the Taylors arguing in the basement apartment below, as Con packed a bag. It was about a woman, naturally.

So here I was. And my landlords were fighting. And they were keeping their basement apartment. And I was supposed to say fine. I raised my glass of Scotch to toast the waxing moon. Below, Con Taylor came out slamming the door to rush down the walk and take a horsecab to the ferry. The moonlight was beautiful on the susurrating waters of the little harbour.

CHAPTER THREE

I pleased my Greek housekeeper enormously by telling her she didn't have to cook dinner for me. I ate a plate of lamb-stew guk at the lighted taverna across the vacant lot. I was again standing on my cavey porch with a glass of Scotch in my hand looking at the moonlit harbour, when Georgina Taylor called up to me from below.

'Are you up there all alone?'

Politely I invited her up for a drink. It was a definite mistake and I knew it. Inviting people in for a nightcap is one of the slower forms of suicide.

She was already a little drunk. And once she was there, inside, she began to put the Scotch away like an NFL linebacker on the night after a losing season. It was Scotch they had thoughtfully provided for me, along with the bill. She got quite drunk on it, quite soon.

It was as if she could hardly wait till the amenities were over before plunging in and pouring out her story.

'It's a shame you should be here all alone like this on your first night here.'

'I don't mind it,' I said.

'How are you finding the house?'

'It's a little big for one man.'

'I told them that. You must have done something quite remarkable for Freddy Tarkoff.'

'We're old friends.'

On the second large whisky she dispensed with the subterfuge of soda altogether, but did accept ice.

'Are you really a private detective?'

I gestured.

'I ought to hire you to get the goods on Con for me.'

'I don't take divorce cases. They get too messy.'

'No? Doesn't matter. I've got the goods on him myself, anyway. He's never bothered to try and hide them.'

'What you need is a lawyer, then.'

'Oh,' she said inconclusively. Then, 'I suppose I shall never do anything about it. It really is a lovely night, out.'

'Lovely.'

'You don't talk a great hell of a lot, do you?'

I didn't answer that.

She thrust out her glass. She accepted a third large one, with ice, before launching herself.

'Con is having an affair with Sonny Duval's wife.' She twisted the word wife savagely, to make sure I understood Jane Duval wasn't one.

'And I'm supposed to say I'm sorry about that, is that it?' I said. I made it blunt.

She ignored it completely. 'They aren't really married, "*the* Duvals",' Georgina Taylor said. 'They don't believe in getting married.' She looked at me, evidently for some comment. I didn't make any. At this point it wasn't going to make any difference whether I did or not.

'This is not the first affair Jane Duval has had on the island. But this time she seems to have flipped. I suppose that's my Con. He could honey-talk the devil himself. Anyway, she claims Con promised to take her away. Away from "all this". Con, who has no intention of doing any such thing has had to flee to Athens. And now Jane is threatening to follow him. And, as usual, it's being left to me to get him out of it.'

She looked at me again. I didn't say anything. Her voice took on a plantive wail.

'I think this is all very un-chic of Sonny and Jane, who are millionaires incidentally. American millionaires. And who claim to believe in free love and free sex all over the place.'

This time she didn't hold out her glass but reached for the bottle herself, on the little tray. 'Don't bother with the cubes,' she said hoarsely.

I got up, hoping she would get up too. She did. But then she took a step toward me, still holding tight to her glass, and leaned against me.

Where I come from women don't lean against you indiscriminately. If they do, they live to think about it, if they don't regret it.

Her unbound breasts in her faded shirt jiggled against my lower chest. 'I guess you must know there's not anything at all I can do about it,' I said, and pushed her gently away from me.

She was wiping her eyes with one hand, and sipping Scotch with the other. 'I'm sorry. I apologize. I really do. I shouldn't come up here and lay all this on your back. Please believe it won't happen again.'

'I do. I believe it. After all, all I did was to come here and rent your house,' I said.

She laughed.

'I'll be going.'

But it took a while to get her out. She was required now by something or other to maintain a pretence that she came up only to see how I was making out and not to confess her current misery and she would not stop talking.

I learned several things. I learned that Con was short for Constantine, and not for Conrad. I learned that Georgina Taylor was indeed English and had met Constantine Taylor in Alexandria during the war, where he was a naval officer. I learned they had a twenty-two-year-old son, now living in London.

When she finally went out the door, she staggered a little as she handed me the slim remains of her fifth large whisky.

I shut the door. I thought I could see now why the cabman made his malicious laugh.

I turned off all the lights and took the whisky bottle upstairs with me and went down the bare hall hung with bad paintings to my bedroom. I was sleeping in the bedroom over the living-room, overlooking the harbour. I did not turn the lights on and stood looking out over the still-moonlit harbour and tried to calm my ears. I was wide awake. I poured myself a stiff drink, while listening to my insides complain to me that I had poured too much whisky in them already today.

From down below, I could hear music playing on Georgina's record player. Then a bottle clinking. I stepped out on the flat porch roof with my drink and stood a long time, brooding. The yacht harbour was still beautiful in the moonlight.

Some vacation. I could boot Freddy Tarkoff right in the butt. All the unpleasant things were clamouring in my head again. My life. My job for Tarkoff. My divorce. All jostling each other to be the first one out.

I still wasn't ready to think about any of it yet.

Among the yachts and boats in the harbour was one big one, a beauty. A ketch. It was all dark, and looked all locked up. It must have had a 90-foot mast, and had the long lines of an ocean sailer. You could go anywhere on that. As it rocked, its huge mast made an enormous arc across the bright star-marked sky.

I tried to imagine what it must be like to have enough money to own a boat like that, and failed. Enough money to live on it, and go where you wanted, and leave when you felt like it. I couldn't imagine it. I couldn't imagine having that much money.

After a while I went back inside and got into the rather lumpy bed.

All I did was toss among the lumps. So I made myself think about the yacht again. It was either that, or the other stuff. I went over every line of her, and every cable, and every stay. I went over every furled sail on her, and over all their lashings.

Then I went over every extra sail that must be in her sail locker. I went over every cabin in detail. I had never seen the cabins. It didn't matter. I made them up as I would have had them and went over them.

It was a trick I had learned during the war. My war. When you did not want to think about something, think about something you wanted. But it had to be something you wanted badly. Back then it had been a cabin I had once seen up in the Wind River Range. I had never seen the inside of that, either. But I had made it up a thousand times. And it had worked back then.

Now I did the same thing with the yacht. It worked again.

It took a long time. But my head stopped, and I got to sleep.

CHAPTER FOUR

The next morning I felt a lot better. With the beautiful yacht harbour before the house, and the boats, and people working on them, and the sea far off, it was hard not to.

The sun woke me early and I sat on my porch with strong Greek coffee prepared by my housekeeper and watched the activity of the harbour below me.

Jane Duval sat with her head down looking sullen and mistreated on the seawall a hundred feet away toward the taverna. The baby played in the dirt at her feet, ignored.

As I watched, Sonny collected his 'wife' and kid and marched away. At the taverna's dock he bustled them into his skiff and rowed them out to his fat, 60-foot, unkempt-looking Greek caique which was springlined to the seawall 20 yards offshore in front of the house. Georgina had already told me this was where they lived. A small but good-looking speedboat was tied up to it.

I watched him put Jane and the kid on board and row back to the taverna. He tied up the skiff and clambered on board a 32-foot fisherman's caique tied up at the dock and began putting it in shape. This was my boat evidently, and he was getting it ready for me.

Behind me, the doorbell rang, and the Greek housekeeper let somebody in. I came back in, half blinded by the supercharged sun. The figure of a woman was coming towards me. It took my eyes a minute to adjust. That's another thing that age does for you. Your eyes don't adjust as fast.

When I could see, I saw the housekeeper had come up the three steps from the hall and into the room, and that she was all blushy and flustered. She made a big thing out of the name.

'The Countess fon Hannders,' she intoned. Her English had a distinct German accent. The same was true of all the older, poorer Greeks on the islands that had been occupied.

The woman, now that I could see her, was wearing a light but expensive summer print. A few carefully selected pieces of jewellery flashed. Her hair was neither short nor long, and fluffed out cutely. A handsome aristocratic woman in her forties, slim, elegant. Elegance wafted from her, as they say. For her age she was still all hung together, at least the parts I could see. Under the elegant exterior there appeared to be a sexy, still attractive female. Just the right age for a broken down private eye turning fifty.

'She makes a big thing out of the name,' I said.

'They all do that,' von Anders said, 'with titles. They love to name them. We prefer not to use them.'

I gave her a grin. 'I never use them myself.'

She didn't know whether she liked that or not. 'Anyway, I don't have any right to it, being divorced.'

So this was the woman Tarkoff had said would take care of me, be my guide and entrepreneur on the island, rent everything for me. This was also the woman who had not met the ferry.

'I'm sorry about not meeting the ferry,' she said as if reading my mind. 'Actually, I got the date wrong.'

'Oh, that's all right,' I said. 'I didn't mind sleeping on the jetty.'

'Good heavens, did you really? Oh, I'm so sorry. Did you really have to?'

'No, not really,' I said. 'I had Georgina Taylor's name.'

She looked relieved. But it was hard to tell if she was out-acting me. 'How do you like the house? Is it adequate?'

'More than. For a lone man.'

22

'Is the housekeeper all right?'

'She's fine with me. I don't know if I'm so fine with with her.'

'Why not?'

'Well, I only brought one suitcase.'

She smiled all the way this time, a perky smile. 'She's a dreadful snob. They get that way after they work a while.'

'We all do,' I said.

She gave me a quizzical grin. 'You're very fast with the wisecracks. Freddy Tarkoff warned me about that.'

There was a fast and easy answer to that: Did Freddy also warn her about other sides of me? I didn't make it. But she didn't seem to be expecting it. She moved around me, to the nearest window. She pointed down at the taverna dock.

'That's the boat I've rented for you. One really needs one here. The man's American. He doesn't really need the money. But he's good enough with a boat, and he has the added advantage of speaking English.'

'Is he a good fisherman? Spearfisherman? Freddy told me he was an expert fisherman.'

'I don't really know that. Shall we go down and meet him, and ask him?'

'I've already met him. And his wife.'

'Ah. You've met Jane.'

'Yes, I've met her,' I said. I said it in a voice that expressed no opinion.

The Countess smiled. It was a pure and pristine bitch's smile. It seemed to light up her whole face with delight, and seemed to show all her tiny little teeth. It seemed to stay on there after it had disappeared. It was the smile of the high-placed lady who loved a good cat fight, and would roll up her sleeves for it.

'Charming thing, isn't she?' she said.

It was my own fault. I had mentioned Sonny's woman. She hadn't. But it was a formidable response just the same.

This was also the woman, I remembered, who Freddy's tone of voice had intimated he knew better than a friend. Was Tarkoff thinking of her along the same lines for me? I didn't like it. I didn't mind the idea. But I didn't like Freddy's presumption. If it was presumption.

'Chantal,' I said, 'That's French, isn't it? Somehow I had the idea you were English.'

She laughed. 'I am English. But my mother was French. And I spent most of my childhood in France. But don't ever think the English can't be as bitchy as the French.'

'So I've heard,' I said. I liked her.

She went on talking about the house, its advantages and disadvantages, its housekeeping problems. She talked about the housekeeping part as if she was an expert housekeeper herself. I was sure she was. But underneath all the housekeeping talk she seemed very jittery, nervous. And seemed to get more so. Then she asked me to lunch.

'It won't be exciting,' she added hastily. 'It's only a bunch of old biddies that I call my Greek Chorus, and one old gent. But the food is good. And I want to talk to you about something.'

'Why don't we talk about it here?' I said. 'That doesn't sound much like my kind of lunch.'

'I don't want to talk about it here,' von Anders said.

I was beginning to recognize symptoms. Being a private dick is a lot like being a doctor. Whenever a doctor shows up at a party, the people all start telling him all their newest symptoms. When a private dick shows up, they start telling him all their secret worries. It gets to be an awful drag. I put up my hands.

'Look, I'm down here on vacation,' I said. 'I'm not down here looking for business.'

'Is blackmail bad enough?' von Anders said.

That was certainly straightforward enough. 'All right, I'll come to your luncheon,' I said. 'But I won't promise any more than that. Okay? Now you should go home. And I want to go to town in my new boat with my new boatman.'

She held out her hand, in a sudden shy way. It was warm and dry and lean. An expensive bracelet winked at me. She was certainly an attractive woman. At least to older men like me. Or Freddy. As she walked away, I found myself wondering if her bottom was as firm as it seemed in the dress. There was only one way to find out and clothes, even a thin summer print, were not part of it. Cut it out, I growled at myself; go and get dressed for the boat.

I was not down here to play games with countesses. I

didn't know what I was down here for but it wasn't that. Engage in hit-and-run short-term love affairs that squirted emotion all over the place. All that was just ego-tripping, as the kids said. Not for me. Not for a hard-nosed old romantic. I would be laughable.

CHAPTER FIVE

At the boat, which was called the *Daisy Mae*, Sonny Duval was ready and waiting for me. He hauled the boat in to the dock by its painter, and held out his hand to me. I ignored it and long-stepped aboard quite handily by myself.

I figured we better get this point about my knowledge of small boats out of the way right at the start.

'Thanks,' I said.

He just looked at me. Then shrugged. He went aft and backed the boat and threaded his way out through the boats and anchored yachts, and started to run down along the shore lined with the high-walled white houses that I had passed along in the horsecab the night before.

'You know boats, hunh?' he said after a while, amiably enough.

'I used to do a fair amount of small-boat running,' I grinned. The truth was I was happy as hell to be out in one again.

Sonny studied me. 'A lot of people say that.' Under his bushy brows, which echoed that Elliot Gould moustache, his small eyes looked away from me. 'You like to try her?'

I wasn't expecting that. 'Sure. Why not?' I said. 'If you wouldn't mind.'

I moved aft and he passed me the helm and I settled down to get the feel of her. It was not a wheel helm but an old-fashioned bar helm: a two-by-five adzed down to round it off and bolted-in into the rudder. I used to love them in the Caribbean.

It was a nice smooth boat. All those Greek boats were. After a minute I manœuvred it, running out deeper and quartering the incoming swell cleanly. When I turned

25

her, I did it on the top of a swell, instead of turning her in the trough and taking the swell broadside and making her roll. She winged back nicely. So I took her closer in, and did the same thing to starboard, and brought her back out. I gave the bar back to him.

'That was nice,' Sonny said. 'Very deft. Very deft. You want to try docking her, when we get to the Port?'

I was not expecting that, either. 'Sure. I guess so. If you think I can.'

'I think you can.'

'Aren't you afraid I'll smash up your boat?'

'I don't think so. You won't smash it.' He grinned. I did not know what he was trying to prove. He seemed indifferent, not even to care. Maybe it was because he was so rich and he could afford to buy another boat, or two of them. I knew I certainly would not let any new man run my boat in to dock it until I had tested him more than he had tested me.

It was all more than I could fathom, around here. I didn't know what was going on. You gave people a paradise like this and they immediately tried to turn it into a club, with all sorts of secret games. I didn't like it worth a damn.

'Okay,' I said. 'I'll take her in, then.'

We settled down to the ride. I stripped off my shirt and stretched my arms along the rail behind me. I am built pretty rough, and I noted Sonny noticing this. He was strongly built himself, but had gotten flabby. I looked back at the land, and at all of the different houses. No two of them were even remotely alike. I liked that. All of them were pretty in the sun. At one spot there was an Orthodox church, with widely spaced olive trees in its sere yard down the slope to the road and the water, and a low whitewashed wall around the yard. A goat was tethered in the yard by the white wall. All the masonry around here was white-lime-washed.

It was a beautiful day, and a beautiful view, and a beautiful ride.

I didn't know why my problem of Freddy Tarkoff's job I had done for him picked just that moment to seize me, and come to the fore of my mind, and demand to be looked at. But it did.

CHAPTER SIX

I guess I had already looked at it from most of the possible positions. No matter how you looked at it I didn't look good. No matter how I tried to dress it up, it was not going to win me any gold Oscars for liberal humanitarianism.

You had to have some kind of code. The only code I had ever found that worked was that as long as you worked for him and took his money, the client was right. If you didn't think the client was right, or if you didn't like what he wanted you to do, you didn't take the job.

Tarkoff's case was simple enough. Tarkoff had a lot of money invested in Greece. A part of it was handled for him by a wealthy Greek attorney. The Greek had power of attorney. With it, he embezzled $130,000 of Tarkoff's money in a year, put all his own property in his wife's name, and absconded from Greece, all Tarkoff's money spent. On women and high living, apparently. This did not keep him and his wife from sticking together, when it came to his own estate. Tarkoff, unable to get anything out of the still wealthy wife, had the Greek traced and found him to be living in Paris, broke and working as a concierge in a cheap hotel in the rue Amsterdam in Pigalle. A hard situation. The Greek was out of the country safe. The wife refused to assume responsibility for his debts. Nothing could be done in the Greek courts.

It was a pretty slick job. I was a graduate lawyer myself; so was Tarkoff. We could both appreciate the cheap, snivelling, very crooked, very shrewd, lawyer's dexterity of it. Undoubtedly, the Greek put it together after the money was already spent, in order to save his family.

Tarkoff was not the kind of man to accept such crooked treatment passively. He was not known as one of the young Turks of Wall Street for nothing. My job was to find the Greek and somehow, no matter by what means, get the money back, or as much of it as possible.

Clearly the money must be squeezed from the wife some

27

way. 'There's no reason you shouldn't have the job and go over there and do it,' Tarkoff said. 'Instead of my paying someone else. Some international type. In fact, you're probably the only one who can swing it. I don't think any ordinary guy could.' Freddy liked to make a tin hero out of me. He would pay me a lot of money, and expenses.

I accepted the case. I accepted it because I agreed with Tarkoff's analysis of it. He said the Greek was depending on human decency to let him off the hook. There was no question I was working for the right side. He had embezzled other people too, it turned out, for smaller sums.

I had known Freddy about five years by then. He was probably the richest man I knew in New York. He had looked me up first because of his secretary. Some satisfied client gave him my name. The lady was being blackmailed by a former boyfriend turned smalltime hood, and Freddy hired me to get the guy off her back. He liked the way I handled that and we became friends. He found it funny that a graduate lawyer with a degree could be a private eye. So did I, sometimes. I did a couple of mainly research investigations about business deals for him. I never asked him why he was so interested in protecting his secretary. He was married, very socially, to a very social girl, but he liked to hang around with me on my beat in the hood bars. A lot of my time was spent hunting lost kids down in the East Village and Freddy liked to tag along with me down there.

I do not know if our friendship had very much to do with my accepting. I could try that on for size as an excuse, but I won't. He was offering me an awful lot of money. And right then I needed it badly. My divorce had gone through, and I was having to pay through the nose. Though it was my wife who had wanted the divorce. That plus two teen-age daughters going to ritzy schools made a considerable lump I was having to lay out every month. Freddy knew all this, of course.

I left for Europe prepared to do anything I had to do to complete my assignment. In New York, where except for professionals like myself it's not safe to walk the street at night, and where even for us it sometimes isn't, I was feeling more and more like a displaced person. I was glad to get away.

But when I stepped off the plane in Europe, I felt more displaced. Standing in the Orly Airport I realized suddenly that all Europeans were displaced persons. They had lived like that for a hundred generations. There was no security and they didn't expect any and it showed in their faces. They looked as though they were born knowing at birth that even their own relatives would screw them. I felt right at home.

In Europe, I took an exploratory trip down to Athens, and looked up the wife. She had a town house in Athens, an imposing seaside villa, and a lot of valuable farm land. There was no knowing what she had put away in cash. But she had a lot more than enough to pay back Tarkoff.

Back in Paris I hunted down the Greek. He was still there in the same sleazy hotel in the rue Amsterdam. He was a fat little man with a mean smile. He was willing to admit everything. He would even sign a paper admitting everything. But he couldn't pay any of it back. He had no money. We both looked around the damp little room. How could he pay? And there was no use trying to get anything from his wife. She hated his guts. 'Naturally enough,' he smiled. 'Wouldn't you, sir? If you were she?'

He smiled his shrewd mean smile at me. He had it all figured out. He had had his fun while it lasted. And he had given everything up for it. And here he was. There wasn't anything more to do to him. He had forgotten one thing. A man named Freddy Tarkoff, who never forgot anything.

I hadn't talked much. There wasn't much point. I had just made my points, carefully. Without any warning I hit him. Then I proceeded methodically to beat him up. As he probably expected me to. I didn't honestly know what he expected. That I would go away and leave him alone, maybe. But he knew the underworld rules as well as I did.

I knew all the tricks. You picked them up. I did it carefully so as not to cause any serious damage or break any bones. He didn't yell. He didn't fight back. When I left, he was just about unconscious on his flavoursome bed.

There was nothing to fear from the police. The French police knew all about him already. They didn't like him, either. Neither of us was going to any police.

When I went back next night, there was a new man on the desk. The Greek was in his room sick, he said. When I went in, he was there. Only now he was black and blue. He put on his nasty smile like a threadbare trenchcoat. For a lawyer, he pleaded quite a case. Beating him up wouldn't change his wife. I could kill him, and it would not help. I would get nothing. And I could go on beating him up forever, he pointed out.

He was almost eloquent.

I nodded grimly. 'Quite true. And I may. Do you have any children?' I'd already checked.

His eyes widened. 'You wouldn't . . .?'

I didn't answer.

'You would never do that,' the Greek said.

'What you need is some incentive,' I said. 'And don't forget, I can go on doing this forever, too.'

Talking, I gagged him. I didn't even bother to tie him up. I kept telling myself I was doing this for good old Freddy Tarkoff. Then methodically I broke one of his fingers.

He screamed, or would have if it hadn't been for the gag. For a moment I thought he was going to faint. But he didn't. Instead, he fell back on the bed and his eyeballs rolled up white and his eyelids fluttered down over them.

When I ungagged him, he groaned. 'I'll be back tomorrow,' I told him. 'And we'll discuss it more. Maybe you won't need any more incentive. Don't bother to try running away. I'll follow you.' I left him moaning.

Outside in the street I was sweating. My hat felt as if it didn't want to stay on straight. This kind of work just wasn't my best thing. I hoped I had hidden that from the Greek. Because I knew I could never do it again.

It was a chilly spring night in that awful, evil part of Paris. There was a steady French mist falling and the street cobbles were slick and dank and shone. Hookers were standing in the doorways of other sleazy hotels, with their teased hair high and their big purses hanging on shoulder straps. For a second I thought of going up with one of them, to forget about the whole thing, and then wanted to gag. I stopped myself from slamming my fist into the clammy brick wall. Melodramatic self-indulgence. I didn't want to damage my hand. And the hookers were watching. I walked away.

Down at the first lighted corner I stopped in a little café-bar filled with pimps to have a couple of stiff drinks.

The only real thought I had in my mind at the time, as I remember, was that I thanked my good luck that I was not him. I would not have wanted to be him, in that sour-smelling, awful, evil, lonely area of Paris, for anything in the world. If I had been him, I would have been totally terrorized.

I suppose he was. When I returned, he was willing to talk to his wife, anyway. He had his hand in a cast. I was as polite as hell to him. A meeting was arranged with the wife in Zurich.

Talk about a displaced person. He had it over me. But he, at least, had gotten to squander $130,000 for his. I had gotten to take care of a wife and two kids for mine.

The wife was about as sorry a human specimen as the husband. After a long talk with him in a café, shadowed by me, she asked to see me. Was I the man who was threatening to kidnap her children? I didn't know what she was talking about; I was only a friend. She snorted and said $80,000 was all she could scrape together. I asked about her seaside villa. 'Not my seaside villa!' she cried. Anyway, she would have to sell it, and that would take time. I pointed out it wasn't mortgaged; borrow money on it now and sell it later. I wouldn't give her an inch. Inside of a week, the full sum was transferred from the wife's Swiss account to a Swiss account I opened, the little Greek was back in Paris, and I was back in Athens arranging transfer of the money to Tarkoff the way he wanted it.

He congratulated me profusely on the phone. He suggested the Tsatsos vacation. I had told him I had no desire to go back to New York just yet. I suppose he thought it had to do with my divorce. Well, maybe it did: Too: In a way. It also had to do with my whole life.

Sitting on Sonny Duval's boat, and moving with the delicious motion as he quartered the swell, I clamped down the lid on my mind, and blocked off the other two items. My divorce. And my life. I had already let

31

one of my imps out of the box.

I was sweating in the heavy sun. The motion of the boat was delicious. We were just about to come in. I put my shirt back on.

The thing that kept coming back was the way his eye-balls had rolled back, and how his eyelids fluttered down over the whites, when I broke his finger.

The terrible thing was I could do it again if I had to. If I ever got myself into the same situation. I intended never to get myself into the same situation.

You did their dirty work for them, and then you were supposed to take your money and shut up. That was part of the contract. They didn't want to hear the gory details. Well, hurray for them.

We were just coming to the end of the long concrete jetty which protected the Port from the swell. The long swell slapped against it and splashed white water as high as its floor, and ran rolling down its length to the shore.

CHAPTER SEVEN

We came around the jetty and at once the swell stopped and we were in quiet water.

So here I was. I much preferred thinking about how to go about enjoying my vacation. Enjoy some of all that money Freddy Tarkoff was laying out on me.

The boat moorings of the Port were a couple of hundred yards ahead of us. Sonny Duval slacked off on his throttle and grinned at me. He still wanted me to dock his boat. He waved for me to come aft.

I took my time, and looked at the Port first. It was a lovely little port in the daytime. I had only seen it at night. Bright-coloured caiques bobbed at their moorings. The two lines of trees shaded the café-terrace, along the top of the wall. Useless ancient cannon peered out myopically through the notches on its crenellated top. Awnings had been run out over the tourist shops and other cafés. There was a sense of everything baking cleanly in the still, clean sun. I got up and went back aft.

'You're not very nervous, are you?' Sonny said.

'Should I be?'

'Here,' he said, grinning, and gave me the helm.

Was he testing my nerve? Trying to break me down and make me chicken it? He didn't know me very well. I would rather ruin his boat and kill us both. But you wondered didn't he care about his boat? Or was he too rich for that? He had stepped back, but not very far back.

The moorings were in a man-made hollow with rocks on both sides that made a slight bottleneck. I went through that.

'See that empty slot? There? Twenty-five yards out from it, you drop your anchor. Then use the anchor line to snub her up as you go in.'

I nodded. 'I've done it that way in the Caribbean.' My mouth was tasting truculence, and aggressiveness. Maybe my adrenalin was up. He must know I was out of practice.

Anyway, I felt like doing it so, suddenly, I looked up at him from the helm; and gave him my solid-gold, No. 1, sudden flashing, bloodthirsty grin. That was the one I usually saved back, and reserved for hesitant teetering clients, where it might earn me a retainer. If he thought I would back down at the last minute, he had lost his bet.

It was easy, if you were calm. Even without practice I didn't have any trouble. His throttle was a difficult-looking home-made affair but it worked fine. Throttle was controlled by a long-armed wing nut on a long screw-tapped rod. You screwed the wing nut down for more throttle, and unscrewed it upward to let off. It made it hard to gun the motor, but I didn't need that. I simply kept slacking off on the wing nut. When she was twenty feet out I put the motor in neutral and let her glide in. When her nose was a foot or two from the stone wharf, I simply tightened my grip on the anchor's line. I had already dropped the anchor over. I didn't even have to belay the line on the cleat.

Sonny just stood and looked at me. Then he ran forward and warped the bow line to the big iron ring. I backhitched the anchor line to the starboard cleat. She was neatly snugged in between the two caiques on both sides, with a foot to spare on either side, without having touched a thing.

'Very deft,' Sonny said coming back. 'Very, very deft.' That seemed to be a word he liked.

'In my misspent youth I was a bootlegger off the Florida coast,' I said.

He stood and looked at me. 'Aw, come on,' he said. 'You're not *that* old.' I decided he was not long on the wit, Sonny. It irritated me. Was he kidding me?

He was only about five years younger than I was. When he grinned and pulled up his mouth, you noticed how old he was. Despite his hippie outfit and the long hair and moustache and the big peace medal. The grin made wrinkled pouches of it under his eyes and at the angle of his jaw.

'That was a strange thing to do,' I said. 'Let a total stranger run your boat in like that.'

His eyes glinted at me. He did not answer.

Suddenly, across the Port, a tall, handsome, sunburnt young Greek standing in the sun on the raised poop of a large caique name-plated *Polaris* started to work a huge klaxon horn fastened to his taffrail. A small mob of people were waiting to board his boat. As the klaxon belched its message, more started to come down from the rise of tree-shaded terrace. Over the gangplank was a sign painted in English saying, PICNIC-SWIMMING-LUNCHEON TRIPS TO GLAUROS, PETCOS, ETC. He seemed to be enjoying the noise he was making. Naked to the waist in blue jeans and sideburns and barefooted, he looked clean and healthy and graceful. Looking at him made me suddenly remember my age again. Sonny shouted and the Greek grinned and waved back but didn't stop working the klaxon. Its eructations shattered the quiet sunny air of the Port like huge glass slivers.

'See that guy? That's our local pusher,' Sonny said beside me when the klaxon stopped and we could hear again. He made the gesture of someone smoking a reefer. 'That's Girgis. He's a local star. Screws nothing but blonde English and American tourist girls. Girgis is not only Master of the *Polaris*. He is also quite big in another business.' Again he made the gesture of smoking a reefer. I was beginning to get the point.

'Looks healthy, doesn't he?' he said with a kind of bitter relish. 'He's about as healthy as a syphilitic spastic.'

He nodded. 'Look at him. Girgis is blowing his klaxon.

Girgis wants his people there. But he won't leave for another hour. The people will sit there. Girgis covers every loophole.' He grinned.

We climbed up on to the stone wharf. The quay we stepped on to immediately swallowed us into its live activity. Tourists and hippies strode up and down, buying fruits and vegetables from the little caiques like ours, which had brought the stuff to town. One of the ferry ships was in and loading cargo, and a gang of local men carried crates of melons and huge tomatoes and green vegetables out the jetty to it. Right in front of us was an ugly building marked BANK.

'I've got to present some letters and open an account,' I said. 'Where shall I meet you?'

Sonny pointed. 'Up at one of the cafés. I've got some friends I want to see.'

The man in the bank had the cold watchdog stare behind rimless glasses of all loyal bank clerks who love protecting their bosses' money from the depredations of tongue-tied working-men. I stared back at him just as hard, and cut him off when he started to give me his lip about his regulations. Hell, you'd think it was his money. When I stepped outside several minutes later, something made me stop dead. I stepped back into the shade of the bank front.

Just in front of me on the wharf, just going down the stone steps to the little embarkation stage, was Jane Duval with her child. The child had difficulty with the high wharf steps. They got on to the boat which – the sign said – was loading passengers to take over to the little airport on the mainland for the morning small-plane flight to Athens. I stayed in the doorway while the boat backed and turned and headed out. The local plot at Georgina Taylor Haus was thickening, it looked like.

I stepped back out into the sun. Well, it wasn't any of my business. The Port was infested with hippies. I made my way up the rough cobbles of the little rise to the terrace of cafés under the trees. It was hard to find a table. Seated, I saw Georgina Taylor stand up across the terrace and shout at me, and motion me to come over.

Sonny Duval was with her, and a whole raft of the kids. Three of them stood out. A tall, skinny youth with very thick glasses and close-cropped hair; a blond Adonis with a sleepy drugged-out stare, and a lion's mane of hair; and another sullen girl in another shapeless robe, like Jane Duval. They seemed to be together. They all three stared at me, as I waved back at Georgina and shook my head.

I had no desire to talk juvenile philosophy. Briefly, I wondered if Sonny knew his wife was fleeing the coop. I suspected he didn't.

After I ordered coffee, I asked the waiter for the men's room. This turned out to be a noisome stall back in a narrow alley and behind the café, a lean-to against the back wall with a plank door that wouldn't close. It smelled like a Dow Chemical plant. Coming out of it, I heard voices, and the sound of a woman crying, and stopped.

In the alley Girgis was being importuned by an American hippie girl who wanted to buy some hashish on credit. The girl was sniffling. Girgis spoke good English. But he was rude and tough with the girl. I stood and listened. I didn't like it. After she left, crying, he became aware of me.

'You were pretty hard on the little girl, weren't you?' I said. 'For a little hash?'

He looked me over. He moved like a star rooster. I would have dearly loved to hit him. 'Her boyfriend sent her,' he said amiably, 'not having guts enough to come himself. And it was not hash they wanted from me, as the gentleman seems to think, but to rent my boat *Polaris* for what they call a picnic. But which usually ends up to be an orgy. I have no use for the hippies, and they like me as little.'

'Do you have to have a licence to sell hashish on this island?' I said. 'Or can just anybody sell it?'

'Selling hashish is strictly illegal, and that is why I would never touch it.'

'But I could sell it. If I wanted to,' I said. 'If I had some with me?'

He grinned. 'The police are very tough here.' The grin widened. 'If you do not know them.'

'I'm sure it helps to know them,' I said.

He was looking threatening, with his grin. So I smiled and inflated my chest a little for him, too.

He came a little closer.

'You are new here,' he said. 'I have not seen you around Tsatsos before.'

'Just arrived,' I said. 'Here on a vacation. But that's the only thing that's new about me.'

This time his inspection of me was a little more professional.

'You have moved in at Georgina Taylor's house.'

'That's me.'

He was taller even than Sonny Duval, and had a tendency to seem to tower over me. But I could left-hook him in the belly beautifully from just where I stood. He bared his teeth at me but I couldn't honestly call it a grin.

'There have been rumours in Athens about a new American narcotics agent, moving around. Who might pay us a visit in Tsatsos.'

'You don't say so,' I said.

'We are very small here. Being small makes us close together. We do not like strangers, unless they are tourists coming to spend money. People have been known to disappear and never be heard again. The sea around us is very big. If I were you, I wouldn't even finish my vacation. I would turn around and go right back to Athens, Mr – ?'

'Davies,' I said. 'Why, I do believe you're threatening me.'

'Not threatening,' Girgis said. 'Just advising.' He stepped back and bared his teeth again. Then he stalked off, still graceful as always. There was a big bare dry field back there they had labelled a park. He went across it.

Back at the alley entrance I found Sonny Duval had been standing here, apparently ready to help me fight. I began to like him better.

'He's a tough guy,' Sonny said.

'Sure. They all are,' I said, and began to like him less again. I had heard that descriptive definition used of men about as many times as I wanted to. Usually it was true enough. You had better believe they were, in any case. It was safer than believing you were tougher. 'Sit down and have a drink with me, Sonny,' I said.

'I can't. I have to get back to the yacht harbour and make sure Jane is okay,' he said.

I looked at him. I did not mention I had seen Jane. He

didn't seem to know about her.

I asked the waiter for a Scotch and sat back down. Sonny told me how to get to Chantal von Anders's house back up in the town, pointing out the street I was to take up the hill, and left.

I fingered my cold glass and sat looking after him, puffing out my lips thoughtfully. It was a habit I had. I did it when I was thinking and the thinking was not too fruitful nor too joyously elated. I usually only did it when I was alone.

CHAPTER EIGHT

I sat and watched the Port's harbour bake. The glare of the all-out sun was harsh, retina-stunning, from the shade. There was something funny about this island that I could not put my finger on, and I didn't like it. I paid the liverish young waiter and left.

The town climbed steeply from the Port. I walked uphill on narrow walled cobbled streets. As soon as I left the district of shops the number of hippies got noticeably less. The heavy sun bore down on the white houses and walls, and leaned hard on me. It was quiet. Some gardens had green showing over their walls, but most of them looked dry and tinderish, as if they would go up at the touch of a cigarette butt.

Von Anders's house was nearly at the top of the town, and it was some house. It looked as if it had been the old time castle of the place, from which the head brigand sortied forth to make all the other littler brigands cough up and pay off, and they couldn't do a thing about it because he could sortie right back in again and they couldn't touch him.

It had thick, ancient, stone rooms with lancet arches over the doors and arched ceilings, a portion of old crenellated wall between the house proper and a low tower in the garden, a stone terrace on one level, a well-tended garden on two levels, a couple of ancient unused wells. It was definitely not the house of a poor girl.

I was let in at the garden door-gate by an enormously

fat, sombre Greek woman of about twenty-four, who waddled. The assembled company was already assembled. They were on the stone terrace, under vine-covered lattice, and were drinking Bloody Marys. I figured a little tomato juice on top of my Scotch wouldn't hurt anything.

In the living-room, which was all stone, hung a portrait of von Anders when she was young, under what was a perpetual light apparently. The dimness of the living-room with its small windows almost warranted the eternal lamp, but not quite. If that was what she looked like when she was young, she must have been really something. That apparently meant a lot to her.

'I hope you'll survive the luncheon,' she breathed after she greeted me. She was cute with two strong Bloody Marys under her belt.

The luncheon was even worse than I expected. The main topic was the hippies and dope. The four old biddies were hard to tell apart. I had difficulty separating one from another. The fact that they all thought exactly alike didn't make it easier. The old gent was easier to distinguish because he had short hair, although one of the ladies almost matched him there. He was a retired American Diplomatic Corps fella. They all called him Ambassador because he had been one. Ambassador Pierson. He was a nervous old gent, and said little. If he hadn't been an ambassador I would have bet he was some kind of hophead.

'It is the dope they bring in, rather than the young vagabonds themselves, that is scary,' one of the ladies said in synthesis.

'Absolutely,' said the Ambassador.

'Dope?' I put in. 'Or hashish?'

'Hashish!' the lady said. 'Isn't that dope?'

I decided not to go into that with her. I knew about a million people who no longer considered hashish and pot to be serious dope. Just about everybody I knew in New York smoked both.

I shut up and listened and learned this was the third year they had come, the kids. Like migratory birds. There never used to be a hashish problem. Now all the children had access to it, if they wanted it. Most of the ladies had teenage children, or grandchildren, who came in the summer. The older people didn't like the influence. They were losing all their control over the young. It was getting worse every year. Et cetera, et cetera. I felt like a fish who has just been jerked out of the water and left to flop on the bank when all he did was bite at a worm, his natural function. I didn't know where all of them had been the last few years. But their concern was genuine.

Afterwards, when they all left, von Anders took me for a walk up the hill to an old temple ruin. A lovely place, and stony quiet. It was another one of those sites that had been an ancient-Greek pagan temple. But here even the later Christian Orthodox chapel had been let go back to grass and mould.

The Countess seemed to be quite taken with me. 'You were really something. Freddy Tarkoff told me you were something different. But he gave me no idea how much.'

'Didn't I do my part well?'

'Too well. You were so polite.' Suddenly she giggled. 'You were like a big black bear in a kindergarten. You looked as if, if you took one deep breath and forgot yourself, you would blow them all away. And my luncheon table, too.'

'Light lunches with old ladies is not my best thing.'

'It certainly isn't.'

'And you find that exciting about me?'

'Well, it's certainly all male.'

Well she was certainly all female. There wasn't anything overt about her come-on. If it was a come-on. But there was a deep glow in her eyes of flirtation. She was even willing to imply, by the way she used his name, that she knew Tarkoff on better than just friendly terms. Women don't often do that.

I steered us back to the reason I was here in the first place.

'What about this secret that's so deep and dark you can't talk about it in front of my housekeeper?'

'It's just what I said. I'm being blackmailed.'

'For a lot of money?'

'Quite a lot. Enough.'

'Yes,' I said. 'Well, let me tell you about blackmail. Blackmail is always dirty business. Because the person being blackmailed has always done something bad. Something against the law or something he doesn't want people to know about. Otherwise, the blackmailer couldn't blackmail him. Could he?'

She looked perplexed.

I spelled it out for her. 'Do you want to tell me what you've done bad? Maybe you'd rather not tell me.'

'I want to tell you everything.' But she seemed hesitant. I didn't say anything. 'The bad thing I've done is that I've been buying some hashish,' she said finally. 'There is a man in the village called Girgis.'

'I've already met him,' I said.

'You do move fast. Freddy said you did. Well, he has been selling me hashish, and now he is threatening to tell people. And I am paying him not to.'

I waited. 'Is that all?'

'Isn't that enough?'

'It doesn't sound very bad.'

'You don't understand. You saw those people at lunch. What if they found out? Those people, and others like them, are my whole social life on this island.'

'Countess, if those people are your whole social life, I would say you are in deep trouble. Blackmail or no.'

She simply stared at me.

'A woman with your looks,' I added.

She flushed. But she came right back. 'This isn't something to joke about. I want to retain you. I want you to do something about that man.'

'You're sure that's all there is?'

She didn't quite bite her lip, but she wanted to. 'Yes, that's all.'

I had no doubt she was lying, now. I leaned towards her, and took her hand. 'Countess, my retainer is fifteen hundred dollars. I don't think you want to pay me that. Besides, I'm on vacation. I'm not here to work. Besides, private detectives never, never charge their close and dear friends. I suggest you just stop paying this Girgis. If that's all it is. I will take a look around. I promise nothing bad will come of it for you. Okay?' I grinned.

'You're a mean man,' she said. There was a distinct impression that she would allow her hand to continue to be held. 'Please don't call me Countess. Call me Chantal,' she said in a weak voice. That was the only signal she would allow herself, I guessed. But there was a distinct impression she would even allow herself to be kissed, maybe. I let go of the hand.

Off in the distance was the 'Construction' where the hippies had installed themselves. I had had a good view of it from the ferry coming in. But here the view of it was superb. An abandoned government building project, started by the state as vacation apartments for government workers apparently, or so they'd said at lunch.

'So that is where the celebrated hippies have taken up abode?' I said.

'That? Yes. They just seem to come. It's like those caves in other parts of Greece. They hear about it. And they come. It's changing the entire island. It's to them that Girgis sells his hashish.'

'Where did you get your hash before the hippies?'

'Oh.' She looked flustered. 'From Girgis. But it wasn't a big business then. It was just a – just a favour. So to speak.'

'I see.' I folded my arms and went on looking at the 'Construction'.

'How much do you charge, Lobo?' She let her voice play with my name a little.

'Hundred and fifty bucks a day, and expenses,' I said without moving my gaze. I unfolded my arms and smiled. 'We better go down.'

'Yes. I – I still want to retain you. But I can't pay that much.'

'Don't worry about it.' I could so easily have used the old line about taking it out in trade. I almost did. 'And don't you be terrorized by such a little thing.' I gave her a quizzical look.

'I have gotten you invited to one of the summer resident dinner parties tonight, with me,' Chantal said. 'I'll meet you at the taverna by your house at eight.'

We were almost at her house.

I walked back down the hill alone, whistling ominous ditties to myself under my breath. She was probably mixed up in something. What could you be mixed up in living on a Greek island vacation paradise?

I wondered a little at the fact that she said she couldn't afford to pay me my regular fee. A lady who lived in a house that fantastic, and lived there that well, should certainly be able to pay my fees. How bad could it be, whatever it was she was mixed up in? Well, I had told

42

her I would look into it.

Back at my own rented mansion, that I rattled around so in, another instalment in the Taylor-Duval drama was on, playing to a capacity audience. A bunch of kids I had seen that morning in town were sitting around, in Georgina's yard. Sonny was out on his big caique, and Georgina was at the seawall shouting at him. I nodded to her and went straight on inside and got myself a drink. I prepared to watch the show from my porch.

Below in the harbour, Sonny flung himself over to his boarding ladder and got angrily into his speedboat and zoomed ashore in it. He went charging up to one of those public phone booths. Georgina left the seawall and followed me into the house.

'Jane has followed Con to Athens,' she said with mild hysteria before I could even offer her a drink.

'Has she?' I said. 'How about a drink?'

'Yes. She has. I don't want a drink. She flew up this morning on the local morning plane.'

'And Con called you about it,' I said softly.

'Sonny is trying to call the hotel in Athens where he and Jane usually stay. He simply has got to do something about it. Or I'll do something drastic.' She was very angry. I didn't know what was drastic by her. She was too thin to do anybody much harm unless she caught them asleep.

'Come on,' she said abruptly, 'I want you to meet some friends of ours.'

'Do you mean those scabby-looking hippies down in your yard? Thanks, I'd just as soon not.'

'You're a reactionary,' she said. It was not a point for discussion. It was a statement. 'And don't call them hippies. They hate to be called that.'

'What do they like to be called? This year. It's getting harder and harder for them to think up new words to call themselves.'

She looked startled, momentarily. 'Young people is what they are, and young people is what they ought to be called. You could try remembering that. The trouble with you is you're too old and you've gone sour.'

'I'll try to remember, Georgina,' I said.

She stared at me a moment and then started to grin.

'You're a cynic. Those young people are the last hope this horrible old world has.'

'My God, I hope not.'

'Oh, shut up.' She was really grinning now. I had gotten her down off a bad hump. Not that it mattered. She would get herself up on another one in fifteen minutes. Her kind always did.

'Just shut up, and come along now,' she said.

'Whatever you say, Georgina,' I said. 'Aren't you glad you've got me around here to holler at with Con away.'

'Oh, you're impossible.'

I followed her out.

CHAPTER NINE

I guess I wanted to go, or she couldn't have made me. But it was quite some scene just the same. There was a gang of seven or eight of them congregated in the yard. They all acted as though they were quite at home at Georgina's. It was hard to learn so many new names at the same time but I noted the three that had stood out that morning at the café on the town terrace. The skinny myopic boy was called Chuck; the blond Adonis, Steve; and the super-sullen, lumpy-looking girl in the Mother Hubbard, Diane. They were all passing reefers around and drinking immoderately from an apparently inexhaustible supply of Georgina's local white retsina. Poor Georgina darted anxiously around, serving them. They listened to her record-player she had moved outside for them.

They all seemed to get stiffish when introduced to me. But the girl Diane was the worst with it. She seemed to take an active and open dislike to me. I guess she thought I was some kind of a Puritan. She seemed to dote on her own two men, Steve and Chuck, like a slave; and then would stare at me as if daring me to disapprove.

The forty-four-year-old Sonny came chugging up from the taverna with news for Georgina. He had gotten the hotel, and Jane was staying there; but she was out. 'Now leave me alone, will you?' he said, and seated himself among the hippies as if one of them. A kind of chorus of 'Hey, man!' and 'Hi, man!' and 'Find the chick, man?' greeted him. It was quite a contrast to the way they treated me.

I bristled a little under all that belligerence. So, when the passed reefer came to me I deliberately sat back and shook my head. There was an exchange of superior glances among the hip. I put on a dumb face and after a moment I said, 'Are you people what is known as hippies?'

There was a general stiffening. And Georgina passed me a warning look.

'Some people call us that,' the nervous, myopic Chuck said. 'We don't call ourselves that.'

'I see. What do you call yourselves?' I asked.

'God's Chillun,' the Adonis, Steve, said. 'We call ourselves God's Chillun.' He had vague blue eyes that did not seem to see you. They were very cold eyes.

'You come here every year?' I said.

'We *live* here! We *live* here!' Chuck said, agitated. '*Live* here, man.' He began to snap his fingers. From the uneasy looks I could tell the finger-snapping was some barometer of Chuck's agitation.

'Take it easy,' Steve cautioned him. 'I own the bar,' he said to me.

'What bar?'

They all looked surprised, as if everybody should know that.

'The Cloud 79, up on the hill,' Georgina put in urgently. 'It's a new bar, the biggest thing on the island.' By now she was passing me looks like a machine gun passes rounds.

'And you own it? I thought you couldn't own property unless you were Greek,' I said.

Steve blinked. 'Yeah, well, I got a Greek partner,' he said.

'And you smoke a lot of this hashish?'

'Yeah, we smoke it,' Steve said. 'A lot of it. And don't go telling us it's illegal. We know.'

'And you all get it from this guy Girgis?' I asked.

'Well, no. Not all anyway. He's a fink. He works for the Syndicate.'

'What Syndicate?'

'Bunch of Greeks,' Steve said, and shrugged. 'How do I know? Anyway I got a bunch myself. I bring it in with me.'

'Where do you get it?'

'Here and there,' he said secretively.

'Athens?'

'You can always get it, if you know the right people,' Steve said, and smiled.

All the others were watching him and they smiled too. Their assumption of superiority would have infuriated a saint. It was at least as bad as that of the bourgeoisie they hated so much.

'And it's one hell of a big business,' I said. 'Is it pretty good shit? Here, give me that.' I took the nearest reefer from someone who had it and smoked it, deep and long, sucking it back and holding it in while I talked. 'Yeah, that's good quality. Good shit. Is that yours? Or Girgis's?'

'Well, that's Girgis's,' Steve admitted. 'That belongs to Georgina.'

'So you're smoking her hash, as well as drinking her wine?' I said. I took a number of quick long drags, and passed the cigarette, or what was left of it, to the next person. Then I slapped my knees and stood up.

'Well, it was nice to talk to you all. You're all very nice people. I can see that. See you around,' I said.

Near me the skinny Chuck said suddenly, in a sort of low-volumed but high-pitched scream. 'In our society, there ain't going to be any pigs, man. No *pigs*! Won't need them in our society. Get it? No *pigs*?'

'You're a nice person, too,' I said. 'See you.' On the walk I turned back. I could feel the slightest tiniest buzz at the base of my skull from the hash.

'I'm not a pig,' I said. 'I'm more what you'd call a wart hog, I guess. Or a werewolf.' And suddenly, because I just felt like it, I put my head back and let out a wolf howl, the long, drawn-out quavering cry of a mountain wolf, alone at night on the mountain in winter under a moon. I had learned to do it from an old trapper in Wyoming as a boy. It had at least as much vital energy in it as all of them put together. Not only did it startle the kids, but I heard a rustle of quiet pass over all the people down at the taverna across the vacant lot as well. I turned and left.

Later, while I was sitting on my porch, I saw Chuck,

Steve and Diane go out the garden-gate door, and over towards the taverna. They moved in the stiff slow way people do who are well-stoned. Some curiosity made me go down and follow them. In the yard some boy with a high, not strong but pleasing voice, was playing a guitar and singing folk songs evidently of his own creation.

'You know who that is,' a boy standing by the garden door said to me, in a celebrity-worshipping tone. 'That's Jason. He's a recording star in Paris.'

I peered at Jason in the gathering dusk, and saw a thin-faced, haunted-looking boy with a straggly beard. I nodded, and went on.

At the taverna, almost before I could reach it, there was a sudden scuffle and altercation. Myopic Chuck was standing screaming, in a karate man's stance, his glasses carefully placed on a table. He had just smashed the nose of a much larger boy, who was being helped up, dazed and streaming blood. Steve and another boy had grabbed Chuck, and Diane had thrown her arms around his neck from behind. 'Nobody's gonna talk like that to my friends! Nobody's gonna talk about my friends!' cried Chuck's wild high voice. Steve and the others pulled him away into the dark. He reached out with one hand and grabbed his glasses and placed them on his nose.

A figure had moved up beside me. It was Sonny. His smile behind his bushy moustache and brows was in-gratiating. 'You sure got to them with that wolf howl of yours. Where did you learn that?'

I didn't answer.

Sonny nodded after Chuck. 'He's sort of Steve's body-guard. But he's a little excitable.'

'A little. Does Steve need one?'

'Not really. They – Steve and Diane – sort of picked him up somewhere. Diane likes him. They brought him here with them last year.'

'Which one is her lover?'

Sonny grinned. 'Steve? Or Chuck? We don't think in those terms any more. You're old-fashioned, Davies. Who knows? Probably both. Or neither. We've found out that sex isn't that important to a couple. That's what the whole thing is about, man.'

'That, and cops.'

'Are you really a – uh – private eye?'

'Is that what Georgina told you?'

Sonny nodded.

'Whatever I am, I'm on vacation.'

We walked out a little way away from the taverna, and sat on the seawall.

Sonny wouldn't let go of it. 'No. We believe in sex for everybody, with everybody. If so desired by the participants.'

'I believe in that. As long as I'm not married. I'm not married.'

'Do you like my wife?' Sonny asked suddenly. It had a peculiar tone.

'Like her? I don't know. I guess so. I've hardly met her.'

'You have to understand her. She's young. Reason I asked, she likes you. That's rare. She doesn't usually. She thought you were sensitive.'

'Look,' I said. 'If you're pulling some kind of John Alden routine between me and your wife, the answer is no dice. Anyway, she seems to be too preoccupied at the moment. And I'm busy.'

Sonny's big jaw hardened. 'Are you kidding? We don't go in for stuff like that. But Georgina gave you a bum steer about Jane, I think. She didn't follow Con Taylor to Athens. She went because she felt she owed it to Con. He begged her to come. Said he needed her. She went to try and let him down easy.' A pause, and he said obscurely, grimly. 'They don't any of them understand her.' Another pause. 'Anyway, I've chartered a plane. For early tomorrow morning. I'm flying up to Athens to get her.'

I nodded brusquely. I didn't really want all these confidences from everybody. 'Must be expensive, all those planes. Do you have to chase her often?'

'I've got money,' Sonny said in a kind of arch way. 'I'm not proud of it. But it enables me to live like I want to, live in a way that keeps up with the future.' A slight, polite hesitation. 'Didn't Georgina tell you?'

'Yeah. She did. You're a millionaire.'

'That's right. But I'm not proud of it. Just like I'm not proud of being an American. I just happen to be born both. My old man made his loot in the Chicago stockyards, of all places.'

I grinned mirthlessly. 'Blood money. Well, the blood

washes off of properly made currency. Almost everything does. That's one philosophy.'

'You're quite a philosopher.'

'Sure.' I got up. 'It costs very little.'

'Listen. Let me tell you something. I live off of what I earn. I believe in living off what you earn. We drink the cheapest retsina, we eat what the locals eat. I live off what I earn on the *Daisy Mae*.'

'Maybe that's why your – "wife" is so unhappy.'

'Who says she's unhappy?'

'I sort of got that impression.'

'Well, she's not. She believes the way I believe.'

'Well, I hope you find your girl. She's not your wife, is she? I mean, you're not married?'

'We don't believe in all that.'

'Well, I've got a date,' I said. Then I said, 'Where'd you go to school?'

'University of Chicago.'

I nodded. 'And Jane?'

'Jane's Bennington.'

'You moved East, hunh?'

'Everybody moves East.'

'See you.'

'I hope we become friends,' Sonny said.

'Why not?' I said. 'I thought we already were. – Listen, what about the boat? What about *Daisy Mae*? I made a date with Chantal von Anders for lunch on her tomorrow. And now you're going away.'

Sonny reached in his pocket. 'Here.' He tossed me the keys. I caught them. 'That's what I came down here to see you for, actually. She's yours. Take her wherever you want. Do what you want with her. You know enough.'

'Okay,' I said grudgingly. I studied the keys. 'And thanks.' I put them in my pocket. 'I'll take care of her.' I waved, and moved away.

Five minutes later a horsecab clopped up with von Anders in it and I got in.

CHAPTER TEN

The dinner party was at some impoverished Danish Count's. His family had lost everything to the Germans, von Anders told me. I figured his mama must have kept back a little of the family jewellery, when I saw the house. It was on one of the narrow, walled, cobbled lanes half-way up the hill. Inside, geometric figured tiles stretched away gleaming under high ceilings. It was a long way from the hippies I had left down in the Port. It was another world. I was bored with it even before we got inside the big iron-studded door.

We ate outside on the terrace. I sat between two ladies who tried desperately to find some common ground to talk to me about. It was sheer hell for all three of us. We went back inside for coffee, and four fat hairy Greek maidens started cleaning up the terrace behind us. Inside, the Count brought out a large silver tray on which was laid out a liberal amount of hashish, pipes, picks, cleaners and matches. This was the lark of the evening.

I had been introduced to a number of people, all in violently coloured sports clothes. One of them was the tall, self-assured, white-haired gent I had met at lunch, Ambassador Pierson. When the tray came out, he came over to me and shook hands again. A record player was playing rock music.

'You're Freddy Tarkoff's business friend, am I right? I somehow didn't get that at lunch.'

'Yes,' I said. That was certainly one way of describing me.

'I thought so. Well, it's nice to have you aboard.' He smiled again, at his little joke. 'I'm just saying good night. I hope we'll see each other again while you're here.'

'I hope so,' I said. It was a barefaced lie. 'You're leaving so soon, Ambassador?'

'Yes, I am. I don't hold with all this hashish business. I know it's supposed to be chic. But as long as it is against the law, I don't feel I can hold with it. Come on, Liza.'

His handsome wife smiled and shook hands with me.

Several others were leaving, too. I didn't know if it was for the same reason. An awful lot were staying, too, and helping themselves to the pipes. All that baloney von Anders had been giving me in the afternoon about her social disgrace over buying hashish looked like a pretty large-scale exaggeration. Technically, you could call it a lie. When the Count, who was a big meaty man and rather pompous, offered a lighted pipe to me, I smiled and shook my head. 'I'll take a good stiff drink instead.'

From somewhere von Anders came towards me holding a glass of her own, her eyes unnaturally bright. She had been at another table at dinner and I had hardly seen her. I shot her a sudden sharp glance, and she flushed. She knew what I was thinking, all right. I said only, 'Having fun?'

She nodded hard. 'Yes, I am. But it's a problem. Some of us are dead set against smoking hash.'

'A lot of you think it's a great lot of fun.'

She nodded again. 'I'm in that part.'

I looked around. 'Pretty hip bunch of people. I just left some of the real ones.' There wasn't a soul under forty in the room. Let alone under thirty.

Von Anders gave me a long, calculating look. 'We're not really hip. And most of us know it. Do you want to dance?'

I shook my head.

'You don't dance rock? Do you mind if I do?'

'No.'

'You're not having much fun, are you?'

'No. But that doesn't matter.'

'But you're not having fun.'

'I'm having as much fun as anybody.'

She looked around. 'You know, it's true. They all look laboured, don't they? They labour at the dancing, and labour not to look self-conscious. They look awkward and unsure about smoking their hash. They're a little ridiculous.'

She laughed. 'What can I do to make you have fun? Shall we go talk somewhere?'

'If you want.' But I didn't move. She was still wanting me to take care of her 'blackmail' case. And I knew I was going to do it. In spite of myself. It was already all set up. And now my feet seemed reluctant to take the first step into it all.

Beside me, von Anders seemed to gather herself all together, as if consciously fitting herself deliberately to my mood. She leaned back against the wall alongside me.

At the record player the rock music stopped and some Greek songs were put on. A line formed, mostly of women, and began to do one of the complicated Greek dances, led by one older woman. A few of them did it quite well. When the number ended there was a gay call to all go off to what they called the 'dancing taverna', a place called Georgio's. A phone call was placed for horsecabs.

'It'll take a while,' von Anders said beside me. 'Let's go out on the terrace.'

Outside on the terrace it was beautiful. We could see over most of the town below, and the harbour with its yachts. The moon was there. Far down, the light from the little lighthouse winked regularly like a pulse. The four hairy Greek maidens had cleaned up the terrace and there was nobody out there but us.

'I thought only the Greek man did those dances?' I said.

'In the old days. Not any more.'

'Women's lib, hunh?'

She laughed. 'Greek women's.'

We sat on the parapet and she began asking me questions about myself.

'You're certainly a peculiar man.'

They were interested questions. She was fitting herself to me the way only an expert woman can, when she seriously sets her mind to a man. It was easy enough to see through it, but all your meat and your glandular system responded to it just the same anyway.

I was reluctant to talk about myself. All this stuff was part of what I had been trying to keep out of the front of my head since Athens. Slowly, I let a few facts about me emerge. I told her how I had come home to Denver from the Second Great War itchy. I told her how I had studied law in Denver on the GI Bill, and then gone into practice. How I was attracted to private investigations work more and more, instead of to pure law, because it was more exciting. How I drifted from Denver to Chicago to pick up more business, and picked up a wife and one daughter. How I moved on to New York, and picked up

52

a second daughter. I didn't tell her about my partner, and his death in Chicago. I didn't tell her about my wife and the divorce. I didn't tell her about Freddy Tarkoff and my latest job for him.

'And twenty years later, here I am. Not much of a story.' I swallowed from my drink. 'About the same as any middle-aged man. Who outgrows both his wildness and his optimism. And finds himself in a profession almost by accident. Finds out that his youthful dreams can't stand the mass of weight life loads on them. In general, human beings seem able to afford almost any luxury except ideals. I guess next to children, ideals are about the most expensive luxury there is.' My smile felt tough enough.

'You make me feel my age,' von Anders said. 'I try to forget it. I shouldn't have asked.'

'Whatever your age is, you don't look it.' I paused like a pro actor. 'At least, not in this moonlight.'

I thought she might grin. She simply shook her head and looked at me. After a moment she said, 'I know what you're going to say to me. You're going to say I lied to you this afternoon.'

'It looks that way. Doesn't it?'

She spoke stubbornly. 'I told you the truth.'

'Not if you told me you were being blackmailed for buying hashish. These people all have it in the house.'

'Does that mean you won't go on with my investigation for me?'

'I never take clients who aren't honest with me.'

'You're cruel.'

'And you're pretty. Very pretty. But whatever you're afraid of, it's not what you told me.'

'Me? Pretty?' She looked down at herself with mock dismay. 'I'm only an old married woman, divorced, living on a substantial alimony I mean to hang on to.'

'But very pretty.'

From inside somebody called to us. The horsecabs had arrived. We went in and trooped out with the others. Somehow, by some ploy I was unable to divine, Chantal managed to get us a horsecab to ourselves. I was already thinking of her to myself as Chantal, now. It never took long, did it?

In the cab, when we had jerked and swayed and tottered

away and the horse had worked himself into a gait, she slipped her hand into mine. I let it lie there.

She said, 'You've been married. Are you still?'

I shook my head. 'No.'

'Divorced?'

'Yes.'

'Why?'

I didn't know whether to answer that at all, or not. 'Incompatibility,' I said shortly.

'Sexual or social?'

But before I could react, she raised her hand and said, 'Don't answer that.' The hand found its way against my cheek as if by accident; for a second. 'That was an unfair question.'

'I'd just as soon not talk about it,' I said.

'Was it recent?' She answered herself, 'It was recent. Freddy Tarkoff told me.' A pause. 'That's how I knew. So you see? I lied to you another time.' Another pause. 'You're really quite a fellow.' She leaned forward and kissed me lightly on the cheek.

I didn't respond. She was hitting a lot closer to home than I felt comfortable with, whether Freddy Tarkoff had talked to her about me or not. The horsecab was just arriving at the lights of the 'dancing taverna'.

It was all very moving, all very romantic, and it was all too easy. As we got out of the cab I said, 'Did Freddy tell you anything else?'

'No. Nothing. And Freddy doesn't know anything about me ever buying any hashish.'

'I've had lots of people tell me I'm quite a guy. Almost always they had some ulterior motive.'

She flushed. 'You *are* a bastard!' She turned and ran away from me toward the door. But at the door she stopped and waited for me. So that when I came up we could be seen walking in together. Fine.

We passed through a tiny restaurant with a zinc bar and about four tables, all closed up now, and came out into a huge barn-like patio which was entirely roofed over with a corrugated plastic roof. A massive jukebox sat against the back wall, and a badly poured concrete floor stretched away. There were a lot of cheap chrome-and-Formica tables. A lot of them were occupied. It was tacky and cheap but that didn't bother our mob.

Many people from the party were there ahead of us, and were laughing and calling out to each other as they were being seated at one big long table that was being made up for them out of. empty singles. They were treated with extreme deference by the owner and his waiters. Like local gentry come down among the commons. And they were all very aware of their higher status. So was Chantal. Subtly, in front of my eyes, von Anders changed her colouration like a lizard and became a 'Countess'.

I had already spotted Girgis at a table with a pretty American girl. Girgis grinned and nodded at me. But Chantal's eyes passed right over him as if he wasn't there. At the table we ordered a drink which it seemed to take an hour to get.

The whole foray was a bad idea as far as I was concerned. I was embarrassed by the airs put on by our big table. Everyone at it treated the rest of the place like peons. Especially the Danish Count, who treated the waiters – and the owner – with indulgent contempt, as if they were his personal serfs. The waiters seemed to like it but I wanted to slug him.

The only thing interesting was the Greek dancing. But few were good at it. Girgis, though, stood out as a beautiful dancer, and as a sort of natural leader. He was a cock of the walk, here. He wasn't showing off for the gentry or Chantal. He was simply enjoying himself. But even watching him palled in that place, with that bunch of aristocrats.

'I'm going outside a while. Breathe some air,' I said to von Anders. She looked at me. A kind of contained panic came on her face. 'Do you want to come?' I added.

'Oh, I –' She looked at the other women near her. 'I shouldn't really. But – all right.'

Outside, she took my arm. 'I was terrified you were going to leave me there.' She paused. 'They are going to think we are starting an affair.'

'Let them. Maybe it's a good idea,' I said.

'That's easy for you to say. But I have to live here.'

Nevertheless, she held on close. I felt the weight of her one breast lying on my arm. She must have felt it. Out here, there was another, open patio, and below it a few steps down to a beach, and beyond the beach the sea. I walked us down to it.

At the edge of the sand I let go of her and stepped back and looked around.

'I didn't expect to find the sea here,' I said. 'I thought we were going inland.'

'Everyone thinks that,' she said. 'No, we really only crossed a neck of land from the yacht harbour. That's all.'

Then, without any more words at all, she had slipped into my arms and I was kissing her deeply on the mouth without having expected to. I was surprised. It was as if the two innocuous comments about the sea had meant something else. Tentatively I put my tongue in her mouth and she received it hotly, moistly; so hotly, so moistly, and with such an eagerness that it brought a sexual metaphor image into my mind. After, she put her ear against my chest. 'I can hear your heart,' she said like some damn adolescent kid. Then, 'I'm afraid. He's got me scared.'

'I don't think it's him you're afraid of,' I said.

'Oh, but it is.'

I let go of her, and without either of us suggesting it we walked back inside.

In the huge covered space the others were getting ready to leave. 'I'll take you home,' I said.

'Oh, no. No, no. I have a ride home. With the Sandersons. Thanks just the same. But they live just above me.' And she walked over to them. 'Good night,' she said brightly. 'Thanks for coming.'

I was not about to let the others see my surprise. So I nodded. 'Don't forget our lunch date tomorrow.'

'Yes. All right. Call me.' She took the male Sanderson's other arm.

The others were trooping out. I was nonplussed by the suddenness of her leaving me. I sat down for a few minutes, almost ordered another drink, then didn't.

Out on the concrete floor the poor people went on dancing Greek dances.

CHAPTER ELEVEN

I must have sat there five or six minutes. I was still a little punchy from von Anders's retreat. It was amazing how the atmosphere of the place changed when the richies left. Constraint disappeared. Everybody relaxed. Apparently I didn't count.

I could not think of a place in the U.S. where the coming of a party of rich gentry to a low dive could cause a comparable reaction. But maybe I was just being chauvinistic. I was sure as hell feeling chauvinistic.

I was still sitting when a young man who looked like one of the kids from the Construction slipped in and spoke to Girgis. Girgis got up and followed him out. It pulled my mind back to pertinent things. I had thought of talking to him.

Girgis had left his American girl behind. That meant he meant to come back. I gave them a couple of minutes to transact their business, then got up and followed them.

Girgis was standing in moonlight about half-way down the walk to the row of waiting horsecabs. The boy was walking off up the road, starting what was a two-mile hike back to town with no horsecab stations in between. Well, good for him. He was young and healthy. I took myself a good deep breath and let it out slowly, then moved up on Girgis's right side. A right-hander turning to his right has to have a pretty good left hook to catch you flat. And Girgis didn't look like any fist fighter.

'Excuse me,' I said.

He turned slowly. Without fear. But I had a sudden, etched impression of an only half-domesticated animal who was all poised, all balanced on the toes of his hoofs or paws ready for flight or combat as soon as his computer nervous system fed him the right combination of necessary sensory information. A half-tamed deer, perhaps. Like the ones we used to have at my dad's Wind River Range camp.

'Oh, Mister Davies. Hallo. I did not know who you were this morning. Allow me to excuse myself.' He made a deprecatory gesture, putting himself down for his failure at information-gathering. 'Are you looking for some hashish?'

'No. I'm not,' I said. 'But if I ever do, I'll come to you. Okay?' I let a beat pass. 'How long were you in America?'

'Two years. Almost.' He grinned. There was a likeable quality about him. 'You could tell, hunh? By my accent?'

I nodded. 'Tell me, do you make more money from selling hash, or from blackmailing women?'

He stared at me and his jaw came out. Casually, he shifted his weight on to his right leg, and put his right hand in his hip pocket.

'I wouldn't,' I said.

Just as casually, he put his other hand in his other hip pocket. The move shifted his weight back on to both feet. He grinned. But there was nothing placating in his grin, and no scare. He was furious. 'Chantal has been talking to you, has she? She's a nice lady, but you do not want to believe everything she tells you. She has the big imagination.'

'I told her to quit paying you,' I said. 'So quit asking her. If you don't, I'll hear about it.'

He laughed, harshly. 'You pretty tough. Okay, I quit asking. You tell Chantal.' He snorted again. 'There's a lots going on around here you don't know.'

'May be. If there is, I'll find it out.'

'You tell Chantal I quit asking, hunh?'

'I'll tell her.'

'You be sure and tell her, hunh?'

'And if I want any hash, I'll call you. Don't you call me,' I said.

Grinning, Girgis nodded his appreciation of my little insult. But his eyes were cold and thinking as he turned away, his hands still in his two hip pockets. I could see the bulge of the sap under his fingers in the right one.

I rather liked him. He was taller than me, and a whole hell of a lot younger, but I thought I could take him. I was ready to try anyway, if he had pulled the sap. I was ready to get in close and tie him up so he couldn't hit with it, and I thought I could still take him. I turned away myself, down toward the row of horsecabs, letting out another good deep breath. I could feel energy sparkling at my fingertips and wrists and the insides of my elbows, pulsing to get out. I still liked it. I swung up into the first cab.

I was still confused about von Anders. About Chantal. I still couldn't believe Girgis was blackmailing her about anything as petty and commonplace as buying hashish from him. On the other hand Girgis hadn't said he wasn't blackmailing her, when I put it to him. He had been pretty insistent that I tell her he was 'quitting asking'; he had repeated it three times. Why?

I was beginning to become intrigued in a purely professional way. What was going on on this wacky ancient island? I tried to let the regular clopping of the horse's feet put my mind into a rhythmic pattern of thinking. But it didn't work. Nothing came, I couldn't figure any of it out. I didn't have enough facts at my disposal yet.

Back at the house, when the drowsy cabman and his drowsy horse let me off, everything was wrapped up. Sonny's caique was dark, Georgina was probably fast asleep, Dmitrios's taverna across the vacant lot was all closed down. Then I noticed one thing. The big sailing yacht out in the harbour was all lit up, and men were scrambling around on it as if making it ready for sea.

It seemed a curious time to be making a yacht ready for sea. I went inside without turning on any lights, felt for the whisky bottle and a glass, and went upstairs and down the hall in the dark to my bedroom. I got an old pair of binoculars Con Taylor had left on the bedside table and studied the yacht. They were indeed making it ready to sail. I counted five or six crewmen. The crewmen all wore blue turtlenecks with the ship's name, *Agoraphobe*, in white across the chest. The captain was distinguishable from them by the white shirt he wore, and a rakish white captain's cap. He was a big man with a big behind almost as wide as his wide shoulders, and he kept the men humping. As I watched, he told them all off on some job or other, then ran down the hanging ladder and took the ship's launch to shore.

The sound of the launch's motor carried up to me in the quiet night. Somewhere within the ship a pump or generator throbbed steadily. I put down the glasses and picked up my drink. I had time for a couple. Twenty minutes later he was back and I heard the launch motor. I put down my drink and picked up the glasses. When he mounted the ladder, he was carrying a carpetbag type satchel which looked suspiciously like it might contain money. Whatever it contained, it was something he was being very careful with, and would not allow anybody else to handle. He took it below himself to stow it.

I watched a while longer and then put up the glasses and went to bed. Once again my internal systems told me I had drunk too much during the course of the day and the evening. In the night I half woke and thought I heard a ship's motor throbbing, and getting fainter. When I woke in broad daylight, the *Agoraphobe* was gone. Otherwise, it was an ordinary, lovely morning. A number of speedboats were out beyond the harbour, hauling water skiers. I noted that Sonny Duval's speed-boat was gone, and his big caique all locked up.

CHAPTER TWELVE

Whatever else happened on this wacky island, it was an intense pleasure to have my morning coffee on the shaded porch above the harbour in the bright morning sun.

On my way down to Sonny's boat I stopped at the taverna and had a coffee there, at a table out over the water. I wanted to talk to the old man.

There was nobody else there that early. When I'd paid, with the keys of the *Daisy Mae* tinkling deliciously in my pocket, I asked old Dmitrios about the big yacht.

The old man had just openly and outrageously cheated me and overcharged me twenty cents for a bad cup of instant coffee in lukewarm water. He peered at me with the peasant's squint of eternal greed in his eyes, wiping and wiping his hands on his apron. He had the limitless patience of ignorant acquisitiveness. I just waited. When he couldn't find a way to milk a quarter or a dollar out of me on this, he finally shrugged. It had gone away, he said.

'I see that. But to where?'

He shrugged again. I could virtually read his slow-witted mind: Did I have some special reason for wanting to know? How could that be made to pay? I understood all about his deprived childhood. He made me mad, anyway.

To Athens maybe, he told me finally. It sometimes

went to Athens. To pick up a charter party of French or
English to cruise in the islands. The captain was an
American. Name of Kirk. Jim Kirk. He had been the
captain for almost two years now. The *Agoraphobe*. A
beautiful ship. The owner had a sense of humour, naming
it thus.

'Who is the owner?' I asked.

He shrugged. And wiped his hand. A Mr Kronitis. Mr
Leonid Kronitis. A Greek. A very rich Greek. Owned
ships. Not like Onassis, or Niarchos. But still very big.
Dmitrios sailed on one of his ships once. To California and
Hawaii. Very big.

'Does he live here?'

Oh, no. Not him. Tsatsos too small for him. Lived in
Athens. But he had a big villa on the mainland, there,
somewhere behind Glauros, the town there.

I squinted at it, the town, a mile or two away on the
mainland shore.

But he was never there, Dmitri said. He used his *Agoraphobe* sometimes, but he chartered it to pay for its
maintenance. A very careful man with money, Mr Kronitis.

'That's probably why he's so rich,' I said.

'You did not give a tip for the coffee,' Dmitri said.

'No,' I said. 'Because you charged me too much for it in
the first place.'

He shrugged, and wiped his hands. On that apron. He
did not even get angry. I turned on my heel and got
away from there.

On the dock I stood a minute and looked at the *Daisy
Mae*, Looking at it, I could forget the Dmitris of this
world. I felt like a kid whose daddy has given him fifty
cents to spend at the candy store any way he wanted. She
lay there, floating and tugging at her mooring on the
slightly moving, dirty harbour water, touched lightly by
the soft air of early morning. I pulled her in, long-stepped
on board her, unlocked her with the keys, and went about
the ritual of getting her ready. Almost automatically I
began to whistle. Working, I could not remember having
had so much fun in a long time. And all alone. I
washed down the deck, which didn't really need it, and
then swabbed it and then washed down the coach-roof
and swabbed that. I checked out the toilet in its cubicle and
cleaned it. I got the ice for the ice chest at the taverna,

replenished the bar, stowed my shirt and shoes below, and checked out the motor. I unmoored her and pulled myself out hand over hand along the anchor line, freed the anchor, shipped it and washed it down. In the swiftly heating sun I left for town, threading out through the other craft.

The run up to the Port, along the blinding, white-white, sun-laved face of the town, was delicious.

In the Port I ran her in alongside a vegetable caique, and climbed up on to the stone, cobbled wharf of the shopping district, still infested with its hippie kids, and bought a paper and went up to the shaded terrace of cafés.

No sooner had I ordered a Campari-soda and settled down with my paper than the blond-named Adonis Steve and his short-haired sidekick Chuck with the thick glasses sauntered by, in embroidered Mongol vests and shorts and sandals.

It was as if they had been looking for me. Apparently, they had been strolling up and down, waiting. As soon as they saw me, Steve came walking over, Chuck at his heels. Steve slipped into a seat at the table, and Chuck slipped into another. Without asking.

'I want to talk to you,' Steve said.

'You do?' I said. 'Then why don't you sit down? Better yet, why don't you ask? Though I'm not sure I want to talk to you. I see your boy Cyclops here found himself a nice pigeon to beat up last night. Hallo, Cyclops.'

'Listen, mister,' Chuck started, and pushed his glasses up with his middle finger.

'I see you take good care of those glasses,' I said. 'Is that the only pair you've got? You'd be in trouble if somebody ever broke them for you, wouldn't you?'

'Mister,' Chuck said.

'They look like they're made from the bottoms of two Coca-Cola bottles,' I said.

'Mister.'

'Say one more word to me,' I said pleasantly, 'one more word, Cyclops, and I'll break them for you myself. I'd be pleased to.' I really meant it. I was boiling angry.

'Shut up, Chuck,' Steve growled.

'That's better,' I said. 'Then next, why don't you two ill-mannered loutish children just bug out of here. Before you get me irritated and I wrap this iron table around your collective heads. I'm perfectly capable of it.'

'I said I wanted to talk to you,' Steve said. He looked at me with his strange, sort of sightless, non-seeing eyes. 'Cut the funnies. You were seen with Girgis last night.'

'Your intelligence service reported that, did they?' I said.

'I don't know what your action is with him,' Steve said patiently. 'But I want to warn you. Don't go getting any ideas about tying up with him. Or about going into business with him, see? You will only do your*self* harm. He's very likely to be going out of business, very soon. He's going to find himself in some trouble. None of the kids like him. He's nasty to them. And he's starting to over-charge them. He can't last long without some boom being lowered.'

'And who is going to do the lowering of this boom?' I said.

'I'm going to see to it myself. So if you have any ideas about fading some of his action, forget it.' His sightless-seeming eyes stared at me.

'Or I'll get the same treatment,' I said.

'That's *right*.'

'And what kind of treatment is that?'

'Never mind. It won't be pleasant. And it'll be ex*pen*-sive.'

I looked at him thoughtfully, or pretended to. 'I'll keep in mind what you said. I will keep it well in the forefront of my mind.'

'You do that.' He made as if to get up. So did Chuck.

'Tell me,' I said. 'You said you had to have a Greek partner in that bar of yours.'

'I didn't say it. You did.'

'Okay, I said it. Who is this partner? What's his name?'

'Uh, who wants to know?'

'I want to know. Me. I'm curious.'

'You wouldn't know him, anyway. Name's Kronitis. Doesn't even live here.'

'Oh, I know him. Leonid Kronitis. Has a big villa over back of Glauros,' I said. Steve looked surprised. 'Owns ships. Owns that big sailing yacht *Agoraphobe*. Sure, I know Kronitis. Matter of fact, I was with him at a party last night,'

For a moment doubt flashed on his face. Then he shook

his head. 'No you weren't. You couldn't have been. I was with him myself.'

It looked like it was two liars each trying to outbluff the other, to me. 'I see. Maybe it was two other people.'

'You remember what I said.'

'I'll remember, son.' I gave him my No. 2 amused smile. The one without the contempt. 'You know, I don't see any difference between your generation and any other generation. There isn't any, is there?'

'Sure there is. For one thing, we don't believe in violence,' Steve said flatly. He grinned at me.

I laughed. 'So long, Cyclops,' I said as they moved away.

I sat and finished my Campari and thought about this new wrinkle for a while. Nothing much of any importance came to me. The shaded, half-crowded terrace of tables was pleasing. My Paris *Herald* and Rome *Daily American* had lost their flavour, but I was damned if I would let them ruin my Campari-soda. Were these dumb kids trying to muscle in on Girgis's business? It looked like it. And if so, how did that – or how would that – affect my client Chantal and her problem? Now I was thinking of her as my client. And who was this Kronitis character who kept cropping up?

Across the terrace I saw Georgina Taylor sitting alone, at a table full of empty cups and plates as if her hippie bird creatures had eaten fast and flown off in a flock. I watched her pay the not inconsiderable tab. By the cheques they pay Ye shall know them. I paid my own and wandered over and asked her if she wanted a ride home on the *Daisy Mae*. She seemed delighted by the prospect.

'I see you're making friends with the young people,' she said brightly, as we walked down.

'Well, yes,' I said judiciously. 'I guess they're not as bad as I first thought.'

'I'm so glad,' Georgina said.

On Sonny's boat with her, after helping her aboard, I watched Steve and Chuck pile into a handsome speedboat and roar out of the Port going west away from the yacht harbour. The back was full of expensive water skiing gear Their precipitate departure set all the boats in the Port to rocking and knocking against each other. Across the Port, as they pulled out, rocking in the wash created by the speedboat, was the *Polaris*, with Girgis at the helm, preparing to sound his klaxon. He grinned and waved at them.

'Tell me, Georgina,' I said as I pulled us out beyond the jetty-breakwater and turned back east. 'Who *owns* the *Polaris*?'

'Mr Leonid Kronitis,' Georgina said proudly.

'I thought maybe,' I said, and devoted myself to upping the throttle.

'Mr Kronitis is our local philanthropist,' Georgina said, almost possessively. 'As well as being a big source of help with capital to people starting out in business. Like Girgis.'

'Is he?' I concentrated myself on enjoying the run back. After all, I was paying for the fuel. Or Tarkoff was.

It gave me some time to muse about Kronitis. Was the local shipowner into everything on the island? Was it possible he might not know his two captains were engaged in a local but profitable hashish smuggling operation? And if so, what did I care? Was it any of my business? Only insofar as it affected my client. My damned client. Did my damned client know Kronitis? In any business way, that is? I was sure she knew him socially.

I pulled in at the dock at Dmitri's taverna and let Georgina off and had another cup of bad coffee and waited for Chantal. This time Dmitrios charged me the same price he charged the locals. I suppose he would have gone on overcharging me twenty cents a cup forever if I did not complain. He was incredible.

Chantal was stunning when she finally appeared. She hopped down out of the horsecab in big glasses, a cute sun hat cocked on her head, a long Indian cotton print knotted around her waist over her swimsuit like a skirt open to the hip, and a blue fisherman's shirt with the sleeves rolled up. The driver handed her down a basket crammed with other clothes, towels, and lotion bottles. 'You look stunning,' I said. 'But you look like you came prepared to stay a week. Aren't you afraid people will talk about us two going off all alone for that long?'

She smiled happily. 'Not really. I think they all know that I'm your official vacation guide.'

Her sudden defection of last night had left me a little wary. I took the basket. Only a little of the flab of age showed on her slender thighs. There was only a very little of that pecky, flaky look on her forearms that ageing skin gets. Her upper arms were firm. You wouldn't have noticed any of it five yards away. 'What have you got in here, for God's sake?' I said. I added, 'I thought we'd go to a taverna around the island.' But up close you noticed it.

She was on board and seated, and all spread out and arranged in the sun, before she noticed there was no boatman.

'Where is Sonny?'

'He had to go to Athens. I'm running the boat today.'

Doubtful looks. 'Well, do you know how?'

'No. But I pick up things fast.' I paused. 'Are you scared?'

'I don't know. I never know what to expect from you.'

'Keep them guessing,' I said.

I fired up the engine with a flourish. After she saw me thread out through the other craft and all their lines, she smiled. 'I might have known.'

I took us out and around the lighthouse point, the other way from the Port. The sea was sparkling, the sun was bright, the water plashed against the bows. High above us through the incandescent air were the green fields of the hillsides and the stands of pine and the white spots of the ancient chapels. Plash was a good word, I thought.

'Have you decided to tell me any more about your secret life?' I said.

Her face fell and clouded over. 'I've told you it all.'

'I had a talk with Girgis last night,' I said. I was watching her from the ends of my eyes. The helpless look of contained panic from last night came over her face.

'What did you say?'

'I told him I told you to stop paying him. I told him to stop asking you for it. He laughed, and said to tell you he was stopping asking.'

There was no look of relief on Chantal's face.

'As a matter of fact,' I said, 'he told me three different times to tell you he was stopping.'

She didn't answer that either.

'I thought you'd be pleased.'

'Well, I am.' But she didn't look it. Then, in a lower voice, 'Do you think he really will?'

'If he doesn't, you tell me.'

'I don't trust him. I know him, you see. It's going to

66

take a lot more than that.'

'I can't do any more until you tell me more,' I said in a carefully flattened voice.

'Oh, let's not talk about it!' she said explosively, and threw her head back in the sunshine. 'It's such a lovely day out!'

It was indeed. The sun bathed everything. The island rose on our right, brown fields down below, then green fields higher up, then the emerald green of forests higher still, and the vast blue seascape sky backdropping all of it. The blinding whitewash of the little chapels dotted fields and woods alike. On the beach the low shape of Georgio's 'dancing taverna' of last night was visible off our quarter.

'You're not the most helpful non-paying client I've ever had,' I said. 'Hey!' I said. 'What's that?' I had seen something. 'See it?' I pointed out something, an object, floating in the water far off. It did not seem to be under way and moving. After a minute, I eased the bow over toward it.

CHAPTER THIRTEEN

As we drew nearer, the floating object became an orange float with a little spar sticking up. As we got closer still, a figure rose to the surface in a black mask, black foam rubber helmet and wet-suit, rolled and lay face down, breathing through a snorkel. Then it rolled up and dived again, the flippered feet rising above the water and sinking silently.

The sun was numbing now; eye-stunning, the way I had seen it yesterday. The sea was as flat as a glass plate. We had been out about a half hour, and it must have been nearly noon. No breath of air stirred anywhere across the glassy surface. Hardly a ripple moved it. No living thing moved anywhere within eye range. We were all by ourselves and an enormous stillness had descended over everything. Only our motor disturbed it, drumming against it without breaking its tough skin. The sun seemed actually to burn the sea's surface, making the surface water

67

more sluggish than the water a few inches down. The diver surfaced, rested, then dived again.

It was kind of awesome. Even though I knew how easy it was to do alone like this. We were far out to sea, no boats were visible anywhere, the shore well over half a mile away. And here was this figure all alone.

'That's Marie,' Chantal said.

'Marie? A girl?' I said.

'Yes. It's that American girl. One of the hippies.' Her nose sounded a little out of joint.

'I think I'll stop,' I said. I suppose there was a half-admiring look on my face. Chantal looked as if there was. 'I've done quite a bit of this,' I explained.

I jockeyed us closer to the float.

The figure rose from the depths again, visible now coming up, with a dreamlike slowness. Its head broke the surface and looked at us, non-human and expressionless in the mask; an alien Martian, with the face mask-covered and the snorkel mouthpiece distorting and hiding the mouth. Then a brown hand came up and removed the snorkel and pushed up the mask and a strikingly attractive girl's face appeared, smiling.

'Get him?' I called.

The girl shook her head, and began to haul in the spear of her gun at the end of its line.

'Come on aboard,' I called. 'Can we take you anywhere?'

'No, thanks,' the girl said. 'But I'll come aboard.' She placed her speargun crosswise on the doughnut float. Three good-sized grouper lay in the rubber sack in its centre. I was scrambling to put the swimming ladder over.

The girl came up it, awkwardly walking backwards in the flippers, an apparition in black: wide shoulders, long waist, swelling hips, long lovely legs. In the wet-suit jacket was a flattened double swell of her breasts. She sat on the railing and stripped off the mask and helmet and the apparition became a real girl, with long straight sun-streaked hair, hippie style to below the shoulders.

'Hallo, Chantal,' she said.

'Hallo, Marie.'

'Do you want anything?' I said.

'I'd like some water, please,' she said. 'It gets dry down there. Have you got any sandwiches?'

'I happen to have some sandwiches,' I said. 'I had a sack made up at the taverna.' I got the sack, and a bottle of water, and gave them to her. 'I thought we might need them,' I said to Chantal. She just looked at me.

I was being apologetic. I did not know if it was coming from within me myself, or if Chantal was imposing it on me. But it was making me half sore. What the hell? I loved diving. I could certainly admire a young girl who had nerve enough to be out here alone miles from everywhere spearfishing with nothing but a diver's float.

Suddenly I had to laugh. All those years of marriage had trained me. And I hadn't even slept with this lady yet.

'Do you want one, too?' I grinned.

'No!'

The girl sat on the boat's rail and munched her sandwich, unaware of byplay. 'This'll save me swimming in afterwhile,' she smiled. She had a strange, sad, still, acquiescent quality about her.

'I used to do a lot of that,' I said. 'Stay in the water all day.'

'Where?' the girl said.

'In the Caribbean. But I rarely went out all day alone.'

'There are more sharks there, I hear. I've never done it anywhere but here. Why did you stop?' It seemed as if she was not really with us, but back there somewhere in the water, in her mind.

'I'm a private detective. I was on a case in Jamaica. My work took me elsewhere. I still do it sometimes. Vacations. But it's not the same.' I paused. 'It's like any sport. You have to do it all the time.'

'I guess.' She began putting back on her rubber helmet.

'Didn't I see you at Georgina Taylor's yesterday, with that gang?' I said.

'Yes. I was there. You didn't notice me. Well, thanks for the meal.' She wasn't wanting to talk much. The mask went back on, then the snorkel. She was the sexy Martian again. Casually, she dropped the seven feet over the side, holding mask to face with both hands.

I stood and watched her swim back to her float for her gun. Then I started up the motor and put it in gear. The float diminished sternward. We didn't say anything for several minutes.

'That's the first time I've ever seen you like that,'

Chantal said finally after a while.

'Like what?'

'Eager. Excited. Interested. You were almost warm, for a few minutes.'

I grinned. 'I guess I forgot myself. I loved skindiving.'

'Why don't you do it then? If you love something that much? Just give everything up and go and do it?'

'Anngh,' I growled. I thought about my wife. My ex-wife. 'I've got a very big alimony to support. I have two teenage girls in school.'

'Responsibilities, in other words.'

'Call it guilts. What's the difference? The effect's the same. I figure I owe it. It was my own fault.'

'Like all the rest of us,' she said softly.

'No, not like all the rest of you,' I said. 'One thing about me you'll learn. I always pay what I think I owe. I'll pay it if it kills me.'

'Which in your business it might just some day do.'

'A gross canard,' I grinned. 'People in my business never get killed – unless they drive their own cars or fly their own helicopters. I always travel by public conveyance whenever possible.'

She looked like she didn't know quite how to take that. My unwillingness to play serious talk games with her still irritated her.

'Listen, where is this place we're going? How far is it?' I said.

She had looked away from me. As if I had insulted her. 'Not too far now,' she said over her shoulder. She went on looking ahead of us. So I looked ahead of us, too. The boat ran on, over the glassy water, under the dead-quiet stunning sun.

I could remember that long, slow, silent, dreamlike ascent swimming up. You could look down between your feet and see the bottom diminishing and fading, or look up at the wavery glare of the surface far above and see the boat's bullet-shaped shadow over you. I expected that, as well as needing to come up for air, she wanted to see who was visiting; because she would have seen us above her. Down below you could hear a boat's motor a long way off, warning you. In the States the little spar on Marie's float would have had on it the red diver's flag with the diagonal white slash across it, but not here. Not

70

in the Caribbean either, where I used to dive. Always, coming up from any of the deeper dives, your mask, pressurized at depth with air from your nostrils, would belch out air bubbles of its own, and you could look up and see them rocketing and dancing up to the surface above you like flattened balls of mercury. I had been able to do eighty and ninety feet before I left Jamaica. Under the tutelage of one of the Caribbean masters. An American, who had stated emphatically that I was the best pupil he had ever had. But that had been ten years ago. And I had been ten years younger.

'Tell me about this American girl,' I said.

'Her name is Marie something. Sweet Marie, the hippies call her. She makes her living selling the fish she spears. She is also the hashish runner for Girgis.'

'Girgis uses a runner? There isn't that far to run, around here.'

'He doesn't like the hippies. He also doesn't like to be seen with them. So he hires her to deliver the stuff and collect the money for him.' Her voice sounded reproving. 'And she also has slept with everybody on the island. And I mean everybody. Boys and girls alike.'

'Are you being jealous, Chantal?' I teased.

'Of her? I guess between her two jobs she makes herself a good enough living. For her. Last summer she made enough to stay on through the winter.'

'It takes a lot of nerve to stay out offshore alone like that all day swimming without a boat. Almost as much as it would take to stay here through the winter, I'll bet,' I said.

Chantal shuddered. 'You're right about that part. I don't think the diving takes much nerve on her part. I think it's an escape for her. From something.'

I looked at her curiously. I felt she might almost be talking about herself without knowing it.

'Aren't there any police around this place?'

'There are four. One fat chief, and three muscular young morons hoping to get fat. They're called the constabulary.'

'Is that all?'

'There's a real Police Inspector over at Glauros on the mainland. When he's not in Athens.'

'Well, there isn't all that much money, or interest, in

71

hashish anyway. Heroin is the big deal.'

I didn't particularly expect any reaction to that from Chantal. I didn't get any. 'I suppose,' she said. 'There's our taverna up ahead.'

The taverna lay in the middle of a long shallow beach between two hills. The hills fell in cliffs to the sea and were covered with pine woods. The place looked cool and inviting in that sun. I unscrewed the wing nut on Sonny's throttle. Then I saw that Girgis's boat the *Polaris* was one of the three tourist boats tied up at the single, rickety jetty.

'Would you rather not go in here?'

Chantal's chin came up and her face took on its aloof Countess look. 'Are you joking?'

'I can't tie up there by the other boats anyway,' I told her, and ran us in thirty or forty yards down.

'Swim a little?' I said, when I came back.

'Yes.'

We did, and the water was delicious and crystal clear. All around us in the water and on the beach were tourists from Girgis's boat, and tourists from the other boats, mostly Greeks from Athens, fat big-bellied women, paunchy vain men, loud-mouth teenage boys and girls. Under an inadequate pine tree two sunburnt autobuses owned by the municipality languished in insufficient shade. The taverna tables were crowded under their vine-covered lattices.

'I think if we stay here and have a drink and wait,' I said, 'the boats will go soon.' They did, all but *Polaris*. The two hot, overcrowded autobuses left on the dusty gravel road, groaning at the steep climb. As the two of us walked up the sand of the beach toward the taverna, a figure rose languidly from the bench below the *Polaris*'s rail. It was Girgis, in diminutive trunks and his raunchy black captain's cap. He leaped down agilely on to the shaky jetty. Behind him a blonde, a new one, rose adjusting her hair and her swimsuit.

'Going to eat?' He flashed white teeth at us from his tanned face. 'Going to eat myself.'

But that was all he said. He and the girl, who sounded English, joined a group of Greeks. Chantal led us to a table much farther away. There was plenty of room, now.

'He has a new one every week. Always blonde. Always

72

American or English. He teaches them the Greek dancing. It's his equivalent of showing etchings. It's a joke all over the island.'

'Why not?' I said. 'It's a big romantic lark for them. A handsome Greek boat captain, with his own boat.'

'He had quite a fling with Jane Duval last year.'

I felt my ears perking up. 'He did, did he? And did she try to run away to Athens with him, too?'

'No. There wasn't any question of running anywhere with Girgis, I'm afraid.'

I was studying her quizzically. Maybe for the first time it entered my head that she might have had an affair with him herself. 'He doesn't seem like a bad fellow.'

'Bad? Bad is not even the word for it. He wouldn't have been a bad fellow if he had stayed a fisherman. America ruined him.'

'Your title is showing again,' I said. 'Don't blame America, either. He looks like he might ruin easy. America gets blamed for everything nowadays. My God, even Girgis.'

She laughed, her eyes bright on me. Then openly, for him to see, she put her hand on my bare forearm on the table. I looked at it, looked up at her, then winked. Helping her out, I put my own hand over hers.

'People see the good things in life all around them, and they want to get some of them,' I said with my No. 2 sorrowful smile. 'It's what keeps me in business.'

The lunch was nothing to brag about. But it was good to eat it out in the open under the lattice and the trees, with the sea nearby. The highlight of the lunch was when Girgis got up with his new girl and danced to the jukebox. The girl was hopeless but Girgis put on a superb exhibition of the Greek dancing. The tourists from his boat clapped and pounded their tables with their wine glasses in approval. I appreciated his grace, and his superb reflexes. He did not glance at us, and he did not seem even to know we were there.

We lingered on a while after Girgis's boat left. I tied us up to the jetty and we lay on the cabin roof under the tarpaulin.

'There are a couple of blankets down below,' I said. 'We could take one of them up on that hill and lie under the trees a while.'

Chantal seemed to stiffen. 'Certainly not,' she said, in her Countess voice.

I was surprised again. 'Oh,' I said, amiably. 'Okay.'

After a minute she said, 'Did something, or someone, give you the idea I am some kind of an easy lay?'

That angered me. 'Oh, come off it. I'm not trying to corrupt you. You're old enough to know what you want. You don't want? Fine. Leave it at that.' I paused. 'I'll still protect you from your blackmailer. I'm that kind of sucker.'

'That was nasty.'

'I meant it to be. Okay, we go back, hunh?'

After we were back out on the water, she seemed to relent a little. She seemed pensive. She came and sat by me in the stern. 'I'm sorry.'

'Oh, forget it.' I was getting bored with the subject of her ass.

'No. I don't want to forget it. I've got a dinner arranged for us again tonight. At Tarquinia Hall's. She's the older one who leads the ladies in Greek dancing. You come up to my place after dinner.'

'You mean I can take you home from dinner?' Big deal.

'No. That's just what I don't mean. I'll go home with the Sandersons again. Then around midnight you come to my house.'

I thought about that for half a minute. 'Okay. Fine. But let me beg off on the dinner, then.'

'You don't want to come?'

'No. I don't get any kick out of that. That's no vacation. Sitting around watching those people struggling to have a good time. They work as hard at it as those poor people on the beach. I appreciate the poor ones better. I'm more nearly one of them than I am your rich friends. I only work for the rich.'

'Just tell them you can't come?'

'Tell them whatever you like.'

'You are strange.'

'Only to a social butterfly like you.'

A pause. 'What you like is skindiving. And girls in tight black suits.'

I grinned. 'Sure. And in bikinis. All men do.' I reached

74

and snapped the leg elastic of her suit gently. 'If women could only realize how much pleasure they give men, they'd be – furious.'

Chantal laughed out loud. 'You didn't imagine I would go up on that hill with you with a blanket with those taverna people all watching us, did you?'

'I never thought about it,' I said. 'One way or the other.'

I gave her a wink. She was mollified. I was mollified. What a pair of middle-aged fools. We were running closer to shore than on the way out and a little farther on we saw the float again, farther out, small. Marie was still out there fishing. She had covered a good five or six miles.

Almost immediately after, we passed a small, tight, rocky little cove, with an elaborate concrete landing dock built in it, and a tiny beach beside it. I hadn't noticed it before because we had come by it much farther out. A tumbling rolling cliff led up to an old-looking, locked and shuttered villa, high above. Concrete steps had been built up the cliff face to an open veranda beside the villa. It was quite a cosy place.

I might have never noticed it at all, or paid any attention to noticing it, if I hadn't happened to look right at it. But having noticed it, I studied it closely. Somewhere in the back of my old cop's nose something seemed to twitch, and tickle at my mind. I guess because it was so damned cosy.

'Is this place by any chance owned by Mr Leonid Kronitis?' I said.

Chantal looked surprised. 'Why, yes. It is.' Then she looked perplexed, and corrected herself. 'Actually, it's not owned by him personally. I think it's owned by some corporation he's vaguely connected with. Rich men come down from Athens in a big boat apparently, with lots of blondes, and have big parties there occasionally. The gossip is that some big businessmen bring their American associates there to wine, dine and woman them.'

I nodded.

'How do you know about Kronitis? What do you know about him?'

I shrugged. 'Me? Nothing. People mentioned him. He's

supposed to be the great local philanthropist. He owns Girgis's boat, and he owns that big yacht *Agoraphobe*. He owns the hippies' bar. He's rich.'

I made a little circle with the *Daisy Mae* and went back past it a second time and studied it again. It certainly was a great place for some kind of nasty skullduggery and chicanery, my nose told me. It was so damned cosy, and here on the other side of the island all by itself. The villa, too. Smuggling, for example. But smuggling what?

Well, it wasn't my affair. I ran the boat on.

'But what made you guess this place might be owned by Leonid Kronitis?'

'Just a hunch.' I grinned at her.

Behind us the little cove wheeled out of sight behind the headland it nestled against. The same headland hid the villa from us up above. The tremendous, heavier-than-air sun heat had diminished considerably, I noticed. Out in the water the little orange float of Sweet Marie the hippie skindiver had disappeared from our sight, too.

'Do you know him?' I said. 'Kronitis?'

'Why, yes. But only very slightly. He comes to parties here on the island sometimes. But he doesn't live here.'

'I know. He has a big villa over behind Glauros on the mainland. Right?'

She nodded. 'That's right. My God, Freddy Tarkoff said you were a nosy individual.'

I just nodded. I screwed Sonny Duval's wing nut throttle down a couple of turns tighter.

CHAPTER FOURTEEN

Sonny Duval was not back from Athens when we arrived back at the yacht harbour. Chantal went on home and I went to work cleaning up the boat. It was just as much fun as when I had done it that morning.

After I finished I walked back up to the house and made myself a stiff drink. We had plenty at lunch, plus some wine, but I felt I needed another. Thus I was in position in my regular grandstand seat to see and hear

Sonny's return.

His speedboat came roaring in from roughly the direction of Glauros over on the mainland. Both Jane in her grubby Mother Hubbard and the baby in its grubby face were in the boat with him. Sonny ran the boat right on in to the dock and gassed it and then took it out to the big caique off the house and tied it up. At this point I ducked back in off my porch and watched the rest through the french doors. I suspected he might come looking for me and I didn't feel up to him yet.

At the caique they all three climbed up on board and went down below. Sonny seemed to have a grim look on his face. In a few minutes Sonny came up on deck and got in his skiff and headed for the dock. At that point I beat it upstairs to my bedroom and lay down.

When the doorbell rang I did not get up and I did not answer it. After a while it stopped and the ringer went away.

I made a half-hearted effort to get up and go take a bath in the tub, but gave up on it. The dried saltiness from the sea water felt crinkly and good on my naked body. Why wash it off?

I drifted towards sleep. My home-made computer went over and over all this new information about this man Kronitis and always came up with the same key: insufficient data. My old copper's instinct was getting enlarged with age to the point of mild paranoia. What did I care anyway? This rich old man. I automatically thought of him as *old*. Anybody that rich ought to be old if he wasn't.

What about Chantal? What was I going to do if this Girgis character did *not* stop hitting her up for money? I hadn't decided on anything yet. What *could* I do to him?

And what about Chantal herself? There wasn't any question she was still lying to me about something. And protecting her sweet favours, at the same time, like some tiger kitten. What kind of subterfuge and evasive tactic would she come up with tonight?

I made up my mind that if she pulled one of her routines on me tonight I would give the whole thing up for good. I didn't really care all that much about making her, anyhow. Her island society dinners and lunches bored the hell out of me.

Chantal irritated me. A woman her age being that coy like that. Anyway, did I even care that much?

Would you believe a raunchy Midwesterner who was true to his wife for fifteen years of marriage? That was me. And in the last three of the eighteen-year span, which hardly counted due to our increasing estrangement, my infidelities hadn't been all that frequent, either.

I still felt I'd failed with Joanie. That was part of what I wanted to avoid thinking about, too, in Tsatsos. She was a cold woman. God only knows what kinds of checks and blocks and snaffles and bits they'd put on her when they saddle-broke her. She became another of these social butterfly types. The right guests at dinner was more important. And down inside this woman was that other woman just begging to get out, be let out. Totally un-aware of itself, and only I knew it.

I tried to arouse her, and failed. Maybe she wasn't arousable. Or maybe, just because I was her husband, I wasn't capable of accomplishing it. I appreciated the irony that some other man who didn't care for her could, and probably would, accomplish what I couldn't. In spite of that, we probably would have stayed together if it hadn't been for my work.

Chantal had been a lot more right in her analysis of our peculiarly American difficulties than I was willing to admit to anybody. But what did that make Chantal to me? The other women I had had in the last three years didn't make that much difference one way or the other. They didn't count. They were either good, or less good.

Sex had just about become a lost cause with me. There didn't seem to be any way you could win with it. I had gone through most of the ages and stages. I had been young and ashamed and apologetic. I had been the wild unrepentant rogue with whom nice girls would do all kinds of things they would not do with their decent boy-friends who loved them. I had in Denver been wildly in love with and lived with one girl for a long time, and stepped out on her on the theory that what she didn't know couldn't hurt her. After that disaster, I had been the dedicated married man with Joanie, faithful for fifteen long years, and that hadn't worked either. Sex and me had about had it with each other, in any non-mechanical, non-sensory way.

My sleepy mind came forward with the theory that Kronitis was really Sonny Duval wearing a disguise, and would wind up owning all three of Sonny's boats, too.

I yawned. I took a nap in the slowly cooling late afternoon.

CHAPTER FIFTEEN

When I woke, it was black dark and my watch said it was 10:15. I pulled myself up and sat on the edge of the bed in the dark.

Dmitri's taverna was all lit up and alive and loud and swinging, down across the vacant lot. Sonny's caique was lit up now, and so were other boats in the harbour that were lived on. There was a feeling that people had come back to life and come out of their holes and were ready to play, now that the heat was gone and the night had come.

I stepped out on to the open, unroofed bedroom veranda to breathe some night air and saw that the *Agoraphobe* was back. Apparently she had just pulled in. She was lit up and they were still jockeying her back and forth to moor her, and as I watched, a man rowed in in a skiff to the seawall to make fast her springline.

I stood in the dark and watched. While the man in the skiff was rowing back, the big fat-bottomed captain, Kirk, went down and came up from below with nine or ten objects which looked like frozen fillets of beef sewn into white cloth, and packed them in a seabag. I knew enough about hashish to know that was eactly what it looked like in the bulk. Kirk with his big ass took the seabag down the hanging ladder and stowed it in the ship's launch and took the launch in to the dock by the taverna. I was glad I had not turned on any lights.

On board the men went on working. At the dock Kirk disappeared up the gravel walk on the other side of the taverna to the street above with the seabag, without ever coming into the wash of the taverna's lights.

Christ, these guys made it look so easy.

I went back inside and made myself a drink from the bottle beside the bed and sat with it in the dark. Almost

79

certainly Kirk was tied in with Girgis, supplying him. Did that mean that old Kronitis was working with them both and masterminding and financing the whole deal from afar? No, nobody as rich as Kronitis was going to be involved in a small-time smuggling operation with Girgis and Kirk. Chantal had never mentioned Kirk to me.

I decided I would eat my dinner at Dmitri's again tonight. As I walked out through the yard there was another hippie party going in Georgina's garden. I walked along the seawall in the dark listening to it. But before I could even get to the taverna I was stopped by Sonny Duval's big figure.

'Hi, there. I'm back from Athens.' He made it sound like a world-shaking event.

'So I see.' I dug in my pocket. 'Here's your keys.'

'Did everything work out with the boat?'

'Yeah. Fine. I didn't damage it.'

'I see you cleaned it up great.'

'I always do that.'

Sonny moved his leonine head. 'I'll bet you do, at that.'

'Did you get your girl all right?' I made as if to go on. I wanted a quiet dinner by myself, and some thinking about the island. But Sonny fell into step with me.

'Naturally. I had to have a talk with Con Taylor, though. Say, I'd like to have a talk with you.'

I was already edgy. That made it more. Being asked to 'have a talk' with somebody always boded something ill. I had forgotten in a day just how childish, how kid-like he could be.

'Yeah?' I said. 'What about?'

'Oh, several things.'

Great. Have a talk. About several things. That boded even iller. We had reached the taverna. I took a table that was empty, down by the water, and motioned for the waiter.

'Do you mind?' Sonny said, and sat down too.

They were all doing it to me, it looked like. I must have something.

'Would it matter if I did?'

He only grinned. 'Anyway, I had a long talk with Con.'

'What did you do? Beat him up?'

'That's what you would have done.'

'Maybe. And maybe not,' I said. 'It depends.'

'Well, I didn't. Nothing like that. But you don't understand. I don't think a man ought to threaten a girl with committing suicide to make her stay with him. Do you?'

'Did Con do that? He doesn't seem like that type.' Sonny put up his hand. 'And that's not the way Georgina tells it,' I finished anyway.

'Naturally that's not how Georgina tells it.' He paused. 'And you mustn't tell Georgina what I've just told you.' He put the hand on my arm to emphasize what he'd just said; and he looked in my eyes, assuring himself of my essential human honesty and decency.

After he assured himself, he went on to explain that he had decided he and Jane would just ignore the whole thing. They would be polite to the Taylors, they wouldn't cut them or anything, but they wouldn't run around with them like they used to.

'By the way, where is Jane?' I said. People always acted so predictably, in situations. Sonny was going to be one of the civilized ones.

'She's on the boat. I thought she ought to stay on board a few days.'

'Punishing her, hunh?'

That made him angry. 'No. I'm not punishing her. I don't punish Jane. All that is old hat crap, man. This is the new age, man.' His face seemed to clear. 'But what do you think about that solution? What I said?'

I was getting seriously irritated. They couldn't any of them get it through their heads that I didn't care about their alliances and misalliances. Besides, the waiter had been standing there patiently waiting for my order, and now had gone away without it.

'Look. I'll tell you what I think. I think all of you people are crazy. Everybody on this whole island. I think there's something wrong with the water on this island, or something. When people go to bed together, they're taking a big chance on getting involved with each other. Period. Nine times out of ten they do get involved. At least, one of them does. Unless they're paying cash for it. And even then they get involved. No "new age" or new phony philosophy is going to change that.'

'We already have changed that.'

'No, you haven't. If you think you have, you're kidding yourself. Now, go away and let me eat my dinner, will you?'

'But we *have* changed it. You talk like a man out of another century. You're not much older than me. Wake up, man. Get with it.'

I tightened my lips and took a breath. 'Possession,' I said calmly 'The desire for possession. It's not that easily eradicated. You can't just whistle it away. A couple of badly written phony manifestoes aren't going to change it.'

'It's starting. Today the university, tomorrow the world!' He raised his arm with the fist clenched, and laughed.

'Horse shit,' I said. 'Listen. Will you bug out? And let me eat? Just bug out.'

'Don't get sore, don't get sore.' He got up placatingly. 'I'll talk to you later, when you're in a better mood.'

I didn't answer this, and he started away. I signalled the waiter. 'I'll see you early tomorrow morning,' I called.

The dinner was the same lamb stew goop, heavy with grease. This time heavily hottened with cayenne. I liked the cayenne. But the tomato and goat cheese salad was good. Afterwards, I stood out on the dock a while. Lights were on on Sonny's caique. Lights and music came from Georgina's yard, and the basement apartment. I stood looking at them all and thinking.

I had almost an hour and a half to kill. Down beyond Dmitri's, behind a spur of land which hid it, was another night club. The music thundered across from it out of amplifiers to me on the dock. I turned and walked down that way. It was only a short walk. Beyond the spur was a brackish inlet along which were built all the shipbuilder's sheds. One of these doubled as the night club at night.

The huge double doors were rolled back, to make the stage. Chairs and tables were set up on the gravel haulway, which was tilted slightly, between the doors and the water. A trio of young Americans was playing terrible folk rock music as I walked in. Not many of the tables were occupied, only three. At one sat Girgis, all slouched down beside his new blonde. At another Jason the recording 'star' from Paris was seated with two hippie boys and one girl. At a third Sweet Marie the diver was sitting with a sloppy-dressed hippie.

I hesitated, and almost left. Then I thought better of it and took a table and ordered a drink.

As it was being served, a tall long-haired figure came around the end of the boathouse on the path and into the light, and stopped coolly to look the place over. As if spotting what he wanted, he looked directly at me.

He was a man I had seen around, perhaps even been introduced to. Maybe he had been at Georgina's the other afternoon. His long hair was rather elegantly parted on the side and hung in loose waves clear to his shoulders. There was an unusual elegance about all of him. He had the Gould moustache, and his full beard was cropped close. Even in that light he seemed to have brilliant eyes. These were still directed at me; but instead of coming over, he turned his head languidly and spoke to someone behind him and two women followed him into the light.

The man led them in without looking back. He moved leisurely through the tables across the gravel. The women were clearly a mother and daughter. The girl was barely sixteen. Neither had anything like the elegance and self-possession of the man. He led them to a table at the far end. And looked over at me again.

People who stare at me get my hump up. I was thinking of going over and saying something to him.

But just then Sweet Marie got up from her table and her hippie and came over towards me. She was still tall, still wide-shouldered, still long-legged, still looking like her name. She was still beautifully built. She didn't walk like any model. She walked more like some kind of great blue crane. But with her equipment she didn't have to walk like any model.

I decided I liked her even better this way than in her wet-suit.

I relaxed back into my chair.

CHAPTER SIXTEEN

Marie stopped and stood in front of my table on her long legs, smiling. There was a constant tremor in her smile. She had on just blue jeans and a cotton shirt. No underpants, no bra. But what her body did to blue jeans and a cotton shirt made them look like something else.

'Hi there! Mind if I sit down?'

I pushed a chair out with my foot. 'Help yourself. Watching you come over here, I understand why they call you Sweet Marie.'

She blushed. 'That's sweet. Thanks. But I don't feel very sweet right now. Actually, they call me that because I say the word sweet a lot. Just like now I did.' She must have been all of twenty-two.

'What's on your mind?' I said.

'I wanted to apologize. I've been thinking about you all afternoon since I met you, and I guess I seemed awfully distant out there today, and I'm sorry.'

'Don't give it a thought.'

'But I couldn't get you out of my mind. You seem to like skindiving so much, and you seemed to know so much about it. Why don't you do more of it?'

'You have to be where there's water.'

'You could do it here.'

'Not in shape. About the time I got back in shape for it, I'd be leaving.'

Behind us at the tall man's table there was a sudden explosion of loud argument. Both of us turned to look, in time to see the older woman get to her feet shouting. The tall man casually got to his feet too, but without talking.

The woman continued to shout. The words 'fucking son of a bitch', in female voice, came out clear from amongst the gabble. Then the woman drew back and punched him in the side of the head with all her strength. She did not look like any weakling, but it didn't even faze him. Shouting, the woman collected the girl, her daughter, who had been sitting and wringing her hands, and marched her off across the gravel to the path. The tall man sat back down calmly and picked up his drink.

'She ought to pick on somebody her own size,' I said. 'Who is that guy?'

'Oh, that's just Pete,' Marie said. 'Don't you know him? That's a weird story. He came here the tail end of last summer, all alone. No friends. He had quite a bit of loot. He met her and the daughter, and started balling the mother. The mother liked the loot. The daughter was just a kid. Then the daughter suddenly grew up. Meantime, he spent the loot. And the old lady got drunk in all the bars with the fishermen. And Pete started balling the daughter. Now the old lady has found this other fisherman who has money, apparently. But she doesn't want to let Pete have the daughter, anyway.'

'And Pete has descended to being a hash runner for some of the local talent,' I said. I remembered him now. 'Georgina tells me everything about everybody.'

Marie smiled at me. 'What did she tell you about me?'

'Well,' I said, drawling it. 'You're a hash runner yourself. For Girgis. In the summer season. You sell the fish you catch. You make enough to live. You stayed here all last winter.' I stopped, and didn't go on. 'That's all.'

'That's all she told you?'

'All I seem to remember.'

'She didn't tell you I'd slept with everybody on the island? Boys and girls alike? And in gangs and groups?'

'I don't seem to remember that.'

'I think you're just being sweet to me, Mr Davies.'

'What's wrong with being sweet to you?'

'Nothing. I'm just not so used to it, is all.' She went on smiling, and it was an easy, unforced smile. 'Anyway, that's the way they usually say it.' In fact, her wording had been almost exactly Chantal's wording. 'And the thing is, that's all true. Or close enough. It's awful, isn't it?'

'Pretty big rep to hold up.'

She shrugged, and just smiled. 'Well, the locals help me out a lot.'

'I'm more interested in this hash running you do.'

'Oh, that's nothing much. I know most of the students.'

'Are they all students?'

'No. Some are. – And Girgis has a thing about not

being seen with what he calls heepies. So I deliver for him. And he pays me a good bit.'

'And Kirk supplies him?'

'Yes. In the summertime. There's a much greater demand in the summer with all the kids here. Girgis brings it in himself when he can, but he has a lot of other work to do with the tourists. So Kirk brings it in in the *Agoraphobe*.'

'Nice straightforward way of making a little money.'

'It is.' Marie smiled that easy, but always tremulous smile. 'But I'm more interested in you. You know, you ought to do it a lot more. Diving, I mean. Why don't you do it all the time?'

'You're the second person today to tell me that.'

'I mean it. I mean, why don't you quit your job, whatever it is – as a detective – and just go skindive? If you love it so much.'

'Responsibilities,' I said laconically.

'You're married?'

'Wife and two kids.'

'Well, at least you're married and have kids.' There was an open sad look on her face, suddenly. She was as incapable of hiding her feelings, apparently, as she was of not feeling them. 'That's a lot. Don't knock it.'

'Except I don't even have that.'

'Divorced.'

'Yeah. But I still got to pay.' I smiled my rueful smile. 'You wouldn't want me not to put my two girls through school?'

'You've got two girls?' Then, as I nodded, 'You know, you probably won't believe this – and it'll probably make you mad – but one of the reasons I couldn't get you out of my mind after I saw you today is that you made me think of my father. I bet that makes you mad.'

I pursed up my mouth in mock pain. 'Well, not really. Was your old man a cop, you mean?'

'I'm glad you're not mad. No, no. Not that. He wasn't a cop.'

'Well, that's something to be thankful for,' I said.

'It wasn't because you were a cop. It was just your – your *you*; the you I was talking to; make me think of him.' Suddenly her mouth quivered. 'You really made me

86

think of my daddy so much, Mr Davies. And just suddenly it all came flooding back.' Her mouth made that quiver again. 'I'm from California. But my folks come from Iowa.' Her voice went off up higher, nearly broke. 'And it just came roaring back. My dad, and the house, and the yard, and the block, and the kids on the block, and my school, and –. I haven't had you off my mind since I saw you.' She dashed her hand quickly under first one eye and then the other.

'Here, now, here, now,' I said. I had been warming to this girl very swiftly. Suddenly I had a flutter of panic. 'What is this, some new kind of a come-on?'

'That's not very sweet, Mr Davies,' Marie said. She managed a tremulous smile.

Her face seemed to have split wide open right in front of me. She was letting everything all hang out, as the kids loved to say.

Either this girl was living daily just an inch from going over the edge at every second, or she was driving on a set of frayed retreads for nerves, or she was capable of turning herself on and off like a faucet for reasons of her own.

'You're right,' I said. 'It's not. I apologize. The truth is, I *am* old enough to be your father. Give or take a year.'

'Something about your eyes, that level way you look at everybody, it's so like the way my dad looked at people.' She shrugged suddenly, a large wild shrug. 'I've been going over and over my life ever since. Whatever happened to it. How it got in the mess it's in. Gee, I don't know.'

'Is it in a mess?'

'You see that boy over there? With the glasses? The one I'm with? I'm living with him. This month. This week. This twenty-four hour period. They call him Slow John. You know why? Acid. Too much acid, too long. He's very rich. And he's an amoeba. He picked me up here this summer, when he first arrived. He's got lots of money. So what. I know one day, sooner or later, he'll up and leave – when Tsatsos bores him, or some other stimulus moves him in some other direction.'

'Are you in love with him?'

'Yes. No. I don't know. What does it matter? What

difference does that make? That's the wrong question. He doesn't love me. He doesn't love anybody. He can't. He's an amoeba. And he's too worried about his spiritual welfare. And his money. He loves him. And I'll still be here on Tsatsos. And sometimes I wonder where it all went. What happened to it all? I used to think it was such fun. How did it wind up like this? – If it wasn't for my skindiving sometimes I'd –

'Besides –'

'Whoa, whoa,' I said.

She paid no attention. 'Besides, he's an orgiast. That's the only way he can get it up. He likes more than one girl. Okay. That's all right. All that's fine. I've been around a lot. A lot, Mr Davies. But a time comes in your life when you get tired of all that fun and games shit and you want something else. And you wonder where did it all go?'

She stopped. Finally. And I was silent, too. Stunned by her outburst. 'I don't know anything to tell you,' I said in a low voice finally. 'If you're asking me. I wonder the same thing sometimes myself. Where did it all go? None of it turned out like you wanted it to, like you imagined it. But I don't have any answer. I don't know what to tell you.'

The girl dashed her hand across her eyes again. 'Gee, I didn't mean to bend your ear like this. I don't know what happened to me. That something about your eyes. I'm really sorry. I guess that's what you get for making me think of my dad.'

'Would you like to go somewhere and talk about it more?'

'No. No, I can't. I really can't. But you're sweet to ask me. I just can't. He's sitting over there. Old Slow John.' She gave me a long look, and then suddenly reached across and squeezed my hand with both of hers. 'I really can't. But would you mind if I came and talked to you some more sometime while you're here? You sort of do me good.'

I gave her a long look back. 'Not if it will help.'

'God, am I getting incestuous in my old age?' Marie tossed her hair back, and laughed but it sounded hollow. 'You won't mind if I come look you up?' She got up, dashing her hand across her eyes again. I realized suddenly that everything had been said between us in extremely low voices, just like an ordinary conversation. I was surprised.

'I'm really sorry,' she said. 'Please excuse me.'

I made a gesture. 'That's why I have big shoulders.'

'My daddy used to say that to me. Oh, gee. You really – Well, bye.' And off she went, in her long-legged, half coltish walk.

I sat and looked at my drink.

It was as if a tornado had passed. There was always a great calm after, and quiet, but it was a calm full of screaming nerves and broken teeth and limbs, and downed trees, and people's smashed houses and cars and heads, and always there was an ambulance wailing in the distance: Somebody's hurt. That was the kind of calm it was.

Suddenly I puffed out my lips. I puffed them out again and let my breath out through them in a long sigh. I was feeling pretty beat up, pretty much a failure. Pretty powerless to help anyone. Pretty old.

CHAPTER SEVENTEEN

I was not in the best mood to have the bearded gent come over to my table.

Actually, I would have left, but my attention got diverted by the boy singing star Jason who was approached at his table by one of the three scrawny American boys on the boathouse bandstand and asked to sing a song. Jason demurred, but was importuned, and got on the stand and took one of the guitars. Heard over an amplifier his fragile voice was much stronger, had more body and phrasing. He was certainly a lot better than the scrawny trio who, I found out later, not only brought all their own equipment but paid the Greek bar owner for the privilege of playing on his boathouse stand.

It was while Jason was playing that the tall man with the long hair got up and came over. When he got to the table, I realized he wasn't any taller than me but just looked taller.

'You mind if I sit down a minute?'

I just stared at him. I was not feeling very charitable at the moment. 'I don't see why not,' I said finally. 'Everybody else around here seems to.'

That didn't upset him much. The man smiled, and took his time. He slipped into a chair. 'You probably don't remember me. But I met you at Georgina's yesterday. And I was at the table in the plaza this morning.'

'I remember you,' I said grouchily. 'Have you got a name?'

'I'm Pete,' the man smiled.

'Great. Is there any last name to go with it?'

He shrugged. 'They don't go by last names around here much. But it's Gruner. I asked after you at Dmitri's. They said you might be here.'

'Well, I'm here. What's on your mind?'

'I wanted to meet you.' He ordered a drink from the waiter.

'That girl friend of yours didn't seem so anxious to meet me,' I said, and gave him a mean grin.

On the boathouse stage, Jason finished his number and went back to his table to light applause. Actually, he looked too slight, and too beat, to even hold a guitar. Let alone play on it and sing. His whole generation must be thanking God for amplifiers and all the new electronics developments.

'Oh, her. That one never wants to do or meet anything interesting,' Pete said. He spoke like a man who was required to maintain an important but uninteresting bit of camouflage.

'Well, you've met me,' I said. 'What do you want?'

'Just to meet you.'

'And what do you do, Gruner, pray tell? What line of work?' I thought I could already smell it.

'A little of this. A little of that. I'm a dropout from a Madison Avenue ad agency.' It sounded a little like a prepared speech. 'I didn't like the life. I didn't like America much any more. So I cut out for Europe. I'm a cook. On yachts. I worked with a French archæological diving crew, for a while, as cook and helper.'

'And what happened to them?' I said. 'It sounds like something did.'

'Well, they turned out to be running raw heroin stock. The raw morphine base. Stuff from Turkey. I didn't even know about it. And – they got picked up. Fortunately for me, I had already left them at the time. After that, I worked on a couple of private yachts.'

'Very interesting.' I was suddenly back in my old milieu again, the old professional. I took a slow drink from my glass. 'Is that the story you tell around here?'

'Sure. Why?'

'And they believe you? Jesus,' I said. I took another drink. 'You know what you smell like to me, Gruner? You smell like cop.'

Pete smiled coolly, his eyebrows amused. 'How do cops smell?'

'Old,' I said, with a false croak. 'And sore-footed. And frustrated. From either kicking people too much to no avail, or from walking around and around in bad shoes trying to help them and failing. You smell like T-man, or CIA, or a Narcotics man.'

Pete was still smiling. 'Not me.'

'You're not a cop?'

'No, I'm not. You wouldn't expect me to tell you if I was one, would you?'

I was supposed to answer that by saying fair enough. I didn't feel like it. I just looked at him. The three young Americans were playing bad music again. 'What do you want from me?'

'Nothing. I was just wondering if you were down here on something special? Or just looking around in general? Or what? And for who?'

'I'm on vacation.'

'Sure. I heard that. Like every private op from America in Athens comes to Tsatsos on vacation. You are a private op?'

'You want to see my licence?'

'Me? No. I don't have any authority, man. Like I told you, I'm a dropout. I just work a while, until I save some money. Then I come here and stay until it's spent. But I live here, man. I'm interested.'

'Yeah, you live here, and there's an awful lot of hash coming on to this island where you live. But I suppose that wouldn't interest you so much, would it? Heroin might, though.'

He just smiled, and chose to deliberately misread me. 'Heroin I don't know anything about, and it doesn't interest me. I've never tried it. I like to smoke a little hash, though, now and then. But just moderately. Heroin is bad medicine.' He had plenty of cool on him under that little beard.

I wondered what he would say if I told him what my old last-century nose had begun to sniff at suspiciously around the boot-heels of Mr Leonid Kronitis.

'Heroin is bad medicine,' I said. 'But heroin has never been one of my problems. Nor one of my assignments. Does that help you any?'

'Not much.' He was certainly a smiler, this Pete. 'What would help me, maybe, would be to know why an American private cop obviously in Athens for the first time would decide to take a month's vacation on the island of Tsatsos, which has hardly ever been heard of by anybody except millionaires, hippies and Athenian Greeks.'

'Maybe I know a millionaire. It's possible.'

'That could explain it.'

I didn't like his damned officious attitude. 'You really want to know?'

'I don't know if I do or not. It depends.'

'Well, I'll tell you,' I said confidentially. 'I picked it out. By myself. You want to know how?'

'How?'

'With an eyedropper on a map. Now. How's that? I just took the old eyedropper and held it over the map and shut my eyes, and ping. Tsatsos. That answer your question?'

'Sure. That answers my question. Well,' he got up, still smiling. He put money on the table. 'Here's for my drink. Everybody pays his own tab here.' He moved his head backward, to include the town, 'See you around.'

'You'll see me around for exactly two weeks, or three. Till my vacation's over. If I can hack it that long.'

He just nodded. Still smiling. He was certainly good-looking enough, in his hippie outfit. Slowly, still with full self-appreciation of himself, he wandered off toward the path.

I motioned for the waiter and paid. I wandered out toward the path myself. I hoped I did it with one half the dash Pete did it with. I knew I didn't. Marie waved at me from her table.

On the road the others had disappeared. There was

nobody, no Pete, no mother and daughter, no horsecabs, no nothing. I started to walk back towards Dmitri's.

So. Now we had a new wrinkle. Pete Gruner. The dropout cop. By process of elimination he almost had to be a nark. There didn't appear to be anything political around, to call for a CIA. Would the Treasury send a man to check on local summer American millionaires? Not likely, not efficient. So he almost had to be a nark, and that meant heroin.

Was there a big heroin operation going on here? Girgis and Kirk wouldn't fool around with vest-pocket hash running if they were involved in something like big-time heroin smuggling. Would Kronitis be? A man that rich? In something that dangerous? Didn't seem logical.

Or maybe Pete Gruner was just travelling, and sniffing in general, without any specific target? There was probably a lot of stuff going on in all these islands so close to Turkey. Or maybe Pete Gruner was just gumshoeing addicts to make a traceback. How many H addicts might there be up there on the hill at the Construction, I wondered suddenly. There ought to be a few. That boyfriend of Marie's, Slow John. A blown acid head. And rich. He was almost a natural for an H addiction. And if there were some, where were they getting their stuff? Maybe Gruner was working on that?

Hell, it was all beginning to sound more and more like my stamping ground in the East Village.

And why would he come up and expose himself like that to me. Maybe he didn't think he was exposing himself, at first? But he certainly didn't get very nervous when I tumbled to him. But then who would I tell about him? Marie, and Georgina, and Chantal? Ambassador Pierson? Who else did I know? And who was going to believe me?

Maybe he wanted me to tell somebody? Some big shot he thought I might be down here working for. In order to flush somebody?

It didn't any of it make much sense. Ahead of me the lights of Dmitri's taverna became specific lights, instead of just a general glow. There wasn't so much noise from it now, it was almost midnight.

I walked in under the fall of light from the overhead lamps, thinking that I was going to be due at Chantal's soon, and then saw that the big man who was captain of the *Agoraphobe*, Jim Kirk, was standing just at the opposite edge of the lightfall.

It was a curious configuration, Dmitri's taverna. Largely because the one-track seawall road ran right through the middle of it, so to speak. The road ran right against the front of the building, so that the waiters had to cross this hard-dirt-and-gravel road to get to the dining tables which were on the other side and built out over the water. The horsecabs and the few official jeeps and trucks were liable to drive through the middle of your dinner leaving a film of dust on your food.

Thus, Kirk and I found ourselves standing in the opposite edges of the light at the opposite ends of this unoccupied one-laner road, that ran through the place like a tunnel. We looked like the perfectly staged final shootout scene from some Greek Western. And me not wearing any iron.

Kirk wasn't doing anything. He was just standing there and looking at me. He might have been waiting for me to appear exactly where and when I did appear, but I couldn't be sure of that.

The place wasn't crowded, but it wasn't empty. There were three or four occupied tables out by the water, and in the open, roofed-over patio room beside the taverna building under the bright lights there were three or four others.

Suddenly Kirk began to caper. He started to prance up and down on his tiptoes, and fling his arms around over his head, his back all hunched down like some dwarf, an enormous leer of a grin on his face.

Kirk was a big man but he wasn't a very tall man. He was only maybe five foot ten. But he was an enormously broad man, both in the shoulders and in the hips, and meat bulged from him everywhere. His head at his ears appeared to be narrower than his neck.

He certainly looked peculiar. Like that. With legs like tree-trunks and huge bulging arms, he capered up and down in front of me at the other edge of the light.

And more peculiar still, nobody at any of the occupied tables seemed to pay the slightest bit of attention to him.

I didn't know what to do. I couldn't figure out if he was

trying to put me on and make fun of me. Vanity made my ears burn. I couldn't very well turn around and walk away. For a moment my ageing persecution complex, thickened and lumpy from years of being kicked by clients' enemies and clients themselves, made me wonder if all of them weren't banded together in a complot to make me a laughing stock.

I started to walk ahead.

Kirk was still capering, and flinging his arms around. 'Hi, there!' he shouted, in a kind of low-volume bellow, his voice a sort of basso falsetto, if such a thing was possible. 'Hi, there! I'm back from Athens! I had a talk with her! I had a talk with him! Naturally I brought her back with me! Do you think it's fair for a man to threaten a girl with suicide! I don't think it's much class!'

Not a soul at any of the tables seemed to be paying the slightest attention. Then I got what it was. He was mimicking Sonny Duval's conversation with me of an hour before. But how had he heard it? There hadn't been anybody near us. Had Sonny told him what he'd said? Had Kirk been standing out in the dark beyond the end of the taverna listening?

And why didn't the people at the tables pay even the slightest attention to us? Were they used to him as some kind of nut? *Was* he some kind of nut?

I went on walking towards him. He went on capering. He was directly between me and the path to my house, but I could easily walk right around him. Then I decided I didn't want to. Some facts I wanted might come out of this. Chantal could wait a little.

I sat down at an empty table not far from him and motioned for the waiter. Kirk immediately stopped prancing and came striding over to me, and stuck out his hand and sat down.

'Jim Kirk,' he said.

I took the hand. My hand wasn't small, but it seemed to disappear completely. His voice had the rumble of a fired-up volcano. It seemed to come from somewhere down near the backs of his knees. 'Lobo Davies,' I said. But it was a perfectly normal, sane, everyday tone he had; and he wasn't at all grinning.

And all around us not one person had turned his or her

head to even glance at us.

'What do you want to drink?' I said.

'I'll have a double Scotch. On the rocks,' Kirk sa̶
evenly. 'Or, if you think you can afford it, a triple. On
the rocks.'

'That was some exhibition you just put on.'

'I wanted to be sure of catching your attention,' he said
without expression.

I told the waiter a triple Scotch on the rocks. 'Well, you
did,' I said. 'Do you do that often?'

'That depends on the people. You mean because nobody
paid any attention to us?'

'Yes.'

'They know me around here. So they know what to
expect.'

'Well, it's certainly a novel way of attracting someone's
attention,' I said.

'I invented it. It's all my own. Of course I don't always
do it the same.'

'That's good to know.' The waiter brought our drinks.
Kirk drained his in one huge draught, tossed the ice cubes
out over the rail into the water, and upended the glass
upside down on the tablecloth.

'How did you know I was going to appear here exactly
when I did?'

He smiled. 'I can't give away all my little secrets.'

'No,' I said, 'I suppose not.'

'That's some piece of tail, ain't she?' Kirk said.

That almost stopped me, for a moment. 'I wouldn't
know,' I said. 'She looks fat to me. But I've never seen her
in anything but that grubby Mother Hubbard.'

'Wait,' Kirk said. 'Just wait.' That enormous great leer
of before began to come over his face. It seemed to
start at the bottom of his chin and spread slowly all the
way up, broadening his whole face. 'She'll be popping out
in one of her bikinis soon now, and you'll see. I had
a couple of pieces of her myself. Before she started
running around with Con. I think I'll go back to it for
some more.'

'She seems to be pretty stuck on Con,' I said.

'Only for as long as it takes her to change her diaphragm. Then she'll be out patrolling again. I could use
a month or so of her.' The leer began to fade out from

his face, slowly, starting from the top down. 'What do you think it is makes a fellow like that let his woman run around she-catting like that? I'd break her jaw if she belonged to me.'

'Sonny believes in free love,' I said. 'And he's a pacifist.'

'Well, it ain't free for him,' Kirk said solemnly. 'I admit, it's almost free. He bought that big dump of a boat for a little of nothing. And he's got two poverty-stricken Greeks to do all the dirty work on his boats for him and pays them next to nothing. He feeds her swill and rotgut retsina. But she likes to go away a lot. To restore her spirituals. And I don't blame her. If I had to live like that, I'd want to restore my spirituals. It costs him a lot in Athens and Rome. They go to Rome winters.'

'What did you want to see me about, Kirk?' I said. 'Besides to talk about Jane Duval.'

'Well, I thought maybe you might want to charter my ship,' he rumbled.

'To go where?'

'Any damn where,' Kirk said. 'Any damn where in the world. But I'd rather keep her in the Mediterranean. Cruise the Greek islands? Sail down the Turkish coast? Go to Sicily?'

'What made you think I might want to charter your ship?'

'Well, you were asking questions about me around, and all,' Kirk said solemnly. 'Like with old Dmitrios.'

'I just asked about the boat because I thought she was so unusual looking. And so beautiful.'

'She is beautiful. And I thought sure it was something like that with you. Or that you wanted to see about a charter.'

If he thought he was kidding me or convincing me of something, and I wasn't sure he did, I saw no reason to not let him. 'Well, I have to think about it.'

'You do that,' Kirk said, and then winked at me with an eyelid that resembled a furry-edged slab of thin sliced steak. 'And if there's any other questions, you come ask Jim Kirk direct. I'll be glad to tell you the history of the ship. Or make a run up to Athens with you for some broads. Anything. I know some great ones.'

'That might be a good idea,' I said.

'Maybe you're worrying about all that extra carrying

work I do for Girgis? In case you wanted to charter me? Don't you give it another thought.'

I didn't answer that.

'Girgis'll just have to get another guy. He's had to do it before. He's getting mighty cocky, Girgis.'

He leaned forward making the tin table creak, and pointed a finger like one of Darryl Zanuck's cigars an inch from my chest.

'Maybe you want some hashish. Well, you get it from me in a big lot, instead of buying it from Girgis in little bits. It'll cost you a fifth as much.' He sat back expansively.

'What about heroin?' I said.

'What's heroin?' Kirk said innocently. 'Never touch heroin. Too many American Boy Scout agents running around Europe nowdays. And you don't look like no heroin man.'

'Maybe I've got some friends.'

'Sure you have. And I know them all. And I don't think they'd be asking you to help them get their stash. If I may say so.'

'You can say so,' I said.

'Well,' Kirk said, and that enormous leer began to climb up over his face again. He slammed a big piece of meat down on the tin table top. 'Got to go. Better be moving along.' When he stood, he actually made the tin table groan. 'Now you know where you can always find me.' He picked out the moored *Agoraphobe* with his eyes for me. It was all lit up and abuzz with crew, as if getting ready to pull out. 'I'll put in a good word for you with Janie, if you want.'

'Better wait on that last,' I said.

'I guess so,' Kirk grinned. 'Since I'm pulling out again in a few minutes.' And he went walking away into the dark, rolling on his short massive legs, and I sat looking after him. I had the impression he would just bull ahead and do anything, anything that came in his head and that he wanted to do. He would talk or fight his way out of it afterward. If it was necessary. And had complete confidence that he could.

Keep away, was what he was telling me. In his own convoluted and inimitable fashion. Keep your nose out and keep it clean, copper. Nobody around here seemed to understand that private eyes were not cops and that usually, cops were more our enemies than anybody's. Well, he had some kind of weird rudimentary sense of humour anyway. Or he seemed to.

I paid. Again. It always seemed to be me who paid around here. And then went and got a horsecab beside the taverna, to take up to Chantal's.

CHAPTER EIGHTEEN

I told the driver I wanted to go to Georgio's taverna. I figured Chantal deserved that much protection. Since she was being so careful of her reputation.

The night sky was bright above the open cab. The land breeze had brought cooler air down from the pines on the hills. The moon either had set, or hadn't come up yet. It was quiet with the clop of the horse.

Half-way out the one main road that ran along the hill face, I told the driver to stop and paid him off. I waited until he disappeared. Then I started walking straight uphill, on the street to Chantal's.

There were very few street lights up here. The narrow cobbled street was walled on both sides. You could smell the flowering trees and bushes. I was thinking, with my professional's mind, what a great place it would be to waylay somebody when three men stepped out of the shadows into the light of the street lamp thirty yards ahead of me and started to walk down to me.

I felt my native combativeness spring out all over me. A happy red gorge rose at the back of my swallowing mechanism. It always made my ears ring a little, and it always made my jaw come out and gave me a kind of rictal grin. I couldn't help it, I liked it.

Of course, I could always turn around and run back down the hill and let them chase me. I could also get down on my knees and beg them not to hit me. Of course, maybe they weren't after me at all. But I didn't believe it. Maybe it was the way they weren't talking, that tipped it. I licked my lips and grinned up at them as I climbed up to them.

When I was five yards from them the two on the outsides darted in toward me, and the one in the middle ran right at me. I knew what to do with that. I ran head-on straight at the guy in front of me. That already put the other two a few feet behind me. The surprised man in front of me tried to slow up. I didn't give him a chance. I caught him by his shirt front with both hands and yanked him to me and hit him full in the face with the top of my forehead. I got one glimpse of his startled face, before my head hit him. He went down without a peep. I'd heard the bone in his nose break and knew he wouldn't want any more fighting tonight.

The other two had had to change their line of run, costing them a few seconds. I tried to jump over the downed man and move forward to get room to turn around but I wasn't quite agile enough. Age, again. One of them pinned my arms from behind and the other jumped in front of me and began to slug me in the face and belly. I could feel the downed man struggling feebly under us to try and get out of the way.

That kind of thing seems to go on and on. But it doesn't really. Six, eight, ten, twelve punches. Most people don't realize the number of hard punches you can take. Especially if you are moving all the time and can roll with some of them. Both of these guys were young. The one in front, a blond, looked like a semi-moron. I managed to break loose, by bull strength mostly, and swung around and left-hooked the one behind me to his knees, then swung around to the other. The blond was rushing me. Instead of ducking I stepped to meet him, grabbed him by the lapels and jerked him in and hit him in the face with my forehead, too. I didn't get as good a shot at him, and hit him somewhere below the nose in the teeth. But it was enough to put him down and I knew he would have a few loose teeth for a week. The other man was back on his feet and I turned and traded punches with him until he staggered and backed off. The blond, half-blinded, was on one knee when I turned back to him. A switchblade knife glittered open in his hand. I started toward him but the second man called something in Greek and the blond backed away. Crablike, he circled around me to get downhill to his friend. We stood and looked at each other.

The downed man was still feebly trying to crawl away out from under the fight. I backed off a couple of steps, to let them come get their friend, and together they backed off down the street half-dragging the friend, with me standing there watching them. There hadn't been one word said, except that one call in Greek.

At the main road, which was the first corner, they rounded the corner out of sight. But they didn't turn back down towards the Port, they turned towards Georgio's. I did not know what that might signify.

Chantal's was only a couple of doors away up the hill beyond the light. I moved there, and leaned back against the wall for a minute trying to figure it out. Figure it out who these guys were, and what they wanted with trying to beat me up. Obviously they were hired. Obviously the beating was to be a warning. But while these guys might be fairly accomplished street fighters, they certainly weren't professional hoodlums.

Leaning against the wall, I was still breathing raggedly, and bleeding a little. I had cut my forehead on a tooth when I head-punched the second guy. And I had a cut lip and a couple of nice facial abrasions that were beginning to swell. My ribs hurt, too. I hadn't felt so satisfied and so peaceful in a long time. I hadn't felt this satisfied since before the little Greek attorney in Paris.

In fact, I had to keep my teeth clamped together to keep from laughing out loud in the street. By God, I wasn't so bad off after all, old age or not. I could still hit a moving target.

Some people, I knew, like Sonny Duval for instance, wouldn't like to hear me say something like that. Well, I couldn't help it. I tried the garden door and it was open and I went on in and up the steps.

Chantal was there, all right. She was waiting for me all alone on her garden terrace. Apparently the rest of the house was asleep. She was wearing one of those summer dresses and no jewellery. The night was still beautiful. She apparently hadn't heard any sounds of the fight. She motioned with her finger to her lips for me to be quiet. Then she saw my face.

'My God, what happened to you?'

I had my handkerchief out. 'A couple of punks tried to give me a working over. Three of them. They weren't very professional about it. Do you mind if I sit down?' I was suddenly feeling very gay, and had to hold myself down. I gave her a cautious grin. 'I don't come back quite as fast as I used to. But I still like it.'

She looked horrified. 'You look awful.'

'You should see the other guys. Actually, I don't feel bad. I just feel like somebody ran me through the wringer of their washing machine.' I wiped the trickle from the cut on my forehead and patted my bloody lip. 'Who knew I was coming here?'

'Why, no one.'

'You didn't tell anybody?'

'Would I be likely to tell anyone you were coming to my house late at night?'

'I don't know. You might.'

That hurt her feelings. 'Well, I didn't.'

'Then somebody sure made an inspired guess.' I guess I was just barely aware I had hurt her. I didn't care if I had. I was not about to go into another long involved explanation about how I couldn't really trust her because she didn't tell me the truth about herself. 'A very inspired guess.'

I guess she realized how I felt. Anyway, she swallowed the hurt pride. 'How do you mean?'

'Well, who would figure I was coming here? At all? After midnight? Second place, who would figure out I would leave the horsecab on the main road, like I did, and walk up? To protect your "good name"? That's pretty smart figuring.'

'But who would want to do something like that to you?'

'I don't know. Your friend Girgis might. This hippie guy Steve might. But those three weren't hippies.'

I straightened up on the bench and grinned at her. 'It might even have been Kirk.'

'Kirk?' she said weakly.

'The captain of the *Agoraphobe*. You don't know him?'

'I know who he is. How do you know Kirk?'

'He introduced himself to me tonight,' I said, and gave her another grin. 'Apparently I've made a whole raft of friends on Tsatsos.'

Now, why would the mention of Kirk affect her so? I

said, 'My guess is that it was Girgis. But how he would guess I was—'

I didn't finish, because she looked distressed. I looked at her. She didn't seem to want to meet my eyes. And I suddenly knew for no other reason than that, that she had told Girgis, or somebody, about me. She might not have told them I was coming up here on any specific night at any specific hour, like tonight, but she had told them enough so that they could plan out the rest.

'Do you think we could have a drink?' I said softly. It seemed to me I had just divined an old affair between her and Girgis. I had speculated about that once before. But I certainly wasn't going to mention it. 'A Scotch?'

'I've got them all ready for us,' she said stiffly, and got up to go to the rolling bar in the patio corner. When she came back with them, she had straightened out her face. She said, 'You really like it, don't you? This fighting. You don't even mind being beaten up, do you? You enjoy it.'

'I must. Otherwise I'd change my way of making a living, wouldn't I?'

'It's very boyish. It's like a group of boys at boys' school. All male vanity and ego. Pummeling and punching each other.'

'This kind of fighting wasn't boyish,' I said.

'I've never met anyone quite like you.'

'Yes. You keep saying that. Could I have a Band-aid for my head?'

'There are some upstairs.'

'Well, let's go upstairs. That's where we're going, isn't it?'

Chantal looked as if she had been slapped in the face. I didn't care. She half-opened her mouth. But then she closed it. I was glad she did. Because I was ready to tell her to go to hell and leave. If she had gotten indignant and put on her Countess look and started yapping, I would have.

I hadn't intended to insult her. But I was plenty mad. Her secretiveness and her hedging and her lying didn't make any sense, if she really meant for me to help her. And they had very nearly gotten the hell beaten out of me.

But she didn't. Instead, quietly, almost demurely, she

got to her feet. Shyly, almost like a girl – which seemed silly to me, after Freddy Tarkoff, and that husband of hers, and God knew who all else – she led the way inside and upstairs, turning on and off the lights for us as we went. A couple of times she motioned me for silence.

In the arched, thick-walled living-room, I paused a minute, glass in hand, and looked again at the portrait of her when she was younger. She must have been a real beauty back then.

Just what the hell was the matter with her, anyway?

In her bedroom, without a word, her back to me, she began to undress. She took off the summer dress, and the half-slip she wore under it, and hung them up neatly. She did it modestly, quietly, matter of factly, elegantly, with no coyness, just as she might have if she had been alone. I stood and watched her and felt my mad slipping away out of me. She was elegant as hell and I admired it. I noted she had thought to have an ice bucket and booze and glasses on a tray on her dressing table. Whatever else about her, she had real class. Class up to her eyebrows.

'You'll have to be careful of me,' I said with a grin. I could catch glimpses of the front of her in the mirrors.

'Yes. I just bet every woman has to be careful with you. You look as if you would break so easily.'

'I'm pretty sore.'

'I'm afraid you'll have to leave at daylight. I'm sorry about that.' She took off her panties, and then her bra. She put them neatly where they belonged.

'I think I'd better leave a little before that,' I said.

'What are you going to do?'

'About what?'

'About those three men.' She took whatever pins there were in her hair out and shook it loose.

'What three men? Oh, them. I don't know.' I was still catching glimpses of her in the three angled mirrors. She had a beautiful dark bush.

Then she turned around facing me. 'You're really very tough. Aren't you.' Then, the voice softening, and mocking, 'Aren't you? Very tough?'

'Sure. I took a course in it at school,' I said. 'I don't feel very tough at this moment.'

'Now's the time to be tough.' A funny little shy smile played at the corner of her mouth. 'Now, more than any time.' Lithely, without haste, she walked to the bed and curled down on to it. She stretched out on top of the cover and then, with a curious little modesty that had great class, crossed her ankles. Just the ankles. And there she was. She still had a marvellous body. The whole thing was the most elegant damn thing I thought I'd ever seen. 'Will you be tough with me?'

I put my glass down somewhere, and began getting out of my own clothes with a style which, if not as elegant, I hoped at least complemented hers. It was the least I could do. Fortunately, I was not one of those men who at almost fifty had to hold in their stomachs and breathe shallow.

'You're beautiful, Lobo,' she said from the bed.

'Beautiful? Beautiful is hardly the word for me. But you're beautiful.' And she was. But it's always good to tell them that.

When I had an arm around her she turned to me, chest on chest, and smiled. A large, tremulous smile. It had a certain radiance. 'Beautiful? An old woman like me? I'm an old woman. Or very nearly am. I used to be beautiful.'

I kissed her to shut her up.

She was as elegant in the bed as she had been getting into it. There wasn't anything new that either of us could teach the other. But her love-making had the same style and class as the rest of her.

I didn't mind if she squeezed my sore ribs. I didn't mind if she rubbed her head against my facial abrasions. I didn't mind if I got a little salt in my cut lip.

I don't suppose I had ever been to bed with a woman before who could be elegant and animal at the same time.

I woke just shortly before first light, because I'd set my little internal alarm in my head.

The bedside lamp was still on, my empty drink glass beside it. I took it to the bottle and poured myself a measured drink. There was no drink in the world like that one, when after a night of satisfactory love-making you are preparing to get dressed and go home from some lady's private apartment. I took it back to the bed with me and sat down to savour it.

When I finished it, I kissed her gently on the cheek and stood up. When I stood up, her arm came out, and her hand grabbed me by my handle.

Still half asleep, her eyes still shut, she said, 'Don't take him away,' and yawned.

'It's just about dawn,' I said.

'Then goodbye, darling, call me this afternoon,' and she rolled over, with a look of deep satisfaction about her shoulders and her back.

I started to dress. Then I was outside, in the air, and walking down the hill toward the harbour. But outside I wasn't so happy, nor so gentle feeling. I knew I shouldn't be getting involved with any woman. Especially any woman who kept hedging her bets, and wouldn't tell me what she was really into. She was supposed to be my client. And now I'd accepted my fee. Passing a hanging branch of a flowering tree drooping over a wall, I took a sudden savage, angry punch at it, scattering petals.

The blush of first light was just mounting in the east, over the sea and the black bulky islands. I could see it all from up here. Now and then I could see the yacht harbour below me.

By the time I got there the real dawn was growing. The taverna was opening, fishermen were stopping by for a coffee, their oars on their shoulders, boats were coming in from night fishing. I stood for a while at the top of my rented garden, inside the upper street door, and looked at it all. This was what it all was about.

There was always such a great new false hope for everybody. At the start of each new day's dawn. It wasn't a human emotional thing so much as a fact of nature. I walked down to the taverna for a coffee myself.

When I sat down and looked out at the harbour, I noticed the empty space the *Agoraphobe* had left in the harbour moorings. That guy sure liked to do his port making and putting out in the dead of night.

I gave Sonny half an hour. When the half hour was up, I rowed out to the boat and knocked on the hull.

It wasn't Sonny who came up, but Jane Duval. She was just putting on the pants of her bikini. She already had the bra on. Jim Kirk had not been kidding me about her body. It was magnificent, and young. Young, young, young.

'Tell Sonny I'm waiting at the taverna,' I told her brusquely.

'Isn't it kind of early?' she said sleepily. Then she stretched and yawned, and I realized she was aware I was looking at her body. So she stretched it for me and showed it to me.

'I told him I wanted to go early,' I said and shoved the skiff off and set the standing-up-type oars.

'Well, I'll tell him,' she said and went back down below. I didn't like her any better than I ever had.

I rowed back angrily to the dock.

When Sonny came up on deck, I called to him to get the boat ready, and to get a lunch at the taverna. We were going out together, alone. But first I wanted to go to town and buy some stuff

At the house I changed. No one was up. Sonny was at the taverna, but the rest of the boats slept on their anchorlines. I caught myself looking hungrily out at the water. In town I bought myself a mask and snorkel, flippers and a speargun. And a depth gauge. I had to go to every shop in town that handled masks to find the depth gauge.

'No people,' I said to Sonny as we headed out. 'No people all day.' Sonny grinned.

'People are always trouble,' he informed me. 'And they never give a warning. The sea,' he said and spread his arm, 'the sea always gives you warning before the trouble.'

I thought that was pretty pompous. Especially since I'd learned he didn't even do his own dirty work. The big peace medal hanging on his chest on its rawhide cord caught the sun and glinted at me.

'What did you do to your face?' he asked.

'I bumped it on my electric razor,' I said.

CHAPTER NINETEEN

We spent that whole day out. We anchored off a tiny islet Sonny knew about to the east and didn't move except to change the boat. I avoided thinking about Chantal. I spearfished, or loafed and rested in the shade of the tarp. Sonny mostly loafed, and listened to rock music on his battery-operated radio. I kept having to tell him to turn it down.

He dived a little, but it was clear right away he was no adept with flippers or speargun, and had no interest in it. This was Tarkoff's 'expert spearfisherman'.

I tried hard to reach sixty feet. I had set sixty feet as an arbitrary limit because I thought I ought to be able to do that. Though I hadn't done any, for four years. But the best I could do was forty or forty-five. My new depth gauge was calibrated in metres and I kept having to recalculate into feet how deep I'd been. It was a pretty disheartening performance. The bottom wasn't very interesting. There were few fish. My whole catch was two medium-sized grouper. I looked at them ruefully on the deck when we packed it up to go in, and commented that there weren't many fish.

'Boom, boom,' Sonny said. 'The local fisherman dynamite. And of course kill the young fish along with the big fish. They know nothing about ecology or conservation.' Sonny was against spearfishing for sport, too.

I made no comment. I was feeling grim enough already.

'Education is very important to understanding,' Sonny said.

But when he fired up the motor, I looked around at the sea and the rocky islet with real regret. Frustrating as it was, it still seemed the best moments I had spent since I got here. The being without people was the best part. Being without Sonny would have been even better. Unfortunately, he owned the boat.

By the time we got back to the taverna dock I knew what I was going to do about Chantal.

I waited until we had cleaned up. But then I went straight in to the telephone booth at Dmitri's and called her at her house and told her not to expect me at her dinner.

There was a pause at her end. 'Again?' she said. 'All right, I'll tell them.' Another pause. 'Will you be coming by my house later, then?'

'I'm afraid I won't be able to. Something's come up. I'm sorry.'

Silence from Chantal. Then, finally, 'You're a great one for letting people down easy.'

I didn't answer.

'Shall I call you tomorrow, then?' she said.

'Yes. That's a good idea. Call me in the morning.'

'All right. Goodbye.' The phone clicked dead.

I must have come out with a savage look on my face. Old Dmitrios looked at me, anyway. Relief was what I felt, suddenly. With the anger, relief. I took a couple of deep breaths of the relief. Sonny was battening down the boat. I told him I would let him know later what time I wanted to go out tomorrow.

I went back to the house and changed. Then I just went out and walked in the town. There was not anything I had to do. It felt great.

It was not yet six o'clock. At the yacht harbour a group of night fishermen were preparing to go out. At the Port break-water another group of night fishermen were preparing their boats. In between, at the two bathing beaches, people were having an evening swim. The café terrace was crowded. The old-fashioned 19th-century British hotel on the water across the Port harbour had two parties of English middle class out in front having drinks, almost lost in the vastness of its terrace.

Finally I came to the Xenia. Xenia was the same name used for a whole chain of government-owned hotels on all the islands and all over Greece. This was the one I had seen from the ferry coming in. Just beyond it was the hill with the Construction where the hippies lived. Smoke from open fires rose from it in columns. I decided to go there.

The entrance was around the headland on the road, where there was a little cove and a beach. I walked right in. Right away I got myself stared at. Without exception

109

I received a sullen cold shoulder from the hippies, not all of whom were young. If I asked directions or information, I got sullen grudging replies.

It was all like some weird, crazy surrealistic Hooverville. They were cooking their suppers over the open fires. A goodly number of filthy children were running around without discipline. Toilet facilities were nowhere visible; people went trudging off with shovels in their hands. Open construction ditches still passed before or behind, or both, many of the four- and six-family units. People either jumped them or climbed down into them and up out of them and over the hump of earth on the other side.

When I had looked it over to my satisfaction, I left. I did not see Steve or Chuck and their gang anywhere. I did not receive any welcoming rapport of brotherhood.

Back out on the road I stopped a moment. I was curious all of a sudden as to what it was that had irked me so. I had nothing against camping-out. I had been doing it all my life, and using a shovel to dig my own toilet. I did believe that children needed discipline. More, that they actually craved it, desired it. But that difference of opinion couldn't account for my truculence. What put my back up was the sense of unfriendly superiority. They put camping-out up on to a level of moral righteousness like a religious mysticism, and then sullenly waited hopefully for you to hate them and martyr them for it.

Down below where I stood on the road, through the foliage, I noticed the little beach below had a number of late bathers in the evening, fading light. Almost without exception they were nude. A few girls wore the pants of bikinis. A number of children, washed clean by the sea, were running naked and screaming. The girls' nude bodies, long and lean with youth, were exquisitely beautiful in the red light. From where I stood, it was an exquisite scene through the leaves.

Old man that I was, I stood and looked. It gave me an unbelievable gnawing feeling of pain. This scene was something I had never had. I was too warped by my parents', and my society's, foolishness. Maybe I was oversexed because of that but the scene had an enormously haunting sexual beauty for me. I wanted to have each girl. Then I recognized Sweet Marie as one of the girl bathers. Marie was one with nothing on. The dark

110

V of her crotch was tantalizingly attractive. Taller than most, she had a long lean rounded line of flank. After a few moments of watching her in particular through my screen of leaves, I turned away back to the road. I felt put down, left behind, out of everything, pretty damned ancient.

Right in front of me a group in their weird outfits were strolling back from town. Three boys and two girls. The tallest boy grinned at me.

'What are you doing, old dad? Catching up on your peeping?' They all laughed.

I didn't say anything. I went on along the curving road. What could I have said? Another act of gratuitous human cruelty. Who cared? I was used to it.

At least it got my adrenal juices to flowing again.

By the time I got back to the Xenia Hotel it was dark. Stake lights were on in its grounds, which contained large clumps of tropical jungle garden. The gravelled road ran through the edge of its grounds. On an impulse I turned and walked up the stake-lighted walk to the lobby.

Inside, the lush new hotel was weirdly empty. A massive, expensively done ground floor was totally deserted. In the dining-room one lone couple was eating. One clerk stood behind the reception. He had on a green uniform with gold braid. I asked him for the bar. He pointed for me. I followed his finger, down a long luxe corridor-like room with expensive gaming tables down each side, the whole done in rich green and white marble. Every other gaming table light was on, and not a soul sat at any of them.

The whole place was so in keeping with my mood it was almost unreal. Beyond the gaming tables was an equally luxe open patio, equally deserted. The bar was on the right. A young lone barman leaned against the wall with his arms folded, smoking, in the same green and gold braid uniform. I went over.

'A Scotch and soda,' I said.

He put down his cigarette and mixed the drink with a professional flourish, without a word.

I crawled on to a stool and drank and then stared down into the wide glass as if it were some crystal ball of my future. If it was, it didn't tell me anything. I looked back up. 'You don't seem to have much business.'

The boy shrugged contemptuously. He had picked back up his cigarette, and refolded his arms. 'There will be some more in August,' he said in perfect English.

'How does everybody stay alive until August?'

With the same contempt he said, 'We are paid a salary, monsieur. A momentous salary. By the government. We were all trained in the school in Mikonos.' The irony was too heavy, and without any humour.

I didn't grin. This whole place was like that. I swung around and, elbows on the bar, looked around at the empty, expensively lit patio.

A tiny bellboy in the same green with yellow braid, but with a green and gold pillbox hat, walked by and smiled at me. He was the only one with any energy I had seen in the place. He went on off the edge of the patio. I swung back around and hunched over the bar.

Just at that second there was a strangled, terrorized yell from the garden. Both the barman and I jumped. The little bellboy came scrambling up the steps out of the dark, gabbling Greek. Behind the bar the barman gripped the edge of the counter.

'What's he saying?' I said.

The tiny boy went into English.

'Please! Come! A dead man!' He paused, his eyes wide. 'He has no head!'

I got him by his arm. His eyes had dilated so that I didn't think he could even see me. 'Okay. Just take it easy. Take it easy. Come on. Show me,' I said.

He led me to the edge of the patio and the steps, and then stopped. 'I can't,' he whispered. He came up exactly to my elbow. He couldn't have been over nine.

'Then point where,' I said.

For a minute I thought he couldn't even do that. Then the little boy pointed out into the dark to a clump of jungle grass. Behind me the young barman made no move to come out from behind his bar and help.

'For Christ's sake, come here and hold on to this kid,' I called. 'He's scared out of his wits.'

I patted his shoulder, and went down into the dark on to the Bermuda grass lawn towards the grass clump.

At first I couldn't see anything in the darkness. Then just inside the clump I spotted a bare foot. I parted the tall grass and peered inside. Beyond the foot was a leg, and beside that another leg drawn up, and beyond that was the body. Where the neck should have been there was nothing.

For half a minute I just stood and looked at it. The neck had been cut off at the base, and whoever had done it had not done a very good job of it. In the darkness it was impossible to see if there was blood on the ground, or on the grass. I stepped a little farther in and felt the grass near the severed neck and looked at my fingers. There wasn't any blood. I stepped back out.

The no blood meant that the killing had not been done here, in the clump. That did not necessarily mean the head would not be here, though. I looked around, and found the sandal that belonged on the bare foot. I didn't touch it. I did not find the head. I was glad, because I thought I already knew who it was.

I came back to the edge of the clump beside the bare foot and stood looking at the body again. There was something very familiar about it. There was a bulge in one of the hip pockets. I snaked the wallet out without touching anything else and took a look at it. A mariner's card stared back at me in the gloom of the bad light with Girgis's picture on it. There was plenty of money in the wallet. I snaked the wallet back and stood up.

Behind me off the patio some American dance music was playing softly on the hotel's intercom speaker system.

It was as if I had known all along that it was going to happen. I hadn't known when, and I hadn't known who, and I hadn't known where, or how. And there wasn't a damned thing in the world I could have done to prevent it. But the whole thing somehow smelled of something like this from the start. And now here we were.

It was an especially gruesome one. I was pretty sure the head had been cut off after the body was dead. It just looked like it. But that didn't make any difference. There was a special indignity about mutilation of that sort.

There was something specially pathetic and indecent about the bare feet of a corpse, too. I had seen that before, and knew about it. A guy who had been blown out of his shoes and socks by a big mortar shell in my war. It was funny until you remembered the guy was dead. I had seen decapitations before, too. We had had some men in my outfit decapitated by the Japanese and left with their heads sitting on their chests for us to find.

I suddenly remembered Girgis standing in his bare feet on his afterdeck in the heavy sun, getting ready to blow his klaxon. The bare feet had looked all right then. I hadn't even gotten to know him. But there was something effervescent and attractive about him, bad boy or not. I didn't hate death. There wasn't much point in that. But I hated wanton death. And murder was almost always wanton death.

I couldn't figure it out. It didn't seem there was enough money in his paltry little hashish smuggling to warrant any murder.

Behind me the young barman, courageous enough now, in my wake, said from the patio steps. 'One is not supposed to touch anything at the scene of a murder, is one?'

I moved my head irritably. 'That's right. Come on, let's go to the desk.'

'Is he really dead?' he said. 'With no head?'

'He's dead, all right,' I said.

Beside him, in his green and gold uniform and his green and gold pillbox hat, the little bellboy began to cry.

In the lobby I told the clerk to call the police. While we waited, I sat with my arm around the unstrung little bellboy trying to comfort him. 'There, now, there, now. Dead people never hurt anybody. Did you ever hear of any dead people hurting anybody?' I wasn't at all sure what I was telling him was the truth.

CHAPTER TWENTY

I hated a killing. A killing always complicated everything. Once a killing got into a case, it became a whole different ball game. Everything else was disturbed and disrupted, by a killing. The local beef trust got called in, and the heavy weaponry – the captains and inspectors – got requisitioned from upstairs. I did not presume it would be any different in Greece, and it wasn't.

The police arrived in their blue jeep, the fat chief and two of his young peasant constables. I had seen him at a distance around town. The chief went out to take a look at our body, and came back swearing and mopping his face. He was in over his depth already. He told us, in English, for my benefit I suppose, that he was going to call the Inspector, in Glauros. 'God only hope he are there,' he said.

When he came back from the phone, he said the Inspector was coming. Should be there in an hour.

I had my 'client' to think of. I might have stood her up but I still wanted to get to her with the news before anyone else did, and tell her to keep her mouth shut. I stood up brazenly. 'Well, I have a few things to do in town. I'll be back here by then.'

'You? You will not go anywhere.' The fat chief's eyes seemed to come back slowly from wherever they were. His two doube chins shook with outrage. 'You were seen to take the dead man's wallet out of the pocket, and then put it back.'

I smiled a tough, mean smile at the young barman. To the chief I said, 'I thought I knew who he was. I wanted to check.'

'No one touches the scene of the crimes,' the chief said. 'We shall search you.' Then he went into Greek.

I put my hands in my pockets to turn them out. The chief immediately put his hand on his holstered gun and undid the flap. I simply grinned at him. I brought out what I had in my jacket. Then I started on my pants. 'I can't stand to be tickled. Especially by hick cops.'

'I know who you are, Mr Davies,' the chief said. 'This don't give you no special priv'lege.'

One of the younger cops picked up my wallet, looked at my special licence, then handed it significantly to the chief. The chief looked at it, and nodded, and put it back. There was absolutely no reason for them to go through this kid routine. I figured they did it because they were scared.

'Now can I go to town?' I said.

'You will stay here.'

We settled down to wait.

The Inspector, when he arrived, walked in swiftly and

took over smoothly. He did not look like he was yanked away from any quiet dinner, with his wife and seven little Greek kids. He was dressed in a dark blue suit that might have been smartly tailored, before he put it on. It was much too heavy for the weather. He was a small man, but inside his smallness he was heavy and florid. He had at least the authority of an Army colonel about him. He also had the most brutal and rudest set of eyes, nose and lips I'd ever seen even on a cop. Absolutely power-oriented. After a quick look at the corpse, he closeted himself with the chief.

I cooled my heels, and contented myself with staring down the slim sneaky barman. While the chief was with his boss, the barman was called in. When they both came back out, he asked for me.

'Well, Mr Davies. You seem to have upset my constabulary. By taking a peek at the victim's wallet.' He wasn't reproving. But he wasn't on my side, either.

I gave him a shrug. 'I thought I recognized him. I was right.' I probably in all fairness should have warned him that I never did rate very high on obedience tests, even in the Army.

'You knew the victim?' Simply by sitting in it, he had turned the hotel manager's office into his own property.

'I've met him. He seemed like a personable young man. He seemed to flash a lot of money around.'

The Inspector nodded. He constructed a brutal smile with his loose lips.

'A lot more than he could make just running the *Polaris*,' I said.

He nodded again, with the same curled-lip little smile.

'I've heard more. More that I don't actually know.'

'Such as what?'

'Well, it's rumoured he was smuggling a lot of hash on to the island. Which he sold here. To all these hippies up on the hill.'

The sneery smile again. He was being nice to me. But he wasn't sure whether he liked me or not. 'That is my information, also. Though I am not sure all the hashish went to the 'ippies. Anything else?'

'Well, it seems the local authorities are unusually lax about it.' I thought I'd give him a little needle. It was hard to tell how thick that skin was.

It didn't faze him. 'Mr Davies. I cannot control the hashish traffic in my own area on the mainland. They are an island here. It would take fifty men, each with his own boat.'

'Sure,' I said. I figured I was safe enough to say it. 'How much better to have knowledge of how much comes in and who brings it.'

'Yes.'

'There was no problem until the 'ippies came. Now each year there are more.' He shrugged a set of heavy shoulders. He looked like he ate well, the Inspector. 'The word gets around. It is all because of the government housing construction up above, where they can live.'

'But nothing has been done about that. Right?'

'I would not attempt to discuss a complex matter like that with you. However,' – the loose-faced smile – 'let me say that no matter how badly dressed and unwashed, no matter how squalidly they like to live, the 'ippies can spend an enormous amount of money in a place.'

I smiled back. 'Sure. They are not many of them poor. Right? At least, not the American ones.'

The Inspector nodded. 'Don't try to get nasty with me. They like to play at being poor, yes.' His loose-lipped smile could be more ominous than a tight-lipped one. 'But murder is another thing, Mr Davies. We've had a few knifings, a few broken heads, a few that went crazy. Not the same thing. I will get a murderer, in my district. That I can assure you.'

'Will it be that easy?'

The Inspector shrugged. 'I suppose you have not also heard who sells the hashish for this man Girgis?'

I pretended to consider this. Why would he ask me, a three-day stranger, that? I lied. 'Nope. I haven't. I thought he sold it himself.'

He smiled and fiddled with the hotel manager's pencil, which had become his pencil. 'Do you know the Countess von Anders?'

'Yes. She's the lady who's been taking care of me on the island. You don't mean to imply she could be mixed up in this tawdry mess?'

The Inspector looked up, his heavy eyebrows raised. 'Certainly not. I have known the Countess for years, Mr Davies.'

117

'Then why the leading question?'

'No leading question, Mr Davies. I simply wondered if you had met her. Merely being social. She is a friend of Mr Tarkoff. You did some work for Mr Tarkoff in Athens. Mr Tarkoff sent you here.'

'Well, she met me, really,' I said, indifferently. He kept up with things, the Inspector. He did homework. 'Fred Tarkoff wrote her about me, and gave me a letter of intro to her.'

'Yes. Mr Tarkoff. The rich American. I have had the pleasure of meeting him a couple of times. Tsatsos has several rich Americans. We like them.' It was impossible to tell which way he was playing it. Did he know about the hashish group, and intend to attack them? Or was he being paid off, and was protecting them? He pushed the hotel manager's swivel chair back as if that was his, too. 'This is not an interrogation, Mr Davies. Okay. That will be all. You can go.'

'And you don't want me to leave the island,' I grinned. 'Right?'

'It's immaterial. I won't need you any more.' Not the greatest sense of humour in the world.

The two of us walked outside to the lobby. The three constabulary were not there, and the hotel employees were standing in the big glass doorway watching whatever was going on outside.

We walked to the door. Outside on the driveway was parked a sun-faded blue Volkswagen bus, its back door open. Beside it stood a tiny old Greek man, so fragile looking he seemed transparent. The two young constables and the chief were holding a stretcher, and arguing.

I looked at the Inspector, and the Inspector's power-structured eyebrows quivered. 'The local hearse,' he said. 'And the local mortician.'

One of the young constables was protesting about something in Greek. The fat chief overrode him. They all disappeared behind the clump of tropical grass. In a couple of minutes they reappeared with the body on the stretcher, a blanket over the body. The body was in rigor mortis and did not lend itself to stretcher bearing. The knee of the drawn-up leg stuck up like a small mountain. One arm stuck out from under the blanket stiffly. It was obvious they had had some trouble with it

118

and all three were sweating. They heaved it up into the bus and the tiny transparent mortician shut the door. The young constable who had done all the arguing went over and leaned against a tree and began to vomit.

'You can see they are not used to murders on the island,' the Inspector said behind me.

I nodded. 'Have you got all the fingerprints and stuff, already?'

'All that we will need around Tsatsos,' the Inspector said.

I nodded again. I gave him a grim handshake meant to show I understood his problems, and went to the line of horsecabs. My 'client' Chantal was still the first thing on my mind. I had to call the driver away from the row of spectators.

In the Port I paid off the cab, and walked up to Chantal's.

It was full night now, maybe 10 or 10:30.

I did not expect her to be home, and she wasn't.

CHAPTER TWENTY-ONE

I told the maid I would wait.

In the low stone thick-walled living-room I looked again at the portrait of the young Chantal. I thought it said a lot about her life, hanging there with its light that was never turned off. It dominated the medieval room. Not that she had centred everything around it. She hadn't. She had hung it off by itself, and then directed everything away from it. So that it dominated by indirection. Very shrewd.

On an antique table I picked up an expensive illustrated picture-book history of the von Ander family, in German. Obscure publisher. Three hundred numbered copies. Obviously, a paid-for book. I settled down with it. Might as well learn something about my client, if I could. The illustrations went all the way back to medieval engravings. Castles. Ancestors in armour. Later, photographs. War of 1870. War of 1918. War of 1940. Periods in-between. Near the end there was a big family portrait, in which I recognized Chantal, and a guy I assumed was her husband, amongst brothers, sisters, cousins, nieces and nephews. And the stern old patriarchal couple.

Quite a family. I still found it difficult to appreciate Germans. I mixed myself a drink, and went back to the book. I dozed a little. Finally, I heard a door slam outside, some whispering. Chantal came in.

'What a pleasant surprise,' she said, much too sweetly. 'So you did decide to visit me after all.'

I deliberately didn't get up. I slid the book on the table.

'I see you've been reading up on Gunther's family history. It's quite an array of Germans, isn't it?' she added, bitterly, 'German nobility. I think there's even one of me in there.'

'I saw it.'

'I didn't know you read German.'

'I don't.'

Since I didn't get up, she made herself a drink and sat. I said nothing. I studied her openly. I had to admit she was charming, as she blew a strand of hair back out of her eyes and looked at me.

'To what do I owe this great good fortune? Did the other one stand you up? Or did you feel you had to leave her side through pity and come and see me. At least, I am getting to know your preferences. You like them very young, and very long-legged. You like skin-diving dope pushers.'

'Pots calling kettles,' I said. 'Just take it easy. I'm here on business. Serious business, for you.' I paused. 'Do you know that Girgis has been killed? Murdered?'

Chantal's face grew pinched. 'You're not serious?'

I nodded. 'I found him. Well, me and a couple of hotel kids. In the bushes at the Xenia. And the only way we could tell it was Girgis was by his wallet, because there wasn't any head on the body.'

'Oh, but that's *horri*ble,' she whispered after a moment. She wasn't acting this time.

'Horrible or not,' I said. I sighed silently, and blew out my lips. I got up and busied myself making myself a drink to give her a little time. 'So,' I said, my back to her, 'I'm here as your representative. To tell you to keep your mouth shut. About Girgis and everything you might know about Girgis.' I sat back down. 'I thought it important enough to come right away. I feel a certain moral responsibility for you. Since you "hired" me.'

She didn't seem as though she was sure she had heard me. Her face was white, and she had her hands to her cheeks and was staring off across the corner of the floor. I looked at her closely. They will sometimes suddenly get sick all over themselves over a shock like that, sensitive protected ladies like her. I got up and poured her a shot of brandy. 'Here.'

She took it and looked at it and then drank half of it. 'I'm, uh – . I'm all shocked. It's hard to believe. I don't know what to say. I can't understand it. Why would somebody want to do that to him?'

'I don't know. I don't care. Drink the rest of that. It's not any of it my affair. Except to protect you and help you keep out of it as much as they will let you. Of course, they may not even bother you.'

'But cutting off his *head*? Why do a horrible thing like that?'

'I admit the head part's pretty gruesome. I haven't the slightest idea about why,' I said.

She drained off the rest of the snifter of brandy. 'What's going to happen?'

'I haven't any opinion about that, either. I thought you might be able to tell me more about that than I can.'

Chantal swung around in her chair to look at me, and set the glass down. 'Well, surely you don't think *I* did it?'

'No. Not unless you're a lot stronger than you look. There was almost no blood near the body. That means somebody had to carry Girgis quite a way. And he isn't small. Even without his head.' I grinned bleakly at her.

'You're horrible. You have no sensitivity at all.'

'It's all been knocked out of me over the years.' I peered at her over my glass. 'Now, are you going to do what I tell you?'

'Well, naturally, I'll do what you tell me.'

'Good.' I put aside my glass and got up. 'First, don't talk to the police or any of your friends. The other thing is that I want to know everything that took place between you and Girgis. And that means everything.'

Chantal leaped to her feet. 'I've told you a hundred times.' But she stopped when I seized her by the elbows, and squeezed her just a little.

'I said I meant everything. And I'm perfectly capable of shaking it out of you, if I have to.' I moved her gently back and forth. 'So start. *I* think you've been *working* for him, in some capacity. So does Inspector Pekouris, I would bet.'

Chantal's head drooped and she looked at the floor. But now she was acting again, I suspected. 'Well, it's true. I have been. I was his "contact", his "carrier", for my friends on the island who wanted hash.' Her face brightened. 'You'd be surprised. There's a lot of them. Then she drooped again. 'And – And I had an affair with him.'

'What else?' I said.

'That's all.'

'Are you sure?'

'I didn't want to tell you that last part. You can appreciate that. I'm not too proud of it. I'm not too proud of either, for that matter.'

'I think there's more,' I said grimly. But I let her go. She sank on to the couch.

'There isn't.'

I shook my head slowly. 'It doesn't make sense that way. Not any way I can figure.'

'He was blackmailing me with it! How do you think I would feel to have people know I had an affair with that upstart fisherman? That I was actually peddling hashish for him, and taking money for it?'

'Let's start with that part. How did that happen?' I said.

'It was simple enough. I winter in Paris every year. I leave here in November, and I come back in March.'

'That's expensive,' I said. 'That takes money. If you can't afford to pay me fifteen hundred dollars, and you need money from Girgis, how can you afford to winter in Paris every year?'

She just sort of looked at me and went on. I didn't think it was a good idea to stop her.

'I smoked hashish in Paris. Everybody does. And I liked it, so I thought I'd try and buy some here. I asked Girgis one time, when I was renting his boat for a party, and we were discussing the arrangements. He said he'd sell me some. People smoked it at my place, and asked me if I could get them some. It just sort of happened. I never went around with it soliciting. They always came and asked me. When Girgis realized it, he was pleased. It opened up a new market for him. He said if I would handle it for him, talk about it, promote it sort of, he would give me forty per cent.'

'That sounds like a lot.'

'Actually, he said twenty per cent at first. But I held out for forty.'

I looked at her in disbelief, then had to laugh. I shook my head. 'I thought you didn't need the money.'

'I always need money.'

'I thought you got a big alimony.'

She made a helpless gesture. 'I entertain a lot. It goes. Honestly I don't know where it goes.'

'And you can still afford to winter in Paris? All right, what about the affair?' I said.

Chantal looked appealingly helpless, like a small child caught at something innocently bad. 'Actually, I'd rather not talk about that.'

'Okay,' I said. 'Don't talk about it.'

'It happened at the beginning of last summer. In the spring, really. When I came back. I had been "working" for Girgis for a year. I was just getting over a thing with Freddy Tarkoff. Freddy had sort of left me. Well, I had always known he would. I expected him to. But it hurts just the same. And Girgis was there. I saw him a good bit because of the hashish. And he is good looking.' She paused.

I didn't say anything.

'He came here a few times, very late at night. We met in chapels in the hills. In the woods. Sometimes on the mainland, back in from Glauros. It was all so sort of exciting, at first. For me. The selling hashish part, too. It was a lark.'

For a woman who didn't want to talk about it, I thought she was doing a very good job.

'But as a lover, he was a good bit of a peasant,' Chantal said, and looked at me.

For a second I couldn't believe it. It was so outrageous and such a ploy. I wondered what she would say about me some day. I had to grin, then had to laugh. 'Is that supposed to imply that I am not?'

She looked at me a long moment. 'Well, yes. It is,' she said defiantly. 'If you insist that I spell it out for you. Anyway, why not? It's the truth.'

I did not react. I was still trying to sniff out the truth of the whole thing. There was something wrong with it somewhere. But I couldn't put my finger on it.

'What happened to stop it?' I said.

'He started to blackmail me,' Chantal said promptly. She was incredible. But then, she went on. 'And I was tired of him. Oh, I'm sure he was tired of me, too. But I told him I wanted to stop working for him.' She seemed to perk up suddenly. 'You see, that was what the blackmail was. He wasn't blackmailing me only for the money. He was blackmailing me to go on working for him.'

There was a silence. She seemed to be waiting for me to react. I pursed my lips. 'Well, you're out of it now. Stay out.'

Another silence. 'Do you think they'll try to involve me?'

'Honestly, I don't think they will. But that's what I don't know. If they go digging deep into his hashish operations, you might become involved. Who else knows about all this?'

'No one. No one at all.'

'How about that Greek sidekick of his, that works on the *Polaris* with him?'

She shook her head.

'How about Kirk.'

Suddenly she had an odd alert look about her, like that of a startled deer.

'That was why I wanted to tell you first,' I said. 'If there was any shock. It's a good thing I did. If you reacted like you did.'

'I'm grateful. I'll be careful.'

'I wanted to tell you not to say anything. To anyone. About any of it.'

'Were you planning on staying?' Chantal said. 'I mean, after you finished your business?'

I turned my head to look at her. Actually, I hadn't been. I thought I had made up my mind on that in the afternoon, when I had called her. But it took a lot of balls, or whatever the feminine equivalent, for her to come right out and ask me.

I knew damn well she wasn't doing it to pay me anything. For all my trouble. I remembered the satisfaction her back showed last night when she rolled over to go back to sleep. She just liked to have a man around.

Chantal swung on me suddenly. 'Let me tell you something about you,' she said, defiantly. 'Why can't you just screw me and stop worrying? You Americans are all so much alike. You don't *owe* me anything. Any more than I *owe* you anything. I haven't asked you for anything, have I? Why do you Americans all have to go through all this self-torture? You all have had the same thing beaten into your heads by somebody.'

I had to grin. I hoped my face didn't look haggard. 'You're absolutely right,' I said. I nodded. 'You are. Absolutely.'

'Well?'

'Yes,' I said. 'I was. In actual fact. I was thinking about staying.'

'And that's what you've been standing there brooding about so lugubriously?' she demanded.

Actually, it wasn't. Actually, I had been thinking about that nude bathing scene I had witnessed so long ago, this evening. Sweet Marie sweetly nude, and all those other girls nude, and all of it. Youth. What was it about a young body? Why did a young body seem so much better than an old body?

'Yes. No. Actually,' I said, 'I was worrying because I was afraid of becoming too involved with you.'

'Well, don't. I wouldn't have you on a platter. As a husband. And you don't have to be afraid of me.' She came across to me, and crept herself into my arms. 'I'm glad you're staying. I'm all shaken up. I'm a little scared.'

I looked down at her, and then gently, wrapped her up in my big strong manly arms.

I was pretty sure it was going to be as elegantly animal tonight as it had been last night.

I wasn't disappointed.

CHAPTER TWENTY-TWO

My Greek housekeeper woke me at 8:15 by knocking on the bedroom door to tell me Inspector Pekouris was waiting downstairs to see me.

Over a scalding cup of her powerful Greek coffee while I shaved in the bathroom down the hall, I called down to him I would be with him in five minutes. As I stretched my face in the mirror I asked it what this could be about.

He was standing on my porch, looking at the prettiness of the harbour. But he wasn't enjoying it. His attitude stated emphatically that he personally allowed these grown-up children to be out there, to water ski and play with their sailboats.

'This is a professional call of courtesy,' Pekouris said in his brutal way. 'We are going to have a look for the head. I thought you would enjoy to come along.'

Down in the road he had parked the blue police jeep in the edge of the vacant lot.

'Well, it's nice of you to ask me,' I said. 'But I don't know what I could do.'

'I do not expect you to do anything. I thought you would be interested. As one professional from another.' He gave me a look.

If I was supposed to understand what it meant, I was flunking the course. 'Well, if you put it that way,' I said. 'I'd love to go. Just give me a minute to tell my boat guy.'

Sonny was at the taverna. I told him I wouldn't need him and that he could take the day off. Then I climbed into the blue jeep beside Pekouris. I didn't feel fully awake yet. But I was awake enough to wonder what had earned me this special treatment. Pekouris stopped along the way for a cup of coffee, but did not enlighten me.

It was another lovely day like the others. They didn't seem to have anything else in Tsatsos. The Inspector seemed to visibly enjoy driving the jeep. We drove in the open jeep along the main road that ran behind the Port, and out the other side of the town toward the Xenia and the hilltop Construction.

The breeze blew the short sleeves of my sport shirt. Inspector Pekouris had his same blue suit on, or another like it. But at least he had changed his tie.

'You think there's any chance of finding it? The head?' I said.

'I doubt it. Still, it does no harm to look. It might tell us something. Or, we might find something else. One thing is certain. The actual killing had to take place not too far away.'

'You mean like maybe up at the Construction?'

He shrugged. 'As you saw, rigor mortis was fully established. The doctor places the time of death at around 3 A.M. the previous morning. Leaving about an hour and forty-five minutes till dawn. Someone had to carry the body to the Xenia garden, crossing at least one major road, and deposit it where it was found. All in the hour and a half before first light.'

'Not an easy job,' I said.

'No, not easy at all. Do not forget he had also to dispose of the head.'

We had reached the Xenia. In the hotel 'parking lot' where the horsecabs usually stood there was a cluster of vehicles: two autos, several horse-drawn wagons. Just beyond it, where the road curved inland to fit itself to the contour of the Construction hill, a group of men milled about.

The Inspector pulled into the lot. 'Oh, something else. Kronitis. Mr Leonid Kronitis. Do you know him?'

'No.' But the name certainly made me alert.

'I received a telephone call from him early this morning, before I left Glauros,' Pekouris said. 'I was asked to give you a message. He would like to see you some time today, if that is possible. He requests you to telephone him about it. Here.' He handed me a slip of paper with the number.

I took it, and studied it, and waited. But Inspector Pekouris said nothing more. He occupied himself with parking the jeep. When he cut the motor, he turned back to me. He still didn't say anything.

'Who is this Kronitis?'

'He has, shall we say, Mr Davies, minor interests in Tsatsos. He loves the island and wants to preserve it. A very wealthy and very respected gentleman. Who has a big villa over behind Glauros.' I got one of his lippy smiles.

'Should I go to see him?'

Pekouris's power-tuned eyebrows went up. 'You ask me?'

'You gave me the message.'

'I see no reason why you should not go see him. He is a very respected man. Also, he owns *Polaris*. Which our dead friend was master of.' He smiled again. 'Maybe he wants to hire you to find his killer.'

'Nobody seems to want to believe I'm down here on vacation,' I said. The Inspector didn't answer that.

Again, I had the feeling he was not saying everything he knew, the Inspector. Or maybe he was one of those who didn't want to know what he knew. That way nothing could be held against him?

'You recommend I go,' I said, finally.

'I recommend nothing.'

I gave him a look but he stared back steadily, with an open-eyed, completely expressionless face. Usually, his eyes seemed half closed. 'But I see no reason why not. Shall we go over?' he said and nodded his head toward the group of men.

We walked it. At the curve the fat chief was supervising the work. He seemed to find me more acceptable, since his boss had given him the word. I had found out since meeting them last night, from Chantal, that all the police in Greece came vaguely under the military, and that the local constabulary were in reality Army militiamen. The Inspector was an Army officer. This did not particularly endear them to me.

I got the picture of the job in progress right away. The in-sweeping curve of the road contoured a sharp little ravine, which below dropped to a small rocky unserviceable inlet of the sea, and above rose in a steep grassy draw. Up on the grassy draw a long line of local peasants and fishermen were working their way upward half way up the steep slope.

The right side of this hollow formed the hill where the Construction was and some of its units with their spindly stilt legs encroached right out on to the steep grass. The right of the peasant line came almost to them.

In amongst the units, as if unwilling to venture beyond their line, some of the hippies had come out to watch.

There must have been forty of them: the men with their long hair and beards and bizarre clothes; the women with their longer hair, and the characteristic part in the centre, and their ugly shapeless long dresses or dirty jeans. They appeared to feel menaced by the search. They were very quiet. The men stood with their arms hanging. Occasionally a woman moved or murmured to quiet a child. They were a pretty unprepossessing-looking lot, not at all attractive; but somehow familiar. Then I remembered. They made me think of the pictures of the people in the German camps.

Although they were here by choice, I didn't like the feeling and the implications that gave me, and I shot a look at the impassive Inspector. He certainly wasn't bothered.

Up above when the peasants and fishermen of the line passed near them, they stared at the hippies and did not speak. There was a definite antagonism, on both sides.

Standing at the bottom I looked the disposition over. Its point reached me quickly enough.

'What if you find nothing in the ravine?' I asked. 'Will you search the Construction?'

'We have to,' Pekouris said. 'But I doubt if we will find much evidence in there.'

'No,' I said, staring up at the hippies.

I didn't know what else to call them, but hippies. I knew they didn't like the term. And I knew it had become pretty much passé. But Georgina called them that, and they even called themselves that, on occasion. They certainly weren't all students.

Not far away in a group of the hippies I suddenly saw the blond-maned Steve and his girl Diane, and Sonny Duval and his wife Jane. A little path led up to the tiny knoll they were on. I started up to them.

'Hallo! What are you doing here?'

Sonny smiled. 'You gave me the day off,' he said amicably enough, in the tone of a man who doesn't really have to work for you.

'We came to be with our people,' Jane Duval said in a clarion voice from behind him, and stepped forward. The runny nosed, not very clean three-year-old was clinging to her long skirt and she put an arm around it protectively.

Her face was a study in self-righteous rage. Black angers roiled behind her frowning eyes like storm clouds, seeking an object. 'We might as well tell each other the real truth for once. We felt our place was here with them.' She looked at me with a kind of aloof defiance. 'Would you rather we cowered in town while our friends are terrorized?'

My face became a patient mask. I didn't answer. This was a look I had seen on the young women's faces before, all over America. And like Jane, they never seemed to know where to direct it, either. The other girl, Diane, beside Jane, had it too. There was a profound hurt in the subtle twist of the brows, as well as the outrage. A deep unhealing wound – or so they seemed to think.

When no one else spoke, Jane Duval said, 'Are you the one who initiated this new terrorization?'

'I'm afraid you'll have to go to Inspector Pekouris, the Police Inspector, for that,' I said politely. 'I just came along for the ride.' I pointed, 'He's right down there.'

Jane's lips writhed as she said, 'Fat chance! And it's easy to see which side of the line your feet are on, Mr Davies, in this new infringement of the rights of our people.'

I remained stolid. 'I don't know if you got any rights, here. Except what the Greek government is willing to donate you. They own this joint.'

'Our rights are the rights of being alive,' Jane said.

'In my book that gets you the right to breathe air,' I said grimly, but politely. 'And nothing more.

'If you can find the air,' I added.

'In your book,' Jane Duval cried. 'The book of the Establishment.' Beside her the grubby child began to cry.

I said, 'Is that the way they read it at Bennington? You're scaring the kid. Maybe you didn't hear, but there's been a murder. They're trying to find the murdered man's head.'

'We heard! And the next step – the real purpose – will be mass deportation of the *hippies* almost surely. But don't think you're fooling us, any.'

'It might be at that,' I said with a stony humour. I'd

talked to so many of them. 'Unfortunately, the murder happened very close to this place.

'Look,' I said to Sonny. 'I came up here to tell you I want you this morning. I'll need the boat.'

Before he could answer yes or no, Jane moved to him and wilting, buried her face searchingly – suckingly like a suckling infant – in the angle of his neck. As if it was all more than she could bear. They formed a sort of staircase of anguish: the little girl with her face in Jane's skirt: Jane with her face in Sonny's neck: Sonny's half angry face at the top.

'Look. You don't have to take me,' I said. 'I'll find somebody else.'

'I'll take you, I'll take you,' Sonny said. His voice sounded anguished, half angry. 'I'll be at the dock in an hour. Half an hour. I hired out to you. All right?' He sort of stepped backwards with Jane, the child following, as if pulling them back out of the self-imposed zone of combat. Jane, without moving her face, and clinging like a leech, allowed herself to be pulled.

Just then, at the top of the grassy draw, which a couple of men from the line had reached, there was a shout. Looking up, we could see the men waving.

'They have found the blood,' the Inspector called up to me from below. 'Do you want to come up?'

'No. That's too much of a climb for a middle-aged man.' I turned back to the hippies. Steve and Diane were still there, with some others, but Sonny had drawn himself and his family back out.

'You feeling oppressed, too?' I said to Steve.

'I don't know.' The vague-eyed Steve looked at me, but appeared to be looking through me, as usual. 'She's probably right. It's easier to blame it all on us. They'll start kicking us out to make themselves look better.' He put out his arm – because the silent Diane had started to move toward him, as if for protection. She crept into it.

'They won't unless they find the murderer,' I said.

'You mean they won't give us permission to leave?'

'I don't know. Might not.' I looked around. 'Where's your sidekick? Old Cyclops?'

'Oh, he's around,' Steve said, too quickly. 'He's around, all right. Somewhere.' Rather thoughtlessly, he pushed the passive girl away from him. He took a step or two down

toward me, lowered his voice. 'Listen, did you tell any of *them* what you and I talked about in the square the other day?'

'I didn't tell anybody anything,' I said. 'I'm not in this.'

'Well, thanks.'

'Don't thank me. Nobody asked me. If they ever do ask me, I'll tell them. Especially under oath in front of a grand jury seeking an indictment, I'd tell them.'

'You would?'

'Under oath? Sure.'

'You give a damn about oaths?'

'Give a damn? I care about *my* oath.'

'That's all crap. Establishment crap. "Before God and my fellow man." You believe all that? They want you to believe that. That's their way of hooking you. I believe in taking their fucking oath, and telling them whatever you want. Establishment crap.'

I simply looked at him. Finally I dropped my eyes and shook my head, is disbelief. 'Lying under oath is also against the law,' I added. As if that meant anything. I might lie under oath myself some day, if it was absolutely necessary. But I never had yet. And I didn't hold to it as a righteous philosophy.

'Okay, pal,' Steve said, in a bitter voice. 'Thanks a lot, man. At least we know where we stand.'

He turned and collected his girl absently with his open arm, and moved away. I started down. 'You know I didn't mean it, don't you?' he called after me, turning back around. I went on. He turned back to the other hippies.

Behind me I heard someone coming down after me. It was Pete Gruner, the high-shouldered, bearded man from the night club. He had been up there with the hippies, apparently. Pete Gruner, the dropout cop. Or was he?

'Hey, Davies. Wait up, man. I want to talk to you.'

'Talk to me later,' I said rudely over my shoulder. 'I've had a bellyful. Of talk. Up to here.' I went on down without looking back.

CHAPTER TWENTY-THREE

Back at the jeep I waited for the Inspector. I sat in the sun-warm driver's seat, fiddling with the faded wheel. For long moments I stared off through the trees, thinking. Mulling it over. I seemed to be getting drawn in in spite of myself.

The morning sun coming in through the trees turned the leaves a yellow-green. It made a hot incandescent halo for itself, passing through the tree branches.

A light little breeze zephyred in under the trees to me from the open water below the hotel.

Already, there was too much material to correlate. Too many people had done or said too many things. I could no longer even remember them all. I'd have had to sit down with a couple of pads and spend a night making notes. Just like I did on a regular case.

Steve and his buddy. Kirk's vague hints. Chantal's continuing reticence. Pekouris. Pete Gruner. This new man Kronitis. Nobody had hired me to work on any murder case. I was supposed to be on a damn vacation.

The Inspector wasn't long. I slid over into the rider's seat, feeling its heat through my thin pants, to let him get behind the wheel. He drove us back to town.

Pekouris talked about the results of his search. He seemed willing enough to talk about it. They had found nothing of any importance. They had found the murder site, or at least the place where the head had been cut off. It was interesting that it was right out in the open, only one hundred yards from the Construction, in plain view. They had not found the head, or any weapons, or any other articles of evidence.

'The men are continuing,' he said like some dictator. 'But they are not likely to find the head, now. He is not likely to bury the head nearby, if he meant to bury it.'

'No,' I said.

'It could be anywhere within two miles. To my thought he had to come down that grassy draw with the body.'

'What interests me is why cut the head off at all,' I said.

133

'To his left was the Construction. On his right were those steep rocks you saw. Impossible. The only other route was to go clear around by the hilltop. A walk of nearly one mile, past half a dozen houses on that little road. Yet we found no traces of blood in the grass down the draw.'

He was nit-picking. 'Was the grass pressed down, as if someone had walked over it?' I said.

'That grass is too short for that kind of an effect,' Pekouris said. 'I too find it interesting why the head was cut off at all,' he said suddenly. 'I also find it *very* interesting that it took place so close to the 'ippie community.'

My comment had finally dawned on him. But by the time it did it became his idea, and he took the credit. That was fine by me.

He let me off where the main road crossed at the back of the Port. 'You are going to call Mr Kronitis? The P.T.T. is right over there.'

I nodded. I knew where the P.T.T. was. But after he drove off, I walked the long block past the sere, thirsty 'park' and past the telephone office, to the café terrace over the tiny produce harbour. He could have my idea. But I wasn't ready to call Kronitis yet, until *I* wanted to. It was not yet 10:00 A.M. I got a Paris *Herald* and sat at my same table and ordered a Campari-soda.

I noticed a lot of the hippies around looking at me. Nobody had seen me get off the jeep. Apparently the news of the search had passed along like a message on the jungle telegraph, and me with it.

I also noticed that Sweet Marie was sitting at a table by herself, with her own Paris *Herald*.

I went over.

'Getting the latest scoop from the capitals of Europe? How's the war going?'

'War's going badly. As usual. The Paris talks are stalled again. Some Prince from someplace is marrying some Princess,' Marie said brightly. Then she smiled that smile that always made me ache.

'Mind if I sit down?'

'Oh, please. Excuse me not asking you. Nobody ever does, around here.'

I slid into a tin chair. She folded up her paper. 'You're

not going out spearfishing today?' I said.

'I haven't thought about it. I'm feeling pretty chipper today. Maybe it's a no-therapy day.'

'When I saw you sitting here,' I said, 'it occurred to me we might go out today together. I bought some stuff.'

'Oh, gee! That would be great.'

'I don't have a wet-suit,' I said. 'So I couldn't stay in that water all day. But we could take my boat somewhere.'

'All right! Fine!' She always seemed to talk in exclamation points, like a teenager. It made me think of my own two teenagers. But they were seventeen and thirteen. 'I'll have to get my stuff,' she said. 'What time? Where?'

'Well, I have a phone call to make. And probably something to do. But I should be finished by 12:30. Let's say we'll meet at Dmitri's at 12:30, and I'll bring along some sandwiches for a picnic lunch.'

'Gee! Great!'

I sat and looked at her a moment, watching her smile. 'You didn't hear about the murder?'

Her face got long. 'Yes. I did. Isn't it gruesome? Who would want to do that to poor Girgis?'

'That's what nobody seems to know,' I said.

'It's so sad,' Marie said. 'The kids have been talking about it.' She didn't seem very upset. And she didn't seem worried.

'Won't you be out of a job, now?'

'I suppose I can do the same job for Jim. Jim'll take over the hash business I suppose.'

'Was there bad blood between Kirk and Girgis?' I asked.

She answered me slowly, her face clouding. 'I suppose there was. Jim felt he wasn't getting enough of the take. But he wouldn't kill Girgis, would he? Wouldn't he be the first one they'd suspect?'

'I suppose,' I said. 'I never thought of it like that.' I was careful not to grin. 'Well. It doesn't matter,' I said. 'It's not my case. I'll see you at 12:30.'

'Okay! But let's not talk about this murder business. Please?'

I shook my head no. It was funny how your instinct just told you naturally that some people were innocent. It would never have occurred to me to connect her with it.

'To tell the truth, the reason I didn't go out today was because I thought it might look unseemly. – ? – ' She looked up at me questioningly.

I just grinned. At my table I paid for my drink, then walked back up to the P.T.T. telephone office. I placed my call to Kronitis. The government clerk was a typical mangy-looking, officious little squirt with one wall eye. Exotropia, divergent strabismus. It took him a little while to get it through. When he did, he ordered me to Booth 2 like a South American general. Being handicapped did not make him any kinder. Instead of Kronitis, I got an uppity male secretary who spoke with an English accent. He told me the great man could see me at 3:30. A car would be waiting for me at the Glauros ferry dock. I disliked him instantly and blazingly.

'I can't come at 3:30,' I said bluntly. 'I've got something else to do. I can come now.'

'I'm afraid, Mr Davies, it's 3:30 or nothing,' he drawled.

'Then it's nothing,' I said. 'Goodbye.'

'Wait, wait. Please hold the line a moment.' When he came back, he said now would be all right. But he sounded like he didn't like it. He sounded as if I had deeply shocked him. When would I be at the ferry?

'In about twenty minutes,' I said, and hung up with no goodbye.

The little clerk was waiting for me to make sure I paid.

When I got back to Georgina's, the first thing I noticed was that the *Agoraphobe* was back, at its regular mooring. Then when I got to Dmitri's, Jim Kirk was sitting at a table over the water. And with him was Jane Duval.

Farther ahead at the boat dock Sonny was on the *Daisy Mae*. When he saw me, he jumped on shore and waved for me to come.

'Okay,' I called. But I stopped in front of Kirk. 'Hallo. I see you're back.'

'My, my. Heavens to Betsy,' he rumbled. 'If it ain't old Lobo Davies.'

Jane Duval across from him, who had not even acknowledged my presence, jerked herself away suddenly in her tin chair so that the back of her right shoulder was to me. Then, as if deliberately to bug me, though I didn't know why she thought it should, she reached out her hand across the tin table and put it over Kirk's big paw. It less than half covered it.

'You got them all straightened out back at the police post?' I said to her.

Jane tossed her head, and her long hair with it. But she didn't speak.

'I guess you've heard the bad news,' I said to Kirk.

'I've not heard anything but. Since I got back this morning. It's all too sad, and too weird. I'm just sorry I wasn't here. If I had been, he would probably have been with me. And I could have helped him.' It was a pretty long speech, for Kirk.

'You would have protected him,' I echoed.

'Well, if I was with him, probably nobody would have jumped him.'

'You got any ideas about who did it?' I asked.

'No,' Kirk rumbled. 'But I'm sure,' he said, and looked blandly at Jane, like a cream-eating cat, 'I'm sure it wouldn't have been any of those nice young hippie people up there on the hill. It's too bad it had to happen there.'

'Inspector Pekouris seems to think it's too bad, too,' I said.

'Ah,' Kirk said, 'I heard the Inspector was over here. Well, I wish him luck.'

This kind of a conversation could go on forever. Besides, Sonny had come up to us from the boat, and was standing just beside me. I had to admit it made me edgy, bugged me a little, to see his wife sitting there with her hand on Kirk's paw in front of him.

Sonny, however, didn't seem to notice it. Or, if he did, didn't seem to care.

'Come on,' I said gruffly. 'I have to run over to Glauros. I'll be about half an hour, or an hour. Then we'll come back, and I'll want the boat for this afternoon.'

On the boat Sonny started his motor and I cast off so he could back us out. At the table Kirk and Jane Duval had stood up. Both of them stood waving.

'Goodbye! Goodbye!' Kirk bellowed across the water. 'We'll see you later! We'll see you later!'

Both of them got on a tiny motorcycle, that was apparently Kirk's, and that he apparently kept at Dmitri's taverna for transportation ashore, and went rocketing and sputtering off along the seawall road toward the Port. The little cycle seemed to disappear beneath Kirk's bulk alone, even without Jane hanging on to his waist behind him.

By this time Sonny had got us out of the nest of anchor lines, and we were heading out of the harbour straight across toward the mainland.

'Can you tell me about what time we'll be coming back?' Sonny asked as we passed the little lighthouse.

'I told you,' I said. 'In about an hour. I think. But I can't be sure.' The irritability in my voice startled even me.

'I wanted to know because I want to go back up to the Construction this afternoon,' he said. 'Jane wants to go, to be with some of her friends. I should go with her.'

I got hold of my irritation. 'Well, I told you I wanted the boat for this afternoon, Sonny. Anyway, it looks like Jane won't be back in time to go up to the Construction with you.' I guess it was cruel, but I couldn't help it. He looked so damned understanding.

Sonny's face stiffened a little, under that ridiculous Elliot Gould moustache. He said only, 'Would you consider taking it out yourself again?'

After asking Marie to go out, the idea had already occurred to me. But I hadn't felt I ought to ask for it a second time. 'Yes,' I said. 'All right. I'll take her myself. I want to take Sweet Marie out diving.'

Sonny just nodded. After a moment he said, 'I guess you think I did wrong, letting Jane go off with Jim Kirk like that.'

'Wrong? What's wrong? Anyway, it's not any of my affair,' I said. 'It's your woman.'

'You don't understand Jane,' he said. He looked off across the water for a long moment, then looked back. 'You don't any of you guys understand Jane. Jane's a free spirit. All of you guys think she's just some neurotic girl with a – with an itchy box. I wouldn't ever want to do anything to destroy that free spirit of hers. It's the most beautiful part of her.'

'Being a free spirit always seems to entail ignoring responsibilities,' I said shortly. 'Was it you who changed the baby's diapers all the time?'

'Jane doesn't ignore responsibilities, she just feels she has certain rights as a free individual. She wants her rights. And she had a right to them.'

'Well, good for her,' I said.

'As a free individual myself, I can't refuse to let her be one.' He looked off across the water again, 'It's you guys who can't appreciate her, or understand her.'

Sonny cleared his throat. 'About this morning.'

'Never mind about this morning,' I said. 'It bores me and I don't want to talk about it.'

'But there's no reason for me and you to be at swords' points over that.'

I thought this over. I rather abruptly felt sorry for him. He had misread everything. 'I didn't think I was at swords' points with you over this morning,' I said carefully. 'If I gave you the impression that this morning hurt my feelings, I didn't mean to. I apologize.'

'But you still don't understand about Jane.'

Abruptly, I was furious. I got up. I was a good bit shorter than he was, but probably stronger. It didn't even matter. I poked a forefinger into his chest.

'Listen, don't tell me what I understand. I probably understand more about "hippies" and the young than you do. Or ever will. Christ, don't you know I live in New York? What do you think I do with my time? You think I'm not down in the East Village? Listen, I'm down in the East Village more than half my time. Doing what? Hunting missing kids. Hunting missing kids is my major source of income, nowadays. Without missing kids I wouldn't be able to keep my two daughters in their ritzy schools. Parents come to me from as far as California. Find my kid. I find them. They pay me. I talk the kids into going home. And you know what it is? Every time? Hurt pride; hurt vanity. I'm grateful for hippies. Every time I sit down to eat a meal. Don't tell me I don't understand hippies. I'm a specialist. And you know what I think? I think they're all goddamned babies. They're running away from growing up. They're terrified of growing up.

'Whatever they happen to feel, they want to gratify it *now*. Nobody ever taught them any self-discipline. That's your Jane.'

I stopped. I was more surprised by my outburst, apparently, than Sonny was. I turned away, and sat back down.

'But,' Sonny began.

And I jumped up again. Again, the forefinger. But this time I made my voice much harder, slower. 'Murder has been done here. You try to understand that. Somebody has killed a man. That supersedes everything. You talk about human rights. The first human right is to not be murdered.'

I made my voice get even slower. 'Murder changes everything. It's got its own alchemy. I've worked on a few murder cases. After a murder, nothing is the same. No peace, no real fun for anybody. From now on, everybody is suspect. You are. Jane is. And your friends Steve and Diane. That guy Pete. Sweet Marie. Every man in the village, and every hippie up on that hill. That's what murder does.'

'There's no reason that it should,' Sonny said.

'No? But it does. Is that some more of your humanism? But that's what murder does. Maybe *you'll* need to have *your* life saved some day. That's what the murderer has done to all of you. You're suspect.'

'What about Georgina?'

'Her, too.'

'What about Chantal von Anders?' There was a subtle change in his voice.

'Her, too,' I said. 'Everybody.'

'What about outsiders, who might have come in?' Sonny said.

'Them, too,' I said, trying to unheat myself, and looking at the Glauros shore. 'Everybody is, as far as I'm concerned. And that's no way to have to live. Believe me. A murder is an affront to everybody. I'm glad I'm out of it.'

'Well, I wish you'd try to understand that Jane's a believer. She believes.'

'That's great,' I said sourly. 'So were the Spanish Catholics believers in the days of the auto-da-fé. Give me a cynic any time. My life's safer with him.'

'I'm sorry you won't try and understand us. I was hoping we could become good friends,' Sonny said.

That was all it meant to him, apparently. That was all he'd gotten out of what I'd said. Or tried to say. Good friends. Or not good friends.

I stood looking at him, and I could feel the corner of my mouth twitch, with irritation, with anger, finally with disgust. I turned away and went and sat down on the coach-roof.

'You're too old to be a hippie,' I called.

'No, I'm not. Nobody's ever too old for anything, to be anything. If they've got the courage.—Here we are!' he called. 'We're coming in!'

CHAPTER TWENTY-FOUR

The Glauros ferry dock was a rough-poured concrete ramp down into the water. I never ceased to be amazed at how badly the Greeks and the French handled concrete. The ferry itself, a U.S. Army surplus LCT painted blue and white, rocked at its dock with its ramp down. Beside this was a normal dock for caiques. We tied up there.

Up on the road where some taxis were parked, the biggest, blackest Rolls-Royce limousine I'd ever seen sat solidly like a tank. The taxi drivers, a sinister-looking lot with sideburns and dark glasses, stood around it. When we walked up the little grade, a liveried chauffeur came forward from beside it. I immediately noticed the extra weight he carried under his left arm. It looked a lot of weight. A .357 Magnum, maybe.

'Mr Davies?'

I nodded, and he opened the door of the limousine for me. Behind me Sonny Duval whistled, a long drawn-out nasty comment.

At the door, I stuck out my jaw at him. 'Just because I have to dress cheap, you think I haven't got rich friends, hunh?' I got in.

Through the tinted window glass, I got some glimpses of the town of Glauros as we went past it, not through it, up the hill. Glauros wasn't big enough to go through. On top we hit the main road—which appeared to be little more than a slightly blacktopped, very hole-filled cowpath. The town below resembled nothing so much as a jerry-built Western town in the Arizona desert country, except for one thing: a big horribly modern glass-and-green-marble tourist hotel, which crouched at the near end of it. There was a row of bars nobody with fifty cents in his pocket would want to go in, a 19th-century brick town hall, and little else. It seemed little more than a way station for the ferry to the islands nearby.

I tapped on the glass between me and the chauffeur. The chauffeur opened it.

'That's Glauros?'

'Yes, sir.' He had an upper-class English accent, too.

'What do they do there?'

'Very little, sir.'

'Then why the hotshot- hotel?'

'People come down from Athens, sir.' He shrugged. 'And there are tourists.'

'To do what?'

'There are a number of ruins in the neighbourhood, sir.'

'How many is a number?'

'In the entire area? Four. Perhaps five, sir. There are two fairly close by.'

'That's all?'

'There is a casino at Petkos, sir.'

'I see. You're English?'

'Yes, sir.'

'Tell me, why do you carry a gun?'

'Orders, sir,' the chauffeur said promptly. 'The country is quite wild hereabouts.'

'Thanks,' I said. 'It's nice to know one is in good hands.'

'Will that be all, sir?'

'Yes.'

'Thank you, sir.' He closed the glass.

He certainly had nice manners. With that cannon he was carrying, I was glad. And he could always be telling the truth. We had been driving mainly uphill, and had reached a plain. From it you could see down to the sea all around. The sea disappeared as the car moved inland. The chauffeur made some confusing turns, then turned off back downhill. Below us a sea vista opened up, in the centre of which was a breathtaking villa. It had everything. It had its own electric plant. It had a king-sized swimming pool. It might even have had its own fresh water plant, to turn sea water into fresh. It was that elaborate. As we got down closer to it, the place looked more and more like an armed fortress. There was a big iron grille gate, chained, with a gateman. There was a whitewashed high wall, with dangerous looking glass cemented on top. I leaned forward and tapped the glass. The chauffeur opened it.

'Tell me, is that the casino?'

There was the tiniest pause, then the modulated voice, 'No, sir. That is Mr Kronitis's estate.'

'That's where we're going?'

'Yes, sir.'

'I forgot to bring my bathing suit.'

Again the tiny pause, before the voice, 'I'm sure there are some available, sir.'

'Thank you.'

I guess he thought me irreverent. I felt irreverent.

This time the chauffeur didn't close the glass. Ahead of us the gateman recognized us and had the gate open before we rolled up to it. He touched his cap like a well-bred peasant as we went through.

'You've got well-bred peasants here,' I said.

'Yes, sir.'

My ire was still rising, as the chauffeur turned me over to a butler. It was enough to almost make you a Communist. The ire went up farther, as the butler led me through an elaborate living area, out beside the big delicious marble pool, and into an annexe and turned me over to the male secretary I had spoken to earlier. He didn't say a word to me, except a polite, 'Mr Davies.' It was a good thing for him he didn't. He escorted me from his own small office into a huge one. Far across it, beside windows that looked on the sea, a tall, stooped, grey-haired man sat behind a desk the size of a small hockey rink.

With an effort, I waded across the thick-napped carpet. Kronitis got up, smiling.

'Please sit down, Mr Davies. Why are you walking so strangely?'

'I always do that when I can't see my ankles,' I said. 'Then, too, I was scared of maybe tripping over a small log that might have been mislaid down in there.'

Kronitis stared at me puzzled, still smiling. 'Oh. Yes.

One of your jokes. Freddy Tarkoff told me about your jokes.' He indicated a chair before the desk, one of several white leather ones scattered about the room. 'Please sit.'

'Well, hardly a joke. Carpets that thick frighten me,' I said. 'Are you sure I won't get this dirty?' I looked at the chair. 'If all this has been done to impress me, I'm surprised.'

Kronitis laughed, 'Ha, ha, ha,' a polite, but rather mirthless laugh. 'Freddy Tarkoff has told me all about you, Mr Davies. But I had rather expected we would meet in another situation, under different circumstances.' He was a very dry man. Sec, the French would say. He probably spoke perfect French.

'You mean like at Ambassador Pierson's for dinner.'

'Something like that, yes.'

'I prefer the ruder, more exotic fisherman's hovel. What do you want to see me about, Mr Kronitis?' I had sat down. Now I deliberately placed one dusty bare sandalled foot on the other knee.

'I want to hire you, Mr Davies. I want to employ your services to find out who killed, who murdered, my man Girgis Stourkos. I'm prepared to pay you handsomely.' He opened a desk drawer.

'Hold on. It's not that easy, Mr Kronitis,' I said. 'I don't usually take jobs I don't know about, from people I know nothing about, either. And you don't know anything about me.'

Kronitis remained poised, hand still in desk drawer. 'I know all I need to know about you from Freddy Tarkoff.'

'He never mentioned you to me,' I said.

'No reason that he should. But I'm prepared to tell you everything about me you want to know. Certain high-finance arrangements of mine, of course, I can't talk about.'

I grinned. 'No. I wouldn't expect that.' I remembered who he made me think of. It was an aged mathematics professor I had at Denver.

'But anything else.'

'I wouldn't even know where to start. You own the *Polaris*, Girgis's boat, don't you, Mr Kronitis?'

'That's correct. Or, rather, I own most of it. I gave Girgis Stourkos twenty per cent of it as an inducement.'

I had been wrong about one thing, anyway. The old

man was no common heroin smuggler.

'Well, would you perchance know that Girgis was running a very profitable illegal hashish-smuggling operation from the *Polaris*? And if so, would you be owning eighty per cent of that?'

Kronitis's face had become very still. He looked genuinely surprised. 'No, sir, I wouldn't. The answer is no to both questions. I had no idea of that.'

He was surprised, all right. 'It seems to be the truth,' I said. 'Would that affect your wanting to hire me?'

'No, it wouldn't. Not in the least.'

'Not even if the smuggling became public?'

Kronitis thought a moment. His hand was still poised in the drawer. 'No. No, it wouldn't bother me. I had nothing to do with it, and know nothing about it. I'm genuinely shocked. And I still want whoever killed him caught and punished.'

I nodded. 'Fine.'

'Well, he worked for me, Mr Davies.' He reached his hand on in the drawer. 'I try to look after people who work for me. Mr Davies.'

I suddenly decided not to mention Kirk to him. The old gent seemed straight enough. Certainly his surprise about the hashish was straight. And I didn't want to lose Kirk his job. Certainly not if he was innocent. And especially not, if he was guilty. Not yet.

Kronitis pulled out a nice sheaf of new $100 bills. 'I have four thousand dollars here, Mr Davies. In cash. Which I'm prepared to give you this morning as a retainer.' He spread the bills in a row on the desk in front of me. They looked mighty good, and mighty genuine. And Kronitis knew it.

I pursed my lips in a soundless whistle for him. 'That's a lot of money to me, Mr Kronitis. That's more than I get for two missing kids in New York.'

'You would charge your usual fee and expenses. In addition to this retainer.' Before I could answer, he murmured, 'I suppose it was all those hippies up there on the hill. He just couldn't resist the temptation.'

'Yes, sir. It would seem so. Well, what would you say if I told you that the prime suspects in the murder case so far are also people who work for you?'

At this Kronitis's eyebrows went up. He still had his

145

hand poised among the $100 bills, carefully squaring them in line, like my mathematics professor used to do his books.

'I'm referring,' I said, 'to two of those same hippies. An American boy named Steve, and his sidekick called Chuck. Would you still want to hire me?'

Kronitis stared at me fixedly, a stormy look. He sat back.

'Some kind of gang killing, then? About who owns the hashish rights?'

'Something like that.'

'You're also referring, Mr Davies, I imagine, to that night club of theirs I helped them start? – Yes, sir, I would still want to hire you.'

'Well, would you mind telling me why you financed that night club, and how much of it you own?'

'I own all of it. That's required by Greek law. But we split the profits of it fifty-fifty. That was my deal with Steve. I thought it would not be wise to favour him too much, and give him all the profits. As to why I did it, this boy Steve came to me about it. I thought it would be better if I financed it, than if some unsavoury element came in from Athens.

'You may not know it, Mr Davies, but Tsatsos is a vanishing type among the Greek islands. It has kept to the old ways, and so far it hasn't been exploited. Mostly that is because it was a resort for Athenian Greeks long before the Americans and Europeans started touristing our country in large numbers. Some of us hope to keep it as the quiet, sleepy, backward place it's always been.

'Naturally, any outside unscrupulous money from Athens getting an opening foothold through a night club, would begin to jeopardize that. Yet there was a natural need for such a night club. I thought backing this boy Steve would take care of it. Also, he seemed to be able to control the hippie colony fairly well.'

That sounded square enough to me. 'Do you have any idea why this hippie colony has been tolerated as long as it has, Mr Kronitis?'

'No, I don't. The Greek government has its own reasons for doing what it does. These are ticklish times, Mr Davies. Almost certainly the present government will not last forever. I am not privy to the government's thinking. But I would imagine the money brought in by the hippies is a consideration. They aren't poor.'

'That sounds fair enough,' I said. I paused. 'If I take your money, and your job, Mr Kronitis – to use a metaphor that may be in bad taste – the heads will have to fall where they may.'

Kronitis wrinkled his nose. A fastidious man, clearly. Well, he could afford it. 'I would not expect anything different. That's the very reason I want to hire you, Davies,' he said just the same. He reached out and shuffled the bills together. 'Here.'

'One minute. I've got another question. Would you happen to know anything about why three men, from off the island as far as I can find, would come to Tsatsos wanting to work me over?'

'Work you over?'

'Beat me up.'

'Is that what happened to your face?'

'Yes. But I thought it didn't show any more.'

'Just a little. A little bruise. Under the skin. So they beat you up?'

'They tried. They didn't succeed. But why, I don't know. Maybe to scare me into leaving?'

Kronitis's big jaw came out. My old maths professor had a big jaw too, when he wanted to use it. Above the jaw Kronitis grinned. 'I would think that would be precisely the way to guarantee that you stayed, Mr Davies.'

'Okay. My fees are a hundred and fifty a day and expenses.' I got up. 'I'll take your money, Mr Kronitis.' I put the money in my wallet and got one of my cards out of it. 'I'll write you a receipt on this.' The money felt nice and thick.

I passed the receipt across the desk. 'Why don't you trust the local police? To get the guy.'

'I trust them. I am acquainted with Inspector Pekouris for a long time. I would also like to know a man of your calibre is working on it, too.'

'Would you mind if I told them you've hired me?'

Kronitis was silent a moment. 'I would rather they did not know. If there is a choice.'

'I'm afraid I'll have to tell them.'

'All right. Tell them, then.'

I straightened up. I took my time putting my fat wallet away. Then I said, softly, 'Mr Kronitis, if I found there was anything fishy about the reason you hired me, I'd drop the case like a hot rock. And you wouldn't get your retainer back.'

'That's fine,' Kronitis stood, and put out his hand, 'perfectly fine. I find you are everything Freddy Tarkoff said you were.'

'If he told you that for my fee I give good service to honest clients, he'd be right, too,' I said. I took the hand. It was as sec as the rest of him. 'Goodbye. I'll be in touch.' I began the long plod back across that carpet.

His head was already bent over his desk as I shut the door softly behind me.

Outside, the man secretary looked at me questioningly, but I stared him down with a blank face.

Then the same routine to get me back out of there began all over again just the same, this time in reverse. The secretary handed me off to the butler. The butler carted me out through that establishment. I went through my momentary Communist proclivities again. The butler passed me to the chauffeur. The chauffeur lateraled me into his Rolls.

I was a football. Or a baseball, in the old double-play routine: Tinker to Evers to Chance.

Back at Glauros I stopped the chauffeur at the end of the main drag, before we rolled out on to the dock. Pekouris had said he was going back to his office. After the chauffeur opened and closed the door for me, still wearing his big piece of iron, he touched his cap.

I gave him a grin, and on the spur of the moment snapped him back a tight little half-military Army salute. I supposed it was all right if a very rich man wanted his English chauffeur to sport a .357 cannon. Especially down here in the wilds of the lower Greek finger peninsulas.

My salute didn't faze him a bit.

I started on into the tiny town, towards the 19th-century town hall of brick.

CHAPTER TWENTY-FIVE

The whole place was deserted, except for a few bored tourists on the veranda of the ugly marble hotel. For a split second down in the dirt street I felt like Wyatt Earp walking down the dusty main drag of Tombstone looking for a showdown with somebody.

Behind me, Sonny Duval came galloping up, and fell into step. 'Where are you going? I'll go with you.'

I stopped in the rutted street. 'No, you won't. I've got an errand to do. I want to do it by myself.'

'Well, gee,' Sonny said. He was putting on a fake boyishness, to hide his anger. 'Gee whiz. Phoo-o. Okay, boss. Yes, sir, boss.' He turned back towards the dock.

I looked after him grimly. Sometimes he could try even my superb patience.

I went on to the city hall. Inside, it was dirty, unswept, empty. It looked and smelled about like any county courthouse I'd ever been in in the United States. Rolls of dirt that my mother used to call slut feathers lay in the corners of the marble floor. Its dimness gave a false impression of cool in the heat. A sign pointed to the Police Inspector's office. I knocked, and went in. Inside Pekouris was at a desk, and one other man sat at a live, but silent radio apparatus. Pekouris had taken off his suit coat but not his tie, and sat in his short-sleeved white shirt.

'Well, Mr Davies,' he said with his brutal smile, and half closed Turkish eyes. 'So soon? Have you solved our murder for us already?'

I grinned, then moved my head at the other man.

'Him?' Pekouris said. 'He doesn't count.'

'Yes, he does.'

He said something in Greek and the man went out. 'He doesn't speak English, anyway.' He pushed back his chair.

'Sit down, Mr Davies. Here you see my tiny, unelegant, unexpensive little domain. It is not as nice as Mr Kronitis's place, is it?'

So he already knew I'd been there. Well, the Rolls was

easy to spot in Glauros. I said, 'I hear you spend most of your time away from it.'

'It is true I am in Athens a lot. On business. But I will not be now, for a while, I think, huh?'

'I just stopped by for a minute. Kronitis has hired me to investigate the murder. Wants me to find the killer. I told him I would have to tell you. I'm telling you.'

Pekouris's power-sniffing eyebrows quivered. He just nodded. It was almost as if he had known it all beforehand.

'Well, we are glad to have you working with us. I'm sure it will all be amicable.' He gave me a big phony smile. 'However, murders are police cases, Mr Davies. We do not enjoy to have private detectives from America coming in and messing things up, and then stealing all the publicity and glory for solving a murder.'

That was more like what I expected to hear. I had begun to wonder if he was ever going to say it. I had my answer already prepared.

'I can understand that. That's why I'm here to see you. I'm not after any glory. And anything I find out will be put at your disposal at once. I'll only be assisting.'

'I suppose I could not stop you nosing around anyway. Even if you were not hired. You are like the old hunting dog. So go ahead.'

He was being so amiable it was almost suspicious.

'But I want to caution you. Do not talk about the case. Play it down, as you would say. Away down. That is of major importance to us right now.'

'Do you think I would go around talking about it?'

'No. Not deliberately. But your investigations may call attention to it. I don't want that now. I have been on the telephone with Athens, and I have a clear directive from them: Solve it, but solve it fast. Whatever I do, hush it up. We have our main tourist season coming up right away now.'

'I'll be careful,' I said.

'It is much more than to just be careful. It is a policy.' He waved his hand. 'As far as I am concerned, it is already almost what you Americans call a case of the open-and-shut, anyhow.' He pushed around among the papers on his desk. 'This young American hippie who runs the Cloud 79 club, and his crazy friend, are the guilty party. All that remains is to find the proof.'

'Well,' I said slowly. 'That's certainly a possibility. But I wouldn't call it a certainty yet.'

'Well, it is,' Pekouris said firmly. 'For me.' He found the paper he was looking for. 'Did you know that this boy Chuck, the one with the thick glasses, was wanted in Mexico, not too long ago, for chopping some poor Mexican up and nearly killing him with a machete?'

I pretended to do a slow take. It wasn't all pretence. 'No, I didn't. How did you find that out?'

'Oh, I have my ways, Mr Davies. I have my ways of finding out all sorts of things.' The superior, dictatorial smile. 'It is true.' He handed me the paper in his hand. It was a cablegram from the Interpol people. I saw the word MEXICO. I read the text. It said pretty much what he had told me. I noted it was dated six weeks before the date of the murder.

'Well, that puts a different weight in the scales, doesn't it?' I said, handing it back.

'We always have our passport check, you know, Mr Davies,' Pekouris said. 'Upon entry. We can keep pretty close tabs on things.' Pekouris sighed elaborately. 'Yes, it does put a lot of weight on the scale, as you say. It was you who suggested we look for *why* cut off the head at all. What better *why* than a man who has a machete and is used to using it. Of course, we still must find the proofs.'

'Yes,' I said. 'That's important, too.'

'Do you know anything about those two?' Pekouris said suddenly. 'Have you ever talked to them?'

'Yes,' I said. 'I've talked to them. At Georgina Taylor's. A couple of times on the town terrace.'

Pekouris nodded. We both knew he knew the answer to his question before he asked it.

'Did they say anything interesting?'

'They sure did,' I said. 'They threatened him. Not in any specific way. I mean, no threat of killing. But they threatened him.'

'As if maybe they did not like the way he ran his hashish business, and were perhaps thinking of taking it over and running it better?' Pekouris said.

'That was it.'

'There, you see? We have our motive.'

'Yes,' I said. 'We sure do. But, as you said, it isn't proved yet.'

Pekouris shrugged.

'Have you picked them up?'

'I'm not ready for that yet.' He smiled that scary smile, 'They won't go away.'

From the door I said, 'Inspector, I'm not telling *any-body* else that I'm working for anyone.'

He looked up at me, then nodded his understanding.

'I suggest you don't, Davies.'

I didn't like that so much. That wasn't exactly the way I had meant it. What was he telling me? Take my money and shut up and don't make waves? Be glad I had Mr K.'s dough and keep out of the way? It sounded like it. But if I ever suggested to him that that was what he meant, he would be perfectly within his rights to deny it. And he would believe himself implicitly, when he did.

Those kids had about as much chance going up against Pekouris as I had getting in the same ring with a cobra. Against him and me, they were like three-year-old babies swimming in the same tank with two old ocean-going white sharks. If they were guilty God or somebody had better help them.

I was inclined to go along with his theory, at least for now. But it was going to take a lot more proof. It was going to take a lot more proof than we had so far, just to convince *me*.

I walked out of the dim, dusty-smelling, dirty-floored town hall into the Greek sun.

CHAPTER TWENTY-SIX

I had plenty to put me into a think-fog on the way back.

But I didn't feel much different. I had a fatter wallet, was all. I was still the same guy.

Sonny was over his sulks, and left me alone. The boat ride was as delicious as ever. The weather was still that magnificent weather, the scenery the same beautiful scenery. The sparkling sea, the bright baking sun, the fresh sea breeze cutting the heat, the green island in front of us and the dun coast behind, the bright dots of chapels on the hills, the scrubbed clean white of the town: the cerulean mask arching over it all an enormous sky, so remote and so tranquil and not caring a damn. Down below all us little worms scrabbling and scrawling away. Sometimes you felt we didn't any of us deserve it all.

At Dmitri's dock Kirk and Jane Duval had not come back yet and the tiny motorcycle was not there. Sweet Marie had not shown up either.

'Well, I'll leave the *Daisy Mae* with you here,' Sonny said. 'I'll wait on Jane.'

'Where's the baby?' I said.

'We left her up at the Construction, with one of Jane's friends. We're to pick her up this afternoon.'

The place was beginning to fill up out by the water with people for pre-luncheon drinks. Every time a new motorbike or cycle came up Sonny looked hopefully down the seawall road.

'Come on, Sonny. I'll buy you a drink,' I said, feeling sorry for him. 'But only if you promise not to talk any of your damned hippie philosophy to me.'

When we had ordered, Sonny said, 'What were you doing over there this morning? Whose limousine was that?'

'I'm sure any one of fifty people on this rock will be more than glad to tell you whose limousine it was,' I said. 'So I won't spoil your fun in finding out, by telling you now all at once.'

Before it could get any farther, somebody called to me from the roofed-over patio room that was a part of the building. It was the bearded Pete Gruner, the cop, or ex-cop, or non-cop, in a brocaded embroidered Turkoman jacket that must have cost $500. 'Hey, Lobo! Hey, Davies! You think you got a little time to talk, now?'

I started to refuse. Then I reminded myself I was working now. No source could afford to be neglected. 'Excuse me,' I said to Sonny. 'I'll be right back.' I went over and between the pillars and into the open room to his table. Except for us the room was empty.

'I'm particular about who calls me by my first name. If you want to talk to me, I could use a drink,' I said.

He ordered drinks for both of us. Then he started right in on me.

'What's on your mind, Gruner?' I said.

'Nothing much. But I'm wondering what's on yours?'

I felt blunt. 'About what?' I said rudely.

'Well, just for example, this killing. I'd like very much to know what you think about it. And I'd like to know how it affects the thinking of whoever sent you down here, to do whatever it was they sent you down here to do.'

I took what I pretended was a deep angry breath, then pretended I was letting it out slowly to keep my temper. 'Look, Gruner. I'm down here on vacation. I already told you that. I don't really give a damn about this killing.'

'Yeah, sure,' he said mockingly.

'That's the fact. I did a little investigations job for a Paris client of mine, in Athens. He liked what I did so much, he offered me a month's paid vacation down here. Otherwise I couldn't even afford it. Now, go and put that in your report.'

'What report?'

'Whatever report it is you're writing for whatever Department it is you work for.'

'Oh. You're still pretending you think I'm a cop.'

'You stink cop a mile away. I'd bet my bottom dollar on it. I don't know how you ever managed to fool these people. What did you pay for that jacket you're wearing? It must have cost $500.'

'$350,' he grinned. 'In Athens.'

'In Athens. If they had them in Athens. It would be $500 anyplace else.'

'I'd seriously like to know what you think about this killing,' he said. 'What do you make of it? Or will you let yourself have an opinion?'

'It's most likely some jealous Greek husband,' I said, 'from what I know about Girgis. If you want my strictly amateur's opinion, it's an Athens gang killing – probably from off the island – to see what petty local Athens crook is going to handle the local hashish trade. That's all it is.'

'You think off the island?'

'I don't see any likely suspects around here, do you?'

'I could see a lot of them. Listen, there's a lot,' Pete said darkly, and looked around, 'a lot going on around here that your simple-minded theory don't exactly explain.'

'You said that before. Like what?'

He would only make an irritated, dark gesture. 'See, I think Girgis didn't work alone. Okay, what about this funny little guy, that was Girgis's assistant on the boat?'

'What about him? I never even noticed him.'

'Well, notice him. What's he going to do now? Is he going to run the *Polaris*? The *Polaris* is owned by some rich guy, named Kroanis, or Kronitis. Does he know what racket Girgis was working? Was Girgis working it on his own? Will this rich guy de-commission the boat now? Or will he let that ugly little mate of Girgis's go on running it?'

'I haven't the slightest idea,' I said.

'This guy Kirk, on this yacht *Agoraphobe*, owned by this same Kroanis, has been Girgis's supplier for the hashish. Does Kroanis know about that? But Kirk can't leave the *Agoraphobe* to take over Girgis's retail trade. He's not here enough.'

'You don't really know his name is Kronitis?' I said.

'Sure, I know. – ? – ' He looked at me.

'So?' I said.

'See, I think I could get that job of Girgis's,' Gruner said. 'Why not? That little assistant clearly can't handle it. He's obviously too dumb.'

I thought about that. 'Are you sure you want to do that?' I said.

We were talking now as if he were a cop. We were talking like two cops together. He had never admitted it, but we were tacitly, without acknowledging it, talking as if he had.

'Why not?' Pete grinned. 'There's a lot of dough to be made, there. And a lot to be learned.'

'That might be one way to explain an awful lot of things.'

'Sure.'

'And you could suddenly find yourself with no head, like Girgis.'

'I don't think so. I'm warned already, by him.'

I thought it was time to stop it. 'Anh, you government people are always looking for some cops-and-robbers game to play,' I said.

He looked at me. 'Damn it, don't say that. I'm a damned dropout, that's what I am. Who has to make his own damned decent – or indecent – living. And I could use

155

some of that money.'

'Do you people get to keep all the illicit loot you pick up on the way, or do you have to turn it in?' I said. 'I've always wondered about that.'

'Lay off me, Davies. I told you I'm not a cop.'

'Whatever you say, Gruner, whatever you say,' I said. 'Well, don't count on me for anything. One way or the other,' I added. 'I'm not playing.'

Pete stared at me and grinned slowly. 'I wish I could be sure of that,' he said, obscurely. 'There's some big stuff mucking around, around here. It would be a shame if we were bucking heads on it.' He got up suddenly, and threw money on the table. 'See you around.' He turned and walked off out into the sun and away. I sat looking after him. I hadn't learned very much. What was all this Big Stuff he was talking about. He had to be a nark. And if he was a nark he had to be after heroin. It didn't fit in with anything I knew. I got up and went back to Sonny.

Sonny was still sitting and nursing his drink. I sat down. All the ice in mine had melted in the hot sun. I drank it anyway.

Before I could get the glass away from my mouth, I heard a motorcycle coming and sensed Sonny in front of me jumping up. I put my glass down slowly and slowly swung around in my tin chair. It was them, all right.

I didn't get up. Jane hopped off and Kirk parked the tiny cycle in its place against the taverna wall. When Jane turned around, I saw that she had grass stems on the back of her brocaded Mother Hubbard and in the back of her long hippie girl hair.

She wasn't covered with them, but it was enough to be noticeable. She hadn't even bothered to brush herself off. Kirk probably hadn't even noticed. If he had, he wouldn't have cared.

She probably hadn't bothered to wash herself, either. I supposed she didn't bother to wear panties. Well, what did I care. I had always liked girls who didn't wear panties. I still didn't get up.

'Well, Sonny,' Kirk rumbled in a magnanimous tone. 'You're back. And here's your lady, back all safe and sound.' He made a sweeping gesture of passing her over, then walked over to me. 'Well, it's old Lobo Davies. Have a good boat trip, Lobo?'

'Tolerable,' I said. I still didn't get up.

'By God, you're as country as me. When you want to be,' Kirk grinned. 'And I am pretty damn country.' He stretched and yawned, flexing his big arms. 'God I'm sleepy. Think I'll go on board and take a little nap.' He gave me a merry wink with that eyelid like a slab of red beef.

'Come on, Jane,' Sonny said from behind me. 'We'll take the bikes up to the Construction.'

I watched the two of them trundle their bikes out away from the taverna wall. They were parked there near Kirk's tiny cycle. Sonny, with all his money, apparently had never invested in a motorcycle himself. Probably one of his phony-liberal theories about living only off of what he made. I already knew that he didn't even do that.

The two of them went riding off up the seawall road. Kirk went down and got in his skiff to row out.

I moved over into the shade and ordered a fresh drink.

I knew one thing. I was glad I was a private eye and not a hippie. But I was probably old-fashioned.

I drank my drink and waited for Marie.

CHAPTER TWENTY-SEVEN

She arrived walking, wearing her skintight blue jeans and the bra-less cotton shirt, and lugging her faded duffel bag of diving gear.

I sent her on board to stow her gear, and went in to Dmitrios to see about our picnic lunch.

When I carried the sacks on board, she had changed to a bikini and was sitting on the coach-roof in the sun. She was burned a deep bronze and there wasn't an excess ounce of fat on her anywhere. It gave her one of those lean, wide-open navels you sometimes see on young girls. You could see right to the bottom of it.

She knew a place up the mainland coast she wanted to try. She had swum there as a guest on boats, but had never spearfished it. Without a boat, she had no way of getting there on her own.

I headed us up that way. There was a shallow reef

three hundred yards offshore, she told me as I worked us out through the web of lines and boats and passed the little lighthouse. The shore had a long, white sand beach, totally deserted, in a long shallow cove between two low rocky points. It was completely inaccessible except by sea. The nearest road was three miles inland, and the nearest farm was a mile away. There would not be a soul unless another boat was there.

'It's about twelve or thirteen miles,' she said suddenly after we had run a while in silence, and squirmed around so that she could sit up clasping her knees facing me. The tiny bikini pants hid just about nothing.

I just nodded.

'You know what I like about you?' Marie smiled. 'It's that I don't feel I have to talk when I'm with you. Most people, you have to talk every minute. With you it doesn't matter, you can sit forever and it's okay.'

I didn't answer that, either.

I was determined I was going to give her a great day of diving and spearfishing. One she could think about. Why, I didn't know. I just wanted to. Also, there might be something I might learn from her about the case.

Somewhere down in the back of that flighty little featherhead of hers, that also carried so much of her own young anguish and a kind of young desolation, there might be some little plum of information she wasn't aware of.

She had lapsed back into silence. I didn't talk either. Around us the summer day buzzed along, friendly, lazy, not at all inimical, making you happy by its existence, seeming to offer you free without charge or work the fruits of nature's growth.

There was a slight swell on the sea, and a light breeze that brought on it the smell of the hot land. Along our left side the dun, sere terrain of the mainland unrolled itself hill after hill. Out at sea mountainous islands reared up a dark blue in the heat haze.

Time seemed to sort of go away. We passed a long low luxurious establishment with its own cove and landing dock that I recognized as Kronitis's.

Farther on we came to a cone-shaped head with a chapel on its top that had just been renovated. The old stones had been reset and pointed, and young trees had

158

been set out around it. A new concrete road ran up to it and circled it to rejoin itself and fade away into the dun thistle-strewn hills. It seemed to wait eternally in the sun for the tourist cars that were supposed to come.

'It's awful, isn't it?' Marie said.

I nodded. 'Yes.'

We lapsed back into our silence.

A couple of miles farther on Marie said, 'Here it is.'

There weren't any other boats. I ran us in almost to the deserted beach for a look at it. It was a great beach. It had to be at least a quarter of a mile long. And not a living thing anywhere in the baking sun except a few gulls sunning on the rocks. At one end a hill that ran back into the land had three gnarled trees on it.

'Some day they'll build one of those roads in here, too,' I said. 'If it looks like it'll pay enough.'

I ran us out to the reef and cut the motor. I was in a somnambulistic sun-hypnotized mood that had taken me over. Even the future road and all the people and crud it would some day bring here did not bother me that much. My anchor made a loud splash in the sun-stillness. I caught it on the bottom, then just sat and looked down through the clear, clean water. There wasn't a sound anywhere except the water moving against the boat, and the cry of a gull now and then.

Behind me Marie took off her bikini and put on her wet-suit. She didn't like the feel of clothing on her under the suit, she explained in a sun- and sea-dazzled voice.

In the stillness I didn't feel like answering her. I was acutely aware of her moving nude behind me. Then she came over to me, metamorphosed into that long black apparition again. She had nothing on under the suit.

'I've got to get in,' she said. 'You can't stay out of the water very long in these things.' She had left the tight helmet off. She lowered her mask and speargun in hand over the side, feet first.

I got my stuff and followed her. The chill of the water brought me out of my dazzlement immediately. I whooped around my snorkel when I came up. Below me the bottom lay at thirty or thirty-five feet. The reef stretched away right and left across the face of the beach. Fifty yards out it dropped down an underwater cliff another thirty-five feet, to a sand bottom which just ran on out to sea until it faded in the haze. Marie had already swum out to the edge of it. I followed her.

I could see right away that she didn't know too much. She swam and surface-dived well enough, but thirty feet was about her absolute limit. After twenty feet she began to hedge and freeze up. On the other hand she was much better at spotting fish here than I was.

'Do you want me to give you a few pointers?' I said.

'Oh, please. Teach me. Everything you can. I want to learn it.'

'I'm not being too dictatorial?'

Under water to her ears, she shook her head vigorously. She had this marvellous quality of putting herself in your hands completely. A lot of people had abused it in her life, I guessed. In me, it brought out all the gentleness I had.

I started showing her some of the things. Hyperventilation, and oxygenation. How to swim down slowly, not swiftly. The slower she went down the longer she could stay. Don't rush for the surface, swim up slowly. I made her ignore the heavings of her diaphragm.

By the time we had done a dozen dives, she was going down and coming up, at thirty-five feet, as lazily and as gracefully as any of the old pros who had tutored me at eighty feet in the Caribbean.

'Ohh!' she said after the last one, treading water to put her head out. 'It's always been fun. But it's never been like this! This is something *else*.'

I felt like I'd picked up a few points for decency, with God or whoever. We swam up and down the reef in the little bay for a while, hunting grouper and diving. It was great fun, in the still, marvellous Greek sun. Finally, when I thought she was ready, I said, 'Come on, I'll give you a demonstration.'

I took her hand and led her out beyond the edge of the reef over the deeper water, and handed her the stringer of fish.

I didn't know how far down I could get, but I knew I could make the forty-five feet I had made the day before with Sonny. I lay on the surface and ventilated, then started down. I amazed myself by going right on down. I didn't push myself but the bottom kept coming up closer and closer until suddenly I was on it, without

160

straining at all.

I reached out and picked up a dead shell half-buried in the sand. I seemed to have all the time in the world. I rolled over and looked up and waved at Marie on the surface. The small figure way up there waved back at me. Just to make sure, I looked at my metre-calibrated depth gauge. It gave me a reading of 20.5 metres. Just about sixty-eight feet. It was weird what you could do when you had an admiring audience to show off for.

I turned over and started back up. About twenty feet up I spotted a big grouper under a ledge, waving his fins at me. I kept on going. I had that feeling I always got swimming up, of an immense regret to be leaving. I swam slower and slower. My diaphragm heaved only a couple of times. The surface came farther and farther down to me. Then I popped out through it and blew my snorkel and lay face down on the water breathing, and looking back down at where I had been. It seemed a long way down there. As always, it was awesome.

'Ohh, that was beautiful!' Marie said beside me. 'Oh, that was beautiful. *You* were beautiful. So graceful. You looked so free. I'd give anything to be able to do that.'

I guessed that was it. You felt so free. Free of gravity. Free of earth. And graceful. Sometimes you felt that, if only you didn't have to breathe, you could stay down forever.

After I rested, I went back down after the big grouper and shot him easily. I saw four or five others, in crevices or under ledges.

On the surface I added him to the stringer and began the job of getting Marie to go down with me. I knew it would be a hard job, it always was. But it proved easier than I thought with Marie. The first time she failed to clear her ears the first try, and jerked her hand free and went up. The second time a sort of just general malaise and panic at being there, being that deep, got her and she went up again. But the third time I got her down far enough to see the big groupers. Maybe forty-five feet. After that, she was over the psychological hurdle.

We had been in the water maybe two hours by then. In the next hour Marie shot four of the big groupers down under the ledge, and I added them to the stringer for her. I didn't shoot any more myself, but just went down with her. Then I thought it was time to call a halt.

Marie acted as if she wanted to go on forever, but I refused to let her. Besides, the stringer was becoming a drag on my streamlining and heavy to lug around.

Back at the boat I passed her up the stringer, which was a lot heavier out of the water than in, then pulled my flippers and climbed up myself.

On the deck my star pupil had dropped the string of fish down, and was swiftly stripping off her wet-suit. She already had the top almost off. As I stepped on deck she threw it down and started on the long-legged bottoms. She had hard, tight, dark nipples, made harder and tighter by the water chill probably. It didn't seem to bother her that she was not alone. She didn't seem to mind if I watched. But I minded. I turned my back.

Perhaps because of me, she put back on her bikini pieces before she stretched out on the coach-roof in the sun, breathlessly.

'Oh, wow,' she said between breaths, stretching her face up to the sun with her eyes closed. 'I guess this is just about the best day in my life. I'm glad you made us stop. I guess I wouldn't have quit until dark.'

I decided not to answer. I got out the gin bottle and the vermouth bottle and ice.

'Oh, gee!' Marie said. 'Me, too! I guess you don't know what you've given me, Mr Davies. You've taught me something I'll be able to use the whole rest of my life.'

I didn't feel much like answering that. I began to swish the martini mixture in the big Mason jar.

After a little bit she sat back up and I handed her a glass. I ran us in to the beach with my glass in one hand, and we ate our lunch on the boat under the tarpaulin. Then we waded ashore to lie in the sun a while.

The meal had made us both drowsy. We were both ravenously hungry from the diving and I had bought a lot. Bread and meat and cheese and mustard and the tomato and Greek cheese salad. And it tasted great, with the bottles of red wine I had dropped over the side earlier to chill and then dived down for.

We were not stretched out on the sand five minutes when Marie began taking her bikini off. She started with the bra first.

I was stretched out on my back, but my face was partly towards her and I could see her from the outside of my eye.

'I would rather you didn't do that,' I said.

She stopped, then turned her head to look at me. 'Oh, but it's all right. Don't worry. There isn't anyone within miles.'

'That was not what I meant,' I said.

'Oh,' Marie said. Then, 'Oh. Oh, all right.' She still had her hands up behind her, at the bra fasteners. She sort of hesitated. 'The bra, too?'

'If you wouldn't mind,' I said.

'Oh, I don't mind,' she said. 'It's just that I'm used to it. Nude bathing. You know? I didn't even think.'

I didn't answer. She left the bra on, and then lay back down sort of thoughtfully and closed her eyes.

After a long moment she said, 'If you want to ball me, I wouldn't mind.'

'Well, I don't,' I said. 'And you ought to be ashamed of yourself. I'm old enough to be your father.'

'Oh, that doesn't matter,' Marie said. She lay still several more moments with her eyes closed. 'That's what I like about it. It's kicky.'

'That's not the truth,' I said.

'No. It's not. The truth is I guess I just like you. Like I said the other night.'

'I appreciate your offer,' I said. 'But I'm shy.'

'Look, you don't have to explain anything. You don't want to ball me, you don't want to ball me.'

'But now I've hurt your feelings.'

'Are you kidding, Mr Davies?'

'Tell me about the kids up at the Construction,' I said. 'Instead.'

'They're just kids.'

'You told me they weren't all students.'

'There're some oldies. But mostly they're just students. College kids. Like I used to be. Kids between years at school. What is it you want to know? They'll almost all go back and finish school. Take a job. Get married. You'd be surprised how many are there because their fathers made them come. A summer on the bum in Europe. But bumming on the old man's money.'

'What about these two, Chuck and Steve?'

'They're different. And that girl Diane. They're worse than just dropouts. They all come from decent families, I think. But they've learned to be con artists. They con the other kids for their living.'

'Aren't they the leaders up there?'

'I suppose. In a way. That's just the trouble. Did you ever see a leader that wasn't a con artist?'

'No,' I said. 'I haven't.'

'Sure. That's what the trouble with the world is that we can't fix. Well, the kids all know that. That's what all the fuss back home is about, really. And they know it up here at the Construction, just like they know it at home in politics. But they don't know what to do about it. Their own leaders do them in, too.'

'Nobody has ever found out what to do about it,' I said. 'Chuck and Steve don't seem much like leaders.'

'Well, they are. They've got the flair. The kids will listen to them and follow them. Steve's the leader, really. Chuck is just his hatchet man. He's even got this machete he's always carrying around and playing with.'

'Oh?' I said.

'The other day they stole a stray goat from the other end of the island and killed it and roasted it. Chuck cut off its head with his machete. Then he went around with the blood on the machete. Wouldn't wipe it off. He's got a thing about blood on his machete.'

I nodded. I couldn't ask her if she thought they had killed Girgis.

'I don't think they killed Girgis,' Marie said. 'Chuck's not like that. He's just a kid. He likes to go around playing cowboys.'

'Sure,' I said, 'I see.' I moved my head. I wasn't going to tell her how he had played cowboys in Mexico. 'Tell me about yourself. How did you wind up in Tsatsos?'

'I'd rather not talk about me, Mr Davies. If you don't mind. It will only upset me and depress me and put me down. And I've had a wonderful day with you. —

'I came to Tsatsos with a boy I met in Paris. He was travelling through. He had heard about Tsatsos and the Construction. We came together. He left. I stayed.'

'How did you get to Paris?'

'From Haight-Ashbury, with another boy. See, I went a year to Berkeley. Then I met this boy and dropped out with him. He wanted to be a rock singer. We lived in Haight-Ashbury for a while. Then he brought me to Paris. I lived with him in Paris for a year before he left me. He said I was disruptive to his art, and he wasn't doing very well. I don't know whatever happened to him.

'Please, Mr Davies. I really don't want to talk about me.'

'And your parents are both dead?'

After a moment she said, 'Yes. For a couple of years. My mother died of diabetes, my father from a heart attack. He drank too much, and she ate too much.'

'Have you ever thought about going back?'

'I have. But it's hard. It costs money. And it's hard, when you haven't got anybody there at all to go back to.

'Please, Mr Davies!'

'Okay,' I said. 'I'm sorry.' I rolled over and heaved myself to my feet. 'Come on. If we're going to do anything more, we better get moving.'

She held out her hands to me. I leaned over and pulled her up. We dived into the clear, clean water over the sand, and swam out to the boat and climbed up dripping wet. It felt marvellous, after the sun heat.

'There's still time to dive some more,' I said, looking at her in the wet bikini. I was starting to regret not accepting her offer on the beach. I did regret it.

She smiled and shook the water off herself. She pulled her long hair straight back. Then she shook her head. 'No. I guess not. I don't want to do anything to spoil it. It's been perfect.'

'Then we'll head on back, then?' I said. Now I regretted it enormously. She was really something. So young. But that was just the trouble. And now it was past and too late. I wanted to swear.

'Yes. And thank you an awful lot, Mr Davies.'

I moved my head. There wasn't really anything I could say to her. Or do for her. I got the anchor up, and we headed out.

Ahead of us the sun had moved west just enough to begin to turn the top of Tsatsos a faint red. Where the people were.

I headed for it.

CHAPTER TWENTY-EIGHT

The lunch crowd was gone and Sonny Duval was sitting waiting at the taverna like a big moustachioed frog, when we arrived back. He and Jane had gotten back from the Construction, he said, and Jane was out on the big caique cooking the baby's supper.

Marie sat and had a drink with us, and spent five minutes telling Sonny what a great guy I was and what a great skindiver. I hustled her into a horsecab with her duffel bag and sent her back to town, and told her I would see her later. I would leave the fish with Dmitrios for her, for her to sell. I paid the driver.

'The police were up at the Construction all afternoon,' Sonny said when I sat back down. 'They went through everything, and everybody, like a finetooth comb. They wanted to know what we were doing up there. They checked our papers.'

'What did you expect? You didn't have to go up there.'

'We wanted to,' Sonny said. 'Jane wanted to.'

'Then don't complain.'

'They're coming down here to the boat so see us. Probably tomorrow.'

I was hardly even listening to him. I was still thinking regretfully about Marie, back there on the beach. And I was thinking about something else: I was thinking about what she'd told me about those two giants of hippie living, Chuck and Steve.

'Listen, there's something I'd like for you to do for me,' I said. 'I want to go up to the Construction. I want to go to Steve's pad. Can you take me there?'

'I guess so. But are you sure you want to go up there? You're not very popular up there.'

'That's why I don't want to ask directions. You can direct me.'

'All right,' he said, grudgingly. 'But it's hard to land the boat up there.'

'We'll take a horsecab. There's a couple here.'

In the horsecab he was silent for a while. If he was embarrassed by my having observed the unsubtle return of Kirk and Jane at noontime, he didn't show it. Then he said, 'When are *we* gonna go spearfishing again?'

'We went yesterday. You weren't even interested. I don't know,' I said. At the moment I didn't care if I ever went spearfishing again.

'I didn't know you were supposed to be so good. Listen, I suppose it's useless, as well as an imposition, to ask,' he began.

'Nothing special,' I said. 'I just want to see him in his natural habitat. He interests me.'

'Sure,' derisively. 'If you want to know what I –'

'I don't,' I said.

'Pete says he thinks you're a U.S. Government man, posing as a private eye.'

I looked at him. 'Pete Gruner said that?' I was mad. If Pete Gruner was going around bad mouthing me as a Government man, it was a sure sign he was one himself. Or was it? And it was about as low as you could get.

'Pete's a guy who's been around. Although there are things about him who I don't like. But I'm beginning to think he's right, about you.' He grinned, 'Jane thinks so.'

'Let me tell you something about Jane,' I said brusquely. 'What Jane doesn't know about everything would fill many large volumes at Bennington. Jane is a spoiled brat.'

'You just don't want to understand Jane. None of you do. She's a threat to all you male supremacists.'

I stared at him in a kind of amazement. I had to snort. 'Male supremacist? That's me, all right.' I thought about Marie. If this was bait for an argument, I wasn't going to bite. But wait till I got hold of damned Pete Gruner.

'Listen, the U.S. Government wouldn't be sending an agent down here because of a bunch of dropouts living in an abandoned Greek construction site and smoking hash,' I said. 'Agents are expensive.'

'There might be other things,' Sonny said with a secretive leer.

'Yes? We must talk about that,' I said. But when he opened his mouth, I put my hand up and added quickly, 'Some other day.'

The horsecab was just passing the good old Hotel

Xenia, scene of so much excitement in the life of Lobo Davies. In another minute he let us off at the foot of the same draw I had stood at the foot of that morning, with Pekouris.

I paid him off. We started to climb the same little path I had climbed in the morning.

It was dusk now, and falling dark fast. We climbed past cook fires, and hippie people moving around them. A smell of stew meat carried to us. We were climbing along the outside edge of the construction site. Sonny stopped.

'It's right up there,' Sonny said, pointing. 'Fourth row from here, the second door in. You'll have to go around to the back to find the stairs.

'I'd stay away from those fires and getting recognized by any of these kids, if I were you,' he added.

'Okay. Thanks. I'll go ahead alone from here.'

'You might get into a fight, you know.'

'If I do, I'll run.'

He scuffed his foot in the raw dirt. 'I suppose there's no use in asking to go with you?' He looked at me and saw there wasn't. 'Do you want me to wait for you down below?'

'There's no reason. I can find my own way back. Assuming I get back.' I grinned.

He stood a moment reluctantly.

'Don't worry, I'll pay for your horsecab back,' I said.

As if that clinched it, he turned and started down off the hill.

I looked after him, then started to climb on. Around me the hippies were moving about their fires. At one fire I saw Georgina Taylor's sun-dried prune face and pop eyes, laughing and drinking something from a tin cup. At another a whole row of young American faces shone at me in the flickery light. Someone chorded a guitar and sang folk music. I didn't know how I could tell they were American, but I could tell. Perhaps because of their inordinate naïveté. Maybe they weren't so innocent, American kids. But they were sure as hell naïve.

Nobody was paying the slightest attention to me. I stopped and stepped in under one of the units on stilts, to watch a moment. It all seemed innocent enough. It certainly wasn't any orgy. Not even of folk music. It was hard to believe that they might all jump on me and start beating the hell out of me, if they knew I was there. But I believed it to be at least a strong possibility.

Then I heard a voice nearby that I recognized. It was coming from one of the housing units over my head, and it was the voice of Chuck, Steve's myopic sidekick.

No one was noticing me, so I sneaked around until I could see into the unit through one of the window holes that nobody had ever put a frame on.

Inside, Chuck and his glasses were sitting on a pile of cushions made from rags and old blankets. They were smoking a hookah and had a home-made turban on their head.

The hookah obviously contained hash. And Chuck was high. Four chubby, wholesome-faced, little American college girls were rushing around ministering to his every demand. And his demands were many. The little girls looked pathetic, as well as unattractive, in their loose-flowing, dirty Mother Hubbard dresses. They all undoubtedly had fat thighs.

The scene was so bizarre that I stood a few moments transfixed, looking at it. One of those aluminium pack frames with sack attached leaned against the wall near Chuck, and leaning by it was a big South American type machete in a wood scabbard. The famous machete. Under the circumstances, it stood out.

I stood looking another minute, mainly at the machete. The police hadn't picked it up this afternoon? Then I slipped away, and headed up along the outside of the debris-strewn construction site, to the row of units Sonny had pointed out to me.

A light flickered from the apartment unit I was seeking, and I could hear voices and the low strumming of a guitar. Farther up and around to the back I found the stairs Sonny had mentioned, and followed them up to the outside terrace along the front of the 4-unit building.

Standing on the porch-terrace I was now thirty feet above the sloping ground. There was no railing.

I made no attempt to hide myself when I came to the right door.

I had no idea what I was going to say. I hadn't come up here with anything in particular to say. I had just decided to come and play it by ear.

The light was coming from two short candles stuck on to saucers. By them, young Steve was reading some kind of gibberish hippie poetry about the hard life of a longshoreman, from a mimeograph-printed poetry magazine.

There were six people in the room. Three young men and another girl, in addition to Steve and Diane. It was the new girl who was strumming the guitar, in a sort of accompaniment to Steve's reading. Steve, bare to the waist, was truly beautiful physically, with his fine build and blond mane, until he looked up with those dead-seeming, non-seeing eyes.

'Hallo! Is this a private party?' I said in a chirpy way. I stepped inside. 'Or can any old square sit in on it?'

CHAPTER TWENTY-NINE

They all looked up at me. There was a sort of silence, and a belligerence blew at me like bad breath from all six of them.

'Why don't you just go away, Mr Davies?' Diane said, in a kind of cold angry wail. It was about the first word I had ever heard her speak.

'I'd love to, sweetheart,' I said. 'I don't like you any better than you like me. But I can't. Unfortunately, I have to speak to your old man here.'

'Listen, the police have been here all afternoon,' Steve said.

'I know,' I said.

'What do you want?'

'I can talk about it here,' I said. 'But you might prefer to talk about it in private.'

'Anything you got to say to me, you can say in front of my friends.'

'Okay. I want to talk about what you said to me in the square the other day.'

'Wait a minute,' he stopped me. 'I'll come outside.' He looked around apologetically at the others, and got to his feet. The other three men hadn't gotten to their feet, but they looked ready to. I followed Steve out.

Outside, Steve led the way down to the ground.

'Okay,' he said in a hate-filled voice. 'Talk.'

'You hollered something after me this morning that stuck in my head,' I said. 'You hollered, "You know I didn't mean it, don't you?" I think those were the exact words.'

He wouldn't look at me. 'So?' he said sullenly.

'I want to know what you meant. It seemed a peculiar thing to say. Under the circumstances.'

'I don't know what I meant. What difference does it make?'

I gave him a mock sigh of disgust. 'Well, let's analyse it. I assume you meant you didn't mean what you said when you threatened Girgis. But how would I know you didn't mean what you said? You threatened Girgis pretty good there. And me, too. And then a couple of days later he's dead.'

'I didn't threaten to kill him. Do I look like a killer?' He was still evasive, wouldn't look at me. I had a hunch he was hiding something. But what?

'You don't look *not* like a killer,' I said. 'Neither does that crazy sidekick of yours. Killers look like anybody.'

'Chuck? Chuck wouldn't hurt a fly.'

'I wouldn't bet a dollar on it.'

'Anh. You're another pig. You're one of them. You were talking me some high-toned guff about a grand jury. Did you ever hear of a grand jury in this country? In *Greece*?' He barked a short laugh. 'The police were up here all afternoon. Asking questions, checking passports, nosing around. They went through our personal stuff. No warrants, no nothing.'

I wondered how Chuck and his machete were still loose? Was Pekouris not picking him up? On purpose?

'Look,' Steve said, 'I don't have to talk to you. You don't have any legal authority.'

'That's right, you don't have to talk to me.'

'If you have any authority, show me. Show me a badge. Or an official paper. Otherwise, why don't you just bug off, you son of a bitch?'

Without a word, crisply, I stepped in and hit him. It wasn't a full punch. It was a short right hand, thrown off the right foot, with the right foot in front. But it was enough to knock Steve off his feet, and down.

It was a calculated risk. I didn't like the way the conversation was developing and I thought a punch on the jaw, if it didn't make him holler for help to try and ruin me, might make him think. Might change the tone and the direction.

'I'm partial about who calls me a son of a bitch,' I said. 'Say I'm old-fashioned. Get up, you.'

He did, rubbing his jaw. He looked surprised and rueful. Although he was built like a muscle boy, he made no move to fight. 'You're a brave guy, man,' he said sullenly, still not looking at me. 'All I got to do is holler, and you would wind up looking like a played-over football field. All I have to do is holler. And not just upstairs. All over this place.'

'Why don't you holler?'

'And have you bring a regiment of cops down on us?'

'Look, I don't like you any better than you like me, bud. If you're an example of the new age, I feel sorry for it. But you're in trouble. I'm trying to give you a break. You better be damn well able to prove you're not a killer. Where is this sidekick of yours? You said this morning he was around. I want to talk to him.' I didn't know why I said it. It was a shot in the dark. But a lucky one.

'He's gone,' Steve said sullenly. 'I sent him away.'

That stopped me. I was dead quiet for a moment. 'You mean you sent him off the island?' I asked, easily.

'No. Are you kidding? He wouldn't make it to Athens. Let alone out of the country. No, I sent him off to St Friday's.'

'What the hell is St Friday's?'

'It's a chapel, in a little cove, around on the other side of the island. It's called Ayia Paraskevi, in Greek. Paraskevi was some woman saint, but Paraskevi means Friday. We call it St Friday's.'

'When did you send him?'

'This morning. As soon as I learned the police were coming.'

'Do the police know you did that?'

'Sure. Of course. I told them as soon as they asked where he was.'

'But you don't know whether they went around there and got him?'

'Not so far as I know. I've still got his passport.'

'You keep his passport for him?' I asked.

'Well, sure. He wants me to.' He avoided my gaze.

That made me think. If Steve kept his passport for him, he was probably crazier than even I thought. 'Tell me,' I said, 'did it ever occur to you that he might come back here from over there, without telling you?'

Steve shot me a sharp look. 'He wouldn't do that.'

'You're sure?'

'Absolutely.'

'Okay.' I stepped back away from him. 'What did you tell the police as to *why* you sent him over to St Friday's?'

'I told them the truth. I sent him there for a three-day fast. Because he's been nervous since the murder.'

'A three-day fast!'

'Yeah. What's so funny? That's what we do, now and then, from time to time. All of us. Now, if you've not got anything further to rap about, may I go?'

'No,' I said. 'One more thing. Where was he the night of the murder?'

'He was with me.'

'Oh, great,' I said. 'And of course you were with him. What a super alibi.'

'There were fifty kids as witnesses who saw us both at the Cloud 79 club until closing,' Steve said.

I just looked at him, and shook my head. 'Girgis was killed at 3:30 A.M.'

'Well, we didn't close at the club until after that, that night.'

'Have you got a lot to learn about Greek justice,' I said. He didn't answer me.

'I hear your pal swings a mean machete,' I said.

He grinned at me mirthlessly. 'You heard that, did you? I figured somebody would get around to bringing that up eventually. Did you tell the police?' It was curious how they always capitalized the word police with their voices, when they said it.

'They already knew all about it,' I said. 'It was them who told me.'

'They did? I bet they did. Now may I go, Mister Pig?'

I felt my lips tighten. I let a long breath out through my nostrils. But all I said was, 'Yes.' Then, just for fun, I added, 'You'll find Chuck down the way, in the third building below here. With four little girls.'

He gave me a look, but didn't say anything. He turned and walked away.

I watched him for a moment, then turned and started on back down the hill.

Down at the other apartment unit, when I stopped and sneaked up again to check, myopic Chuck with his Coca-Cola-bottle glasses was still sitting with his hookah and his turban. The little girls were now sitting in an adoring circle at his feet.

I backed away and walked on down the hill along the outside of the place.

I needed time to think about it. It looked to me like Steve thought his pal had killed Girgis, and was trying to cover up for him. And it was entirely possible Chuck had killed him. Chuck was obviously a crazy, and who knew what a crazy would do? I had seen him break that boy's nose with a karate chop about the first night I was here. It was entirely possible the two of them were in it together.

But what if they *were* guilty? It bothered me why Pekouris had done nothing? Why hadn't he picked them and that machete up? He hadn't even picked up their passports. What was to stop them from taking off some dark night in a small boat for Turkey, with or without passports? That was a cute trick, sending Chuck off to this St Friday's. But that wouldn't have stopped Pekouris if Pekouris had wanted to pick them up.

Down at the bottom on the road, I stopped and turned around and looked back up at the weird place. What a comment it was on the state of our fouled-up civilization. You wouldn't see any places like this in Russia or China, by God. Goofy or not, I was glad we still had them here.

Off on my right as I stood looking up, the loudspeakers from Steve's Cloud 79 had begun to batter the air. I could see the coloured lights through the trees, and the amplifiers would certainly tell me where it was even if I was blind. I was tempted to walk over and look it over.

But I knew I wouldn't go. What was in store for me tonight was not some night club but dead-weight, unexciting, ulcer-making work. That was what was in store for me.

I thought of the money Kronitis had given me. Now I would have to begin to earn it.

I walked over to the Xenia and caught a horsecab back to the house. At the taverna I picked up some sandwiches for my dinner and to keep me going later. At Georgina's another hippie party was in progress in the garden. I avoided it. The old gal had hurried home with a whole mob. In the house I called Chantal to tell her that I would not be up to see her tonight. She had already heard about my skindiving trip with Sweet Marie. I told her I had work to do and if she didn't believe it she should stop by later and see me. Then I got out my locked briefcase and took out some pads of yellow legal cap. I placed them neatly on the desk and after looking around on the ceiling for an excuse I couldn't find, finally sat down with them.

I had made up my mind about one thing. If Sweet Marie made me any more offers, of her carnal form, I was sure as hell going to take her up on them. And to hell with the moral tone.

CHAPTER THIRTY

I couldn't work it out. I couldn't formulate a working hypothesis.

There were two big humps I simply could not get over. First, that every suspect stood to lose, and none of them stood to gain, by Girgis's murder. And, the motive did not equal in value such a drastic act.

There was only one motive available. The hashish trade. And as a motive that just simply wouldn't hold water. Even if it paid ten times the amount I calculated it was paying, it wouldn't be worth the chances you took in killing somebody over it. Killing Girgis amounted to the almost certain ruin of the hash trade itself.

There were only two real suspects. The two hippie boys; and Jim Kirk. There were some peripheral suspicions. Chantal's involvement with Girgis. The fact that Kronitis owned both boats. But they were negligible. Chantal's deep shock when she learned of the murder was completely genuine, if I was any judge. And I would bet my bottom dollar that Kronitis did not know about the hashish smuggling until I told him.

Jim Kirk was certainly a suspect. But he simply wouldn't have killed Girgis over the hashish trade. It wasn't worth that much to him.

That left the two kids. It was possible they were in it together, but I didn't believe it. It was more likely crazy Chuck had done it on his own, thinking in his crazy way that he was helping his pal, the same way he had broken that boy's nose that night, and now Steve was trying to cover up for him hoping to squeak him out of it. Given all the other facts we knew about Chuck, it was a high probability.

That was the only answer I could come up with. And after working on it for eight straight hours, I was inclined to accept it. The thing that bothered me was that it was completely circumstantial.

The only other possibility was that there was another motive, with a vastly greater element of gain in it, which had been so cleverly concealed that I had received no inkling of it at all since I had been here.

In a way I hated it to be Chuck because I hated crazy murders. I would rather it was Kirk. It would have been so much cleaner. So much more human.

It was 5 A.M. when I locked up my briefcase, and locked it away in the lock-up closet. I had eaten six greasy pork sandwiches that had nearly destroyed what digestion I had left, smoked two packs of cigarettes that put me that much farther along the road to lung cancer, drunk five carefully measured drinks that hadn't helped me at all as I intended they shouldn't, and I was tired. Chantal had not come by. I made myself a really important drink and went upstairs and went to bed.

It was after 10 A.M. when Pekouris arrived down below in the jeep with two other policemen, to check out Sonny Duval. He waved up at me, before they walked down to the dock.

I sat on my porch over the harbour with my coffee, and watched Pekouris show-off in his blue suit and row them out, standing up in the skiff with the long, push-type oars. Everybody in Greece, or at least everybody I knew, seemed to be able to row a dinghy like a professional.

The other two officers were strangers I had never seen before.

I watched all three of them climb up Sonny's ladder. It was hot and sunny where we were at the yacht harbour, but off over Sonny's caique above the mainland a long bank of dark yellowish cloud was moving down from the northeast, and there was a stillness and absence of breeze that presaged some weather.

Half an hour later they rowed back to the dock and Pekouris drove the jeep over to my side of the vacant lot and parked it in the grass. He left the other two sitting in the sun. On his way up he made an elaborately polite greeting to the leathery Georgina who was pottering around in her hot garden.

'Do you want a drink?' I said when he came in.

He just looked at me.

He had a genius for rubbing me the wrong way.

'Then to hell with you,' I said. 'I'll have one myself without you, then, Pekouris.' I called to the housekeeper. 'Mama-san. Ice.'

'I came to ask about your investigations. What have you found out?'

'Not too much,' I said. 'I haven't done too much. Did you find a lot of incriminating evidence on Sonny's boat?'

He gave me his superior thick-lipped smile. 'That was only a routine call. He is, as you say, clean.'

'Well, you upset him enough by it,' I said.

He grinned. 'I hope so. He is not a man I find I can like easily. Nor his wife. But he is clean. I did not expect to find anything.'

I smiled. 'So you just wanted to blow his mind a little?' I didn't know if I liked that or not. I guessed I did. 'I've been doing some homework, though,' I said, 'if I haven't done much else. And I've about reached the same conclusion you already arrived at. It looks like it has to be that boy with his machete.'

'I do not think there is any doubt,' Pekouris said.

'He's got a machete with him here, you know,' I said.

Pekouris nodded.

'Well, just curiosity, but why didn't you pick him up?'

'He was not there when we were there. He had gone off around to Ayia Paraskevi.'

I didn't know what it was about him that I just couldn't cotton to. But I just couldn't appreciate him. Couldn't he give a straight answer, once?

'Wouldn't it have been easy to run around there in a boat and pick him up?' I said patiently.

Pekouris made a nastier than usual smile. 'Yes. Yes, it would. But I do not think you understood my Athens directive yesterday, when I told it to you, Davies. I was told by Athens to: Solve it, but solve it *fast*. The The emphasis was on the Fast.'

Apparently calling me just 'Davies' like that was some form of slightly more intimate address that meant equality, to him. But to me it sounded condescending, dictatorial, domineering, superior, and snotty. I didn't like that about him, either.

'I see. So?'

'Well, is it not self-evident? If I pick this boy up now, an American, there would be an enormous publicity in the press, and a long drawn-out court case. I might not even convict him. If he was a Greek.' He shrugged. 'It would be a different matter. But he is not. And that is not solving it *fast*, as my directive ordered me.'

He suddenly looked a little peaked, Pekouris. Like a man being pulled two ways by exactly equal forces. But he wasn't going to admit that to me. There was his duty as he liked to conceive it, and his duty as his Athens superiors preferred him to conceive it. I wanted to feel sorry for him. But it wasn't easy.

'I need some real evidence. Or a confession. A confession would be best. That would be perfect.'

'And in the meantime, these two boys may just up and hightail it out of here on a small boat, to Turkey.'

'Highly unlikely. Believe me, they would never get there.' It sounded like a face-saving pronouncement to me. But maybe he could back it up.

'Well,' I said. 'Listen, speaking of evidence. I happened to be with someone yesterday.'

Pekouris smiled. 'Yes, I know.'

I blinked once at him, slowly. 'And this somebody told me something interesting. Not long ago a bunch of these kids stole some goat and killed it and roasted it. This boy Chuck decapitated it with his machete. Fine. But then he went around with the goat's blood on the machete without washing it off, and bragging about it.'

Pekouris was watching me intently. 'Yes? I do not entirely follow your reasoning.'

'Well. If he would do that with goat's blood, isn't it just possible he might do the same with human blood?'

Pekouris nodded. 'I see. Yes, it's just possible. Especially with a crazy man.'

'Is there any way of separating and distinguishing dried goat's blood from dried human blood on a knife.'

'I would have to ask a doctor about that.'

'I don't know enough, medically.'

'Nor do I. Anyway, do not concern yourself with that. I will find out all about that from our laboratory. It's an excellent idea.

'But I am not going to arrest the boy and confiscate the machete now. First, I want to find out what the laboratory tells me.'

'Well, I can hardly confiscate it for you,' I said. 'Or steal it for me.'

'I do not ask you to,' Pekouris said, humourless to the end. 'This just might solve all our problems,' he said, more to himself than to me. Clearly, he meant *his* problems.

'I'm not holding it up as any great possibility,' I said.

He moved away from the chair he had been standing beside. 'I'll be in touch with you about the laboratory.' He pronounced it like the English: la*bor*atory. Ponderously, in his ponderous way, he moved towards the three steps down into the hallway to the door.

'Hey, wait a minute,' I said. 'What about Jim Kirk? What are you doing about him?'

Pekouris turned. 'He is being looked into.'

'You know he was in with Girgis, don't you? He's a suspect, too, you know.'

He blinked at me solemnly. 'No stone is being left unturned, Davies,' he said. He turned and went down the steps.

I watched him go out. Then I walked out to my porch to watch him drive away. He was just about not believable. I watched him climb into the jeep's driving seat, beside his two hot cops, who were still sitting there obediently in the sun.

After he was gone, Sonny Duval walked up along the seawall from the taverna, looking up at me. He didn't come inside the gate.

'You saw?' he called. 'I've been given a clean bill of health.'

I just nodded.

'Listen,' he called up. 'Will you be wanting the boat? It looks like one of those quick summer storms. We almost never get them. But when we do, they blow like hell for a couple of hours.' As he spoke, the first fingerlings of rising breeze blew dust swirls up from around his feet in the dry gravelled road. It was hotter now, if anything. Muggy heat.

I looked off towards the bank of cloud to the northeast. You could see the blue sheets of rain falling from it in long parallelograms. 'No, I won't want it,' I called down.

He shrugged his shoulders up once, then turned and stalked off towards the taverna again. I went inside and picked a book in English off one of the shelves. It was something called *Bitter Lemons*, by Lawrence Durrell, about Cyprus.

I sat down with it on the porch and told the old Greek woman to bring me some whisky, and that I'd eat lunch there.

CHAPTER THIRTY-ONE

The prospect of a rainy day made me feel I didn't have to do anything. My lunch was the first meal my Greek housekeeper had made for me. It was pretty hard to ruin plain scrambled eggs, but she managed it. I put down a whole bottle of red wine with it, and took my book back out on the protected porch with a brandy.

Chantal had not called. I was sort of glad.

The bank of yellow cloud had continued to come on out of the northeast, and the excited feeling of a storm had fallen over the harbour. A steady rain began to fall.

The wind hadn't abated and the sea was up, making the boats rock in the harbour, and the high masts toss wildly. Everything was battened down and seemed suddenly empty of people. I sat and watched it like you would watch an exciting movie.

Outside in the rain the ship's bell over the upper garden gate jangled, and then the front door bell rang. The old Greek woman opened it. A tallish long-legged long-haired blonde young woman in skintight blue jeans and a braless thin cotton shirt came in. She said hallo to the maid in Greek.

'Hallo there, Mr Davies!'

My dirty black old heart sort of skipped a beat.

I stood up, out on the porch, as she came leggily down the living-room towards me, slightly damp. She obviously knew the house.

And I, standing drink in hand, suddenly saw that long body nude, the way I had seen it yesterday pulling off the black wet-suit. And the day before yesterday, striding naked into the water at the hippie beach. And today? Well, today – such a nice quiet cosy rainy today – was such a great day for it, wasn't it?

'Gosh it's raining!' she said breathlessly, in her half-childish way. 'A lot of wind! But I think it'll blow over by this evening!'

That eternal cheerfulness, on that perpetual brink of disaster.

'Yes,' I said. 'Well, come on out. You didn't go out today, hunh? Didn't go spearfishing?'

'No. Actually, it's all right on the lee side out of the wind. But I don't like it somehow, in the rain. It puts me down. And anyway I somehow found myself thinking about you all morning. Somehow.'

'You did, did you?' I said.

'So I thought I'd come pay you a visit! You told me to, once, if I ever felt like it. And I thought you probably wouldn't be out on your boat, today!'

'It's funny. I was just thinking about you, too,' I said. 'Would you like a drink?'

'No.' She looked down at her body. 'Gosh, I'm all damp.' She was, and it made the cotton shirt cling closer to her. She went over to the railing and looked up at the sky. 'Yes, this'll blow over! Tomorrow'll be clear!' Then, much softer, 'What were you thinking about me?'

'You want me to be blunt?' I said.

'Be blunt,' Marie said. 'I like you when you're blunt.'

'I was thinking about how you're affected by this killing. You're very likely to be out of a job, do you know it? Because this thing is going to put an end to the hashish business for some time. That's going to put a bad cramp in your sources of income.'

'Yes, it sure is. That's what's so good about you, you know it? You clear all the shit away fast. Actually, that was part of what I came to talk to you about.' She looked straight at me, open-eyed, honest. 'That, and the fact that I've been thinking about you so.'

Suddenly she shrugged her hands out, then slapped them against her thighs. 'But I'd rather not talk about it all here.'

'I don't know where we could go,' I said. 'Some bar?'

'We could go to my little place,' she said. 'I have a room in a private house, where I lived last winter. I'm not using it much now in the summer. I stay up at the Construction. But I have the key.'

I didn't say anything. It was funny, you didn't have to do a thing. They would do it all for you. If they decided they wanted a chunk of you.

I gave her a long moment's look. She looked straight back. There wasn't much doubt about the rest of it. The silent rider was attached, all right.

'All right,' I said. 'Let me finish my drink.' I tossed it off.

Suddenly she giggled. I looked up at her in time to catch something dark that flashed out at me from her eyes. For a split second she looked like an old whore soliciting in a dark hotel doorway.

At the door she said, 'You better put something on. In this rain.'

'What about you?'

'I'm wet already. Anyway, I don't mind it. I like it. And I can change down there.' Again the silent rider.

I put on my old trenchcoat. Then my beat-up old New Yorker's hat. In the hall mirror I suddenly looked tougher, older, more mean, more like a cop. The hat and trenchcoat looked weird, over my resort clothes and sandals.

'Now I look more like what I am,' I said.

'And more like my daddy,' Marie said smiling.

I smiled wryly. 'The middle-aged private dick. Who no longer believes in anybody. And wouldn't give his own grandmother change of a dollar. For fear of being short-changed. And rightly so.'

Still smiling she opened the door for us.

Her room was down in toward the town. So we took the upper street, above the house. Twice, when flurries of rain hit us, she huddled against me. But mostly she walked openly in the rain. Twice she put her head back and closed her eyes, lifting her face to feel it. When we got to the house, her hair was wet and her clothes half soaked. But by then I was out of the game.

I didn't know what had changed my mind. Was it the look I had suddenly got of myself in that hall mirror? Maybe it was the way she threw back her head to the rain. I could never have done that, not without laughing.

Whatever it was, I knew I couldn't go through with it.

Maybe it was the way she huddled against me, for protection, when the rain flurries hit us. I remembered my own two daughters huddling against me in the exact same way, when some tiny disaster in their lives had hit them and they didn't know what to do about it. Except huddle against daddy. Like Marie. Only, Marie's disaster was a big one.

Maybe mostly, it was because I was too old. Old enough to be ridiculous.

The house was a nondescript one, with the regular walled garden. She led me back along a walk beside the house to a private door. Inside, it was a poor cheap little room with nothing of anything in it. She had added nothing of herself to it. She could have moved out in five minutes.

The room hurt me, too. Only her diving gear, in one corner, scrupulously cleaned, marked it as hers.

'Such as it is,' Marie said. She shut the door. I turned around and stripped off my trenchcoat and hat, wanting to be rid of the personality they inflicted on me.

When I turned back Marie was standing looking at me with that open, childish face. Maybe she was breathing a little fast. For a split second that same strange, odd, dark look crossed her face. Then it was gone.

To describe it as whorish was too strong, but I guessed

it had that in it. A masochism, maybe. Of some special female kind? A kind of whorish delight.

'I'd better change,' she said, and half-sitting on the little bed, stripped off her shirt and picked up a towel.

She never wore a bra, of course. Her breasts were young, and the size of a large cup. There was a shy, vulnerable movement about her, as she dried herself. She dried the breasts first. She didn't look at me.

'And I'd better dry my hair,' she said. The breasts jiggled deliciously, as she moved the towel. Especially when she bent forward to do her hair.

I felt like a man under some attack. I hadn't had time or a chance to move. I stood with my back jammed back against the door. I felt my face getting tighter.

'Do you want to help?' Marie asked, looking up through her hair.

'No, thanks.' I said it harsher than I meant.

The towel around her shoulders, she tossed her hair back, and stood up. That funny odd 'whorish' look was back on her face openly. She unbuckled her jeans belt and unzipped the fly, and pushed her jeans down and stepped out of them. She began to dry her legs, and her belly.

I just stood there. It was one hell of a body she had on her. If she knew how bad I wanted it, I guessed she would be pleased. My hands were jammed down tight and clenched in my pockets. I relaxed them. She straightened, holding the towel in front of her, but not at all protectively, and looked at me.

'Cut it out,' I said hoarsely. 'Put some clothes on.'

'You don't like me?'

'I like you a lot. Now cut it out. It wouldn't work.'

That strange look went off her face, and the young girl's look came back on it. 'Do you think I'm a whore?'

'If I thought you were a whore, it would work.'

'Well, I am a whore.'

'And I'm old enough to be your father. Now cut it out.'

'I told you I thought I'd try some incest.' She laughed, a girlish tinkle, from that lovely lush nude body that made my teeth ache. Her crotch was lean and sturdy and built for wear and beautifully hairy. 'I've tried everything else.'

184

'It wouldn't work,' I said. 'You'd have a bad feeling afterwards. Little girls shouldn't do things that leave a bad feeling afterwards. Neither should little boys,' I said.

'Did you know I had an affair with Jane Duval?' she said. She half turned. 'Hand me those pants,' she said.

I stepped and got a dry pair of jeans and a shirt lying with them and tossed them to her.

'No,' I said. 'I didn't. But I don't see why not. And it doesn't surprise me. Everybody else has.'

'Except you.' She turned sideways and stepped into the jeans demurely and pulled them up.

'Except me,' I said.

Turning her back, she put the shirt on. Then she turned and sat down on the bed.

'Don't ever do that to me again,' I said, and grinned. 'I haven't got that strong a heart. And I'm no iron man.' The grin felt pretty cracked.

She just looked at me, with that open girlish look, and didn't say anything. She picked up her hairbrush.

'I suppose I should be ashamed of myself,' she said. 'But I'm not. It's a shame, really.'

'You'll feel better about it this way,' I said.

'But you wanted me. Didn't you want me? Terribly?'

'Terribly. As much as I've ever wanted any woman in my life. More.'

'Then why didn't you just take me?'

'Because if I'm going to be your substitute father around here,' I said, 'I didn't think it would look good.'

'I'm really glad that you didn't do it, really.'

'Good. Fine. That's great. And I'm just beginning to feel sorry. Look,' I said. 'You said you wanted to talk to me about Girgis?'

CHAPTER THIRTY-TWO

'I wanted to ask your advice about something. It wasn't really about Girgis. It was about Jim Kirk.'

'So what about Kirk?'

But first she had to get me a drink. She rummaged around, found a bottle of Scotch, and a split of soda. I sat down with it on the one chair. Outside, the rain drummed audibly. My ears had stopped hearing it there for a while.

'I'm sorry there's no ice.'

'I don't need any ice,' I said. 'What about Kirk?'

She had made herself a stiff drink, too. She put down half of it on the first try, then sat on the bed.

'This whole thing has upset me terribly. I've had nightmares about it.' Suddenly, she shuddered. She smiled, but her mouth had that sudden quiver. 'Cutting off his head like that. Anyway, I'm thinking of leaving Tsatsos.'

'I think that's a good idea, personally,' I said crisply.

'Kirk wants me to stay,' she said. 'You said I'd be out of a job running hash for a long time. Kirk says it'll only be for a couple of weeks. Then he will start operating again. And he wants me to do the same thing for him that I did for Girgis.'

'I couldn't advise you about that,' I said coldly. 'Two weeks? That sounds like Kirk's got some kind of special pull around here, that I don't know about.'

'But you're smarter. But maybe he does have pull, as you say. Because he's been bringing some heroin on the island, you know. Did you know that?'

'Has he!' I said. 'You wouldn't know what his source is, would you?'

'I guess, Athens. There're some addicts up at the Construction. Slow John's one of them. Kirk runs in just enough for them. He charges double what it costs in Athens, John says. Jim says it's for the risk he takes.'

'Was Girgis involved in this H deal?' I asked.

'No. Girgis wouldn't touch H. That old Ambassador Pierson is an addict, too.'

'How does Kirk get the H to these people?'

'I carried it for him up at the Construction.'

I shook my head. Then I set my glass on the floor and got up. I was angry, and I had to hold myself down. 'That's pretty damn dumb. You can get busted, and busted bad, anywhere for that. Don't you know that?'

'I only did it as a favour. He slipped me a few bucks.'

'Legally, it makes no damn difference. And H is dynamite right now. That's why they're all so secretive about it.' I was thinking about Chantal, at that exact moment.

Marie just looked at me, then suddenly smiled that

hurt smile of hers that always got to me. 'I know. Oh, to hell with it.' She didn't say anything for a moment.

I was wondering if old Ambassador Pierson and his H supply could be Chantal's further secret? That I never could get hold of? But why would she hide that from me?

'It's all so dirty, isn't it?' Marie said.

'Oh. No more than any other line of endeavour.' I gave her one of my better smiles. 'In my business, you're in danger of getting to believe it's *all* dirty. And every*body* along with it. And that's bad. Don't get like that.'

'It couldn't be all dirty if you were in it,' Marie said.

I gave her a hard look. 'Don't be too sure of that, either, sweetie.'

'I'm sure of it about you. – Anyway, it's because the price of H is so high here, that John wants to leave Tsatsos. And he wants me to go with him.'

Outside, the rain seemed to have stopped.

'John? It's him you're leaving with?' I said.

'If I go. I figured you'd love that.'

'Where would you go?' I said.

'To Capri. He wants to take a house in Capri for a month or two. He's been there before. And he wants to take me with him.'

'What if he takes off and leaves you in Capri?'

'I suppose I could always do something. I guess I could spearfish there as well as here.'

'Capri's a lot different from here. I hear it's a pretty wild, wide open place. It's supposed to be crawling with fags and rich swingers.'

'Fags would never bother John. Or me, either.'

'No,' I said. 'But where there are fags there're also lesbians. They follow each other.'

There was a pause from Marie. 'Oh. Yes,' she said. 'Yes, there's that, I guess.'

I turned on her from the door. 'Look, you're no les. If you were, what the hell? Who cares? But you're not. I'm not thinking of you so much. But if John's propensity for extra girls is as strong as you say it is? He could get you involved with some pretty bad types, like that. They're all leses, those extra-girl types. And then go off and leave you there. I'm not sure you're strong enough to handle those types. A lot of leses work the racket. Rich swingers pay high. And one of the biggest payoffs is for fresh meat. New young meat. Like you. Do you think you could tell the straight ones from the bent ones?' I said harshly.

'I don't know,' Marie said from the bed. She wouldn't look at me. 'Probably not.'

'Well?' I said. 'Look, have you thought about what I said yesterday? About going back home?'

She pushed her hand through her hair in a sort of distraught gesture. 'It's all such a mess, isn't it? –

'Yes, I've thought about it. But it's so hard. It's not only just the money. Where would I go? I wouldn't know anybody? I'd be starting all over, cold turkey, in a cold new town? It's too much.'

'All right, damn it, I'll help you get out of it,' I said grimly. 'I'll give you my address in New York. If you can get the money together, you come back to New York. You look me up. You won't be alone that way. You ought to be able to hold down some kind of job. I'll help you get one. Hell, I'll even spring for the money.'

'Would you really do that? I can get the money. I'll make John give it to me.'

'It would seem he owed you at least that much,' I said. 'But I wouldn't bet on getting it.'

'You'd really do that?'

'Sure.'

'Can we talk about it later? I'm all confused right now. But I think I'll do it, if you really mean it.'

'I mean it.'

'Not about the money. That other part, I mean.'

'I mean it.'

'That's the most important part, is having some friend.'

I opened the door behind me, and gave her a grin. 'There must be some decent husbands still left around somewhere. We'll find you one.'

'Look, I'm going spearfishing tomorrow. Do you want to go out? And talk about it then? We could take the boat.'

'I can't. I've got things I've got to do,' I said. 'Another day, though.'

From the bed she smiled her wounded smile at me. It looked better than it usually looked. 'All right. All right, Big Daddy. You really are Big Daddy, you know that?'

'Oh, nuts,' I snarled, and stepped back outside and shut the door.

CHAPTER THIRTY-THREE

The squall was swiftly blowing itself away behind the hills. I folded my trenchcoat into a roll under my arm and carried the hat. It was so dry the rain seemed hardly to have dampened the bare dirt along the edges of the cobbled street. The air had a fresh smell.

I guessed I looked pretty ridiculous. With Marie, either way I went I had to look silly. Nobody in his right mind would turn down a girl that lovely. Instead, me, I had to go and acquire myself another responsibility.

I could afford her plane fare, and a little living money. We'd let Mr Kronitis pay that. I had several younger friends, girls, in New York. Where she could bunk up for a while. It wasn't the first time I had done something like this for some kid. It was just the first time any of them had ever had a body like that.

But that wasn't the whole problem, and I knew it. The whole problem had to do with something else. That was the part I hadn't wanted to think about, and still didn't. The whole problem had to do with age. My age. I was having serious difficulty avoiding it. I supposed it was a problem everybody had to face, if he lived long enough. That didn't help me. I still didn't like it. And I still didn't want to think about it.

The rough cobbles under my feet were already bone dry of rain. With the storm past I felt I ought to get back to doing something. But what? Nothing Marie had told me about Kirk had made me feel any different about the murder. I decided to go up and have a look at the Cloud 79 night club tonight.

I walked on home and called Chantal. She was home. She had another one of those dinners of hers on for the evening. I certainly didn't want to go to that. I told her I might be up to see her late, but that also I might not.

'Is she as good as I am?' she said.

I didn't answer her.

'I'll bet there are a couple of things she can't do as well as I do,' Chantal said.

I expected she was right. There were a couple of things I could think of. Marie certainly couldn't do them any better.

'I don't like your social dinners, sweetie,' I said. 'And I don't have to go to them. I've made some friends of my own, on my own level, down here in the Port.'

'All of them with long long legs, no doubt.' Her voice sounded sharper.

'I'll try and get up there late,' I said. 'But if I shouldn't, don't fret over it. There's nobody down here who's looking for an ageing private dick as a lover.'

'Well, if I'm not there when you get there,' Chantal said in a lofty Countess voice, 'and I may not be, just go right on in and make yourself at home. I'll get there eventually.' She hung up.

I hung up myself, and walked out on my porch. I'd gone as far as I could with her. I supposed I could have told her I was working for Kronitis. But I had promised Pekouris I wouldn't tell *any*body.

Actually, I intended to get up there if I possibly could. If Chantal was carrying even small bits of H for Kirk among the high-born, the way Marie was among the low-born, it was something I wanted to talk to her about.

On the porch I leaned my hands on the thick stone railing. At the taverna across the vacant lot Pete Gruner and his beard, in another expensive coat, were sitting at a table.

I thought a minute, then went out and down the walk and over to the taverna to join them. I waved at Georgina as I went past her little outdoor living-room.

Gruner had clearly seen me coming. I took a table off by myself. He came over and slipped into a chair.

'Okay, what did you want to see me about?'

'What makes you think I wanted to see you?' I said. 'I thought you wanted to see me.'

'Because I happened to be sitting at your private taverna here? Sure.'

Strangely enough I was beginning to kind of like him, in a masochistic way. 'Well, you don't generally hang out down here. It's more your style to hang around up at the Construction with your buddies.'

He grinned. 'Well, actually I did want to see you.'

'Let's take mine first,' I said. 'It seems you've been going around throwing eggs on me telling people you suspected I was some kind of a Government man.'

'I don't think I said that.'

'It seems that you did,' I said. 'I haven't thrown any eggs back yet. But I'm all ready to. I'm eager to. Can you tell me anything that might deter me?'

He gave me a snide grin. 'I did say something to one person. Jim Kirk. But it wasn't Government. I said I thought you were down here working for some very big outfit.'

'Big enough to be the U.S. Government,' I said. 'He told it that way to at least one other person. One more little piece of gamesmanship like that from you, and I'll ruin your image good, friend. I haven't done it yet.'

He grinned. 'I knew you were a good guy. Underneath that phony heart-of-gold routine of yours. I'm sorry about that other. I had to do it. If I could tell you why, you'd understand.'

'No, I wouldn't. And you may find out I'm not the sweet-tempered boy you think I am. Now, what's your bad news?'

His face took on the flush of a crowing rooster. 'I wanted to tell you I've got that job I was telling you about. I'm going to work as Mate on the *Polaris*. I talked to the big man.'

That slowed me. 'You saw Kronitis?'

'I talked to him on the phone. I'm to see him in a couple of days. If it works out, I'll be promoted to run the boat.'

'Where are you meeting him? At his villa?'

'No, in Glauros. At that big hotel. It was easy enough to get hold of him. I just called him up, like this kid Steve did, about his bar.'

I made no comment on any of that. 'Why are you coming here telling me all this?'

He grinned. 'I just wanted you to know. If anything should ever happen to me, you'll know where to look. Start looking for what's left of me on that *Polaris* boat.'

'I'm not going to go looking for you anywhere, bud,' I said grimly. 'I'm not getting paid to. Do you want to tell me *why* you're doing it?'

'I'm going into the hashish business. With Kirk. That

was why I had to lay a little heavy on you with Kirk. Kirk carries a lot of weight with Kronitis, and I'll need Kirk to bring in the stuff. Kronitis doesn't know, of course. I had to promise him I wouldn't indulge in any hashish smuggling. Kirk and I will split fifty-fifty. Kirk is satisfied, Kronitis is satisfied, and I'm satisfied.'

'That's not the *why*,' I said. 'That's the *how*.'

'It's the *why*. Hell, in a year it'll net me enough to buy me my own boat. And I'll be all set to live in the Greek islands forever.'

'And I'll be able to fly over here from New York and charter your boat for years to come,' I said. 'Go ahead, con me some more.'

He just grinned. 'Maybe some day I'll be able to tell you a little more, Lobo. About my plans.'

'Sure,' I said. 'You can tell me the next time I'm in Washington.'

He shook his head. 'Just remember what I told you about the *Polaris*,' he said, and got up. He threw some bills on the table. He was about the only one who ever paid a tab around there, except for me. That alone made him rare.

'See you,' he said, and winked. He went walking away with that long-waisted athlete's walk of his, his well-kept long hair swinging.

I just sat and looked after him. I'd sort of hate to see him dead. It was beginning to get a little dark. I moved from my bare table over to one of the tables laid with a cloth for the dinner trade and motioned the waiter.

CHAPTER THIRTY-FOUR

I didn't know what kind of trouble to expect up there at Steve's Cloud 79, so I didn't eat a big dinner. I put away a few extra Scotches, instead. I expected some kind of a jolly reception. I figured I could handle five of them. But I couldn't handle ten. It would take a Ray Nietschke or a Mean Joe Green to handle ten. I carried a flathead sap in my briefcase, but I didn't take it. It was a precision instrument. I didn't want it against these kids. In a wild mêlée you could accidentally kill somebody with it, very easily.

The horsecab from Dmitri's parked me at the foot of the path up to the club. The path led up through some trees and rocky outcrop to a little plateau below the Construction. I took it. Down below the horses' hoofs and cab wheels had beaten down a parking space for half a dozen cabs to wait. You could hear the blare of folk rock at least as far away as the Xenia hotel.

It was a pretty place for an outdoor club. On the little plateau, above the screen of trees, you could look out to sea and the nearby islands, and to Glauros on the mainland.

But they hadn't done much with it. Steve was saving Kronitis's money for himself, I guessed. Three plywood and tarpaper shacks had been thrown up, and a rickety fence strung between them, to get inside of which you had to pay. I paid. When I handed in my sixty drachs, the long-haired boy on the gate gave me a startled, hard look. I grinned at him, and winked.

Inside, everything about the place had been done on the cheap the same way. A warped wooden dance floor of junk lumber had been laid down in sections. The junk tables and chairs, throw-aways from the cafés and tavernas in town, looked dangerous to use. In spite of that, or perhaps because of it, the place was doing an enormous business and everybody seemed to love it. A lot of young Greek locals were there, a lot of rich kids of summer residents, and a lot of the Athenian tourists. And, of course, a lot of hippies from the Construction. A number of kids danced barefoot on the packed dirt around the edges of the dance floor.

The word that I was there went ahead of me. As I'd expected. The boy at the door had passed it on. A wave of sullen anger passed across the dance floor and through the tables, when the hippies saw me. The others, the locals and the rich kids, didn't notice me. I sat down at a rusty table, and stolidly ordered a Scotch. I hadn't expected any different.

A lot of people I knew were seated around. Steve and Diane were at a sort of favoured, owner's table. Myopic Chuck was with them. Georgina Taylor was sitting with them, too. Georgina got a hollow-eyed disturbed look, when she saw me and avoided looking in my direction. Right next to them were Sweet Marie and Slow John. With John and Marie was Jason, the Paris 'recording star', so stoned on hash he kept falling over. John and Marie had to keep propping him up. Nearby was the elegantly bearded Gruner, smiling as always.

On his way to the dance floor with some hippie girl type Gruner paused, with a sardonic grin, and said hallo.

'I won't sit,' he grinned. 'You understand why.'

'Sure,' I said, and grinned back. He was a good-looking guy, Gruner. Be a shame if anything happened to him. But I couldn't worry about that now. I tossed off the rest of my drink and ordered another.

When I re-ordered, Steve got up and sauntered over. With a flick of his blue eyes Steve stopped my waiter.

Behind him at the table Chuck got up, too. But Diane grabbed him by his shirt tail. Apparently he'd been told to stay away. She tried to make him sit back down, but he refused.

There was a definite authority about Steve, here in his own joint. I could see why Marie said he had the flair. It was a little flagrantly displayed maybe.

'I'd rather you didn't order that second one.'

I looked up at him. 'Oh? How come? You mean you're buying one?'

'No. I'm asking you to leave.'

I pursed out my lips. 'What if I don't want to?'

'It would be easy for me to have you thrown out.'

I let my eyes run around at all the hippies all around me. One by one they dropped their gaze, as mine swept past them. 'I don't think so. I don't think you've got the muscle. Certainly not without creating such a rumpus you'd get your joint closed down. They're just waiting for something to jump on you with, chum.' I turned suddenly to the waiter, another youngster from the Construction. 'Here. You. Young man. Bring me a bottle of Scotch.'

The waiter looked at Steve.

'Tell him not to bring it,' I said. 'Go ahead.'

Steve stared at me, expressionless. With those weird, stoned eyes.

'Go ahead,' I said.

His knuckles were resting on the table top. I watched

them turn white. For a long moment he didn't move a muscle. Then slowly, he lowered his eyelids in a slow blink of assent to the waiter.

The waiter nodded a jerky nod, and went off to the bar.

I grinned at Steve. 'Why don't you sit down? Take a load off your feet, and save a little face at the same time.'

He slid into one of my chairs. Behind him Chuck had come up in a slow, consciously ominous way. He made as if to slide into another.

'Not you,' I said. 'You don't sit at my table, Four Eyes.'

It was an appellation I suddenly remembered from my childhood. Back then, it was the worst insult you could call a boy who had to wear glasses. I didn't think things had changed that much in a generation.

He reacted just the way I hoped he would. Behind his glasses his magnified, enormous eyes went a wild, crazy enormous fiery red. A bubble of spittle pooled at a corner of his mouth. As he hunched forward, his voice came out in that high, low-keyed, falsetto scream I'd heard before.

'I don't have to take that from you, you punk bastard! I'll break your face. I'll break your teeth! I'll pop out your eyeballs! You won't have a solid bone in your punk body!'

I just looked at him. But I had my feet together under me. I'd looked him over and he didn't have anything on him except his karate lessons, which of course didn't show.

But before either of us could move, Steve was on his feet in front of Chuck and pushing against him with his chest, pushing him backwards.

'All right, now. All right, now.'

'Tell him to go away and sit down,' I said, calmly. But the crazy murderousness I'd seen had my heart thumping regularly in my ears. I'd found out what I'd wanted to know, anyway. He was perfectly capable of what I thought he was capable of. Especially if insulted properly. Girgis was a greater insulter of hippies.

'You heard what he said,' Steve said. 'You go and sit with Diane. Take care of Diane for me.'

'I don't have to!' Chuck whispered. 'I don't have to take it!'

'Go on,' Steve said. Slowly, he bellied him back away from me. And after a moment Chuck turned and walked away. But he didn't go back to the table to Diane. He walked to the entrance lane, and then out through the fence and into the night.

'Where's he going?' I said. 'To get that machete of his?'

'You think about that machete a lot,' Steve said. He sat back down, and grinned, and shook his head. But his face was white under his tan.

'Machete? What machete?' I said. 'I don't know anything about any machete.'

'He wouldn't need that machete to take you,' Steve said seriously. 'He's tough.'

'He's also crazy,' I said. 'As a bedbug.'

'You take an awful lot of chances, mister.'

'That's how I get my kicks,' I said. 'Because I really honestly don't give a damn. And I like to fight. Especially kid karate experts.'

Steve looked at me with contained, but unconcealed hatred. 'Do you run over everyone the same way?'

'No.' I grinned. 'Just the lucky chosen few.'

Behind me the young waiter came up with the bottle I had ordered. He put it on the table with some new glasses. He didn't set it down lightly. He was as angry as the rest.

'You took an awful chance just coming here, you know.'

I poured a drink for myself. Then I poured one for him. He didn't touch his. 'I figured you wouldn't let your pals beat me up right in your joint.'

'No but I'm not responsible for what happens to you once you're outside that fence.'

I just grinned at him. 'Of course not.'

'Would you mind telling me how you knew he wasn't at St Friday's?'

I borrowed a line from Pekouris. 'Oh, I have my little ways. Of finding out all sorts of things. Why don't you go and get him for me? I would like to talk to him.'

'Are you crazy? After what you said to him? Go and get him yourself. If you think you want to.'

I smiled. 'No, I guess not. I don't want to give away any more odds, to go up in there alone this late at night. I figure I've given away enough, coming here.'

196

'You sure have.'

'I don't see how you figure it,' I said. 'You two boys are prime suspects in a murder case. You ought to go to the police and prove your innocence.'

'I figure if we sit tight, we'll be all right. We're not without friends.'

'You mean like your rich silent partner?'

'He's one.'

I didn't disillusion him. 'You want to know what I think? I think probably you two did it together.'

That got to him. For the first time. He didn't like for even me to be thinking that. 'Did it ever occur to you we might both be innocent?'

I grinned at him. 'I've thought of that. It's not a good money bet.'

'You're one of those people who instinctively hates any life-style that's not his own, Mr Davies.'

'Is that the way you figure it, huh? But what interests me is what're you going to do. You can't hide him. Not here.'

'Who says I need to hide him?'

I shrugged. 'Nobody. And he could never make it to Athens and get on a plane.'

'There are other things.'

'Sure. If he runs – and even makes it somewhere, like Turkey, on a little boat – Interpol will have his picture all over Europe and the Middle East in two days. You want him to live on the hop in the Middle East? I don't think you've got the connections.'

'I've got money, now.'

'You'd be robbed blind in five days. You'd never be able to trust a soul. You've never really lived in the real lower depths. I have. There's no milk of human decency down there.'

'It's a good thing for us the police didn't hire you, isn't it?' Steve said. He got to his feet.

I looked up at him quizzically. 'Tell me something, are all the hippies like you two? Where's all this peace and human kindness stuff I've been hearing so much about?'

'We offer. It isn't often accepted.'

'So you start hitting back. Like everybody else. Hunh? Like me. What's so different?' I looked around the place.

All I saw was sullen anger. 'You want to know what I think? I think you're all hypocrites. All of you. And all of these.

'Take away the long hair and the wild clothes and you're nothing but a small-time hood, who sells marked-up booze and hash to,' I looked around again, 'a bunch of ordinary middle-brow suckers – who think they're different too because their clothes and hair are different. Hypocrites.

'And your sidekick is just a punk, a paid gunny, a bodyguard who happens to use a machete instead of an iron.'

Steve's knuckles, resting on the tin table, clenched themselves into a fist. He nodded once and walked away without a word. But at least I had gotten my little speech in. Why not, since I was going to pay up for it in a little bit? I gave myself the right.

Feeling savage, I poured myself another drink from the bottle and looked around. The hippies around me all looked away sullenly. The others, the locals and the rich kids, didn't even know what was going on. I didn't see how. The atmosphere was as charged as an electrical storm cloud bank that hadn't flashed yet.

Across the way Sweet Marie got up from her table and came striding over in her coltish walk and sat down.

'I think you ought to leave, Mr Davies.'

'I'll leave in a little bit,' I said.

'Please, I wish you'd leave now. They all hate you. They all think you're some kind of cop. I'm afraid something will happen if you stay.'

'Nothing'll happen as long as I'm here,' I said. 'It's after I leave that it'll happen.'

'Please go.'

'Have you thought about what we talked about?'

'I've thought about almost nothing else. I'm going to do what you suggested. But – ' she shrugged guiltily. 'I can't get the money from John. He won't give it to me.'

'Then take it from me. Like I said. Consider it a loan. You can pay me back when you're settled in New York.'

In her open sweet way she squeezed my hand lying on the table, and smiled her wide smile. 'You're really something special, do you know that?'

'I see you've got that boy Jason on your hands.'

'He's going back to Paris,' she said. 'He's broke.'

'I hope he can still sing, when he gets there.' I looked over at Jason. 'It always seems to come down to the money, in the end, doesn't it?'

'It seems to. It shouldn't. Now will you please go?'

'Yes.'

She gave me a long, worried look and left, and I poured myself another drink. After drinking it, I left money, picked up the bottle and started to make my way out.

As I got up, two of the hippies sitting farthest from me slipped out of their seats and slipped off into the dark around the dance floor the other way. I grinned to myself after them.

At Steve's table I paused. Suddenly, I tossed the bottle to him. He either had to catch it, or let it fall and smash.

'Here,' I said. 'A present.'

I waited. But Steve, the caught bottle resting on his lap, didn't say anything. It was childish of me, but that was what I wanted from him. Feeling quite calm, I left.

They let me get below the rocky outcrop before they hit me. I didn't know how there were so many of them. I had only seen two leave. But there were plenty.

Three of them came at me from the side. I tagged one with a left hook right on the button that put him out of it all. Another I missed on his jaw, but caught him square in the Adam's apple, which was just as good, and he fell down choking. The third ran right on past me and didn't turn or stop.

By this time another had jumped on my back from behind. By now they were coming in from everywhere. They were dropping from the chandeliers. I reached back for his shirt and flung him off over my head, and into two others who were running at me from the front. All three went down, but they all got right back up. By then two more were on my back from another direction behind me. I carried them out into the beaten-down parking lot where there was better footing, and managed to throw them off. I took two punches in the face doing it, and tagged one of the swingers with a right. Suddenly, without ever intending to, I yelled. A kind of combative bellow. And slugged somebody in front of me. I certainly didn't have to worry about hitting any

199

friends. I wasn't scared. I was having fun. The yell had just popped out of me. Actually I was enjoying myself. It seemed I'd been waiting for this a long time. Then another lit on my back, and at the same time still another dived in with a football tackle and the three of us crashed down.

On the ground I tried to kick my feet loose, but the boy who had tackled me held my legs tight against his chest. I kept punching away with both hands, at anything that got in front of my face. I connected four times. I could hear muffled voices yelling, 'Get him. Get him. Grab him. Hold him.' They were all in English, and they all had American accents.

In one of those moments of absolute quiet that come in a free-for-all like this one, I found that odd. And somehow strange.

Somebody was cursing and booting me in the side. Between bodies I caught a glimpse of the scared, light faces of the Greek cab drivers all turned toward me, from where they sat up on their coach boxes. Then something hit me in the side of the head and bells rang and coloured lights exploded, and wheeled in the dark sky, and burned themselves out and down to zero lighting in the black night like a dying pyrotechnic display. Very beautiful. Very satisfying.

CHAPTER THIRTY-FIVE

When I came to, it was Sonny Duval's hairy face I saw. He was kneeling above me and gently slapping my face.

'Let me alone,' I muttered. When I moved my jaw to speak, I could feel it was okay. So I added, 'Can't a guy take a nap around here?'

'What happened?'

I ignored him and started doing a little assessing. There was a throb in my right temple, from a small knot just above the ear. My arms and legs seemed okay. My teeth were okay. My face felt puffy again, like that first night at Chantal's, but there was only a tiny spot of blood. Lobo Davies, the Tsatsos Tackling Dummy. Sixty drachs, step

200

up and take your shot. I could charge admission.

I had jammed my left thumb hooking. There was a sharp bite of pain in my left side every time I breathed. That would be from the kicking I remembered, before I went out.

Wearily, I forced myself to sit up and made myself cough, and hawked and spit on the ground. There was no blood in it.

In all, I was in pretty good shape. They hadn't chest-stomped me afterwards. Hadn't kicked in my jaw. I felt a kind of liking for them. No maiming; just good, clean old American fun.

'The cab drivers said a gang beat you up.'

I made myself roll over on to my hands and knees, trying not to wince from the bright pain in my side. I got one foot under me, then the other. Sonny stepped to help me. I waved him away.

'Damn it, what happened?'

I pushed myself up, and a bright spotlight of pain in my side made me go lightheaded for a second and made my scalp tingle. If there was anything at all, I might have a cracked rib down there. But that was all. I wasn't feeling the best I'd ever felt. On the other hand I'd taken a lot worse beatings than this in my time.

I looked at Sonny, and gave him my No. 4, tough-but-pitiable grin. 'Where did you come from?'

'I just got here. The cab drivers told me you were over here in the weeds.'

'Ah, yes. The happy cab drivers. The grandstand seats.' I looked over at them. They were back on the ground, smoking.

'Will you tell me what happened?'

'Nothing. A bunch of the hippie kids. It's my own fault. I asked to see some guts and muscle, and I got shown some. If any of those boys are draft dodgers, it's not through any lack of desire to fight.'

'Draft resisters,' Sonny said. 'There's a difference.'

'Have it your way,' I said. 'Draft resisters. I'm too tired to argue.'

I forgot about my side, and took a weary, deep breath which made me jump and cut it off half-way in. 'Let's get something straight. I'm not against draft dodgers. I wish I'd had the guts to be one myself. I just wish everybody in the world would be a draft dodger. Instead of only just Americans. Now leave me alone,' I said. 'I'm sort of tired.'

'You don't seem to be very upset by it all.'

'I'm just wondering if I should go back in there and have one drink,' I said.

'I'll go in with you, if you want,' Sonny offered.

'You would, hunh? You're a regular fire-eater, aren't you?'

'Sure. I've been beat up before, myself.'

'Where's all this peace and loving kindness of yours?'

'A fist fight is not a dehumanised imperialist modern industrial war,' Sonny said.

I just looked at him. He had an infallible ability for ruining the nicest of gestures with some slogan. 'That's true,' I said. 'You're absolutely right there.'

'Do you want to go back in there?' Sonny said.

'I guess not.' I looked up at the lights through the trees. 'It wouldn't add anything. I got what I wanted. I guess I'll go on home.'

'Come on. I'll take you.' He put out an arm.

'You will like hell.' I waved the arm aside, and winced. 'Where were you all evening?'

'I was home. To eat. I just came out. Jane, uh,' he half hesitated, 'Jane didn't want to come.'

'Jane. Dear Jane. How is dear Jane? You go on up there with your friends.'

His face clouded at my ironic mention of Jane, but he said only, 'What shall I tell them?'

'Tell them whatever you want. Join the celebration. It won't bother me.' I turned away towards the cabs. 'Tell them Lobo Davies survived.' I stopped. 'They're not bad kids,' I said. 'Most of them. Just misinformed by Stevie-boy. And I deliberately antagonized them.'

'I guess you won't be wanting the boat tomorrow,' Sonny said.

I grinned. 'No. I guess I won't.'

He stood looking after me reflectively. When I got to the stand of cabs I walked on past them.

'Aren't you going to take a cab?' Sonny called.

'To hell with them. Anyway, the walk will do me good.'

I hoped it would. But I wasn't sure. At least it would loosen me up. But my side was hurting more and more.

Every breath was an agony, as they say. Actually, it wasn't all that bad. It hurt, but I had learned about pain that if you would only go down inside of it, and sort of rummage around down there, and feel it in all its corners, it hurt much less than when you drew back from it and tried not to feel it at all.

It was about a mile's walk back to the edge of the Port, and it was quiet and tranquil in the night air. The cooler night air had freshened whatever flowers there were blooming and their odours mingled faintly in my nose. It wasn't really all that late, only about 10 o'clock.

I had almost reached the end of the hotel grounds, and was passing under one of the infrequent street lights, when there was a soft sound like a hard puff of air and a whack, and a piece of the whitewashed wall four feet from my head popped out and fell on the ground. It didn't take vast experience to know what that was. Someone was shooting at me with a silencer.

Another puff, another smack, another piece of wall popped out almost beside the first and a little higher.

I didn't wait. And didn't stand on dignity. I cut and ran. In the old days discretion might be the better part of valour, but at the end of the 20th-century publicity was the better part of heroism. And I didn't have any P.R. people with me.

There were two more puffs, two more pieces of wall popped out. I made a couple of zigzags. Wherever it was exactly, it was coming from inside the Xenia hotel grounds. I reached a corner and ducked around it.

The gate entrances and doors were all barred or locked along here, but up the side street I found a deep-set one and flattened myself in it.

Everything was still as I stood in my doorway. I saw no one. Nothing moved. The extreme corner of the Xenia gardens with their dark vegetation just overlapped the entrance of the side street. I had about as much chance of finding somebody in there as you would in any other jungle. Even assuming I could get back down to it, in safety, which I couldn't.

In the dimness down below nothing moved. After five minutes I took a chance and sneaked out of my doorway. I hotfooted it on uphill, hugging the wall, and holding my left arm against my side. Nothing happened.

Nobody followed. There weren't any more shots.

Up above, on one of the cross streets, I walked back to my house thoughtfully. I was pretty careful at all the crossings.

CHAPTER THIRTY-SIX

As far as I was concerned the shooting made it a whole new ball game. Four feet from the head at twenty yards was pretty close for scare shooting. It implied something more was involved than I had yet figured out.

Would Chuck have gone off and got a gun and come back to take a crack at me? It was entirely possible.

At the house the first thing I saw as I came in the upper garden door was the yacht *Agoraphobe*, all lit up again out in the little harbour as if she might be getting ready to go to sea again.

I went on in and wearily climbed the stairs with the ice bucket to see what I had to repair. I examined myself in the bathroom mirror, then started methodically to work. Icepacks for the swelling, a Band-aid for a cut. I had gotten good at it over the years. My face wasn't as badly marked as it felt. It would be nearly normal by tomorrow. The worst thing was the pain in my side but I could live with that. Anyway, I couldn't do anything about it now. Maybe tomorrow I could get Georgina to help me tape it. That ought to titillate her.

It was not yet eleven o'clock. Dmitri's across the way was lit up and going full blast. With a drink in one hand and the icepack in the other I went to my bedroom and undressed to the skin and then turned off the lights. Then I stood in the window with my icepack to my face and watched the *Agoraphobe*.

Whatever they were doing, they weren't getting ready for sea. As I watched, the lights began to go out and the generator motors were turned off. As I stood there, I heard Kirk hail them from the dock and one of the crew men ran down the ship's ladder to the launch and went in to get him. I put down my icepack and got Con Taylor's binoculars.

I gave Jim Kirk a close looking at with them as the launch burbled back to the ship. I wanted to see if he had a gun on him. He didn't. Not one that I could see. Then I turned them on the crewman, and received a slight shock of recognition.

I was looking at the smartest one of the three men who had jumped me outside Chantal's house that night. The one who had called off the moronic-looking blond boy when he flashed his knife.

I supposed I owed him a small debt of gratitude. I didn't feel like it.

It had never occurred to me to look for my would-be muggers in Kirk's crew. I swung the glasses back to the ship, and right away spotted the moronic blond boy in the crew on deck. The third man, the one whose nose I'd smashed with my forehead, wasn't among them.

I put down the glasses, and got my icepack and my drink. On board the yacht the rest of the lights went out, and I watched the crew pile into the launch and head for shore. Only Kirk and the blond boy stayed on board. I watched them go down the forward hatch to the crew's quarters, where two lighted portholes stared back at me like eyes – the only lights left on the ship.

With my icepack and my drink I sat down on the bed and sat there for a while, thinking. Down below the crew tied up the launch and dispersed. It was funny, but I hadn't spotted a one of the three in town.

I thought some more.

After a while I got up and painfully began to dress. I didn't want to. I went downstairs and got out one of my snub-nosed .38s from my locked briefcase and put it in my belt under my shirt. Then I took the flexible flathead sap from the briefcase and put it in the hip pocket of my jeans. It was old-fashioned, my flathead. But I preferred it to the round club-shaped ones. It was more precise, and it didn't fracture as easily. One way or the other I meant to find out why those three had jumped me, and who had given the orders.

If I found out something about the murder too, that was all to the good.

CHAPTER THIRTY-SEVEN

There was a lot of chatter and laughter and clinking of cutlery out in front at Dmitri's and the jukebox blared some Greek song out over the water. Nobody paid the slightest attention to me.

The dock was beyond the taverna's circle of light. I untied somebody's skiff, and sculled it standing, out past the gabbling terrace towards the quiet yacht. Every stroke of the oars built a new fire under my left arm.

I didn't head for the ship's ladder. It was strictly illegal, what I was doing. At the stern I grabbed hold of the springline and stood in the skiff a while listening. Then I tied it and climbed stiffly but silently over the stern, trying not to grunt from the pain in my side.

The door to the big deck house was wide open. I looked it over, then silently descended its set of ship's stairs into the hold. I found myself in a long corridor running forward, with four cabin doors opening off either side. At the forward end light shone through a curtained half-door. From beyond it came low voices.

It was certainly my dream yacht, all right. I'd have given just about anything to have been its master and owner. My forehead had broken out in a sweat from the pain of that climb over the stern.

I didn't know what I expected to find. Certainly no million-dollar caches of heroin, even of hash. Not, anyway, without moving a lot of gear and floorboards and making a lot of noise.

Up forward the low voices hadn't stopped. The galley was on my left and I looked it over with a pocket flash. Then I started forward through the cabins. The first one on the right was locked. I had looked into two of the other cabins when the overhead lights went on and a voice behind me said, 'All right, hold it. Just told it right there. Don't reach for anything.' It was Kirk's voice.

I put my hands up to my shoulders and turned around. Kirk stood at the foot of the stairs wearing a mean grin, a big Luger in his hand.

'Stephanos!'

Behind me my moronic blond friend from the street fight appeared at the half-door. Kirk said something in Greek and the curtain dropped, and I heard feet scrambling up the ladder and running along the deck.

'I told him to keep talking,' Kirk grinned. 'Know how I cottoned to you? I felt it. The balance of the boat changed. I didn't hear you. Yes, sir.' He looked pleased with himself.

I walked along towards him. If I could get close enough. I wondered. My side was still hurting brightly from the climb over the stern. I wasn't in my best fighting form.

'There's been a rumour going around Athens that there was some kind of an agent floating around Tsatsos,' Kirk said.

The moronic blond boy had appeared behind him down the ship's stairs.

Kirk snorted. 'That's far enough. Let me just feel you up a little, Mr Lobo Davies.'

He patted me, found the pistol in my belt, stuffed it in his own belt, seemed about to quit, then felt behind me and found the sap.

'Oho. A regular arsenal. You all ready to go to war, Mr Lobo Davies.' He put the sap in his pocket and stepped back.

'You look like somebody else has been using you for a punching bag too,' he grinned. Suddenly he stepped in, fast as hell, and slugged me on the jaw with a left hook. I lit on my butt, my side screaming, and slid a few feet along the corridor. I sat still, shaking my head to clear it.

'You wouldn't be that agent, would you, Mr Lobo Davies? Get up, Mr Lobo Davies. What happened to your face?'

I got up, using my left arm and side and turning to the left, although it hurt like hell. I didn't want him to know I was incapacitated there.

'A bunch of your hippie clients tried to remodel it for me,' I said. It was the first I'd spoken.

'They're not my clients.' He looked as if he was going to hit me again. Instead, he reached behind him with a key and unlocked the locked door I had tried earlier. 'Let's just step in here. This is my country. Stephanos!'

The blond moved around behind me. Kirk backed into the cabin, the Luger steady on me. There wasn't much I could do. The blond boy pushed me roughly. The push made my side flare with hurt.

The cabin was almost severely austere, and scrupulously clean. The only furniture in it besides a tiny desk and chair was the bunk. The only adornment was a lovely colour photo of *Agoraphobe* under full sail and heeled over. Kirk put my gun and sap up on a little shelf behind him over the bunk, then pulled the little chair out to sit on.

But the captain didn't sit on the chair just yet. As he straightened from pulling the chair against the outside wall, he extended the movement, turned it into a swing, and belted me on the side of the jaw again with his left hand.

'Now, what are you doing on my ship?'

The blow was half strength but it knocked me into the corner of the bunk, even though I rode with it. My side sent me several wild signals of pain. I straightened up, shaking my head. The punch carried a value ratio of about ten of the hippie blows earlier.

'I want to know whether you're that agent I've been hearing about,' Kirk said. 'Are you?'

'I'm a private detective,' I said. 'On vacation.'

He belted me again in the same place. I sat down on the bunk. I knew if I was going to do anything at all, I was going to have to do it soon. I clamped my teeth down on the pain from my side, holding it in and not letting it swerve me, and made myself get up.

'I can hit a lot harder than that,' Kirk said with a flat mean grin. 'And I can slap you around some with this,' he lifted the Luger. 'That marks good. I can even shoot you, if I want. Nobody would ever know. Put a coat of chains on you and slip you over the side, they'd never find you. Water's sixty feet deep here, and nobody ever goes down in it. Harbour's too dirty. And nobody knows you're here. You didn't tell anybody you were coming. Now, say something. And say something important.'

'I don't think you'll shoot me,' I said, making my voice hard. 'I don't even think you'll pistol-whip me.'

'You don't, hunh?' Almost without lifting his hand, he hit me again, harder this time. I was knocked back into the corner, this time off my feet and on to the bunk.

I sat up, shaking my head. My head was buzzing that sleepy buzz right behind the ears. Always a warning. The bright red and white flag of pain in my side was streaming in the wind again. But this time when I got on my feet, I was standing where I wanted to be. To the left and just a hair in back of the blond boy – who now was grinning all over his moronic, vicious face.

'I can put this thing against your skin when I pull the trigger and nobody'll ever hear it,' Kirk said. 'I said, what are you doing on board my ship?'

'I came here because I recognized two of your crew,' I said. 'They're two of the three guys who tried to beat me up the other night. I'm not in the habit of letting people get away with that. I want to know why.'

'You want to know why, hunh?' Kirk snorted. This time he drew his fist back. Not much, but it was enough. In the cabin's close quarters I slipped half a step to my right, grabbed the boy and shoved him at Kirk. The punch glanced off his shoulder. I pushed him harder, into Kirk. My side seemed to shriek out loud. But the two of them fell into a tangle on to the bunk, the Luger caught between their bodies.

As they struggled, I booted the kid hard in the tailbone with my left foot, slammed my left knee into his back and stood on the knee, and reached my gun and sap down off the shelf above the bunk. I stepped back.

'Let go of it,' I said. 'Let me hear it hit the floor.'

As I spoke the boy got his feet under him and sprang back up, turning. The kick on the tailbone had hurt him bad, and there were tears of pain in his eyes. That made me feel fine. That made me feel excellent.

As he turned at me, I rapped him sharply on his right wrist with the sap. He collapsed to the floor, nursing a paralysed hand. Behind him the Luger thudded on the deck.

I scooped it up, straightened and stuck it in my belt. From the floor the kid started at me again. This time I rapped him hard on the point of the left shoulder. He collapsed again, with a paralysed left arm. He sat holding his two arms in his lap.

I had already sensed Kirk moving at me from the bunk. Tall or not, he loomed up like some kind of colossus. I stepped to meet him, and laid the barrel of my little .38 on him.

He was anticipating the sap, but I didn't want to knock him out. I hit him on the left side of his neck, just where the neck meets the skull. He sat down on the bunk, his eyes glazed, his mouth open and his tongue sticking out.

'How does it feel?' I said.

'Thanks for not cutting me,' he said in a dulled voice. It would have knocked any other man unconscious.

. 'Go screw,' I said. 'You're entirely welcome.' I stepped back to the wall behind me, and put my back on it.

'You take a lot of chances,' Kirk said from the bunk.

'Not really,' I said. 'You were handicapped. You didn't want to shoot me. Even if you only cut me up with it, it wouldn't do your reputation any good. I'd show it to Pekouris.'

'You think he would help you, hunh?' Kirk said dully.

I noted this little slip, if it was a slip. Maybe it wasn't. Maybe it was deliberate. I tried to ease my left side by pushing my back against the wall with my legs. 'Now, maybe we can talk a little,' I said.

Dully, Kirk nodded slightly towards the blond boy. 'I don't like to talk too much in front of him.'

I looked at the boy. 'He doesn't understand English, does he?'

'He's a wharf rat from Piraeus. You never know with them. He may have enough English to figure out what we're saying.'

'I'll fix that for you,' I said crisply. 'I'll be pleased to.' I shifted the gun and sap and stepped to the boy and rapped him with surgical precision above the left ear. Horrible to Chantal, maybe. Or to Sonny Duval. But it wasn't horrible to me. And it wasn't to Kirk. The boy's head dropped like a stone, without a sound.

Kirk grinned dully. 'You're pretty good with that sap.'

'He won't even have a headache,' I said. 'At least, not any worse than the one you gave me.' I shifted the gun and sap. 'Now, where were we?'

'You were just saying maybe we could talk a little,' Kirk said. He rubbed his neck. 'I think that's a good idea.'

I pushed my back against the wall again with my legs. My side was giving me real bloody hell. It was making my scalp tingle again. And Kirk's face danced a little in front of me as I looked at him.

'You know, somebody shot at me a while ago,' I said.

He only grinned. 'They did? Somebody must not like you, hunh?'

'I guess not. They seemed pretty serious about it.'

I pulled his Luger out and sniffed it. It didn't smell strong, but it had been cleaned recently. With Hoppe's # 9.

'It wasn't that one,' Kirk said.

'First,' I said, 'I want to know who was behind your three lovable characters trying to knock me over the other night.'

'I don't mind answering that. That was Girgis.'

'Blame the dead. Why haven't I seen any of them in the town?'

He grinned, and hitched himself up a little on the bunk. He was coming out of it. 'I thought I'd better give them a few days off.'

'Where's the third one?'

'He didn't come back. You gave him a pretty sore nose. They had to pull a lot of it back out of his eyes.'

'Girgis wanted to scare me off of him, was that it?'

'That was the general idea. He asked me to do it. I did it for him as a favour.'

'And he asked you to have your hard boys handle me. And you did it as a favour. But your boat left Tsatsos for Athens that same evening. Before I got jumped, Kirk.'

'I stopped at the next port ten miles up the coast, and came back and picked them up. It's an easy run back down here in the launch.'

'And Girgis was killed the same night. It would have been easy to do both jobs on the same trip. Or even to make a second trip in the launch, alone,' I said.

'It would have at that. But I didn't do that. Hell, I told you, Girgis and I were pals.' He grinned.

'I heard you were such good pals you might have wanted to take over that paying trade of his for him.'

Kirk shook his head. 'You didn't hear that. Who would have told you that? It wouldn't have worked. I'm not here enough. I don't know any of these kids here the way Girgis did. You have to be here. That was his

211

problem. He couldn't get away enough to get all the stuff he wanted. So I started bringing it down from Athens for him.'

I tried another tack. 'Did it ever occur to you that the person or persons who knocked off Girgis may be trying to muscle in? And that you might be on the list?'

He grinned benignly. 'No. It didn't. And it still don't. There's nobody here that big. And there isn't that much money in hash. Nobody gives a damn. Nobody would risk a murder for it.'

I couldn't fault that. So I gave him the rest of it. 'That's the point. That's a very good point. But there is also a little heroin involved, it seems.'

'I don't know anything about that,' Kirk said promptly. 'If Girgis was selling H, I never heard about it. And I wouldn't touch it. Heroin is dangerous stuff nowadays. With all these American agents running around all over Europe.' He looked at me sanctimoniously.

I didn't answer. Marie had explicitly said he was bringing in small amounts of H for those who had to have it. And more, that Girgis himself refused to touch it.

'If Girgis was selling H, I don't know anything about it,' Kirk said again.

'What about this boss of yours?' I said. 'What's his name? Kronitis? Is he in on this whole deal? He owns the *Polaris*, too.'

'Mr Kronitis? If he found I was in anything like selling hash, he'd fire me like a shot. The same goes for Girgis.' There was a sudden fervency in his voice, that made it sound like the truth.

I probed it further. 'Kronitis must know about the hash you guys have been handling.'

'For God's sake, don't go and tell him,' Kirk said. 'You'll have me out of a job.' He meant it.

Beside us on the floor the blond boy began to stir a little. He groaned. I looked down at him. My legs were beginning to tremble. Partly from holding my back so tight against the wall.

'I guess I might as well be going,' I said. 'His anæsthetic seems to be wearing off.' I grinned at Kirk. 'Unless you want me to put him to sleep again and talk more.'

He didn't answer me. He just looked down at the boy, apparently lost in thought. Then he shook his head.

212

'But get one thing straight,' I said. 'I'm no agent. I'm a private detective. I've been hired by a client to find out who killed Girgis Stourkos, and that's what I'm trying to do. I don't give a damn about anything else.'

'It's easy enough to guess your rich client,' Kirk said with a leer. 'Chantal von Anders's been screwing Girgis for over a year. I know all about that.'

I shook my head. 'Wrong guess. Anyway, I never tell who my clients are.'

'Well, I'd like to find out who killed Girgis, too. I'd like to help you. Why do you think I'm talking to you?'

I wanted to laugh. But I was afraid of what it would do to my side. I was remembering when he had had the gun, and the drop, and the upper hand. Some help. 'I ought to break your jaw with this,' I said, pulling the Luger out of my belt again. 'I'll leave it up on the wheel housing for you, instead.'

I pushed the blond boy out of the way with my foot to get the door open. The movement sent a pain shooting through my side again. It suddenly occurred to me that if Kirk had wanted to talk longer, I couldn't have done it anyway. I opened the door and looked back at them.

'Hey, no hard feelings, hey?' Kirk said. He rubbed his neck. 'You're a tough hombre. You hurt my neck.'

'What do you think you did to my jaw?' I said. 'No. No hard feelings,' I lied. I shut the door behind me.

Up on deck I ejected the magazine from the Luger, and looked at it. It was full except for one. I drew back the elbow-type receiver, and a shell popped out on to the wheel housing. He had had it loaded, all right. I left the three objects on the housing.

When I climbed down over the stern to the skiff, I thought I wasn't going to make it. It was all I could do not to groan out loud. When I sculled the skiff back in, standing up, the lights of the taverna danced wildly in front of my eyes. I gritted my teeth and kept sculling.

After I tied the skiff, I walked quietly through the still-rioting late drinkers at the taverna and went home and went to bed. I wouldn't be any good to Chantal or anybody else, this night.

I had been beaten unconscious, rib-kicked, shot at and missed, then beaten nearly unconscious again on the jaw until I could hardly touch it, and then threatened with killing. I had certainly earned my pay from Kronitis today, even if I hadn't found out anything significant. What else could happen to me?

What else could happen to me was that I couldn't sleep. Whenever I moved the pain in my side woke me. My whole side was hot with fever when I touched it.

I passed a fitful night, as they say in the newspapers about sick Presidents and other world leaders. Nobody came by and wrote it up.

CHAPTER THIRTY-EIGHT

The bad thing about injuries and bruises is they're still there when you wake up the next morning. They don't go away. I was barely able to crawl off the bed, in the morning. Shaving loosened me up a little. But my side made it almost impossible for me to move. I hobbled downstairs and downed some strong coffee and went down to the basement apartment to Georgina.

'Do you think you could help me tape up my side,' I said, 'if I showed you how?'

'Why, of course.' She was delighted, in fact. 'What's wrong with it?'

'Just a bad sprain,' I said. 'But it's uncomfortable.'

Con Taylor had all sorts and sizes of adhesive tape lying around. I chose a roll of $2\frac{1}{2}$ inch Johnson & Johnson's. I tore the strips off the roll for her, stuck them by their ends to the edge of the table, had her put the scissors beside them.

'My God, you're beat up,' Georgina said when I took off my shirt. She touched my shoulders. 'You have a very manly torso, sir,' she said. 'I've never been up this close.'

She loved every second of it. I stood in the middle of the room with my arms up like some grotesque flower stalk, while Georgina buzzed and darted around me like a hummingbird on a flight mission in a stand of hollyhocks. She tried to pump me about the fight, but I clammed up.

Women always seem to love to help you, when you've

been hurt; much more than when you're unhurt. I think it gives them some kind of weird, secret sadistic sexual gratification of some sort.

I kept up a running comment of instruction.

'That's it. No, start around farther to the back. That's it. A little lower. Now, pull it tight. Pull it as tight as you can. That's it. Never mind about hurting me. Now, smooth it down. Never mind the loose ends. We'll cut them later. That's it. Now, put the next one two-thirds up the first one, overlapping it. That's it. Pull it tight.' I didn't know if she knew this particular bandage was the bandage for busted ribs. She didn't ask. And I didn't tell her.

When we finished, I was trussed up my left side like some mummy. But I felt almost immediate relief. In the mirror I looked like some right-handed gladiator putting on his suit to go out in the ring. I put my shirt back on.

I figured, with a little rest, I could get by like that and do almost anything I had to do. I certainly wasn't about to give Kronitis back his retainer.

I kissed Georgina on the forehead, thanked her and went back upstairs.

About ten minutes later Pekouris roared up down below in the police jeep. He was alone this time. He wasted no time on preliminary ceremonies.

'Is this what you call keeping your investigations quiet? Getting in a public brawl with that gang of hippies?'

'I'm sorry about that,' I said. 'There wasn't anything I could do. They jumped me.'

I had already decided I wouldn't mention my set-to with Kirk, nor the shooting either.

'My informants inform me you provoked it so strongly no one but a saint could have avoided fighting you,' Pekouris said coldly.

'I guess there's some truth in that,' I said after a moment.

My unwillingness to leap in with irrefutable explanations seemed to set him back. He was too used to the European style, I guessed, which considered vehement counteraccusation the best defence for everything.

'Do you want to prefer charges?'

'No,' I said. 'I wouldn't remember any of their faces.'

'Against the hippie Steve? Or the place?'

'It happened outside his place. No,' I said. 'Unless, of course, you want me to prefer charges.'

'I confess I do not understand you, Davies,' he said. 'You are certainly not the Greek idea of what a police officer should be.'

I felt like saying thank you.

'I found out what I wanted,' I said. 'Which was that this Chuck is crazy. I think homicidally crazy.'

'I told you all that,' Pekouris said. 'Before. I did it by deduction. You did not have to prove it. –

'Well, I have some news for you in this department, Davies,' he said. 'Some good, and some of it bad.'

'Let me have the bad news first,' I said. 'What did the laboratory say?'

'That is the good news. Our laboratory in Athens thinks it is highly probable that they can find and distinguish any human blood that might be on the machete mingled with goat's blood. They are not sure they can determine the human blood type, though, under those circumstances.'

'That's good news. Are you going to pick him up?'

'I would not have done that in any case,' Pekouris said disdainfully. 'If they could not determine the blood type. But all this is an academic question now.'

'What do you mean, academic?'

'I have been on the telephone twice with Athens this morning,' Pekouris said. 'In addition to the laboratory. They are dropping the case. They have ordered me to close it out as unsolved and to send in the dossier.' He looked dismal suddenly, Pekouris. Not in any moral or idealistic way. But like a bloodhound who has suddenly been pulled away off a hot scent and put back on the leash. Like the bloodhound, his jaws appeared to ache.

'Closing it out!' I said. 'But it's only been three days! What the hell?'

'There is no mystery about it,' Pekouris said. 'Our main tourist season for the summer begins in ten days. They do not want to risk the bad publicity and the resulting cancellations. Our tourist season is very important to us.'

I turned to stare at him. My belly began to tickle with wanting to laugh. I couldn't help it, I began to laugh out loud. 'Poor Pekouris,' I said.

'Not at all,' he said stiffly. 'I am the same thing as a soldier. I obey my orders. Theirs is not to reason why. Theirs is but to do, and die.'

'I didn't see the movie,' I said. 'But I read the book.'

He only frowned. 'In fact, I quite agree with them. Our national tourist season is much more important than the murder of some petty hashish smuggler. Right at this moment, a rumour is going out that it was not a person who was killed in the Xenia gardens at all, but a white hairless monkey from South America which was somebody's pet. And that the boy who found the headless body was confused.'

'It's you who is putting this out?' I said.

He simply blinked at me, and pressed his thick lips together tightly. 'It will confuse. It will inject an element of doubt. Right now, it is being spread around all day. By tonight two-thirds of the people on Tsatsos will believe there was no murder. The other third wouldn't care anyway.'

'Too bad Girgis's so well known,' I said dryly.

'Yes. But that can't be helped.'

'I'm being paid to find the killer,' I said.

Pekouris leaned against the wall with folded arms. 'I've been ordered to tell you to stop your investigations.'

I gave him a look. 'You know I'm not going to do that.'

He nodded at me, 'You have no choice. I already have been given the authority to put you on a plane and throw you right out of Greece, if you do not. To make sure, I am placing a telephone call to Mr Kronitis this morning.

'Officially; officially, you are ordered to cease any action of yours having to do with this murder.'

'Go ahead and call him.'

'I mean to.'

'Well, this is a gas,' I said, and grinned at him. 'You and me enemies, Pekouris.' I pouched out my lips. The whole thing sounded like something out of Dick Tracy. That rumour, about a hairless South American monkey, that knocked me out.

'Unofficially,' Pekouris said. He looked around for the housekeeper. 'Unofficially, there is still one thing that might be done. Just between us two chickens.'

'And what's that?' I thought I could guess.

'If I can get hold of that machete,' he smiled. 'Some

way or other. If I can have it tested, and the tests come out right, there is a good chance I can cause the thing still to work. I think Athens would back me up, with evidence like that. But, naturally, I cannot confiscate it, myself.' He suddenly looked like some Lebanese banker.

'You're asking me to steal it for you?'

'I am asking you nothing. I am not even offering a suggestion. And if you say I did, I –'

'I know. You'll deny it,' I said. 'Hell, Pekouris, I can't do that. I'm liable to get myself killed, if I go up in there again. The younger generation takes a very dim view of me. You saw what they did to me last night.'

'I don't mind admitting it would be a large feather in my cap in Athens,' he smiled.

'I'll bet.'

'You would not get credit. But you would have the satisfaction of a job well done.'

Before I could even jeer, he put his hands up and tilted his head on one side, like some character out of *The Merchant of Venice*. 'But I'm *asking* nothing.'

'You're appealing to my conscience? You're a bad judge of character. I'm famous for not having any.'

'No, but you want to keep on getting paid by Kronitis.'

'Of all the Machiavellian, Levantine, middle-European,' I had to pause, 'shenanigans.' I was forced to grin. 'I'm promising nothing, Pekouris,' I said.

'No one is asking.' He pushed away from the wall and straightened his blue suit coat. 'Just remember, any bit of notoriety attached to you, any word about you investigating those boys again *or anybody else*, just one bit, and –' He jerked his thumb in the direction of the sparkling horizon we could see through the open doors, out beyond the shaded porch, and the sun-faded little harbour.

'I'm expecting to go to Athens in a couple of days. On business. For quite some time.'

'I see,' I said.

'Anything that happens must happen before then.'

I walked out on the porch to watch him drive away another time. Portly, heavy-shouldered, an excellent eater, Pekouris. He sat his jeep like it was some old-time charger, and herded it down the road the same way.

I went back inside.

He wore with enormous vanity his certain measure of

power, did Pekouris. And he would use it without scruple when he could. He was willing to swallow it down humbly when he couldn't. He was the personification and spit and image of my picture acquired over fifty years of what the whole human race stood for and was worth.

It was a pretty dismal image to put up against fifty years. If you couldn't laugh at it, you would want to go away and shoot yourself.

I sat down and called Chantal. My mind was a complete blank. I had no plans towards any scheme. And I wasn't going to work up any for Pekouris.

Morning was the only time to be sure of getting Chantal, and she was in. But she had a lunch date, a date to play bridge in the afternoon, and a dinner for the evening.

'I didn't get up there last night,' I said.

'I know all about it. You got yourself into another fight. The great tough private detective. Fighting with a bunch of children.'

I was a little stung. 'They didn't hit and kick like children,' I said mildly. 'Anyway, I didn't come.'

'You were too bruised and wounded. I know. Nobody's talking about anything else. I've had five phone calls. They're all delighted to call me. My new boyfriend. And out fighting with children.'

'Lay off it about children,' I said sharply. There was a slightly startled pause. I can make my voice quite sharp. 'I wanted to come. And while we're on it, I'm getting tired of seeing you only late at night, after your social evenings, like some hired stud. Lobo Davies Stud Service. Available At All Hours. Satisfaction Guaranteed.'

That slowed her down a little. 'That's a nasty thing to say. But then you never were noted for your manners.'

I wouldn't answer that.

'Well, do you have another fight scheduled for to-night?' she said in a less bitchy tone.

'No,' I said. 'But I'm not coming up to your house for just a little late sex after the servants are sent off. You want to see me, you can have a date with me.'

'I can arrange it for you to come to this dinner party. Very easily. But you don't like my dinner parties.'

'No. I don't. That's not good enough.'

'Well, do you want me to meet you somewhere after?'

'I'll meet you at Georgio's,' I said. 'The one you call the dancing taverna. That's near where you'll be.'

There was a pause. 'All right,' she said. Another pause. 'But you had better be there when I get there. I'm not going to go in and sit at a table alone, there, and wait for you.'

'Whatever you say, Countess,' I said.

We arranged the times, and hung up. I went across and lay down on one of the couches in front of the fireplace. I didn't know if I was up to meeting anybody anywhere. The constant hot scream in my side was gone. But it was replaced by a vast monstrous toothache down there, with roots all the way down to my crotch.

I had not been down long enough to doze, when the phone rang. I got up stiffly and went over to answer it. It was Kronitis.

Pekouris had called him, all right.

But first I had to go through the long and dismal formalities the old man seemed to dote on. First, I had the male secretary, who meticulously checked if I was me. Then the old man himself, with all his how-are-yous.

'What do you think you ought to do?' he asked me finally. It sounded very cautious.

'Well,' I said irritably, 'it would seem to me that when the police are dropping it is when you ought to want to go ahead. Assuming you want the murder solved. But I'll do whatever you instruct me. I can return your retainer tomorrow.'

'No, no. No, no. That retainer is yours. That was the way I made the arrangement.' A pause. 'As for the rest, I guess I had better just leave it up to you – .

'But Pekouris said he would throw you out of Greece if you didn't stop your investigations. I wouldn't like that to happen. Nor would Freddy Tarkoff.'

'I'd like to keep on nosing around,' I said. 'For a few days. If that's all right with you.'

'You don't think it would be better to just give up the whole thing?' Again, it sounded excessively cautious.

'Only if you say so.'

'Very well. I'll authorize that,' he said. 'What you said. It's whatever you think, Mr Davies.'

'You know, I got myself shot at last night,' I said.

There was a sharp intake of breath at the other end. 'You mean, with a gun?'

'Yes, sir,' I said. 'With a real gun.'

'Isn't that awfully, uh, professional?'

'I don't know,' I said. 'They missed me. You wouldn't have any ideas on that, would you, Mr Kronitis?'

'No.' A pause. 'No, I certainly wouldn't.'

We went through a long and excessively courteous formality of saying goodbye which could have been done in two words.

I lay back down on the couch. Finally I was able to doze, after a couple of stiff Scotches.

I ate the old woman's lousy cooking for lunch again, and hobbled around the house most of the afternoon. My side hurt too much to read with any pleasure. I slept a little. For dinner I ate the same greasy lamb stew at the taverna. The Greeks never seemed to have any other kind of meat. My teeth and jaws were beginning to hunger after a good thick sirloin. American-style.

At eleven I caught a horsecab in front of the taverna to take me up the hill and across the point to Georgio's.

CHAPTER THIRTY-NINE

I hadn't been back there since the night I'd accosted Girgis outside. The place didn't seem to remember me. It didn't remember Girgis, either.

The huge jukebox still blared the same Greek songs interspersed with foxtrots.

There were a lot of the Greek tourists. After a little, you learned to recognize them. I took a table where I could watch the door for Chantal.

I had to admit she was a beauty, when she came in. Her shortish hair looked just right for a hot summer night. And she always had that look of class. She was dressed ingeniously in an outfit that did not look out of place at Georgio's, and at the same time would look right at home at the Danish count's. At that distance, with make-up, and with clothes on, you could never have told her age.

I saw her before she saw me. My table happened to be camouflaged from her. So I watched her change her roles at the door.

It was like watching an actress shake herself and change her personality before stepping on stage. From a hard-eyed, suspicious, acquisitive European woman, totally self-concerned, she became a youngish, carefree, flighty, rich man's plaything, too cheerful and spoiled to remember her last bank-account balance.

I got to my feet.

She had been so openly hostile and angry the several times on the phone that I had forgotten the feeling of deviousness she always gave me when she was in front of me in the flesh.

'This isn't the place I would have picked, but it doesn't matter.' She gave me a cute grin. 'It's good to see you any way at all.' She was a little high.

I got my drink and we moved to a table at the very back, where we could look out over the outdoor patio and the sea beyond. The moon made a twinkling ladder at us off the water.

'I'm drinking cognac,' Chantal said.

I ordered two.

'I've got a few items of news for you. Then I've got a couple of things I want to talk to you about,' I said.

She was looking around the place. She seemed hardly to have heard me. 'I didn't know you had taken up the Greek dancing?'

I shrugged. It made me wince involuntarily.

'Oh. You're really hurt.'

'Nothing that won't heal overnight,' I said.

She looked at me with large eyes. 'You're so stupid, really. They all say you were knocked completely unconscious.'

I made a face.

'What is hurt?'

'My back,' I lied. 'I sprained it.'

'Must we go through all this dating routine, before I can get you home and get my hands on you?' she smiled. 'I suppose we must. The male vanity must be appeased.'

'It's good to see you outside your bastion once in a while,' I said. 'I was beginning to forget what you looked like with clothes on.'

She was smiling. 'Oh! You really are the bastard. Aren't you?'

'If you say so.'

'And that's what women love about you; and you know it; and you play it; Lobo Davies, the lovable bastard. What's all this news you have?'

I looked out at the yellow moon path. 'Would you like to take a walk outside first?'

'If you like.' She got up.

I followed her. The waiter arrived just then with the cognacs. I motioned him to leave them. Outside we walked back and forth on the stone patio. It was a little cooler out there, but not much. When I turned to her, she reached out to put her arms around me. I steeled myself not to wince when she squeezed me. But she drew back.

'What's this? What's that on your side?'

'Adhesive tape. For the back. It's nothing.'

'Oh, you really are such a fool. I'm not even going to ask you why you were up there. Or what you did, to have a fight.' This time she put her arms around me carefully, and didn't squeeze. I kissed her. She felt good, and natural, under my hands; as if it was on a woman her age that my hands belonged. But I couldn't forget that first look on her face back there at the door.

'Oh, that's good!' she said when I let her go. 'Come on, let's go back inside. I want my cognac.'

As we walked back to the steps, I looked down at the water and saw something floating in the edge of the moon path that looked like a log. The wavelets nudged it repeatedly against the sand. I stopped, but my side was hurting too much to bother going to look at it. Anyway, I wasn't doing any driftwood sculpture this year. I followed Chantal in.

She grabbed her glass. 'What's all this news, now?'

'Well, first, I've been hired by someone, to find Girgis's killer. And for a goodly sum.'

'Oh, really?' She kept on looking at me. She didn't seem so surprised. 'Who might that be?' I had a sudden, weird hunch that she already knew.

'You'd never guess in a million years.'

'I might.' She looked at me speculatively. She seemed to be deciding whether to make her guess. The only one who could have told her was Kronitis. He was the only one who knew, besides Pekouris. She dropped her eyes. 'No, I guess I couldn't guess.'

'Try,' I said.

'No. I never would guess it,' she said without raising her eyes.

I chalked up one for my side.

'The second thing, that I found out,' I said, 'is that Jim Kirk has been pushing a little H on Tsatsos.'

'Jim Kirk?' She looked up, and her eyes had that startled-deer look I'd seen them get before at the mention of Kirk. I chalked up another one. 'You mean the captain of the *Agoraphobe*?'

'The very same,' I said mildly. 'I wonder if old Mr Kronitis knows about that?'

'I have no idea,' Chantal said. 'I wouldn't think so. I would think he'd fire Kirk right away.' She looked away from me, outdoors. 'Isn't the moon path lovely?'

'Did you know that old Ambassador Pierson is an H addict?' I said.

She looked back at me crossly. 'You really are a nosy bastard, aren't you? Freddy Tarkoff was quite right about you.'

'That's what people pay me for,' I said.

'Well don't be proud of it. Nobody's paying you to check up on poor old Ambassador Pierson.'

'I haven't told anybody but you,' I said. 'And you already knew.'

She jerked her shoulders at me, as if something had pricked her in the back. 'All right! I did it as a favour to Kirk. He asked me because he knew about the hashish and Girgis. I also did it as a favour for the old Ambassador. But I didn't get a penny for doing it!'

'That doesn't make any difference in the eyes of the law.'

'And I know all that, too. I'd still do it again!'

'How long have you known about the old Ambassador?'

'Oh. Oh, a long long time. Everybody I know on the island knows about it.'

'But how did Kirk find out about it?'

'That, I don't know. Maybe the old gentleman went to him.'

I didn't try to refute that, but it wouldn't hold water. If Pierson went to Kirk himself, Kirk wouldn't need Chantal as a carrier. I said nothing.

'Sources for heroin have been drying up in Europe lately, with the Americans running all over,' Chantal said. 'I guess the old gentleman was having trouble getting it through his regular channels.'

'It interests me how Kirk gets it so easy.'

Again she got that still, startled-deer look. 'Kirk apparently has all sorts of avenues for all sorts of things in Athens. And I'm sure Leonid Kronitis doesn't know about any of it.'

'I'm sure he doesn't. Was that the, quote, further secret, unquote, that you've been holding back on me all this time?'

She looked at me as if she didn't understand me.

'You could have told me that,' I said gently.

She still looked as if she didn't understand. Then she drew in a deep, deep breath, which she held for several long seconds before she finally spoke. As if thinking, or deciding. 'Yes. Yes, as a matter of fact, it was. I wanted to tell you about it. I wanted to tell you that same night I told you about the hashish and Girgis. But I just couldn't stand the thought of implicating the poor old Ambassador. I'd do anything in order not to hurt him.'

Lying, again.

'Don't worry about me hurting him,' I said.

'But how did you find out about it?' she said thinly.

I was getting irritated. All these damned convolutions. But I swallowed it down. Chantal obviously didn't know about Sweet Marie's carrying H for Kirk to the addicts at the Construction, or she wouldn't even have asked me that. I fell back on Pekouris another time.

'I have my little ways,' I said.

'Yes. Yes, you certainly do,' Chantal said. 'Sometimes I wish you'd never come to this island. Sometimes I wish you'd go away. Just leave, right now, without worrying about finishing your vacation. You're like a damned bulldog. When you get your teeth into something.'

'A moray eel,' I said. 'They won't even let go when you cut off the head. You have to pry the jaws apart with a knife or a screwdriver. And their bite is poison.'

'Ambassador Pierson picked up his heroin addiction in the Far East, when he was serving your country there,' Chantal said.

'A casualty in the line of duty,' I said.

'Exactly.'

'It's what we call the Oriental's Revenge,' I said. 'It's the way they figured out to get even with us, for all the terrible things we've done to them.' I grinned. 'It's all a Chinese plot.'

She just looked at me.

Maybe it all seemed too tough to her. But I was beginning to feel tough. As far as that went, she was pretty tough herself.

But there was no opportunity to go any farther into all that. So I did not get to tell her how I was against the Vietnamese war, just on military principles alone, the logistics, the length of supply line, if for no other reasons, and that we had no business there, and never had had, and that we were maintaining a criminal government there, which was also making a fortune selling us heroin on the side, as well as ruining our own economy on the operation.

There was no opportunity to tell all that, because outside on the edge of the outdoor patio by the water a man had started to holler something in Greek. In a voice of awful urgency.

'Voitheia!' the man hollered. 'Voitheia, voitheia!'

I had picked up a few Greek words and I knew that word meant Help. 'Help, help!' he was hollering.

'Voitheia! Voitheia!' he called again.

I was on my feet before I remembered Chantal. There was no mistaking the urgency. Or the shock. It was a young couple who had passed our table going out to walk on the patio the same way we had. On my feet I could see them both standing silhouetted against the twinkling moon path. The man was by the water, the woman a few yards back.

'Wait here,' I said.

'No, I'll come,' Chantal said behind me. I didn't stop to argue.

I didn't know how, but I knew before I got there. Probably it was a combination of associations. The sea. Sonny's boat. Seeing the low taverna from out there on

226

the water. That was when I had first seen the figure. Coming back we had passed the building again, but the black figure and its little float had been miles away by then. This stretch of coast was apparently her private bailiwick.

It was her, all right. The man had rolled her over face up, and then seen there was nothing to do. She was wearing the foam rubber helmet and the wet-suit. The mask was gone.

In the moonlight, against all that black, the skin of her face was as pale as tanned skin can get. Paler than ivory. It was easy to see why. There wasn't any blood left in her.

I could hear people running up behind me, as I had run. I had forgotten my side. I knelt on one knee in the skim of water.

It was easy enough to read. The wet-suit was buoyant. She wore enough lead to give her a hair less than neutral buoyancy. Dead, she had floated a foot or two below the surface, until the wind and the sea had rolled her up here.

Her left arm had been nearly amputated at the elbow; and her right shoulder had been torn wide open, down into the neck. A rubber wet-suit was no armour for the kind of force that had hit Marie. I looked at the wounds closely. She had been bled completely empty long before the sea rolled her up on this sand.

Nothing, no fish, had touched her or nibbled her. She had not been in the water long enough yet to begin to swell. Except for the wounds, she lay there just as perfect as she had ever been. Except, of course, she was dead.

'Oh, no,' I heard Chantal say behind me. 'Oh, no.'

The nail polish on the manicured fingers looked black in the moonlight, against the paleness of skin. I felt sick. There wasn't anything, not a damn thing I could do for her. My stomach seemed to have fallen completely away out from under me.

There was a growing murmur of other voices behind me. 'Karcharias, karcharias,' some of them were muttering. Shark, shark. I looked around at Chantal for confirmation. 'Shark,' she said. I nodded, and looked at the wounds and the rest of her again. They were dead wrong. I knew better. I had seen shark bite. A shark's serrated teeth were as sharp as a well-honed knife blade. And no shark in the world would swim off and leave all that dead meat uneaten.

What had hit Marie was something heavy, and blunt-edged, and turning at high speed. Like a boat propeller. And it hadn't hit her just once but twice. The boat driven by the man, or woman, who had hit Marie had turned and come back and hit her a second time. She hadn't been killed by any accident. She'd been murdered.

I got up and walked away. My wet pants leg slapped against my shin. Water sloshed in my shoes. I had a sudden flash memory picture of her striding nude into the sea at the hippie beach that day, and went sick again all over. Those heavy-hanging, pointed breasts, and the lean rounded rump. That beautiful lifeful stride.

Everybody had used her in her life. She had been used, and cheated, by just about everybody she had ever come in contact with. Now, somebody else had used and cheated her in the final, worst way possible.

And I had been worrying about Pete Gruner getting it.

'Perhaps you had better take us home,' Chantal said quietly from behind me.

'Yes. Come on,' I said.

Well, I had just saved myself several hundred dollars of Kronitis's retainer money, I thought. I gave Chantal a bleakly bitter smile.

Down by the water a pompous little man with a watermelon paunch was taking things over. He was a doctor, apparently. He motioned the crowd back, and said something to two big fishermen. The fishermen went obediently into the water to haul Marie out for him.

I suddenly wanted to go down there and slug him in his pompous paunch and then break his jaw for him.

'Come on,' I said, 'let's go.'

'There's nothing we can do.'

'Not a thing,' I said. 'Nothing at all.'

We passed the chief of police and two of his young men. They were carrying their inevitable stretcher and blankets. The chief nodded to me. He had started smiling warily at me since Pekouris had adopted me.

I thought he must think I was doing a bang-up job of being around to find his bodies for him.

CHAPTER FORTY

We didn't talk in the horsecab. I was in a state of semi-shock. Chantal was sensitive enough to know that and kept her mouth shut.

I couldn't get over it about Marie. I couldn't come out of it. I was in that state of straining disbelief, where you try to reconstruct the sequence of reality. You want to make events that have already flowed past you in the time river take a different pattern, so they will cause a different ending, which itself has already flowed past you into inevitability. I called it the *If Only Blues*.

If only I had gone out with her when she . . .

If only I hadn't got hurt and stayed in the . . .

It was a fruitless process. But I couldn't come out of it. Your language got jerky, battering against that brick wall of passed reality. You didn't finish sentences.

At the house Chantal set out a full bottle of brandy on the polished, heavy table in the stone living-room.

I gave her a silly grin and said, 'Thanks but I'm going back to Scotch. It's better for me for long-range imbibing.'

She poured and downed two quick brandies for herself, then got a Scotch bottle and put it by the brandy bottle, softly. 'And you're going to do some long-range imbibing?'

'You understand she was killed, don't you?' I said. 'Murdered?'

She stared at me. 'No. I didn't understand that.'

'She wasn't hit by any shark,' I said. 'She was hit by a boat. Which then turned and came back and hit her a second time – probably as she was struggling in the water with her amputated, or nearly amputated, arm. Which arm she had thrown up, for protection, to ward off the first pass. Probably, she saw the second pass coming, and was able to jerk her head out of the way, but in doing so bobbed her shoulder up into the propeller.'

Chantal didn't say anything.

'That's the way I piece it together,' I said. 'From the evidence.'

'God,' she said, in a long sigh.

After a moment she put her glass down. She picked up the brandy bottle as if it seemed too heavy to lift.

'You're sure it was a boat?'

'No question.'

'And you're sure they came back, and hit her a second time?'

'No question, either. A double-motored boat couldn't have hit her on both sides at once just like that. Too far apart. Even a double outboard couldn't.'

She downed the third brandy.

'Whoever killed her is also the person or persons who killed Girgis,' I said.

'I think you've got murder on the brain,' Chantal said in a low voice.

'If I find Girgis's murderer, I'll find Marie's. I know that.'

'You thought a lot of her, didn't you?'

'Yes. I didn't sleep with her, though. If that's what you mean.'

'Then you were the only one who didn't.'

'She was young. When you're that young, and Marie, you don't realize you'll survive the anguish of being young. That it will pass and you'll survive it.'

'Survive it,' Chantal said. 'But survive it only to gain another anguish.'

'But of a different quality. Less intense. One that you can live with, and know you can survive.'

'Sometimes, I wonder.'

'No you don't. You've never wondered for a second.'

She picked up the brandy bottle and looked at it and waggled it, thoughtfully. 'Aren't you going to have a drink?'

'Sure. I'll have one in a minute,' I said. 'I think I'll have quite a few.'

She sighed, and brushed her hair back with the back of her hand. 'I don't blame you.'

'She got cheated again,' I said. 'Marie always got cheated by somebody. The really young almost always get cheated. That's how they pay their dues. They don't like it. I don't like it. There's nothing anybody can do about it. And now somebody, somebody or other, has cheated her again. She never got her chance to learn you can survive youth.'

'I suppose this is become a vendetta for you, now hasn't it?'

'It sure has,' I said.

'I think I'll leave you down here,' Chantal said. She lifted her hip off the edge of the big table where she'd been sitting, still waggling the brandy bottle, and studying it. 'But I'll be upstairs. If you want me for anything. Anything at all,' she added.

'Thanks. I'd like to be by myself a while.'

'I understand.' She went to the stairs, and started up with the brandy bottle.

I got up and got myself a glass. I got a big one. I filled the crystal tumbler two-thirds full of straight whisky. I didn't want any ice in it. I wanted it to burn.

I took the whisky and walked over with it to the lighted portrait of Chantal as a young woman, and stood looking at it and put down two hefty belts of the Scotch. Chantal must already have been three or four years older than Marie, when this portrait was done. The whisky burned, all the way down, satisfyingly.

I turned around and saw she was still standing on the stair, looking at me looking at her portrait. When she saw me look at her, she said simply, 'Good night,' and went up one step. Then she stopped. She came back down three steps.

'I'm afraid that I think I'm falling in love with you, Lobo,' she said, and smiled, and ran up the stairs. I listened to her go on up.

I took my glass back to the table and reloaded and sat down in one of the big chairs.

There wasn't any question in my mind that she'd been knocked off. There wasn't any question in my mind that whoever had done her in had also done in Girgis. But from that point on it began to go haywire. Just like with Girgis's case. I couldn't read it.

On the surface of it, it had to be tied in with the hashish racket. But I believed the local hash trade wasn't important enough to kill one person over. And now there were two killings.

That seemed to lay it right back at the feet of my young friend Chuck.

I was sure he was perfectly capable of it. But why?

Why Marie, too?

I didn't think Jim Kirk was a killer. I didn't believe he could so wantonly do in a young looker like Marie. Kirk appreciated ladies as much as I did. Certainly he wouldn't kill two people over this petty hashish racket. That brought me right back to where I'd started.

It had to be a speedboat that had done her in. Kirk had one. But Chuck and Steve had one too, I remembered. A boat as slow and hard to manœuvre and with such a deep draught as the *Daisy Mae* couldn't have done it. I had checked her face carefully, and had not found a single scratch or abrasion like a deep draught boat would certainly have made. A speedboat could skim along over the surface like a razor blade cutting through face hair.

But just about everybody on the damned island had a speedboat.

Maybe there was something in this heroin business. They were all so close-mouthed about it. Could there be some kind of big heroin operation going on in conjunction with, or even totally separate from, the hashish? Going along parallel to it, separately, but involving the same people? Personal relations were always so insanely hard to unravel. They were never simple. Mainly because everybody lied.

The heroin business was something I was going to have to look at closer. I could start tomorrow with Pekouris. He was so circumspect, Pekouris. Maybe he knew something. And I could talk to Pete Gruner.

I got up and went over and reloaded my crystal tumbler another time. She had very nice glassware in her medieval fortress, Chantal. What had she said? Falling in love with me?

I knew one thing. I was going to get the son of a bitch if it took me ten years, and every nickel I could scrape together.

I sat back down. I was inflicted with – penetrated by, as they say – a mental picture sequence, like a series of movie shots, of Marie's last moments in the water. It was as if some fanatic automatic button pusher ran it over and over.

I was the man strapped in the chair and being tortured. She probably didn't even know what was happening when they made the first pass. Probably thought it was an accident. Then, suddenly, no arm; or nearly none. Would she even have been able to take care of it, in the water? Hurt bad, like that? Did she know about pressure points? How to keep swimming with a severed artery. Probably she would have died from the first pass anyway. The best bet would have been to use the line from her speargun for a tourniquet. Would she have thought of that? But by then they would have turned and been coming back. Did she see them far off? Or only up close, at the last moment? Maybe she thought they were coming back to help her? Then they didn't. She had had the presence of mind to jerk her head aside. Did she know by then?

Over and over. My mad Nazi SS colonel with the red armband wouldn't stop pushing the button.

But the whisky was beginning to bring me down off it a little. Slowly my mind stopped yawing and plunging around out of control. And after that I just sat.

And then it all began to well up in me. All the stuff I had tried so hard to keep down so long. I had known a moment was coming, sometime, when it would all come out.

Apparently, the moment was right now. It poured down over my head, and over me, like the contents of a tenement dweller's slop bucket over the head of an unsuspecting pedestrian.

The little Greek man in Paris; my divorce; my life, and the virtual dissatisfaction it had become; my bad marriage; my virtual estrangement from my daughters; the enormous sums I didn't have and was having to lay out anyway to keep the whole mob in the style to which they wanted to become accustomed: it went back a lot farther even: to my partner and his death in Chicago in 1955; to the move from Denver two years before; to my subsequent heroization in Chicago after I'd caught and killed his murderer; to my whirlwind courtship, and my involvement in Chicago that followed it; to the move to New York five years after that; to the grim years in New York that followed.

There was no one spot, one moment, that I could point my finger to. That was the bitch. No one act, no one decision was bad. No one major move or change was wrong. And yet here I was, sitting here, just the same.

Why had we gone into the business in the first place? We wanted adventure. We were young, and we wanted action not contemplation. Natural enough. We moved to Chicago simply because there wasn't enough to keep us occupied in Denver, and we were getting bigger. But my partner wouldn't have been killed, if we hadn't gone into the business. Probably, he wouldn't have been killed if we had stayed in Denver. It was my three months as a Chicago hero — 'PRIVATE EYE SHOOTS MAD DOG KILLER IN FLAMING GUN BATTLE' — that introduced me to my wife.

The three months as local hero put me up there. And I couldn't stand it. After Chicago, I always left a place for the right reasons morally, and the wrong reasons financially. At that, it took me five years, a marriage, a wife and one daughter later, to leave Chicago. Joanie tagged along, papoose on her back, reluctantly.

Probably I should have given in to her and become a corporation lawyer then. That was when that corporation lawyer fight began. And it had never ended. I could have made the switch then. I had all the opportunities. I could have made it later. The opportunities didn't stop. Probably, I should have given up, and settled in, and become a stuffy whatcha-ma-call-it, living off of other people's fat.

Because being morally right, didn't get me anything. People didn't admire you when they didn't know you were a failure by choice, for moral reasons. They didn't admire you even when they knew it. They thought you were a nut. Or a fool.

Instead, I threw it all up, and moved to New York, and hung out my little sign, and started over.

But I couldn't stand Chicago. I couldn't stand the bigshots. I couldn't stand what you had to do to be one. Also it was boring. And I was haunted by my partner, and his death. Jeff Watson. Who was Jeff Watson? Who ever heard of him? Jeff Watson, Wasp. Another Wasp. Another Wasp from Denver. Denver in the Heartland. Jeff Watson, another Wasp from Denver in the Heartland. Shot dead by a doped-up Negro gunman on South State Street in Chicago. That was back before it was even fashionable.

I never should have sent him out. I should have gone myself. The guy wouldn't have killed me. I wouldn't have trusted him. Like Jeff Watson Wasp from Denver in the Heartland did.

234

And in New York? Deterioration. The life of Lobo Davies, in a word. Deterioration, here. Deterioration, there. Water, water, everywhere. East Hampton for expensive summers. Living above my means to be bored by the expensive rich. Deterioration. An apartment in the East Sixties. Deterioration. Two lovely young daughters totally estranged from their father by their mother, going to ritzy schools, hunting the rich husband.

Deterioration.

Fortunately, my wife had fallen heir to a little money from a maternal uncle, late. After Chicago.

I got up and got myself another crystal-tumblerful of whisky.

They weren't even hippies, in revolt, my kids. Sometimes I wished they'd run away and be hippies. At least, then, I could go and find them. I knew how to do that. But not them. Nothing but Princetons and Harvards around the house. And not your ordinary Princetons and Harvards, but your Groton and St Paul's Princetons and Harvards. Deterioration.

Deterioration in everything but the work. And even that was a joke. Lobo Davies, Finder of Lost Children. Lobo Davies, nursemaid to the hairy. Find your children cut-rate and quicker, with Frank 'Lobo' Davies – another Wasp from Denver the Mile-High City in the Heartland of the West.

Sometimes I felt all the Spades and Jews and Puerto Ricans, Japs and Chinese on the West Coast, Wetbacks from the Texas border, had all formed a circle, and stood and pointed their finger at Frank Davies and hollered, 'Wasp!'

Every con-man and teenage drifter in the world pointing in shame and hollering 'Wasp!' with one hand, and reaching for my pocket with the other.

Because I owe it to them. They said.

Poor old Lobo Davies, who couldn't help it if his family had been in America before the Revolution. Who was ready to apologize for being born White, but couldn't find anyone to listen.

I was ashamed and embarrassed for having been brought up not to lie and steal. Nobody cared.

Once I had had some vague hazy ideal about helping

people and having some fun and notoriety at the same time.

Instead, here I was. A rather vulgar Wasp private eye descended to breaking the fingers of little Greek men in shabby hotels.

I couldn't even protect the only bit of true gentility and integrity I'd found here, in their lousy country. Couldn't even save it from being chopped to shark meat, by some vicious speedboat's propellers, in the azure Grecian sea.

Vanity. I was willing to admit that. But there wasn't even any satisfaction even in that. Vanity had also got me moving in the first place. I couldn't even get any relief even in that. Vanity giveth; and vanity taketh away.

Who cared?

Only Lobo Davies. Lobo Davies down in Greece, in the sumptuous medieval fortress living-room of a genuine bona-fide Countess he was studding for, sitting in a big deep chair, drinking her Chivas Regal Scotch by the crystal-tumberful. Hot damn.

I got up and put my crystal tumbler carefully on the heavy polished table. What had she said? She was falling in love with me? That was a hot laugh.

I wandered up the old stone staircase and down the old stone corridor upstairs, to her bedroom. She was asleep, brandy bottle at bedside. I shook her shoulder gently until Chantal opened her eyes and looked at me.

'No, don't move over.' I coughed.

'How would you like to hear the story of my life?' I said.

I pulled up the chair.

CHAPTER FORTY-ONE

I told her most of it. I didn't tell her about the little Greek in Paris. I figured she might know the man or his family, and anyway it was Freddy Tarkoff's private business with me. But I told her about the big Spade on Chicago's South Side. The one who killed my partner, and that I went down into the South Side after, myself. The police were looking for him and couldn't find him. I found him because I had close friends on the South Side. I told her there was one moment when I probably could have saved his life. For about thirty seconds during our discussions he'd been about ready to give it up and turn himself over; if I'd asked him. I didn't ask him. Instead, I let him think he'd fooled me into trusting him. I did it deliberately. So he went on sweetmouthing me, with his slippery mean eyes. Until he thought he could get the drop on me, like he had my partner. When he went for the gun he had hidden in the back of his belt, I was all ready and waiting. The luridly described 'FLAMING GUN BATTLE' of the headlines was only three shots really, one from his gun that went past my chest as I turned sideways, and two from mine.

'Probably I wouldn't have done it that way, today,' I said. 'I was younger then, and I was angry. Today I'd probably take him in. And six months later he would be back out on the Street, terrorizing and extorting other black people, and bragging about how he fooled us whiteys. If he ever went to jail at all.'

'I don't understand you,' Chantal said crisply, from the bed. 'I would have killed him without any compunction. He killed your friend, didn't he? And tricked him?'

'He was black.'

'Why does that make any difference?'

'It shouldn't. I kind of liked him,' I said. 'And he probably had had a hard life. Liking him was about comparable to liking a rattlesnake you found by the road.'

In the bed, she shrugged.

'And you were a local hero for a while because of this adventure?'

'About three months. But I milked it for a lot longer. I could have milked it even longer, and gotten a lot more out of it, if I'd wanted to stay in Chicago.'

'I don't understand you Americans,' Chantal said. 'No European would have left like that. Here you had all this acclaim and opportunity, and you had earned it. You had the right to get everything out of it you could. A European would have.'

'We're an odd breed,' I said. 'Some of us, at least, I guess. Anyway, that was how I met my wife. She was a Lake Forest socialite. Or, rather, she was a would-be socialite. Her grandfather did very well, in Lake Forest, in the 'Twenties. But Samuel Insul's stock mergers put him under. Her father never recouped.'

'So she transferred all her social ambitions on to you?' Chantal said.

'You might say.' I took a long, deep breath, and drank down some whisky, then pouched out my lips and blew the breath out through them.

'You said you were falling in love with me. I thought I'd better tell you all this.'

'So that it would make me fall less in love with you?'

'It ought to, shouldn't it? All this old dirt? It's not a very heroic tale.'

'You're either dumb. Or else you're a lot smarter than I've given you credit for: That kind of life story, told by a bundle of muscle like you, only makes a real woman fall more in love. Not less.'

'You're awfully sure you're a real woman,' I said.

'That's one thing I've never really had to worry about,' Chantal said. She slid over in the bed, and touched the place beside her. She had nothing on, under the sheet. 'Come on in. Do you want me to prove it?'

I stood up and began taking off my clothes. I was suddenly dead beat and dog tired.

'My God, look at that side of yours,' she said.

'I'm not sure I can do you any good,' I said as I got out of my pants. 'After all this whisky. And after this—' I didn't know what to call it. I didn't want to say, Murder. 'After what's happened.'

'It doesn't matter,' Chantal said softly. 'Shh. Shh. Just rest a while.'

I started by kissing her, and running my hands over her breasts. They lay a little flatter than a young girl's, maybe. I didn't mind that. I liked it better. I put my nose against her hair by her ear. The faint odour of perfume and light female sweat in the night heat was soothing, and delicious.

'Don't worry about making love,' she said. 'Just lie quiet.'

'I'm sick,' I said to her ear without moving my nose. 'I'm sick all over. I get sick in my heart and sick in my guts and sick at the base of my skull, when I think about her out there in the water, bleeding, and that damned boat propeller coming down on her a second time.

238

It makes me sick in the middle of my crotch and right under my toes on the soles of my feet. My toes curl up.'

'I know. It's sad. It's terrible,' Chantal said. 'But there's nothing we can do.' One of her hands was kneading the small of my back. Right where the tension was.

'Not a damn thing,' I said. 'Not for her, anyway. But there's damn sure something I can do for me.'

'You'll do it,' Chantal said, soothingly. 'You'll do it.'

'I mean to.' I ran my hand over her left breast again. Its nipple was puckering up and tightening and rising. Almost of its own volition. As if it had its own little mind. So it seemed.

And oddly enough it was happening to me. I was getting hard. I wasn't even thinking about sex. I was thinking about Marie, bleeding. Bleeding in the water, and the boat turning to come back.

It was as if all the little cells in both of us had lives of their own, without ever caring what we thought or felt. As if both of us were nothing but collections of undersea hydroids and zooids and medusa buds swimming around in the salt water, cells mindlessly mating, mindlessly breeding, mindlessly forming chains, mindlessly producing the polyps that produced the free-swimming medusae that bred polyps again. The picture was so cruel it brought me up short. The ferocity and raw greed and unconcern of simple cellular life shocked me. Poor Marie.

I raised up on my elbow and looked down at Chantal, and suddenly her head turned into the head of my wife. Joanie's head went on talking to me and soothing me.

'You'll do it. It's all right.'

I made myself blink, but Joanie's head didn't change back to Chantal's. It went right on talking to me, trying to soothe. It wasn't any fantasy. It was the real head. The body was Chantal's. I wondered if I was losing my marbles, what few of them I had left.

Before I could react, the head changed again. Joanie's head became Marie's head and went right on talking, crooning to me.

'It's all right. It doesn't matter.'

I decided to risk wiping my eyes with my hand. I did. Marie's head went on crooning to me. And suddenly I wanted to weep, for all of them. For Chantal, for Joanie, for Marie. For everybody. For anybody, and everybody, but mainly for me.

What a situation our race had got itself into. Condemned to separation. Not wanting to be separated. But loving it. Hanging on to it for dear life. Anyway we had no choice anyway. Cellular collections. Zooids and hydroids. We would be laughable, if it didn't hurt so much.

The head on Chantal's body now was Chantal's. I took it in my hands and kissed her on the mouth, before it could get away.

'You don't have to talk to me,' I said.

'I don't mind,' she said. Her hand groped my crotch. 'What do you want? Do you want me to do something special for you?'

'No. I'll do something special for you,' I said. 'Don't do anything. Just lie back.'

I started at her breasts, and worked down. I took a long time. The tiny blonde hairs on her skin, invisible except up this close, seemed to quiver all on their own. Separately. I tried to put into my lips and tongue and teeth and nose all the sad delightful things I'd never been able to say to any of them, to any woman. Women were so valuable – to men. Her navel pulsed, like a pursed mouth, contracted to meet my mouth. From above me she moaned. I had her going, and that was what I wanted to give her. Her crotch hair tickled my nose, crisply, like curly endive lettuce when I'd held batches of it to my face to sniff it. And then the woman smell: faintly perfumed, faintly pissy, faintly polecat, faintly something else.

'Oh. Oh God. It's never been like this,' Chantal said above me. 'Oh God. Oh. Nothing's ever been like this.'

She was right. I'd never done it like this. I'd gone down on a lot of women, but not like that. It was for all of them. For Marie. And for Joanie. And for Chantal. For a hundred others. All the ones I'd failed with, and who had failed me. All the ones I'd wanted, but hadn't got. All the ones I'd wanted and got, but had left, or who had left me. All the ones I'd only seen, and wanted. All the wounded ladies. It was for all of them. Chantal reaped the benefit.

Her legs jerked under my forearms. 'UNNHH. NNHHNN. AARR. NNHHH! NN! AAARRRGGHHH!' Chantal called.

I let my head rest on her belly and through my ear felt the muscle contractions diminish and fade.

'Oh, fuck me!' Chantal said from above me. 'Oh. Fuck me, Lobo, fuck me. I want you inside me. I want to feel it in me.'

I rolled around and mounted her. I could feel the inside parts of her come down to touch. 'Oh. Oh.' Her eyes stared up at me sightlessly. I don't know what she was seeing. Herself, maybe. Her portrait mirrored in my eyes. Then I came myself, exploding.

After a while I rolled off of her.

'If you don't mind, I think I'll stay the night,' I said dully.

'Stay as long as you want,' she said. 'Stay forever,' and she put one arm under my head and pulled my face against the dampness of her armpit.

CHAPTER FORTY-TWO

I was up only a little after the sun was. Chantal didn't mind any more if the maids saw me. But I had things to do. I wanted to see Pekouris about Marie. And I wanted to talk to Pete Gruner about heroin. Also it was time I had some sort of a face-to-face with crazy Chuck. If he was still here, I meant to find him and have it.

I rolled out stifling a groan. The taping had helped my side a lot in a day, but it sure as hell hadn't by any means cured it.

I made the walk down to the harbour in the sun-bright, fresher morning air. At the house I changed to a fresh outfit, and washed the last scents of sexuality off me in the lousy showerless bathtub, being careful of the bandage.

What had she said? Stay forever? Well. It was endemic in people to say things in the sack that they wanted to bite their tongues for later on, when the heat was gone. As for love, love seemed doomed to be crushed by the law of gravity like strength and beauty. All you had to do was wait around long enough. Sometimes it wasn't so long.

I wasn't sure I could trust her even now. Was the old Ambassador's heroin the last of her 'further secrets' she was holding out on me? I had a hunch that it wasn't.

I hadn't seen my boatman Sonny since he helped me

after the fight. I waited around on my porch until he came up on deck and rowed ashore. He came up pretty late. I went and got him and had him take me to town.

Sonny already knew about Marie. He had heard it last night at Dmitri's. But he still thought it was a shark that killed her. Also, Sonny told me, Girgis had not been killed at the Xenia. The true story was that Girgis had fled the country because the police were after him for selling hash, and the headless body found at the Xenia was that of a hairless South American monkey which was the pet of one of the guests.

So much for the truth. I silently tipped my hat to Pekouris.

But at the Port I found the knowledge Marie had been hit by a boat had passed around during the morning. Nobody was talking about anything else.

I took my newspaper across the shade-mottled terrace to the table where I usually sat. I didn't feel much like reading it. I concentrated on my Campari. A longhair with a beard came up the rise from the produce jetty past the kiosk, heading for Georgina's table of kids until he saw me and stopped. After a moment, he came sidling over.

'Hallo?' He said it all like a question, 'It's a nice morning?'

'I guess it is,' I said. 'Who are you?' I asked it with an upward inflection, gently.

He was a scrawny kid. I thought I could probably put one hand around both of his wrists. And my hands weren't that big. Narrow-shouldered. Long thin fragile head, bulging at the top. Enormous eyes. A great plough blade of a nose hanging out. His beard was scraggly and woefully thin.

'I'm Harvey Richard,' he said. 'May I sit down?'

He was the first one who had ever asked me, that I could remember. 'Sure,' I said. 'Sit down, Harvey.'

He eased himself with great trepidation into a chair. And I suddenly remembered his face. He was the young hippie in Georgina's garden, about the first night I was here, the night Chuck broke somebody's nose, who had pointed out Jason the Paris 'recording star' for me with such awe in his voice.

'What can I do for you, Harvey?' I said.

'I think you know my father. I think he's a friend of

yours. In New York?' He smiled nervously. 'Arthur Richard?'

'Hell, yes. Why, sure.' I looked at him again. The resemblance was there, all right. It was just hard to see. He was almost a physical caricature of his father, who was a healthy husky extrovert of a man. Big player of tennis. Arthur Richard owned the Volkswagen distributorship for half the Eastern seaboard. I had known him for ten years. 'Do we know each other? You and I?'

'We've met several times at our house. But I was a lot littler. You probably wouldn't remember me. I didn't remember you either, at first.' He had an authoritative way of talking, despite his nervousness.

'I remember you,' I said. 'Well. What's on your mind, Harvey?'

'I was just down at the police post below,' he said in a precise way. 'They just got a notification that Sweet Marie's death has officially been declared accidental. I heard them talking about it.'

I thought this over. 'You speak and read modern Greek?'

'A little. We have a Greek butler at home.'

I nodded. 'Why bring it to me?'

'I was on my way to tell Georgina and the gang at her table, and I saw you sitting over here.'

'But why tell me?'

He shrugged his thin shoulders tortuously. But his eyes were steady, and rather piercing. 'I thought you'd like to know. I saw Marie talking to you the other night at the Cloud 79. And I saw you talking to her here. I knew you had taken her skindiving. I just thought you'd want to know they said her death was accidental.'

'Do you have any reason to believe it wasn't accidental?'

'Me? Gee, no.' He looked at me with round eyes. 'I just thought you were a friend of hers, and that you'd want to know.'

'Well, thanks a lot, Harvey,' I said. 'Remember me to your father when you get back to New York.'

'I sure will. He'll be glad I ran into you while I was here in Greece.' He made as if to get up, then didn't. 'Mr Davies, I was one of the ones who beat you up the other night. I thought I ought to tell you.' He looked scared, but resolute.

'You weren't the one who kicked me, were you?' I said.

'No. I wasn't. I didn't even see that. I don't know who kicked you.' He made his tortuous shrug. 'But I wouldn't tell you if I did know, Mr Davies.'

'I wouldn't expect you to,' I said. 'Well, thanks for thinking of me just now, and say hallo to your father.'

'I didn't know who you were then, that night,' Harvey said. 'Or of course I wouldn't have done it.'

'Don't worry about it, Harvey,' I said. 'I didn't know you either.'

'Well, see you, Mr Davies,' he said, with his resolute eyes; and got up and started to sidle off. I called him back.

'How are you making out with Jason, the Paris recording star, Harvey?' I said.

He gave me a lopsided grin. 'Oh. Yeah. It was me who pointed him out to you at Georgina's. He sure is drunk or stoned a lot of the time. He's run out of money. He sure wouldn't be much without electronics to bolster up his voice.'

I winked at him. 'What are you studying in school, Harvey?'

'Well, I'm majoring in philosophy, and ecology.' He made the tortuous, apologetic shrug. But his eyes were not at all apologetic. 'With a minor in social studies.

'But what I'm interested in going into is video cassettes for TV. It's going to be a very big thing, soon, and there are enormous technological difficulties to iron out.'

I didn't say anything.

'Well, see you around, Mr Davies,' he said, and went sidling away. Apparently his sidle was a chronic thing, and not just a temporary, acute thing of the moment. It was probably some signal of pacifism he affected. I watched him go, and thought about his father. Harvey would just be beginning his senior year at Harvard in the fall, if I remembered right.

Thank God something or other protected them. Maybe it was just simply their own naïvety. Or maybe their intelligence. It didn't always protect them, though, did it? No, it didn't. So Pekouris had already gone ahead and declared it accidental.

Pekouris's move did not upset me. I had rather expected it. It stood to reason that, if he was backing off on Girgis's murder, he wasn't going to saddle himself with another one to declare unsolved. But young Harvey's information did get me to moving.

There didn't seem to be any more I could learn in the square. Sonny had joined the table around Georgina, and I signalled him. When he came over, I told him I wanted to make a run to Glauros.

Pekouris was in his office, at the end of the Wyatt Earp gunslinger's street.

He was packing. Two huge briefcases lay opened out flat on tables and Pekouris was separating stacks of papers and putting them first in one and then in the other. The radio man was sitting there just like before. The big radio console was still buzzing pregnantly, but not saying anything.

This time I ignored the radio man. If Pekouris wanted him not to hear what we said, he would have to arrange it himself.

'You're leaving a little early,' I said.

'Yes, I'm sorry about that.' He shrugged. 'Orders from above.' He looked at the radio man, and nodded, and said something in Greek. The radio man got up and went out. 'Have you something for me? I do not see any packages.'

'No. I haven't,' I said. 'I haven't been able to do anything about the machete.'

'I will give you a telephone number. It is where you can always reach me in Athens.' He took a scrap of paper and wrote a number down and handed it to me. 'If I am not there, tell them who you are and I will call you. I will fly down as soon as you call me. Or perhaps you would prefer to come up to Athens to me. As my guest,' he added, and smiled.

'Okay,' I said. I put the paper in my pocket. 'Thanks.'

He picked up his papers, and then stopped and looked at me; I smiled. 'Was that all?'

'Actually, I came about something else.'

'Yes? What?'

'I heard you declared the girl's death accidental.'

'That is correct. Why? Does that case interest you, too?'

'No. But I happened to be there when they found her. And I got a chance to look her over pretty closely. It looked to me like she was murdered.'

'Oh? The medical examiner and I did not think so. Nor did any of the other officers who examined her. What made you think that?' He raised his thick eyebrows at me.

He knew I knew the medical examiner on Tsatsos was the tottery old mortician. And I knew the other officers were Pekouris's constabulary: his fat chief and the chief's two muscle-headed patrolmen. That was no great answer to give me.

'Well, it looked to me as if she had been hit twice, two separate times,' I said. 'By the same propeller. Two inboards would be spaced too far apart to do that in one pass. Even double outboards aren't that close together. And those wounds didn't look like they were caused by ordinary outboards.'

'We noted that point. And we took it into account.'

'There weren't any abrasions on her face from the bottom of a boat,' I said.

'She could have been struck from behind.'

'That's true. But the wounds looked to me as though she were hit from in front.'

Pekouris shrugged, and moved his still-raised eyebrows slightly. 'We think she was struck from behind.'

'And of course,' I said, 'there's always the tourist season coming up in ten days.'

'I think you're stepping over the bounds a little.'

'Excuse me,' I said.

'I am still the legal authority here. Your only recourse, if you think me wrong, is to go over my head to my superiors in Athens.'

I nodded. 'I would never do that. I only wanted to give you the benefit of my thinking, since I happened to be there. I was sure you would want to know every opinion.'

'I appreciate your concern. And your thoughtfulness. But I do not honestly feel that anything you have told me changes our opinion.'

I nodded again. 'Well,' I said. I got up.

'The order from my superiors in Athens about you still stands, by the way, Davies. I assume they would include this new case of the girl in it. I'm quite prepared to carry the order out, you know.'

'Don't worry,' I said. 'You won't have to do anything like that.'

'I hope not. You know, we went over the aspect of murder, too. I am not accustomed to ignoring serious murders. But just for example, there is no motive. We were unable to find anywhere any motive for killing the girl.'

'There could be a lot of motives. For instance, this boy Chuck – who we think may have killed Stourkos – might have knocked off the girl for the same goofy reasons he killed Girgis. If he did.'

'If he did, you have no worries.'

'How do you mean?'

'Well, if you were able to get hold of that machete, for yourself of course, and the tests proved out as we expect and hope, the girl's murderer will have been caught, too, will he not?'

'I only used that as an example,' I said.

'You have other theories?'

'No. But I've changed my mind about quite a few things since we talked the other day. Quite a few new little things have turned up.'

'Such as what?'

'Did you know Ambassador Pierson is a heroin addict?'

'Yes. That is well known. Even in Athens. We have done nothing, for obvious reasons. Your country would not be happy if we arrested a former American Ambassador as a heroin addict.'

'Did you know that Jim Kirk has been bringing heroin on the island for the Ambassador?' I said.

'No. That I didn't know. But for myself, I don't mind that very much. A little heroin for the Ambassador.'

'Nor do I,' I said.

'Then how have you changed your opinion?'

'I haven't, really. Not yet. It's just that things seem a little bizarre around Tsatsos.'

'I am aware that you had an, uh, shall we say, certain affection for the dead girl, Davies,' Pekouris said thinly. 'I don't think you should let that carry you away, out beyond your reasoning abilities.'

I gave him a slow blink and just looked at him. I hadn't told him about Chantal. And I hadn't told him about the presence of Pete Gruner on the island. Maybe he already knew both. But if I ever intended to tell him, I sure wasn't going to, now.

'The fact remains,' I said, 'that whoever killed the girl even accidentally is guilty of a crime if he did not immediately report the accident. Doesn't it?'

He moved his head. 'It is entirely possible someone might have struck the girl and not even known it. However, I intend to look into that particular matter when I return from Athens.'

'I'd like to look into it with you,' I said.

'I would be glad to have you do so.'

'When do you think you'll be back?'

'Oh, in five days. Perhaps a week.'

'When are you leaving?'

'This afternoon. On the evening plane.'

'I'll give you a call when you get back,' I said. 'It's certainly an inconvenient time for you to be leaving. And an inconvenient length of time to be away.'

'You might be giving me a call before I come back, mightn't you?' he said, and smiled.

'Yes. There's that possibility, too,' I said. I opened the door.

'I'll call you,' Pekouris said. 'As soon as I return.'

In the hallway, as I left, I looked thoughtfully down at the dirt swirls and lint rolls still on the town hall floor. Nobody had swept out its corners since the last time I was there, it appeared.

As I came outside, the hot sun blinded me again.

'Where to now, Commodore?' Sonny said when I jumped back on board.

I started to tell him to take me back home to the harbour. Then, instead, I changed my mind and told him to take me right back to the produce Port where we had been. I was still looking for Chuck and Gruner.

CHAPTER FORTY-THREE

I got madder and madder as Sonny made the run back to Tsatsos.

I go in there with proof of Marie's murder, and I come out with magnanimous permission to help him in a non-criminal accident case.

Pekouris's slipperiness made me want to bite something. What a poker player he would have made. He was a master at confusing an issue, and a past master at avoiding a straight statement.

It could all of it be due to his precious tourist season. There was no reason to think not. They all seemed to love that tourist season more than life itself.

But if he was involved in a big illegal money-making deal, if he was getting a piece of it, if he was protecting someone, he would have acted the same. I didn't think it was funny any more.

I had felt a lot differently when it was just Girgis's murder. Then it was just a game, and I enjoyed playing it with him. Now was different.

If he was right, and Chuck was the killer, he would have his damned machete. I would get it for him. But if I turned up something entirely different about Marie, I wasn't going to back away from it for anybody. He could go ahead and throw me out of Greece. By then I would have the goods on the case and he wouldn't be able to stop it.

I sat on the coach-roof in the shade and sniffing the occasional mist of spray, tried to assess what I knew. I came out with just about zero. The beautiful summer weather over the sparkling sea was all gall and worm-wood, to me.

When we tied up at the jetty, I bought another paper at the kiosk and walked up and took another table at a café. I had left my first paper in Pekouris's office, from being so furious. I didn't really want to read it, but it gave me a good excuse to be sitting there. I was looking for Pete Gruner.

What I found was blond Steve. He came walking up to the terrace from the other way, toward the Construction, and he was alone. Chuck wasn't with him. He did not even have Diane with him.

He went on past and stopped by a display rack of yellow film at the corner of the little alley I knew. He seemed to be just loafing. He stood looking across the crowded tables out under the trees and over the harbour, with his vague stoned eyes.

I folded up my paper carefully and put it on the table with my Campari, to hold the table, and got up and walked over to him, before he could move away from the alley.

'I want to talk to you, bud,' I growled in my best private-eye voice.

People passing jostled us both.

'I don't want to talk to you, Davies,' he said, and turned his slow sleepwalker's look on me. It was just the response I needed. The one I was hoping for.

I took two steps into the alley and turned and reached back and grabbed him by his Mongol vest, and yanked him into the shaded alley with me. He came, as if launched from a slingshot. I could hear the sheepskin of his vest tearing. That cheap sewing. I got my other hand on him, too, and slammed him back against the building wall so hard his head bounced. I put my left forearm across his throat and pushed, hard. His face turned red. I turned my hip to him so he couldn't knee me if it should occur to him.

He didn't even try. I left him like that for a little bit.

Outside on the sidewalk a few inches away people gabbled and jostled each other, or talked merrily, or shopped at the display rack of yellow film. None of them noticed us. I hadn't thought they would.

I didn't even think any of them even noticed his sudden slingshot launching, and disappearance. If anybody looked in, they didn't interrupt us.

Steve's face was getting the slightest tinge of blue. I relaxed my forearm a little. He made a strangling noise and whooped for air.

'Now,' I said softly. 'I don't want any lip. I don't want any back talk. I don't want any philosophy.'

He opened his mouth. I pushed with my arm.

'No. Don't talk. Don't say anything. Just listen.'

As his face got redder I let up a little.

'I want to know where your buddy Four Eyes is. Your buddy Chuck. I want to know where he is right now, this minute. Not where he was half an hour ago. Not where he'll be an hour from now.'

Steve tried to crane his neck.

'No. Not yet,' I said, and pushed with my arm. 'Don't be in a rush. When I let up on my arm, you tell me where your buddy is. Okay? Now.'

'I sent him over to St Friday's,' Steve croaked.

I pushed down on him by sheer reflex. 'Don't play games with me, son. I'm not here to fart around. Not today. Now where is he?' I let up a little.

Steve tried to swallow. It seemed to hurt him. I was glad. 'It's the truth,' he whispered. 'I sent him to St Friday's. He's been upset about Sweet Marie dying. I sent him over there for another three-day fast. He was beginning to get into fights.'

'How long ago did he leave for there?'

'Maybe an hour ago.'

'How's he getting there?'

'He's walking. Along the coast road. I made him walk.'

'If this is a con,' I said through clenched teeth, and grinned, 'I am perfectly capable of putting you in the local hospital, if there is one. I'd be happy to take you right out of here with me, and take you to find him yourself.'

'It's the truth,' he whispered. 'Honest.'

I jammed my arm into him once more, viciously, and took a step back. I guessed I was feeling bloodthirsty, after all that had happened to me in the past few days. I caught his throat in the crotch of my left hand and balled my right fist.

'Get ready,' I said, and hit him in the belly with my right as hard as I could.

He doubled over, whooping silently. Muscle-boy that he was, there wasn't much of the fighter in him. I put my palm in his face and hooked my fingers under his chin and straightened him up. He was white.

'No, you don't,' I said. 'You're not going to vomit, and you're not going to fall down. You're going to walk right out of here, just as if you were a big grown-up man. Because if you don't I'll kick your teeth in.'

He turned without a word and walked towards the merrily cackling pavement. I jabbed him in the kidney.

'Straighten it up.'

Outside on the walk he turned right and started blindly toward the newspaper kiosk. I guessed that was where he was heading before I grabbed him. I went back to my table and sat down and picked up my paper and unfolded it.

I was feeling pretty good. Better than I'd felt in days. My side was hurting but I didn't care. I felt fine. But I had to make my plans. I looked around for Sonny.

Just as I did, I saw Pete Gruner come on to the terrace from the direction of the Construction. I folded my paper under my arm and left money on the table and went over to Gruner.

'I've been looking for you,' I said. 'I want to talk to you. It's pretty important. But I haven't got time now.'

'Well, I want to talk to you, too,' Gruner smiled. 'That's the second time. Great minds run in –'

'Never mind the gas,' I said. 'I've got to go somewhere right away. Can you be at Dmitri's taverna in two hours? Better make it two and a half. No, make it three. Three hours?'

Gruner looked at me quizzically. 'I'll be there.'

I nodded, and left him. Sonny was back at Georgina's table, and I went over there. Young Stevie-boy was sitting there too, now. But Stevie-boy was looking glum and wasn't saying much. I touched Sonny and motioned him to come away with me.

'I want to go somewhere,' I said, as we walked toward the kiosk and the cobbled walk down to the jetty.

I wasn't much worried about Stevie-boy getting his speedboat and following us.

CHAPTER FORTY-FOUR

The coast road was easy to follow by boat. You couldn't very well miss it. But west of the Port there were a lot of coves and inlets the road cut inland to skirt. I was afraid we might lose Chuck in one of these and miss him.

'Do you mind telling me what's up?' Sonny asked, as he followed my instructions about going back into the inlets.

'Never mind,' I said. 'Just do what I tell you. That's what Freddy Tarkoff pays you for.' I didn't know what I was going to do with him when I found him. But I meant to find him if I had to walk the road.

We finally found him along a long ugly straight stretch. He was trudging along in the sun with his Kelty pack-frame on his back. Even from a hundred yards out I could see he was wearing his machete. I hadn't thought I'd be that lucky.

'Pull in there. Up in front of him,' I said to Sonny. 'Where there's sand.' The sand, when we got to it, was half mud. That was what made the place look so unappetizing.

'Hey!' I called. 'Hallo!' Under me the bow nudged into the sand gently. Chuck looked at us a minute, then came walking down on to the sand.

'What are you doing out here?' I called.

'Going to St Friday's,' he said sullenly.

'Well, come on,' I called. 'We'll give you a lift.'

'You will? Really?'

'Sure. Why not?'

'I could sure use a ride, man.' He came down to the water's edge. When he got that close, I could see he had been weeping. He was still sniffling, and wiping his nose. Dirty streaks ran down both his cheeks. He kicked off his sneakers.

'Here,' I said. 'Hand me up your pack.'

He came out into the water and passed it up.

'Pass me your machete,' I said. 'So it won't get wet.'

He pulled the scabbard off his belt and handed it up, without a word. I laid it on the seat beside the pack.

Behind me Sonny was keeping his mouth laudably shut.

'Now. Give me your hand.' I leaned down. He came on out up to the bottoms of his shorts. I got hold of his hand and heaved, and he clambered up over the rail.

'There,' I said amiably. 'Sit down. This beats hoofing it.' I moved my head at Sonny, and he began backing us off.

'It sure does,' Chuck said, and sniffled, and wiped his nose. He looked glum. He sat down by his pack and machete.

I sat down myself. But I kept my feet under me.

'Why are you going to St Friday's?' I asked.

'I'm being punished.'

'I see you've been crying,' I said after a minute.

'Yeah,' he admitted, and began to sniffle again.

'Why are you being punished?'

'Because I took the speedboat out yesterday by myself,' Chuck said. 'Without asking permission.'

I felt fire surge up into my ears. I had to do a slow blink, to keep it from showing. 'Who's punishing you?'

'Steve,' he said, amiably enough, and sniffled. 'Steve's my mentor. So now I have to walk to St Friday's and do a three-day fast and walk back. That's my penance.'

'Maybe we shouldn't be picking you up, then.'

'I won't tell him,' he said. He looked up, 'If you won't?'

'I won't tell him. But it seems to me he's a little hard on you,' I said.

He agreed. 'He is, sometimes, man.'

We lapsed into silence. Chuck sat sniffling. Sonny had got us backed off, and was swinging the boat. We started chugging along the coast towards the next point in the hot, orange sun. I was still digesting what he'd said about the speedboat. It was hard to believe even he would volunteer a piece of information like that, without any reference at all to Marie.

I supposed if you wanted to you could feel sorry for him, on a kind of basic animal level. I had friends who would. I didn't want to. He was enough to make you believe in euthanasia. Unless you were a liberal anarchist like me. His mental processes were on about the level of a smart dog.

'Do you have to do many of these penances?' I said.

He shrugged. 'I had to do one couple days ago. I beat up some guy.' He grinned. 'But I fooled Steve. I didn't come all the way. I sneaked back.' His eyebrows popped up. 'I never did figure out how Steve found out I didn't come.'

This made me feel ridiculously pleased, since I was the cause. 'Is a three-day fast hard to do?'

'It sure is, man. But I've got a chicken in my pack, and a couple bottles of wine. Tomorrow, Steve and Diane are bringing me another chicken.'

'Then it's not a real fast?'

'Well, it sort of is. You get awful hungry.' He looked down, and rubbed his hand over the machete, and tears started to run down his face again. 'I just wish he wouldn't make me throw away my machete, though.'

'You mean he's making you throw away your beautiful machete?' I said.

'Yeah. He said I got to throw it away, man. It's part of my penance. I'm supposed to take it up on the bluff at St Friday's, and throw it out in the sea as far as I can. It's a propitial offering to the One God for my penance.'

He looked at me.

I didn't have any ready answer to that one.

'He's going to buy me another one,' Chuck said, his face strained. 'But I want to keep my old one.'

'Yes. I suppose if you've had it a long time,' I said. 'I suppose it gets to be, like, part of you.'

'That's it, exactly, man.'

Whether had had killed Girgis and Marie or not, it was plain as hell his buddy Steve sure as hell thought he had.

Suddenly, he started pouring out to me all the troubles of his life. First he looked at the stern to see if Sonny could hear. In his simple-minded distress, he seemed to forget he had ever been mad at me and was supposed to hate me.

He had plenty of troubles. I got a picture of a kooky kind of semi-religious, knock-up kind of cult worship, not organized at all, cemented together and laced with an almost constant smoking of hash and pot. It sounded like enough to crack the nervous system of a lesser nut than Chuck.

They believed in the right of freedom from work. They also believed in the moral obligation to steal, no sexual repression, love of nature and the protection of the woods and rivers. Chuck had been appointed grand vizier. By Steve.

But that wasn't all his troubles. Not by a long shot. There was Diane. He was Diane's second husband, he explained to me in a garbled way that made historical reference to polygamy, polyandry, Moslems and harems, only he didn't use the big words. Steve was Diane's first husband. He was second husband. One husband couldn't take care of her, in the sack. But now he, Chuck, was falling in love with Diane and it was making his life a torment. Now in addition to all that, Steve was making him throw away his machete.

'Let me see your machete,' I said. 'May I?'

'Sure, man.' He handed it over.

'It sure is a beauty,' I said. I drew the blade half out. There were the celebrated bloodstains, rust-coloured and brown, on the blade near the haft. The blade below was clean.

'This looks like bloodstains?'

'It is,' Chuck said. 'That's goat's blood.'

'It ruins a blade to leave blood on it. It rusts it.'

'I know. I know all that, man. But that blood's special. I had to fight a man once with that machete in Mexico. A Mexican. Blade to blade. He had his machete and I had mine, and I won. I swore I'd never wash his blood from my sword. If I washed that goat's blood off there, there by the hilt, I'd wash his blood off, too, see?' He peered at me. 'I keep the rest clean.'

'That's quite a souvenir,' I said.

'Yeah. You see? You can see why it's so hard for me to throw it away. Even as a penance.'

I pushed the blade back in and hefted the scabbard. 'I'll tell you what. Why don't I keep it for you? I'd hate to see you lose a souvenir like this. I think Steve's wrong. This time. Let me keep it for you and in a couple of weeks, when Steve isn't mad any more, I'll give it back to you.'

He thought it over. If you could call it that, with him. 'Okay,' he said. 'That's a deal.' He got up, and walked up to the prow and back a couple of times, agitatedly. 'I think it's a great idea, man. And I won't tell Steve?'

'No,' I said. 'Don't tell him.'

'You don't know what a help you are to me, man.'

'It's nothing,' I said. 'I'll take good care of it.'

I had been wiping the machete's grip with my shirt tail. I held it out to him, holding it by the scabbard. 'It'll be safe for you with me.' He took it by the grip. Gently I pulled it back. He let go.

'I'll just put it where it's safe,' I said, and got up and took it aft. I ran down the hatchway stairs and put it in the toilet cubicle, got the key from the inside and locked the door from the outside. I put the key in my pants pocket, and patted it. So I had it. And with it a perfect set of prints, if Pekouris wanted them. I came back up.

'How long to St Friday's?' I asked Sonny.

'About ten minutes.'

'Well, hurry it up. As much as you can.'

I went back forward. Behind me the motor went up in pitch several tones. Chuck was sitting with his arms spread along the rail-rope, happily smoking a cigarette and looking as if a great load was off his mind. I just hoped it would last. But I was afraid it wouldn't.

St Friday's was just as pretty as they had said it was. The fine sand beach ran on back to become a sandy loam strewn with rocks, on which grew a grove of high old pines that soughed gently in the sea breeze. A carpet of brown needles covered the loamy ground. The chapel was a low one-storey building of whitewashed stone with an ancient red tile roof and a Greek cross at one end tilted slightly askew. It gave the chapel a rakish look, as if it were winking at you. Somebody had tried to steal it apparently, but hadn't been able to get it loose.

There wasn't a living soul anywhere.

In all that tranquillity I made the bow line fast at the concrete dock built against one rock wall of the little cove, and put over the bumpers while Sonny made fast the stern line.

Then I helped Chuck off with his pack. I brought him up a couple of extra bottles of wine from my store below. He took the bottles and set them on the dock by his pack and then turned back to me. I stepped off on to the dock.

'I've been thinking,' he said sullenly. 'And I've decided I want my machete back.'

CHAPTER FORTY-FIVE

I guessed I was more or less expecting it. I wasn't exactly surprised. Just too much time had passed. Even he could figure it out in ten minutes.

'Oh?' I said. 'How come?'

'Well, I've been thinking about it, man. And I'd rather have it myself,' he said.

'If you do, you'll wind up throwing it out in the sea like Steve wants you to.'

'There're plenty of places here I can hide it.'

'You bury it and you'll ruin it. It'll rust.'

'Don't kid me, man.' He made a little half smile that was more a snarl. 'I want it. It's mine.'

'I think you'd be a lot smarter if you let me keep it for you,' I said.

His voice started to get higher. 'You think you're fooling me? You talked me into giving it to you. You even got me to put my fingerprints on it.'

'Come on,' I said. 'I wouldn't do that.'

'Listen, man. That's my machete. Just give it to me, man.' He began to snap his fingers, both hands, the way I'd seen him do, the way Steve was constantly watching him for. He started to bounce agitatedly up and down on his toes.

'Well, I guess I can't do that,' I said. 'I'm going to keep it for you, anyway.'

He began to yell a stream of curses at me. 'Motherfucker. Cock-sucker. Shit-eater.' A string of variations. 'That's cheating. It's not fair. You're a sneak. Give me my machete.'

'I'm keeping it,' I said.

'I'll *make* you give it to me,' Chuck screamed.

'Okay,' I said. 'Make me.'

He was really very fast. One second he was standing in front of me. The next second he had danced in, delivered me a front groin kick in the crotch, and danced back out. All before I finished getting the words out of my mouth. I just didn't see it. Maybe I'd been expecting to talk a little longer.

Pain engulfed my crotch and shot up in rays through my groin like an aurora. Right after it came the slow, sick nausea in the pit of the stomach that you get. But the kick seemed light. As if he'd pulled it to get back away.

My instinct was to retch and try to vomit. But I was damned if I would. I wasn't Stevie-boy. I wasn't one of his punk kid opponents at the Construction, either. I gave him a grin and went after him, and I could see the surprise in his eyes. He'd expected me to keel over.

He came at me again, all set to groin kick, by his body stance. I slid left and leaned in to him and hit him with a hard left jab that went through his guard to his nose and rocked him back. His kick missed and he danced back. I followed him.

I was more than just furious. I was crazy mad. The pain in my crotch and the pain in my side were already enough. But I was thinking about Marie and Girgis, and all the rest of it. There was a kind of crazy joy in it, too, that made my head burn as if seared. I didn't care if he killed me. If he did, I'd kill him along with me.

He came in again, and I did the same thing: slid left and jabbed. After he missed that kick and I had punched him again, he slammed a right-hand chop into the side of my neck that did me no harm at all. I hit him in the belly with a right that hurt him. When he danced away I followed again.

He was losing ground to me. And his nose was already swollen from my two jabs. I noticed something else. He was fast but he didn't carry much weight behind his punches and kicks. Curiously, his blows didn't carry much conviction, or authority, as if his heart wasn't really in fighting, like mine was. I gave him a mean grin.

He was 'Hoo!'-ing and 'Hah!'-ing, like they teach you in the suburban karate classes, but I saved my breath. Silence can be as scary as noise. And karate was like with everything else. You had to be good at it, to be effective. That was why I preferred fist fighting. It was natural to me. Chuck wasn't that good. He was good enough to terrorize some kid at the Construction, was all.

When he came in again, he tried to tag me with a leaping high kick. I reached out my left and swung it up under his ankle and dumped him. He lit on his back. It knocked the wind half out of him, but he rolled free and up to his feet very fast. I gave him another grin.

This time he had desperation on his face when he came in. He was going to give me a front groin kick with his right foot, from the way he moved. I moved to get inside it, taking a chop to the cheekbone that numbed my cheek, and he shifted his weight and kicked out with his left foot again. Just like the first time. I seemed to be a patsy for that one.

Pain exploded in my testicles, but I was where I wanted: inside. I hit him with a left hook in the belly that knocked all the wind out of him, and then sunk my right fist into the side of his head as hard as I could hit him. He went flying, and lit on his back two steps away. I took the two steps, though it hurt me, and grabbed him by his shirt and jerked him to his feet and hit him with everything I had, just above the angle of his jaw, and let go. He went sprawling, and I followed and got his shirt and jerked him up again. I was intending to do the same thing. I was willing to keep on doing it just about forever. But something stopped me.

He was out on his feet. His glasses were long since gone, knocked off somewhere, and his eyes were glazed and rolling around in his head. Fine. All that was fine. But syllables came out of his mouth that didn't make any words. It sounded like, 'Tra ga go ka gye dye.'

I suspected he was still cursing me, or thought he was.

I wanted to break him apart. I hoped Pekouris gave him everything he could give him. I didn't care if they gave him the firing squad. But I made myself put my hand down.

There was no point in breaking his jaw for fun. Instead, I grabbed a handful of his shirt with my left hand, and softly shook him back and forth. He just sort of dangled. I let go of him and he sat down.

I walked away toward the boat, waddling from the pain in my crotch, wanting to vomit, my side shooting pains every time I breathed. What a way to make a living. I was getting too old for it.

Behind me Chuck began to come out of it. He struggled to get to his feet, and made it as far as his knees. The syllables he had been mouthing turned back into curses, which he now screamed at me like a girl. He didn't have a lot of grace in defeat.

On the dock his glasses that had been knocked off in the fight were lying there, somehow miraculously undamaged. That seemed grossly unfair to me. Almost automatically, I made as if to grind them under my heel. He'd have one hell of a time replacing them, here. But the same something stopped me.

Instead, I picked them up and looked at them. They were sure thick.

Holding them up for Chuck to see, I whistled. When I was sure he was looking at me, I snapped them in two at the bridge, and tossed them into the seven-foot-deep water and said,

'Dive for them, you son of a bitch.'

Chuck peered at me myopically with his bad eyes, then peered myopically at the water. 'I'll get you for that,' he screamed. 'I'll get you for everything.'

'You do that,' I said. 'Bring all your friends.'

I nodded to Sonny. 'Let's get the hell out of here,

260

Sonny, for God's sake.'

As we rounded the far point of the tiny cove out of sight, Chuck was rummaging in his Kelty pack and pulled out a face mask.

CHAPTER FORTY-SIX

'I never saw anything like *that*,' Sonny said to me admiringly from the helm. 'I didn't think a boxer could whip a karate man.'

'I'm not a boxer,' I said. 'And I probably couldn't whip a grand master of karate. I couldn't whip Cassius Clay, either.'

'Well, I never saw an exhibition like it. Don't your balls hurt?'

'Yes. They do. Now shut up and leave me alone.' I turned away, then turned back.

'Listen, I want you to take me straight over to Glauros. When we round the end of the island, head straight over.' I still had just time to catch Pekouris before his plane left.

'Does this mean the Girgis case is closed?' Sonny said.

'This means nothing. At all. And the Girgis case is already closed,' I said. 'Pekouris closed it himself. Remember?'

'I guess you've heard the story about how Chuck killed some Mexican with that machete,' Sonny said.

'I have,' I said. 'You just told it to me. Chuck told it to me. Pekouris told me. Just about everybody's told me. Now, shut up and let me alone. And you just keep your mouth shut about this fight.'

I waddled forward and sat down gingerly on the coachroof. As bad as my crotch was hurting me, my side was worse. It sent stabbing shooting pains clear through me each time I had to breathe.

In spite of that, something was tickling at my mind. I sat still and reached down in and fished around for it. When I brought it up, I found it was a conviction that had been forming, that crazy Chuck the karate man wasn't guilty. I knew he just hadn't killed either party.

I just knew he wasn't guilty. And I knew it strongly enough to be willing to act on it.

I didn't know how I had arrived at it. It was another of those obscure combinations of associations. Like my premonition about Marie's body. Chuck's nut's face. Steve's fear, of everything. How Chuck talked about the speedboat. How he tried to keep on cursing me when he was out. How he was smart enough to figure it out about the fingerprint bit. How he admitted his intention to throw away the machete.

Any two, any three, yes. Acceptable. But not all of them together.

Whatever the reasons, I was convinced Chuck hadn't killed Marie, or Girgis either. Someone else had done that.

That presented me with a beaut of a problem. What if I went ahead and delivered the machete to Pekouris? Would Pekouris go ahead and try to use it anyway? I didn't like Chuck worth a damn, but I wasn't going to be an instrument in railroading him on a murder rap just the same. And now I knew there was human blood on the machete. The Mexican's. True, it was old. But what if the lab experts were able to isolate it? What if they couldn't tell the blood type? Or what if they could tell the blood type, and the Mexican's was the same as Girgis's?

I was still full of fury. I sat on the coach-roof, brooding. I was feeling the let-down that comes after the end of a fight, and you don't feel the satisfaction you thought you would. Was I feeling a little sorry for goofy Chuck? Was I thinking about Marie, who couldn't be brought back, whose murder couldn't be undone even if I solved it?

After a minute I got up and waddled back to Sonny in the stern.

'I've changed my mind,' I told him. 'I don't want to go to Glauros. I want to go straight back home to the yacht harbour.'

CHAPTER FORTY-SEVEN

Because I didn't go over to see Pekouris with the machete, I had an hour to wait before Pete Gruner would show up at Dmitri's.

I locked the machete in the lockup closet with my locked briefcase. I had carried it up unobtrusively from the taverna dock, and nobody had even noticed it. I didn't know what I was going to do with it. But I wasn't going to turn it over to Pekouris.

With all the rest that had happened to me, now I was guilty of secreting evidence. In America that would make me an accessory after the fact. In Greece I didn't know what it would get me, probably decapitated.

After the machete was taken care of, I went through my first-aid inspection routine. It was getting to be a daily thing, just about. Like having to shave, or change my underwear.

I went in the bathroom and locked the door and inspected my testicles. They weren't swollen up, thank God. But they were sore as hell. I could hardly stand to touch them. The nausea was gone, and the sharp pain. But there was a constant ache in them, especially when I strained or tensed my thighs or walked. I wouldn't be of use to Chantal tonight.

My side seemed to have gotten worse, and felt inflamed. But there wasn't much I could do for it. The bandage was still in good shape, and still tight. I couldn't do much for my balls, either. I could hardly bandage them. I didn't know any bandages for testicles.

The rest of me was unmarked. The right-hand chop to the cheekbone had caused no swelling. The left side of my neck was a little sore from the chop to the neck.

I felt I was certainly earning Mr Kronitis's retainer and my hundred and fifty dollars a day. I ought to up it to two-fifty.

The worst thing of all was that I didn't have a murder suspect any more. Chuck was out. So I had to start over. What was left? Jim Kirk. I had Jim Kirk, and this

263

clandestine heroin business that was going on, or seemed to be going on, but never seemed to be more than vaguely alluded to.

I was hoping Pete Gruner could clarify some of that for me. I sat on my porch and rested my poor balls, and waited for him.

He saw me up on the porch when he came by, and waved. But he didn't come in. He went to Dmitri's and took a table, back in the arched, open room. If that was a signal, I respected it. I walked down, gingerly, and took a table in the open-sided room myself. It was empty except for the two of us. Everybody else was outside in the sun. After a minute he slipped over to my table.

'What's the matter with your balls?' he asked.

'I picked up a dose in Glauros,' I snarled. 'Now, let's cut the funny stuff. What I'm here about is serious. At least, to me.'

'I know it is,' Pete said, and gave me a look.

'You mean you know what's bugging me?'

'Well, I've got a pretty strong suspicion.'

'You figured it out about the girl?'

He moved his head and neck in a way that was not quite a shrug, but was more of a gesture of sympathy. 'Well, I didn't exactly figure it out. I'm not a homicide man. But I made a pretty strong guess.'

'Well, your guess would hit pretty close,' I said, and made a snarly smile. 'I won't go into the details about it. It's too complicated. And it'd only bore you. But for reasons of my own, I've run into a wall. I thought I had a suspect, a good one, but it petered out. –

'Well. What I'm interested in right now, is heroin. And what is going on around here about it. I'm pretty sure that something is.'

He looked down at his drink, and turned the glass on the table a while. Finally he looked up and said, 'I don't know anything about any heroin.'

'Okay,' I said. I couldn't keep a certain bitterness out of my voice. 'If that's how you want to play it.' I started to get up.

'Hold on. Hold on,' Pete said. 'Wait a minute. My God, you're short-tempered. You fly off the handle before they can turn the crank. Just sit down, now.'

'I don't want to play games,' I said. But I sat back

down. 'If you don't want to admit you're a nark, and tell me what you're jackassing around after down here, I might as well be on about my business. I know you're a nark. You know you're a nark. What the hell? To hell with it.'

'I've never said I was a nark,' Pete said. 'It's you who keeps saying it. I deny it.'

'Okay, okay,' I said wearily.

'It's the truth.'

'Okay.'

'What do you know about heroin around here?' he said.

'I know that Jim Kirk of the *Agoraphobe* has been toting some H around here, for special clients. Like the old American Ambassador, and a few people at the Construction. It's supposed to come from Athens. He charges double Athens prices. But he doesn't seem a pusher. I know that Girgis was not involved, and wouldn't touch heroin. I know that Kronitis, who owns both their boats, is not involved.' Gruner looked at me sharply. 'Or I think I know that,' I added.

He turned his glass some more and pursed his mouth as if in a whistle and thought a little while. 'That's all you know?'

'That's all I know.'

'That's all you suspect?'

'I have no reason to suspect anything else.'

'All right,' he said, and tossed off the rest of his drink. 'Now, if you'll shut up and not go off half-cocked and let me just say something – ' He motioned the waiter.

'Okay,' I said and scowled. I set my shoulders and jiggled my butt, in a parody of concentrating, and both my side and my testicles hollered at me. 'All right. I'm ready. Shoot it.'

'It's a good thing for you that I'm leaving, or I couldn't talk to you at all,' he said, and grinned. 'Now don't interrupt. I'm leaving here, probably on the evening flight tonight. That was why I wanted to talk to you.'

'You'll have Pekouris as a fellow passenger,' I said.

'Fine. I've never met him. Now don't interrupt any more. I'm leaving here and going back to the States. I'm leaving because my mother died. Don't interrupt. So I wanted to see you. As an old islands hand, not as a nark, I can tell you maybe a little bit that might help you

265

out in what it is you want to do. Which is, presumably, to catch whoever it was who killed Girgis. And probably the girl.' He paused to take a breath. 'Okay?'

'Why did you say you were leaving?' I said.

'Because my mother died. I'm going back for the funeral. I may be back here, and I may not.'

'Where did your mother live, in Washington?' I said.

'No.'

'How about Marseille, or Paris?'

'No. She lived in New Hampshire. And that's where I'm going.'

'Why do they do this to you?' I asked.

He shrugged, and deliberately misread me. 'Mothers die. It can't be avoided. And it's something that can't be controlled.'

'So you're going to just pull out, and just leave me here, with the whole thing in my lap?'

'When your mother dies, you go home. Period.'

'Don't you even care?'

He grinned. 'Sure, I care. When my mother dies. Everybody cares when his mother dies. As for my new boat I told you about, well, I'll just have to wait. I'll get a chance at another boat, some other day somewhere else, on some other island.'

'All right,' I said. 'All right. What were you going to tell me?'

'Nothing much,' Pete said. 'I don't really *know* anything to tell you. All I really *know*, is that I had a nice cushy job lined up on the *Polaris*, and that I was going into business with Kirk. And then my mother went and died.'

'Sure, sure,' I said. 'So?'

'All I really *know* to tell you, is one little thing. Listen to it. Remember it. Record it. Use it. I won't tell it again. One piece of information. Keep your eye on that *Polaris* boat. Keep a *close* eye on it.' He stopped, and picked up his one of the two fresh drinks the waiter had left us.

'That's all?' I said irritably.

'That's all. But it's important. Or maybe it isn't important. But that's all I *know*. What I suspect is another thing, and I'm not at liberty to discuss that.'

'Because your mother died,' I said.

He ignored me. 'My leaving is going to put a moderate-sized hole in the machinery. I was already hired, and I

266

think they were already counting on me. With me gone, somebody else'll have to do it.'

'Do what?'

'Work on the *Polaris*.'

'Does Kirk know you're leaving yet?'

'No. Not yet. I was going to tell him while I was down here. But he's gone off.'

'And you really don't care? At all?' I said.

'There's always another island.'

'Where is Kirk now?'

'If you want to know, I can tell you exactly. He's gone off up the mountain road on that tiny cycle of his, about two miles up in the hills and off to the right in the woods. And he's got Sonny Duval's wife with him. Okay? Enough? I'm waiting around for him.'

I looked around for Sonny. He had gone back on board his big caique, when I left him earlier. I supposed he was still there. I didn't care where he was.

'And that's all you've got to tell me? Watch the *Polaris*?'

'That's all I've got,' Pete said, and nodded.

'Okay.' I got up. 'Give my best to your dad when you see him, will you?' I said. 'I just hope he doesn't have to die on your next job.'

'Actually, my father passed away last year.'

'I hope you've got enough aunts and uncles for the future,' I said. 'Okay. Good luck. I'm sorry you're running out on me. I'll be seeing you. In Washington. I'm going into Indian Affairs myself, when I get back.' I started to stick out my hand, but then didn't. It seemed too much. 'So long.'

'Oh, Lobo,' he called after me.

I stopped and turned around.

'I know from experience that if you will buy a jock-strap, smallest size they have, it will help a lot for the first couple of days. But get it small.'

I just looked at him, then gave a small snarl and went on.

'Good luck,' he called. 'Keep after it.'

CHAPTER FORTY-EIGHT

Watch the *Polaris*, he'd said. As far as I knew, the *Polaris* hadn't stirred from its dock space since Girgis was killed.

Also, I was sure Marie wouldn't have lied to me about Girgis's refusing to touch heroin.

But if Watch the *Polaris* was what he'd said, then Watch the *Polaris* was what I'd do. I'd do anything, at this stage.

I suddenly had my old mad on at cops again. They were all so damned superior. The only thing they really had going for them, besides the badge and the pension, was their great ability for blindly taking orders. I had failed every obedience test they'd given me since I was a kid.

The idea about the jockstrap was a good one, though. I had to admit it. It irked me that I hadn't thought of it myself. There was a little Greek notions store not too far beyond the taverna, and I walked down there to buy one. It would save me having to walk, or take Sonny's boat, into the Port.

When I passed the taverna, Gruner had left. Jim Kirk had ridden up, with Jane Duval on behind, a while before. I assumed Gruner had talked to him and gone. To pack his bag, and catch his plane.

The jockstrap helped a lot, right away, when I got it home and put it on. I was feeling pretty damn good with a drink in my hand when the phone rang. I should have known better.

It was Kronitis.

I had to go through the whole rigmarole. The suspicious male secretary, the old man himself, his arsenal of formal salutations.

'I'm calling to see if you have, uh, made any progress. On our case,' he said at last.

'I'm making some progress,' I said. 'I've found out that one suspect isn't the murderer.'

There was a pause. 'But you haven't found out who is the, uh, murderer?' he asked.

'No, sir, I haven't. But I've been doing an awful lot of

work. And I've been spending a good deal of physical effort and energy.' I thought that was fair to say. 'I've got a lot more work scheduled to do in the next couple of days.'

His voice got more steely. 'I see.'

'You may not know it, Mr Kronitis,' I said, 'but there's been another murder over here.'

He sounded shocked. 'Another one?'

'Yes, sir. That young American girl, the skindiver. She – '

'Oh, I know all about that. The girl who was hit by a boat. The police have declared her death accidental.'

'Well, I think it was murder,' I said. 'And I think the same person who killed Girgis killed the girl.'

'Well, I'm sorry about all that,' Kronitis said. 'Naturally, I'm sorry the girl was killed. But I'm not interested in the death of this girl. I'm only interested in the killing of Girgis Stourkos. And I'm afraid I'm going to have to terminate our little affair.'

It was my turn to pause. 'Has Pekouris been talking to you?' I said sharply.

'Pekouris? The Inspector? No. No, I haven't spoken to him since the last time I telephoned you, Mr Davies. No, that's not what the problem is. The problem is the, uh, tourist season.'

'Well, that's the axe Pekouris is grinding,' I said.

'The tourist season is of interest to other people. Much bigger than Pekouris.'

That gave me the right to another pause. 'I see,' I said finally. I couldn't think of anything else. What I was wondering was whether I could trust Kronitis or not. I was remembering Gruner's sharp look when I'd mentioned him.

'So I'm afraid I'm going to have to un-hire you, Mr Davies. I'm sorry about that. But I'm un-hiring you as of right now. As of this phone call. It'll do no good to discuss it more.'

'All right, sir,' I said. 'If that's the way you feel. I'll have my cheque for your retainer in the mail to you tomorrow. I'll include a bill for what my services are. You can mail me a cheque here.'

'No, no,' he said. 'No, no. I don't want the retainer.'

'You'll be getting it anyway,' I said.

'No, no. That was a calculated risk I took with you, Mr Davies. We took a gamble together. It didn't work out. Fine. I lost it fairly and squarely. You are to keep it.'

'I'm sending it back anyway,' I said shortly.

'I insist that you keep it.'

I didn't answer him.

'Are you planning on leaving the island right away?'

I thought that was a funny question, coming from him. 'No. I'm not,' I said. 'I thought I'd stick around a while. At least until my vacation is over.'

There was a pause. 'All right. I hope we'll have an opportunity to see each other.' He started in on his interminable signing-off routine. I cut him off.

'Goodbye, Mr Kronitis. I'm busy as hell,' I said, and hung up.

Screw him. The hell with him. I didn't want a client who was always trying to back out. Especially when I wasn't any longer sure I could trust him.

I decided Pete Gruner had told me quite a few things. After all.

So there I was. I looked at the phone. I didn't give a damn about his money. – I stopped myself: That was a lie. I did care about his money. I cared about it a lot. I needed that money; bad. But the worst thing was that now, without him as a client, I didn't have an official status with the police at all. And he must know that. If that was what Pekouris was working for, he had achieved it. I didn't believe Kronitis. I thought Pekouris had talked to him a second time.

I went over and sat down to think it over. My side felt hot, and my crotch ached. And now I was out of a job. As soon as I had myself arranged so that I could rest comfortably, the damned phone rang again. This time it was Chantal.

She didn't waste any time honey-talking me.

'I want to see you. I have to talk to you.' She was using her cold, professional-Countess voice.

'Okay,' I said. 'Don't bite yourself. I'll be up there later tonight. You've got a dinner party somewhere, haven't you? Is it anything that can't wait till tonight?'

'Yes. It is. I mean, it can't wait. I want to see you, and I want to see you right now,' she said.

'Listen. Just cool it. What's so awful?'

'I don't want to talk about it over the telephone. And it's personal.'

I thought it over. I didn't feel much like going out anywhere. I hadn't even wanted to go up there later on tonight.

'Okay, I'll come right up. About half an hour.'

She hung up without saying goodbye. I wondered what that was all about. It couldn't be because she was complaining about last night. But it had to be more bad news of some kind.

I went over to the lockup closet and unlocked it and got out my locked briefcase, where I kept my New York cheque book. My secreted evidence, the machete, was still there, leaning against the shelves.

But as I started to write Kronitis his cheque, it occurred to me there might not be enough money in the New York account to cover it.

I still had his four thousand in cash locked in the briefcase. I hadn't gotten around to putting it in the bank here.

I put the cheque book back in the briefcase with the cash and locked it and locked the briefcase away with the machete again. I'd have to find some way of getting his own cash back to him.

I put the key in my pocket and got ready to leave and went outside and waved to a horsecab by the taverna. I didn't feel up to hiking up the hill to Chantal's on foot.

CHAPTER FORTY-NINE

She was waiting on the upper patio, and she didn't waste any time on amenities or love talk.

'The police have declared Marie's death accidental.'

'I know,' I said. 'But that doesn't change my ideas about it any.'

'Nothing changes your ideas about much of anything easily, does it?'

'I don't know,' I said. 'It depends on the idea. And on the thing. About Marie there's no question, in my mind. The police are wrong. But surely that's not what you called me up here to talk about, is it?'

'In a way, it was,' she said thinly. 'And another way not. I was hoping the police report would make you get off this murder thing you're on.'

'Not a chance,' I said.

'I might have known that,' Chantal said. She made a sort of bitchy face. 'Anyway.' She took a deep breath and sighed it out. 'Anyway, I called you up here because I want to tell you that I'm terminating your employment for me.'

'You're what!'

'Well, I'm firing you,' she said, and blushed. 'If you want it bluntly. I don't want you to work for me any more.'

'Were you under the impression that I was working for you?' I said.

'Yes. You were, weren't you? But now the police have closed Girgis's case, as unsolved. Marie's death has been declared accidental. So I've decided to forget the whole thing. Girgis is dead. Nobody is blackmailing me now. I don't need your services any more. I want you to pack up and leave, get off the island; go away, and stay away, and not come back. You're nothing but trouble here now with your "investigations". For everybody.'

I studied her. We had been slowly moving across the patio toward the house. 'Do you mind if I get myself a drink first? Before I pack?' I said.

I turned and went inside into the living-room and straight to the bar. It was only when I had a whisky in my hand that I turned around, and saw that the portrait of the young Chantal was gone from its place.

It had been replaced by a rather uninspired landscape. And the perpetually burning light above it was turned off. Chantal was still outside. I walked over to the new painting and switched on the light. The landscape of a Greek village scene leaped out at me, even less good in the light. I stood looking at it. Chantal came in and looked at me looking.

'What have you done with your painting?' I said.

'It's gone,' she said, and made a strange smile. It was half harsh, and half pitiable, pleading.

'I see that. But why?'

'Because I don't like it any more,' she said, and her eyes flashed a kind of fire. 'I'm sick of it. I often change my paintings around, when I get tired of them.' It was a cold fire.

I was willing to bet she had never changed that one before. 'So you want me to pack up, and leave, and get off the island, and not come back, do you?'

'I think that would be the smartest, and most gentlemanly, thing for you to do, yes. Under the circumstances.'

'Maybe,' I said. 'But it seems like awfully short notice. Only last night you were telling me how you were falling in love with me.'

Her face got stiffer. 'Maybe that's part of the reason.'

'Maybe. But I think we ought to get this thing straight about me working for you. I'm not working for you. And I haven't been since the day after Girgis was killed.'

'Well, you told me you were going to help me. And I assumed you were going on helping me. I thought if the reason you were involving yourself in all this was that, then I wanted to tell you not to do it on my account.'

'You know better than that,' I said.

'No. I thought even before Marie was killed, that it was me you were protecting; or trying to protect.'

'Assuming I did leave. What would you do about the rest of the rent on the house? What would you do about the rest of the cost of Sonny's boat?'

'I'd try to get what refunds I could on them, and return the money to Freddy Tarkoff,' Chantal said, and smiled.

'Fat chance of getting refunds,' I said.

She shrugged, lamely, and moved her head. She didn't answer.

I stood and studied her, and tried to figure out what it meant. Because it didn't make sense. Even if she had fallen wildly in love with me, it didn't. And I didn't think she was that much in love with me. And I was glad. Because I wasn't that much in love with her. And I thought she knew that, too.

'Have you been talking to Kronitis?' I said.

It was a shot in the dark. Her face suddenly got all funny, and she blinked to try and hide it.

'Leonid? Why would I be talking to Leonid Kronitis about you?' She was lying so obviously that it wasn't even necessary for me to comment on it.

'I just thought,' I said. I grinned. 'You're the second client – if you're a client, and there's some question about that – who's fired me today. Kronitis is the other one. You remember I told you that I had another client?'

'I don't know anything about any of that,' Chantal said staunchly. 'And I don't care. I'm only concerned about me and my life.'

'Sure,' I said. 'Have you maybe been talking to Jim Kirk, too?'

That got her too. Her face seemed to get even flatter, in a valiant but fruitless effort at expressionlessness. She was so expressionless that it expressed.

'Jim Kirk has nothing to do with it. With anything.'

'I wish I was sure of that. Do you realize that Jim Kirk could easily be the murderer I'm looking for?' I said.

'Jim? Jim Kirk could never do a thing like that.'

'Maybe. I'm not sure of it.'

'Oh, I just wish you'd go away,' Chantal said bitterly. 'I just want you to get out, and get off this island. That's what I wish.'

'Not much chance,' I said. 'Believe me, I don't like being here any better than you like having me. As soon as I get this thing settled up, I'll be long gone. But until I do get it settled, you better get used to seeing me.'

'There's another very good reason you ought to leave,' she said.

'What's that?'

'Because I'm going to leave myself. In a very few days I'm going to have to leave and make a trip to Paris. In two or three days probably. A friend there is sick and needs me. I simply can't let her down. So I won't *be* here for the rest of your – ' she paused, 'your "vacation".'

'Well, I'll miss you,' I said. And I guessed I would. It didn't change anything.

'Even that isn't enough to make your change your mind and leave? No me?'

'I don't think you understand,' I said. 'I'm here for what my generation used to call The Duration. I'm not leaving till the denouement.'

'And you suspect Jim Kirk?'

'As a matter of fact, you may be right about Kirk,' I said. 'I may already have found the killer. I picked that boy Chuck up today, and got hold of his machete. It's got blood all over it.' I watched her.

She seemed totally nonplused. 'What? Who?'

'One of the hippie kids. So maybe you can rest easy about Kirk after all. Inspector Pekouris seems to think it was the kid.'

Her face seemed to clear. 'Well, then you've got the whole thing all worked out.'

'Not quite. It still has to be proved.'

She looked completely puzzled. 'Then this boy did it? You think this hippie boy is the murderer?'

'It's possible. It looks right now like it's him.'

'Well, you see? I told you Jim Kirk couldn't do a thing like that. Why didn't you tell me about this boy in the first place?'

'Because you surprised me. When you told me you were going away,' I said.

'And you'll miss me?'

'Yes. I sure will. I sure as hell will.'

She gave me a sudden smile, that was making the corners of her lips tremble. Then she put her hands up to her nose and mouth, and turned and walked away.

She walked clear across the room to the bar, and stood fiddling with the bottles, and a glass. She looked as if she were about to make herself a drink, but then she didn't. Instead she turned around and faced me, and her face had completely changed. I couldn't describe the change. But she wasn't smiling.

'Do you think I don't know why you're doing it?' she said, harshly.

'Doing what?' I said.

'Helping me.'

I didn't answer. She had lost me somewhere, and I wasn't getting the point.

'Looking after me, taking care of me, helping me with all this mess? Making love to me, even? Do you think I'm a fool?' Chantal said. 'Well, I do know.' She stopped. I didn't say anything.

'Old age,' she said. 'Yes. Old age. You see it in me just like you see it in yourself. You're sorry for me.'

She was on the verge of crying.

'Well, I don't want your goddamned pity. Or anybody else's.' Her shoulders drooped and suddenly she seemed to come all apart. 'You and your goddamned old age.'

I was just beginning to get the point, which as far as I could see hadn't followed from anything else we'd said. She was pulling an intuition on me; and a pretty profound one; right out of the hat. I was just getting it and she apparently had finished. She began to weep.

'There's nothing anybody can do about that,' I said softly. 'Nobody's ever found anything to do about it yet.'

She didn't make any answer, and kept her hands up to her nose and mouth. Her shoulders were moving.

So I stepped to her and put my arms around her, and for a moment she collapsed against me. Then she pulled herself away and straightened up.

'I've got to go out to dinner in a few minutes,' she said, glaring at me. 'I'm going to look just awful. I'm going to look like bloody hell.'

'Go upstairs and wash your face,' I said. 'With cold water. And I'll go.'

'Will I see you later on tonight?'

'I don't think so,' I said. 'Probably not.' I couldn't quite bring myself to tell her why. 'But maybe I'll call you late. And maybe tomorrow night.'

As I left, I was wondering if I would get a call from Pekouris in the morning, about young Chuck. It would be interesting to see.

CHAPTER FIFTY

I shouldn't have walked back. By the time I got back to my house, my groin was aching badly. But I hadn't wanted to hang around Chantal's and wait the time it would take a horsecab to come, if I called one. My side was better, though, and less feverish, after the rest I'd been able to give it from violent movement during the afternoon.

There was a note pinned to my door when I got back, inviting me to a party on board Sonny's caique. The note was signed by both Sonny and Jane, and also by Jim Kirk. Apparently Kirk was co-hosting the party. I took it inside with me.

It seemed a bit much to me, having Kirk sign the note

too. But Jane Duval wasn't my business, and never had been.

In the house I put on the lights and got myself a drink. It had been after 7 o'clock when I went up to Chantal's and now it was dark. The party on the caique was both visible and audible from my porch.

I debated whether I should go to it, and decided I probably should. Especially if Kirk was going to be there. I didn't feel like it. I hadn't had any lunch to speak of, but I wasn't hungry. The old woman was gone. I didn't feel like eating the dog vomit old Dmitrios passed off as food, again. Not the way I was hurting.

After a while I got myself a second drink and went upstairs and changed my slacks and got another shirt and put my sandals back on and went down and out and down to the taverna dock to borrow a skiff and row myself out.

The party was in full swing. Sonny came up on deck to get me when I hollered, and took me down. It was so archetypal of hippie parties that it could have been staged. Everybody was below decks, and there wasn't all that much room, so that they were all pushed up together. They liked that. It was funky, unkempt, physically dirty, with overtones of potential orgy. The hash smoke was thick. Bottles of the local retsina were all over. Steve and Diane were there, and Georgina Taylor, Sonny and Jane, and Kirk, and some of the hippie couples from the Construction. Jane Duval was no housekeeper. The baby was asleep in a messy bunk in the roar of the record-player. Life on board centred around the expensive, battery-operated record-player, not around the galley.

The belowdecks was one big room without bulkheads, and the whole forward part of it was one large bed from planking to planking that could accommodate six sleeping people. Four couples were curled up on it. There was a lot of necking and near nude sex play by the couples, and not much reservation about changing partners in the middle. I'd seen it all a hundred thousand times.

The swing-table had been taken down for the occasion, and once in a while two or three couples danced the jerky freak dances in the compressed floor space.

'There's some whisky hidden over here,' Sonny whispered to me, grinning foolishly. He was well stoned. 'But

277

only you and Jim are drinking it. Nobody else knows where it is. I'll show you.'

Sonny and Kirk seemed to be the greatest of buddies. Georgina sat smoking hash and drinking retsina happily. The only one who seemed unhappy was Jane Duval.

I got a water tumbler of straight whisky and put the bottle back in its hiding place and sat down on the edge of a bunk. There were three of them, two of them one above the other, in addition to the huge bed forward. No sooner had I staked out my territory than Stevie-boy came over and squatted down beside me.

Steve was expansive. He was also finely stoned. He had been over to see Chuck, he told me smugly. He seemed very happy about Chuck. Chuck was fine, he told me, except he had broken his glasses.

'Oh?' I said. 'How did he do that?'

'He stepped on them. He put them down by his pack on the dock to go in for a swim, and when he came back out he stepped right on them. Snapped them in the middle. But he's got them taped together.'

'Pretty stupid,' I said. 'Wouldn't you say?'

'No. He can't see a thing when he hasn't got them on. He just didn't see them.'

He could see well enough to ball-kick somebody, I wanted to say. But I didn't say it. 'Mmm,' I said. 'And how is that machete of his?'

'Well, he seems to have lost it,' Steve said and grinned. 'I don't know exactly where. Somewhere in the water. Somewhere in the water between here and St Friday's.'

'It would be hard to find, then.'

'Yes. I guess it would,' he grinned.

I nodded. 'Smart.' Apparently Chuck had told him nothing about our encounter, or our fight. Apparently he had lied to Steve about throwing the machete off the cliff, too.

I didn't say anything, and Steve wandered away. He looked supremely, smugly happy. I got another glass of whisky and sat back down gingerly on my bunk. People seemed to know it was my territory and left it alone. Or maybe it was because I was directly below the snoring little girl. I sipped the whisky and looked around.

Jane Duval reigned over her party with a regal contempt, it seemed. She seemed to have a sardonic, but

278

solid, sense of her total superiority. The contempt, to me, seemed only a very thinnest coating over a real and very deep anger, expressed by those expressive eyebrows of hers. In the heat in the close space she had taken off her tent dress. The scantiest of bikinis showed off that body of hers.

But her attitude toward me was a surprise. After a while she got up and came over and pretended to look at the baby and then sat down by me. Instead of hating me now, she acted intrigued, even flirtatious, in her contemptuous way.

I had assumed it was Kirk who wanted me invited. But now I wasn't so sure.

'I've never met a real "private dick" before,' she said, laying heavy on the Private dick. 'I always thought they were ugly dirty little men with thick glasses. Like shyster lawyers.'

'Not today,' I said. 'Today they all look like CPAs. They're all computer analysts. I'm a vanishing breed.'

'You must have an exciting life. In your grubby little way.'

'In my grubby little way,' I said. If that was what passed for sophisticated repartee by her, Bennington must be worse than I had heard.

'What would you charge me for a divorce case, for example?' she said.

'I never take divorce cases. Too messy,' I said. I grinned. 'Except, of course, if it's a very, uh, special friend of mine.'

'The man? Or the girl?' she said.

I didn't answer her.

'Do you know that I have slept with every man in this room? Except you?' Jane said.

'Bully for you,' I said. 'Were they one-nighters, or longer liaisons?'

'It depended on the man,' she smiled. 'Entirely on the man.'

I didn't feel like going on with it, so I didn't answer. When I didn't, she got up and flounced across the cabin to the other small bunk, waving her bottom at me like a red flag in a bull's pasture.

I couldn't understand her change of attitude. Maybe it was just my continuing indifference. Indifference was one of the best tools to use on women that there was. If they weren't interested in you, they respected and liked your indifference to them. If they were interested, it needled them and fired them up until they were breathing steam.

Anyway, her Bennington credentials were no great thing to me. They didn't aid me at all in what I was looking for.

But it was Jim Kirk not Jane I'd come to watch. And he was very out of it and very cold. He took no part in the sexual antics and he didn't smoke the hash. He stayed aloof and close to the whisky. I still couldn't get a proper fix on him in the whole business.

At one point in the festivities the hash smoke and armpits were getting to me and I went up on deck for some air. A minute later Kirk followed me, and said he wanted to talk to me.

We went out on the point of the bow.

'You're a pretty hard guy to convince,' Kirk grinned.

'About what?' I said.

'About leaving the island.'

'So it was you who got Chantal to jump on me?' I grinned back.

He didn't answer. There was absolutely no fear in him and you could feel it. There was a strong streak of meanness and you could feel that too.

'I guess I am hard to convince,' I said. 'I've been beaten up, shot at, threatened, crotch-kicked, and fired from a job I never got paid for anyway. What else can they do to me?'

'You've been sticking your nose in some things that aren't any of your business. By mistake, maybe. Inadvertently. But some people don't like that. So far you've been lucky. Very lucky.'

I decided I'd try him with the same thing I did Chantal. 'Well, the people you're talking about won't have to worry any more. Because I'll be leaving here soon. I've found the killer.'

He was totally surprised, like Chantal. He began to look pleased. 'You have?'

'I think so. It's one of these kids from the Construction. I won't tell you the name yet, but Pekouris seems to agree with me. The kid had a bloodstained machete on him. I lifted it. I've got it hidden away. He used the same machete to do a guy in in Mexico, it seems.'

Kirk was overjoyed. 'Crazy Chuck. Well, that is great news. So the whole thing is finished.'

'Yeah. I'll hand it over to Pekouris.'

'Fine. I always hoped somebody would be able to pin the guy who did in my friend Girgis,' Kirk said piously.

I wanted to laugh. 'So those people you mentioned can stop worrying.'

'If I knew who they were,' Kirk smiled, 'I'd go tell them myself.'

'Too bad you don't know them.'

Kirk's smile turned into a mean grin. 'Because it wouldn't be wise for you to linger around here too long. In spite of your fantastic luck.' With a delicate movement that bespoke fine reflexes under all his meat, he pulled his hand from his pocket. 'Because see this?'

He appeared to be holding a block of black wood, a little longer than a finger. But then he pushed with his thumb, and a chrome knife blade winked and seemed to dart out of its end all by itself like the tongue of a snake. It wasn't a switchblade. The blade came straight out of the end. Without jerking his hand. I'd never seen a knife like it. It looked positively murderous. He pressed the point against my side.

'A lot of things could happen to you besides being shot at and missed.'

'So that was you, too, was it.'

'Who else?'

'Well, a good knifing's about the only thing that hasn't happened to me,' I said easily.

The blade snicked back into the knife without moving his hand. Kirk put it back in his pocket. 'I just wanted you to understand.'

'Don't ever do that to me again,' I said quietly. 'Or be prepared to push. Because I'll take it away from you and break it on your teeth. So, we both know where we stand, hunh?' I turned and walked away, offering my back.

I threaded my way through the messy tumble of gear and went down belowdecks again. In a minute Kirk came down too and grinned at me.

Two attempts to scare me seemed to indicate a pretty big involvement on Kirk's part of some kind. But did it mean he had killed two people?

The smoky smelly party was still going on.

Finally it was Jane Duval who broke it apart. She stood up and contemptuously removed her bikini bra and said she was going for a swim. She had fine boobs, and apparently was proud of them. She paraded up on deck, with just about everybody following and whooping and yelling, and kicked off her bikini pants. She stood straight and slim for a moment, to make sure everybody got a good look at all of her, and then dived out into the harbour water.

I used the moment to quietly take my leave in the borrowed skiff.

But as I rowed ashore, something seized one of my oars. It was Jane. She floated up on to the surface, feet together, so that the water rolled away from off her dark crotch, and smiled at me a smile that did not change her angry eyebrows.

I didn't respond, and waited patiently, and when she let go of my oar, I rowed on. She swam away with a laugh.

Behind me, I heard other oars and then Sonny calling. He had come out in his own skiff to look for her.

At the dock I tied the skiff and walked on home and went creakily to bed. I didn't call Chantal. She wouldn't even have been home yet, by the time I went to bed.

CHAPTER FIFTY-ONE

Marie's funeral was the next day at noon.

I spent an hour in the Port in the morning, sitting at a café and looking at the *Polaris*.

Watch the *Polaris*, Gruner'd said. *Polaris* was moored at the wharf in the little harbour, exactly as Girgis had left her the last time he walked away from her. Apparently the little assistant was taking care of her, because she looked clean and bright, but I didn't see him. I didn't see anybody else, either.

I found I kind of missed Gruner. He was the only one around here who had ever paid for a drink.

But how the hell was I going to Watch the *Polaris*, without sitting at a café in the Port all day and all night every day?

I had Sonny run me back to the yacht harbour, and put on my city suit and a tie to go to the funeral in.

I probably shouldn't have worn it. It felt strange and foreign when I put it on, and I realized how used I had gotten to being here. When I got up to the local graveyard, on a little knoll above the town, after Sonny had run us back to the Port in the *Daisy Mae*, I found I was the only one there in a suit except for the old ex-Ambassador, Pierson. But somehow I had felt I ought to wear it for Marie.

The old Ambassador was the only one among the rich people and summer residents to show up. I had called Chantal earlier, but she begged off on the excuse that funerals upset her and she hated them. I couldn't blame her for that. I hated them myself.

There were about three Greeks. Almost all the others who came were hippies from the Construction, dressed in their regular clothes. Which was to say, weird outfits. And there weren't too many of them there. But they looked more in keeping with the occasion than my suit did.

Steve and Diane were there, and Sonny and Jane, and Georgina, and some of the others. I didn't see young Harvey Richard. Slow John apparently had already checked out of the island. Marie's landlady was there, conspicuous in a rusty long black dress. It wasn't a great showing for Marie, but I figured she didn't care.

It was the landlady who had done most of the arranging. She spoke a little broken English and told me how nobody had claimed the body. Since there was no known address to send it to in America, she and the local priest had arranged burial here. She had gone around taking up a collection. Mr Steve, the young man from the night club, had given generously. Well, believing what Steve believed, I thought he should. I gave her two thousand drachs from my pocket, and her eyes widened. She thanked me.

It was hot and dusty in the sun. Almost no grass grew in the place. But you could see the green sea shading to blue out below the town. After the ceremony, the old Ambassador came over and shook hands.

'I didn't expect to see you here.'

'I knew her a little,' I said.

'I didn't know her.' He smiled lamely. 'But seeing as it was another American, I thought I ought to come.'

'It was good of you,' I said. 'She would have appreciated it.'

'Oh,' he said vaguely, and smiled.

'How are things with you, sir?' I said.

'Things? With me? Oh, all right. Fine. Just fine.' He straightened himself in his white tropical worsted. 'I've been upset by this murder business. But perhaps it will put a stop to some of this hashish smuggling for a while.'

'Yes,' I said. 'I hope so. But probably not for long.'

'Probably not,' Pierson said, and looked off at the sea. 'Well, it was nice seeing you again. If under these sorrowful circumstances. I enjoyed our lunch that day. I hope we see each other again before you leave.'

I took his hand. 'Yes, sir. I hope so too.'

I watched him walk away in his pure white worsted. His house was only a little way away down the road. I walked back to the Port alone.

Sonny Duval was in a group ahead of me, and when we got back to the café terrace I told him I might need him and to stick around with the boat. They all seemed subdued, as they sat down together at a table. But quite soon laughter was coming from the table crowded with drinks, where Georgina was again playing older sister and picking up the tab. I figured Con Taylor must make a lot of money in Athens, to support her hippie habit.

I took a table alone beside the parapet among the mouldering cannon, and stared down at the *Polaris*.

I had not been sitting there fifteen minutes when Jim Kirk came up to the wharf and boarded her. A minute later Girgis's little assistant came up and went aboard. As I watched, they unmoored her and fired her up. Then the assistant stepped back on shore and Kirk took her out through the harbour entrance. He headed in the general direction of the mainland, and he didn't change course.

Good old Gruner, by God. He hadn't given me any bum steer. I didn't know what it meant but I sure intended to find out, and I was beginning to have a suspicion. I knocked back the rest of my Campari, left money, and went to get Sonny at his table.

'I want you to follow that boat,' I said when we came

284

out of the harbour mouth.

'The *Polaris*?'

'That's the one,' I said patiently. 'That one there. You see any others?'

It was still plainly visible, maybe three-quarters of a mile away.

Sonny only looked puzzled, and settled in to follow her, almost exactly behind her and in her wake over the flat sea. 'I wonder who's taking *Polaris* out?' he asked.

I didn't much like taking him into my confidence, but he was going to find out eventually.

'It looked to me like Kirk,' I said. I was watching him at the helm. He didn't budge it, and after a minute I stepped over to him. 'Here, let me have that helm.'

'Why? What's the matter?' But he gave it to me.

'Nothing,' I said. 'But I don't particularly want to advertise to him that we're following him.' I veered us off to the eastward. Kirk was heading east of north in a straight line for the shoulder of the mainland east of Glauros, probably to round it and head north up the coast. We were headed toward nothing, there was nothing but open sea in front of us; but from where Kirk was, if he should happen to look back and check, he wouldn't be able to read our angle and it would look as if we were heading due east for the Tsatsos yacht harbour.

I let us run like that for a while.

Sonny was watching me closely. I thought he was getting the idea. Anyway, I didn't bother to explain it.

'I wonder where he's going in her?' he said.

'Probably up to his boss's,' I said. 'Kronitis. Up the coast there.'

It looked like I was right. When he reached the shoulder of the coast, *Polaris* cut north right up the coastline, pretty much the same route I had taken that day with Marie.

'Why?' Sonny said.

'Who knows?' I said.

'Then why are we following him?'

'Who knows that, either?' I gave him a grin. 'Maybe I'll think up a reason, if we stay out long enough.'

He shut up.

I let us run a little farther, then cut straight back for Glauros on an acute angle with our former heading.

After half a mile, I headed her east again, but this time almost due north-northeast instead of east-northeast as before. Now we were headed toward the island of Petkos, and hopefully would look like another boat entirely, going to Petkos.

I wasn't at all sure that Kirk was watching behind him.

'Can you get this shade-awning down?' I said to Sonny.

'Yes. I think so. Going this fast the canvas whips a lot, but I guess I can do it.'

'All right. You be ready to get it down when I tell you. Without the awning we'll look like a different boat entirely. Leave the forward part attached and roll it up, so we can just unroll it and put it up again when we want.'

'I'll take a look at it now,' he said.

Kirk was almost below the horizon by now. And if I continued on my present course slightly away from him, *Polaris* would sink out of sight. When she was almost invisible, I turned us slightly north and jockeyed the *Daisy Mae* until we were heading parallel with her.

'Okay, take the awning down,' I told Sonny, and let up a couple of turns on the throttle to aid him. Hopefully now we would look like an entirely other boat, heading north for Hydra which looked faint and blue like a mountain in the far distance.

When the awning was secured, I just stood and let the boat run, the outside of my leg holding the helm steady.

Maybe I was taking too many precautions. There was no reason to think Kirk would suspect he was being followed. But I would rather take a few precautions too many than have him spot us, and be alerted later on.

'That's pretty slick,' Sonny said beside me, the wrinkles of his eyes squeezing up. 'Where did you learn all that?'

'Tailing a boat? I learned it in the Caribbean. From a local Jamaican. On a case I worked on. He learned it from his father, who was one of the slickest rumrunners and hijackers in the Gulf of Mexico during Prohibition.'

'Well, it's pretty sharp.'

Off on our left on the mainland coast Kronitis's villa appeared, gleaming white at us. We watched the almost seadown *Polaris* turn into the little cove.

'All right,' I said. 'Now we wait. We'll run a mile on up

286

the coast, and come back down with the awning up again.'

While we waited I queried Sonny about aqualungs. He had just the one old rig he'd told me about earlier. The regulator leaked a bit, but it didn't matter because he never went down in it more than ten feet, to clean his hulls. There was only one air bottle. It was maybe three-quarters full of air at the moment, he reckoned. The whole thing reposed in the back store-room at Dmitri's right now, he said, apologetically. Because he didn't have room for it on the big caique. It wasn't exactly the rig I would have chosen to work with, if I'd had my druthers.

'Well, it'll have to do me,' I said. 'Our problem now is to get hold of it. Do you think you can find it quick at Dmitri's?'

He was sure he could. He knew just where it was. I told him we were going to wait and see, but if I knew what I thought I knew, we'd have a chance to run and get it when Kirk went back to the Port in the *Polaris*.

I didn't tell him why, which was that I figured Kirk would have to stop in at the Port to pick up Girgis's old assistant, before he could go out and do any diving. If I had told him that, I would have had to explain why he would be diving, and if I explained that I would have had to go on and explain the whole story.

'Was Girgis ever a skindiver that you know of?' I asked him.

'Yes, as a matter of fact, he was. He used to keep two or three lungs, and take people out diving, back at one point. But he gave it up, and concentrated on the tourist boat instead, because there just weren't that many people who wanted to go diving or learn it.'

'And there isn't that much to go diving for, around here,' I added on.

'Will you please tell me what the hell we are doing?'

'No. I won't tell you,' I said. 'Mainly because I don't know what we're doing myself. And I won't know exactly, until we get there and do it.' That was a lie. But he had to be satisfied with that.

Kirk was gone for over half an hour. We made circles and figure-eights to keep way under us in the rising afternoon wind.

Finally *Polaris* came nosing out of Kronitis's cove, and

started heading back. I followed, using the same techniques I'd used to follow him north.

When Kirk rounded the mainland shoulder and headed straight in for Tsatsos Port, and didn't vary his course, I veered us off a little to the south and when we were close to shore ran us in to the yacht harbour at the poor old *Daisy Mae*'s top speed, along the face of the town.

While Sonny was getting his aqualung from Dmitri's store-room. I ran up to the house and got one of my guns out of my locked briefcase. I wrapped it in a polyethylene bag from the kitchen, and tucked it in my belt inside my shirt. When I got back on board, I put it carefully on one of the edged shelves below in the cabin.

We arrived back at Tsatsos Port just as *Polaris* was pulling out of the harbour mouth, and turning west along the island coast. I immediately veered off toward Glauros.

It was great to be back in action and doing something again, after sitting around so long and brooding.

CHAPTER FIFTY-TWO

Kirk headed west. He appeared to be going on around the island, and he stayed pretty close in. I let him get half a mile ahead. Then I turned from my Glauros heading and ran back in close to shore. Until a point put me out of sight of him.

I settled down to following him from close in to shore. I would throttle up along all the concave parts where he couldn't see me. Then I'd throttle down and sneak around each point cautiously. I tried to time it so that he would just be disappearing around the next point ahead.

It was easier tailing, in one way. The bad thing was that he might change course, and turn in somewhere when I couldn't see him; and I might run up on him. That was the chance I had to take.

But he didn't. And I didn't. It worked perfectly.

I noticed Sonny watching me closely. I was having fun, and enjoying myself, and turned my head and winked at him. He didn't grin back. He looked shocked, as though it upset him that I should be enjoying it.

About a mile before he would have reached St Friday's Kirk did turn in. I cut my throttle immediately and cut in to shore out of sight. Under very slow throttle I sneaked up on him until I was only two coves behind him.

We were around on the seaward side of the island now. Around here there was just about nothing. A couple of points of the island stuck way out up ahead. There was a rocky islet about a mile off shore, bare and too small for trees. The rest was open sea. The only other thing visible anywhere was an old freighter beating its way west and flying a Turkish flag.

I figured that had to be the boat.

I had stopped us behind a rock spur that hid us from *Polaris*. Sonny had binoculars aboard and I took them and waded ashore and climbed the spur and stuck my head up over it.

Kirk, with glasses of his own, was climbing up the headland he had stopped at. When he got to its brow he planted himself and put his glasses on the Turkish ship. I lay and watched him through my glasses while he watched the ship through his.

The Turkish ship came on slowly, chugging through the flat sea. At about St Friday's it turned slightly inland and began to make a slight curve closer to the island.

There wasn't any doubt in my mind any longer. I put the glasses off of Kirk and on to the ship, and watched it.

When the Turkish ship was not too far out from the rocky islet, I saw three flashes wink out from its side, and then saw something white hit the water. I marked the spot, as best I could, then swung back to Kirk.

Kirk was watching the ship steadily, marking the spot in his own mind I guessed. Then he put his glasses down on their strap against his chest and started to climb back down to *Polaris*. Out at sea the ship began to curve slowly back on to its former course.

I dropped my own glasses and scrambled down the rocks and waded back out to the *Daisy Mae*.

I had figured Kirk wouldn't dive for it right away, with the ship still there. I didn't know if he would dive for it in a little while. If he did, I was screwed for getting a look at it, and could only continue following him.

What I expected was that he would go out and maybe dive or swim around to locate it and drop a marker buoy on it and come back later and pick it up, maybe at dusk, or after dark without lights. When it was safer. But Kirk didn't even do that.

In a couple of minutes *Polaris* came chugging back, presumably heading back to Tsatsos Port. Apparently he had done the operation enough, with or without Girgis, to know exactly where to look. Or else he had a better sea eye than I did, which was probable. As *Polaris* chugged past our spur, I motioned Sonny down and we both froze. In another couple of minutes *Polaris* chugged out of sight behind the next point.

I waited fifteen or twenty minutes.

'All right, let's got out and have a look at it,' I said.

I wasn't as confident as I sounded. I'd expected Kirk would leave a marker buoy. I had made a rough triangulation by eye between the islet and the nearest point, but I could easily be four or five hundred yards off when I got out there. What bothered me most was how much air I had in the lung tank. I didn't dare use it to search.

The only thing I could do was park the boat and make a series of widening circles around it with just a mask, flippers and snorkel. If I didn't find it, I would have to have Sonny tow me around. That would be even colder. But I was sure the white flash I'd seen hitting the water was a marker panel to the drop itself.

Out by the islet I jockeyed the *Daisy Mae* back and forth, sighting from islet to point until I thought I about had it. Then I put on Sonny's old sweatshirt and went into the water. The water was cold.

I found it on the third pass. I was already freezing cold. Swimming about a hundred yards out from the boat, I saw something white way off to my right. The bottom was eighty or ninety feet. The square package lay edged between two dead coral ridges, the luminous white marker panel floating maybe twenty feet up, above the package. The white panel was what I had seen hitting the water. I waved for Sonny to bring the boat and got into the lung and wrapped a line around my arm and started down.

Almost immediately I had trouble with the leaky regulator. The whole dive would have made a great Red Skelton comedy. With me playing Skelton and Sonny playing Keenan Wynn.

There are two kinds of leaky regulators. One kind is temperamental and cranky near the surface, but gets better and harder and tighter and cleaner the deeper you take it. The pressure helps it. The other kind just leaks more and more as the pressure rises. Naturally, with Sonny, I had the second kind.

By the time I got to sixty feet I was having to gulp a swallow of water with every breath, and breathe very slowly to get any air through the bitter tasting water. I silently cursed Sonny's slipshod way of living and swam on down. His goddamned regulator was indicative of his whole undisciplined life.

But after sixty feet it levelled off and didn't get much worse as they usually do. Good old Boyle's law. I was glad I knew it. The volume of a gas is inversely proportional to its total pressure. If I hadn't known it, I'd have given up at sixty feet.

On the bottom I warped the line around the package's tie ropes. I took a quick glance at my depth gauge and saw it read the equivalent of ninety-two feet. I was shaking so hard from cold I could hardly tie the line.

I left the line warped to the package and started up breathing as little as possible. I watched the boat's silhouette get larger gratefully.

Once again I realized about myself that only a moron would have tried what I'd just done, with a regulator that bad.

On deck I jumped up and down to try and get warm. At least my crotch wasn't hurting me much any more. My side sent me occasional flashes. I ate Sonny out roundly and savagely for his slop-ass, mushy way of living. He only looked at me.

'What do you think he's doing?' he said, when I'd finished. That was all it meant to him.

It was my turn to look at him. 'It's hard to say,' I said.

'Well, you must have some theory?'

'Did you see the ship?'

'Yes.'

'Did you see it signal?'

'Yes.'

'Well, what do you think he was doing?'

'I don't know. Playing some cops and robbers game.'

'Well, what do you think I was doing down there, in

your goddamned leaky regulator, taking a chance with my goddamned life?'

'I don't know. Getting something.'

'Well, goddam it, haul it up, you dumb bastard, and find out!' I shouted.

By the time he got it to the surface I was in better shape. At least I wasn't frozen. It was heavy, and from the surface to the deck I had to help him.

The package easily weighed 150 lbs, and was about the size of a sack of cement. It was elaborately wrapped with waterproof wrapping. I put myself to untying and unwrapping it carefully so it could be rewrapped without anyone knowing. Inside the waterproof wrapping was another waterproof sack. Inside the sack were smaller sacks of waterproof plastic. Inside these was a crumbly brown stuff that had the look and texture of brown sugar.

I picked some of it up and sniffed it.

'Well,' I said. 'That's it, all right.'

'What is it?'

'That's morphine base. The stuff they make pure heroin out of.' I looked up at him, and saw he wasn't getting the import of it. 'They don't refine this. They just change it chemically. In other words, it doesn't diminish in bulk when it becomes heroin. So they've got themselves over 150 pounds of pure heroin here, when they put it through the lab. And you can set up a little lab anywhere. In an abandoned farmhouse,' I said, and looked off into the diminishing afternoon.

The sun was almost down to the horizon. 'Or in an old villa,' I added.

I was thinking about something else, too. Kirk mightn't have killed Girgis and Marie over a petty hashish racket. But he might have killed them over a million-dollar heroin operation.

I began to rewrap the package carefully.

'What are we going to do with it?' Sonny said.

'Nothing,' I said. 'Put it back. Then we're going to watch where they take it.'

'So you are a nark, after all!' Sonny said triumphantly. 'Pete Gruner was right about you all along!'

I just looked at him, and didn't answer. If he wanted to think I was a nark temporarily, I wasn't going to stop him.

'How much is this worth?' He kicked the package lightly.

'As heroin, delivered in France, about $300,000,' I said. 'But the price goes up, when it's delivered in New York. And when it hits the street, it goes up a lot more.'

Sonny whistled. Then he began to slap his arms against his chest. 'Jesus, I'm cold.'

'You're cold!' I hollered. I had to bite my lip.

He was like all the rest of them. They were the ones who were always harping about sensitivity all the time. But when it came to the fact, their enormous sensitivity never extended more than six inches out beyond their own skins.

When we'd dumped the package back in the water, I ran us back to the rock spur we had hidden behind before.

Kirk was quite a long time coming back. It got dark.

'How long are we going to have to stay here?' Sonny said, after the first hour.

'Till Kirk comes,' I said.

'Well, at least let me have one cigarette.'

'No smoking,' I said sharply.

'Well, can't I go below? And have just one puff?'

'Do you want to find yourself in the middle of a gun battle?'

'No.'

'Then don't smoke. I want to smoke myself.'

He complained about just about everything else, too. He was tired. He was cold. He was hungry. He couldn't complain about being thirsty, since there was plenty to drink, water as well as other things. I consoled myself with a couple of Scotches and listened to Sonny, and thought what a great thing a couple of years in the Army would have been for him. Or even a couple of years in the Boy Scouts.

Kirk arrived about an hour after that.

He was running completely without lights. This was strictly illegal, but it wasn't as illegal as what he was after. There were a couple of sudden bright sweeps of a searchbeam out by the rocky islet, that struck at us like screams, in the darkness. Then the motor stopped. I caught a glow on the sea's surface of a powerful underwater flash. Then silence. Ten minutes later the motor started up again.

I listened to the fading motor carefully. It was moving west, on around the island, and staying in very close. I was pretty sure I knew where they were going, if that was their heading.

'Aren't we going to follow them?' Sonny said in a stage whisper.

'No,' I said. In a normal voice. 'I think I know where they're going. We'll go around the other way. It's a lot safer.'

I waited until I could no longer hear their motor and fired us up. For a little while I ran without lights, then switched the running lights on. We were headed back towards Tsatsos Port.

When we passed the town, it was all lit up and alive with people. Music and voices carried out to us across the water.

Farther along at the yacht harbour the lights of Dmitri's taverna came out to us, and the blare of his jukebox.

'It's lonely, isn't it?' Sonny said beside me.

'Like this? No. It's great,' I said.

Around the sturdy little lighthouse, solidly throwing out its beacon to night mariners, Georgio's taverna made another landmark, easy to steer by.

When we were almost to the point at the eastern corner, I let off on the throttle and steered us in, and ran us in on a moonlit beach. We dropped the anchor out behind us into the sand bottom. I tied the bow line to a tree. Before I got off, I got my gun out of the polyethylene kitchen bag and put it in my pocket.

We had to cross two ridges, wooded with scrub and a few low pines. I didn't mind. I might have run us a little closer but I didn't want to take the chance. Anyway, there was a nice comfortable path in the moonlight. Sonny Duval complained anyway.

When we got to the top of the second ridge, I motioned to Sonny and slowed us down.

When I peered over the crest, we were looking down on the old villa owned by Kronitis – or at least by one of his corporations – which I had noted so long ago with Chantal and filed away in my head.

Lights were on in the villa. And in the beautifully appointed little cove lay the launch from the *Agora-*

phobe, and *Polaris*. Both were moored in the elaborate little concrete docks I had noted before. The whole cove was practically invisible, except for a few yards from directly out to sea. And even then it was hardly noticeable.

I knelt by a scrub clump and watched for five minutes. Men moved from the *Agoraphobe* up to the villa carrying things in their arms. At the villa there was an outside cellar door with light coming from it. The men carried whatever it was they were carrying down into the cellar. Then three men ran down the long staircase of concrete steps to the cove and boarded the launch. Jim Kirk and two men stood on the patio at the top and waved them off. The launch pulled out and headed back north, toward the lighthouse and the yacht harbour, the way we had just come. Kirk and the other two went into the villa.

'Okay. Let's go home,' I said.

Three-quarters of an hour later we rolled into the yacht harbour looking like two innocent men who had been out night fishing. It didn't matter, there was almost no one there to see us. The taverna was closing up.

I sent Sonny off. Then I caught one of the last of the horse-cabs left at the stand by the taverna, and told him to take me up to the house of the Countess Chantal von Anders.

CHAPTER FIFTY-THREE

I hadn't telephoned ahead, and Chantal's place was battened down for the night. I didn't mind. It was only a little after midnight. I was sure Chantal wasn't home yet. I banged on the garden door and hollered.

The whole thing was falling into place. I didn't have all the threads yet, but I had enough to see the shape of the tapestry. I didn't have my murderer yet, was all.

In a few minutes the fat, middle-aged Greek maid of twenty-four came waddling down the patio steps. I listened to her putting the chain on the door inside, before she opened it.

I didn't have to say who I was. The minute she saw me she started to simper and slipped the chain. She locked the door behind me and led me up, turning on lights as she went. She had thrown a dingy robe over her enormous udders in her flimsy nightgown and her hair hung in a thick rope over one shoulder. I had only seen her maybe twice, but she knew me. She knew me well enough to know I was Madame's new lover.

That was how she treated me. She simpered and offered to make me coffee or something to eat, and when I said no, left me in the living-room with the bar.

I couldn't stand it in there. I was too highed up from the boat, and following Kirk, and the villa. I got myself a drink and went outside and sat in the overhead swing in the shadows on the patio.

That was where I still was when Chantal came in and locked the garden door.

Her eyes widened when she saw me sitting in the shadows. I guessed I was a formidable figure. I felt formidable.

I didn't beat around any bushes. I told her I knew all about the heroin ring that was operating out of Tsatsos. Her eyes widened again.

'I know more than that,' I said grimly. 'I know where the ring headquarters are. I know Kirk and the *Agoraphobe* are involved. I know Girgis with the *Polaris* was the pick-up man for the operation. I know Kronitis is the money man. Or they wouldn't be using "his" villa. What else have you got to tell me?'

She put her purse down on the outdoor table, and sat down on an outdoor chair. 'There isn't any more to tell, I guess.'

'Oh, yes there is,' I said. 'There's a lot more. Let's start with where you are in it.'

'I'm not in it,' she said in a low voice.

'You've got to be,' I said. 'All right, later. Who's the boss? The big boss? Who's the general?'

She didn't answer.

'Maybe you'd like for me to get you a drink first?' I said.

'I would like a drink.' She was lovely in her evening make-up.

'I'll get us both one,' I said. 'If you'll promise on your Scout's Honour not to run off somewhere. I'd hate to come back and find you gone.'

Her eyebrows fishhooked, and her eyes flashed anger. 'You don't have to be nasty.'

I didn't answer that. If I went into why I thought I had a right to be nasty, it might take a very long time. I went and got the drinks and brought them back.

'I want to know, first off, who the boss is.'

'I suppose Jim is the real boss,' she said.

'No, he's not. Kirk may be the field general. But he's not the big boss.'

'Then I suppose it's Leonid. But he doesn't do anything.'

'Oh, yes he does,' I said. 'He arranges to have shipments of over 150 pounds of morphine base dropped off Tsatsos by Turkish freighters. He pays for that. He puts his old villa, owned by some dummy corporation, at the ring's disposal for a lab and drop-off place. He arranges, I assume, to get the H the lab makes out of the morphine base to Europe, or to America. I would say he does a lot.'

Chantal didn't say anything, and drank. 'Would you get me another drink, please?'

I went and got it. 'What about the hashish operation? Did Kronitis know about that?'

'No. He knew nothing about it at all. He was shocked when you told him about it.'

'So whose idea was it?'

'Girgis's. He wasn't satisfied with what he was making from the heroin thing. He wanted more. He opened up the hashish running on his own.'

'And you went along with it?'

'Yes.'

'And Kirk went along with it?'

'Yes. It was money. It was there. The hippies were there. The market was there. If we didn't do it, someone else would have.'

'And you were greedy,' I said.

'Leonid was terribly angry when he found out from you. He called Jim in and made him swear he wouldn't do anything like that again. Jim lied to Leonid and put all the blame on Girgis, and said he had nothing to do with it. Leonid never suspected me.'

'He was absolutely right, Kronitis,' I said. 'The police were bound to come around eventually, looking into the hashish racket. And if they did, they might stumble on to the much bigger heroin deal by accident. I'm surprised they haven't been around before. Where does Pekouris fit into it?'

She looked up. 'Pekouris? I don't know anything about Pekouris.'

'All right,' I said. 'Forget that. What about the heroin for the Ambassador?'

'That was Jim's idea. He approached the Ambassador himself.'

'He was stealing the heroin from the stock at the villa,' I said.

She nodded. 'Yes. Later, he came to me and asked me to carry it for him, as a favour. He didn't want to be seen too much with the Ambassador.'

'And you did it.'

Again her eyebrows fishhooked at me. 'I only did it as a favour to the Ambassador. Jim said he would stop otherwise. I didn't take any money for it.'

'And Girgis threatened to tell Kronitis about the heroin?' I said.

'No. I don't know he did that.'

'He was blackmailing you, wasn't he?'

'Not about that. He was threatening to tell people I was working for him.'

'There was bad blood between Kirk and Girgis, wasn't there?'

'Yes. Jim wanted a bigger share of the hashish money.'

'And he's preparing to go right back into it, as soon as the heat is off.'

She shrugged. 'Yes.'

'What a lovely trio,' I said. 'The three of you. Even your own crooked boss couldn't trust you.'

She looked up and shook her head. 'But he wouldn't do something like that. Kill him and – and cut off his head.' She shook her head again.

'You think so,' I said. 'Let's get back to where you are in it.'

'I told you,' she began but I interrupted.

'Don't lie to me. One more lie to me from you and I'll lump your pretty jaw. You've got to be involved in it. You know too much, and you're too close to it all.'

She hung her head and looked down at the stone flags of the patio floor.

'I carry it for them to Europe. To Paris.'

I almost yelped. 'What! You what?'

She nodded and looked up at me timorously. 'That was how I got involved with Girgis and the hashish in the first place. That's how I got to know him.'

'How did you get involved?'

'Leonid came to me.' She shrugged. 'About two years ago. He asked me if I would carry something to Paris.'

'Who did?' I said. 'Who came to you?'

'Well,' she said, and swallowed. 'Leonid.'

That was some kind of a lie. But I couldn't tell what about. 'And he didn't tell you what it was you'd be carrying. Is that it?'

'Oh, yes. He told me. He showed it to me. He had had some special Vuitton luggage made with false bottoms. In Rome. He bought the luggage in Paris and took it to Rome somewhere and had it remade. I was to carry those. That was all I did. He handled all the details himself. I just delivered the bags to an address. They were sent back to me later at the hotel. He said I'd make a great carrier for him. With my title, and my style, and my social contacts. I thought it was a great lark. And he paid me handsomely.'

'By God,' I said. 'You've got nerve. So you're the European delivery boy.' I still could barely believe it. 'Do you have any idea what would happen to you if you got caught? How many years you'd be in jail. How did you get yourself mixed up in this?'

She gave me a pale smile. 'Money. It's really very simple: Just money. All I really have is this house here on Tsatsos, and barely enough money to run it. He knew my situation. He knew that I had no money to winter in Paris; would have to live on Tsatsos all year round, unless I had extra money. So he arranged for me to earn it. Can you imagine what it would be like, living here in winter alone, with everyone gone?'

Incredible. 'Your social life,' I said.

She didn't answer. 'I love my social life.'

'What about the rich ex-husband? The Count? What about all the expensive alimony?'

'Nothing,' she said. 'All his money goes to transporting handsome young boys around the capitals of Europe. He's spent his entire fortune on it; and is swiftly spending everything he has left. All I really have is just barely enough to run this house he gave me. Why do you think I told you I couldn't afford your fees?'.

'Couldn't you take him to court?'

'And have him exposed as a homosexual?' Chantal said. She smiled. It was a very European smile. 'Anyway, a court probably wouldn't award me additional money. To winter in Paris every year.'

'So it all comes out,' I said, and grinned. 'The dirt. For money. Like everyone else, it comes down to the money. You rich people ain't much better than us lower classes, are you? When you haven't got the money?'

'In a way I'm glad you've found it all out. I've been trying to quit, but they wouldn't let me. It's not fun any more. Not now, with all the publicity about dope. And all these damned American agents running around all over Europe.

'But I could never quite bring myself to tell you. And it was never that overt. They never tried to threaten me. They were too polite. But when I said I wanted to stop, they always talked me out of it. And I always let them.'

'Sure. Meantime two people have been killed.'

'Do you think I haven't lain awake thinking about it?'

'No. I don't think you have. Not much . . .

'But I don't understand how you could let them run you like that.' I thought a minute. 'They. You keep saying they. Did you have an affair with Kirk?'

'Good heavens, no. Jim? I'd never have an affair with him. Jim thinks he's a ladies' man. Kirk loves them and leaves them. He's an oaf.'

'He's back with Jane Duval now,' I said, and watched her face.

'Oh, her. She's had affairs with half the people on the island. She even had an affair with your Sweet Marie.'

'I know all about that,' I said.

'Jim had an affair with your Sweet Marie, too,' Chantal smiled. 'Did you know that?'

I looked at her blankly. Something had touched at my mind.

'He did?' I said, vaguely.

A fading echo, a lost laugh, a piece of burnt newsprint browning in a fire. I reached down in and fished around for it, and it slithered away from me. Had Marie ever mentioned an affair with Kirk to me?

I remembered her telling me, guiltily, about the affair with Jane Duval. Very clearly.

I leaned against the swing support. I could suddenly see Marie's face in front of me as real as if it were there, clear blue eyes, wide mouth, blonde down on the always tremulous lip. '*Did you know I had an affair with Jane Duval? Hand me those pants.*' Had she ever mentioned Kirk?

'What's the matter with you?' Chantal said. 'What happened?'

'Nothing. I've just thought of something,' I said. 'Something very important. Listen, I've got to go.'

I didn't remember whether she said good night or not.

Outside the garden door I stopped and leaned back against the wall a while and looked up at the clear star-freckled star-marked sky.

It didn't take it long to come. Quite suddenly, like a brick dropped on the top of my head, it all fell into place. And I remembered that Marie hadn't mentioned Kirk.

It had been there all along, plain as the nose on my face, and as close in front of me, all the time I was suspecting that poor crazy dumb kid, Chuck. I wondered if Pekouris had ever suspected it.

I pushed away from the wall and started down the hill to the harbour and the house.

But now that I had the son of a bitch, how was I going to prove it? How was I going to catch the son of a bitch out and prove it?

That was going to take some thinking.

CHAPTER FIFTY-FOUR

Back at the house I put out all the lights but one, and got a new Scotch bottle and ice and a glass. I lay down on one of the couches in front of the fireplace, the Scotch and ice on the floor beside me.

When I leaned my weight on my left arm, or leaned on my left elbow, my side still sent shooting pains through me. Well, to hell with that. I sipped cold Scotch.

When I put it all together correctly, it fell into place so naturally. There was no longer any doubt. When you knew it, you were amazed you hadn't seen it sooner. But they always seemed like that, cases. But how was I going to prove it? I didn't give a damn about their goddamned heroin ring. I could break it up. Or they could go on running it. I didn't care, as long as I got that son of a bitch for killing Marie.

I settled myself, and winced, and sipped some Scotch, and started cudgelling it.

I was still there the next morning at 8:15 when the old woman came padding in and touched me on the shoulder and woke me.

The Scotch bottle was still sitting on the floor, half empty. The ice had melted. The glass was lying on its side in a wet spot.

I was no nearer to my fourth down quarterback's sneak touchdown solution than I'd been the night before.

I had dreamed about Chantal. It was not an original dream. But it was vivid and horrible. I had dreamed she was being caught, and there was nothing I could do to help her. They were going to send her away for twenty years, or some awful term like that. Pekouris was there, and I tried to buy him off with every nickel I possessed in the world. Even my wife's alimony. But somebody, Kronitis, was paying him more. More than I could ever hope to scrape together. And there was nothing I could do.

I got up and went upstairs and took a quick spit bath in the lousy tub and shaved and put on a pair of trunks and a fresh shirt to hide my bandage and came back down.

It was working up to being another hot day. I wondered if there was some way I could use the heroin ring itself? But I couldn't think of any way.

Coffee tasted as bitter as defeat in old age. I got a Scotch and soda, instead. I sprawled on a couch in the living-room. I didn't even want to go out on my porch. I was like a man trying to glissade a curling stone that didn't have any handle. After an hour the old woman got on my nerves so much, padding around and pretending to clean, that I sent her away for the day. I watched her go down the front walk and down the road to Dmitri's where she stopped and sat down. Spending my money. I suddenly hated her. Pointlessly. Outside, people were playing. I hated them, too.

I went back and got another Scotch. If I couldn't use the heroin ring itself, what could I use? There didn't seem to be anything. I sprawled back out on the couch. Then I sat up. Then I lay down again.

There was a discreet knock at the door, and Jane Duval walked in without waiting to be asked.

'I saw your housekeeper at the taverna,' she smiled. 'She said you sent her away for the day.' She came up the three steps from the hall.

'I thought I'd come by and see how you liked our party night before last. You missed the best part. It went on after you left.'

She was in her Mother Hubbard dress, and her quirky eyebrows were at work, and the child wasn't with her. There seemed to be a secret, vastly superior knowledge in her smile she kept turning on me. She was pretty obviously here to be seduced, and there didn't seem to be much doubt in her mind that she would be.

The sheer dumbness of it, or the sheer vanity, whichever it was, was flabbergasting. It was like something out of a two-bit movie, after all the errant subtleties my mind had been playing around with the last few hours.

'You've been brooding about me, haven't you, Mr Davies? Since the other night?'

I was still sprawled out on the couch. She came on in and sat down on the other couch, across from me. I looked at her, and did not get up. An idea had come into my mind from nowhere, from the left-field bleachers. I started playing with it. There might be a way I could use her.

'A little,' I said, and grinned. 'But I guess I'll survive it.' I let an amused look come into my eyebrows.

'I could tell. You know, I meant it when I asked you what you'd charge for a divorce case.'

'You and Sonny aren't married, are you?' I said.

'Oh, we're married. He just doesn't like people to know it. Sonny has a lot of money, you know.'

'Forget it,' I said. 'I'm interested in other things. How old are you?'

'I'm twenty-four.'

'Then, you graduated from Bennington at twenty?'

'Nineteen. I was a prodigy.' She raised her head high on her neck, like some actress in a film take, and looked out the end of the room over the harbour. 'I'm sick of living like this. I want bright lights, and music, and movement, and people. I hate this living like a bum.'

'What about the revolution?'

'You don't have to be a bum, to be a revolutionary.'

'You don't, huh?' I didn't pursue that. 'I understood you were pretty stuck on Con Taylor. Weren't you?'

'Yes. I still am. I like Con a lot. But he's basically a weakling.'

'But you've been seeing Kirk since you got back, haven't you?'

She didn't answer for a long moment. She seemed to be trying to figure out which answer I wanted to hear. 'Of course.'

I gave her my wild old man look. 'I see.'

'Do you?'

'Do I?' I wasn't even having to invent my lines.

She moved, lithely, two steps, and swung her behind from her couch across to mine, and sat down beside my bare feet. 'You liked my little trick, did you, of swimming up beside your boat? I could tell you liked it.'

'I liked it fine. It bothered me a little that Sonny was right behind us. Didn't it bother you?'

'Why should it?'

'Does Sonny know you're here now?' I said.

'I don't know. I don't care. Does it matter?' She started playing with my ankle.

'Not to me,' I said, and grinned.

'Well then?'

I didn't say anything. For answer I put my bare foot against her thigh in the Mother Hubbard.

'It was very dark,' Jane said. 'Did you see all of me?'

'I saw all of you.' Christ, she was writing all of my lines for me.

'Did you like what you saw?'

'Sure,' I said. 'But what will you bet Sonny isn't watching this house right now?'

Jane smiled. 'He would never do that. He "understands" me. Would it bother you if he was?'

'Me? Not me. I would like it even better,' I said.

She laughed, and stood up. 'It's suddenly gotten terribly warm in here.' She stripped off the Mother Hubbard. Under it was the bikini of two nights ago. She sat back down, this time at my waist level, and put her hand up under my shirt.

'Hey. What's this?'

'Adhesive tape,' I said.

'Is that from your fight the other night?'

'Yes. I guess one of the horsecab horses must have stepped on me.'

Jane put her face down against my jawline. 'Poor darling.'

'It doesn't hurt,' I said. 'Do you know where Kirk is now?' I whispered into her ear.

'No. I don't know. He's disappeared, for a couple of days. Since the night of our party.'

'What would you say if I told you where he is right now, and that he's all alone?' I whispered.

She sat back up and looked at me. 'I wouldn't say anything. Not with you here.'

I made my voice as ambiguous as I could. 'If I told you where Kirk was, would you go to him?'

She looked puzzled. She gave me a long look. 'Is that what you want me to do?'

I grinned. 'Maybe.'

She thought a minute. 'Would you go with me?'

I grinned again. 'Maybe. After all, we're all friends.'

A sudden kind of hot rapacious smile of delight came over her face. 'Is that what you like?'

I grinned a third time. But avoided a direct answer. 'He's at an old unused villa around the corner of the island. I think it's owned by some corporation. You know the one I mean?'

She nodded. Her eyes were as bright as museum-lit sapphires. 'So that is what you like. You naughty boy. What's he doing over there now?'

'He's taken the *Polaris* there. I don't know. I think he's just getting away from here.'

Jane touched my chest again, where the tape was. She didn't say anything.

'Have you ever been there with him?' I asked. I was willing to bet my roll she had.

She nodded. 'A couple of times.'

I didn't know whether he had let her in on the heroin lab secret. I expected not. 'I happen to know he'd like to see you.' After a pause, I said, 'Maybe I would come along later.'

Without a word, her eyes even brighter than backlit sapphires now, she stood up and put her long dress back on. 'When?'

'I don't know.' I looked at my watch. 'Maybe right after lunch? Sooner, if I can. But I'm hungry.'

There was a kind of sly look of secret triumph on her face. She started for the door without a word. Then she turned back, 'I knew there was something delicious about you.'

'Maybe it would be better not to tell him about me. Let it be a surprise.'

She thought about this, and frowned.

'You use your own judgment,' I grinned.

She gave me a big rapacious smile. 'A surprise is even better.' She went out.

I walked to the windows and watched her ride off on her bike down below. Then I looked at my watch again. I had all the time in the world. I made myself a drink.

I was suddenly feeling great. I was feeling so great I was half afraid sparks might start shooting out the ends of my fingers, and ignite me.

I went to the lockup closet and got my briefcase out and got my two guns out of it and put them side by side on the green desk blotter. They looked very pretty and very lethal, on the green backing. Display pieces.

CHAPTER FIFTY-FIVE

I had maybe three hours to kill. I spent almost an hour on the guns. You wouldn't think that much could be done to a couple of simple, double-action short-barrelled .38s, but it could. Neither of them had been used in quite a while. I cleaned them, and oiled them and wiped them down, and checked all the moving parts, the cylinder swing-outs, the trigger pulls. Then I did a couple of other little things.

For what I wanted. For the kind of fight I expected, and hoped I would be in control of. If there was any fight at all.

I had once been an ardent student of ballistics and trajectory. I easily found enough tools in Con Taylor's kitchen tool drawer for what I wanted to do.

It was kind of a long shot, my plan. My plan for Kirk. It was one of those dime-novel tricks. But it ought to work. Especially if Jane Duval did her part right, it would work.

I still couldn't be sure she would not tell Kirk I was coming. But the beauty of my plan was that it would work whether she told him or not. It would still work, even if she told him.

I put the guns in one of those little airline satchels that was lying around the house and stowed them on board the boat. I found Sonny, and told him I would want him and the boat a little later. Then I went back to the house.

I sat on my porch a while. I was too keyed up to read. I didn't want to drink any more, not with the job I had in front of me. Finally I remembered my precipitate departure from Chantal last night, and went in and called her.

'How are you feeling?' I said when the maid finally got her on the phone.

'I'm feeling all right,' she said. 'Is there any reason I should not be?'

'No,' I said. 'None at all. What are you doing?'

'I'm sitting in bed, having my mango with lemon juice, and my tea. And reading yesterday's two-day-old paper that was brought to me this morning. The sun is shining in my window.'

I remembered there was a phone extension in the bedroom. 'Sounds great.'

'It is great.'

I remembered that at one point she had lied to me again last night. Something about Kronitis. About how Kronitis inveigled her into becoming his carrier.

'You remember what we talked about last night?' I said. Her voice got guarded. 'Yes?'

'Well, how long does it take them to process the stuff, once they've got it here?' I didn't want to tell her I'd seen them bring it in last night.

'They can do it very fast,' Chantal said. 'If they really work at it. I don't actually know. Why? You're not thinking of trying to catch them?'

'Me? No. I'm no narcotics man,' I said. 'The only thing I'm after is that killer.'

'That girl certainly did something to you,' she said. Her voice sounded plaintive. 'I wish I could do something like that to you.'

Get yourself killed, I thought grimly, and you can.

'Well, you can rest assured Jim is not the person you want,' Chantal said. 'That I can assure you. I know he would never do something like that.'

'I'm glad you think so,' I said. 'Listen, you lied to me again last night.'

'I did? I lied to you?'

'Yes. Something about Kronitis. I didn't understand what. But I noticed it.'

There was a pause. 'Well, I see no reason why I should have to tell you everything, if I don't want to. You don't work for me any more, remember?'

'Do they have a phone out there?' I said patiently.

'No. There are no telephones in outlying houses that far from town. Why?'

'But Kronitis has a phone.'

'I'm not planning on calling him today, if that's what you mean,' Chantal said.

'Good,' I said. 'Don't. Look. The real reason I called you was to tell you I dreamt about you last night.'

'Oh?' Her voice got slower. 'What kind of dream?'

'It was a silly dream,' I said. 'You were going to jail.'

'And you couldn't help me?' she said.

'Look, if you want out of this thing, I'll find some way to get you out,' I said. 'If you really want out of it, I'll get you out of it. For good.'

'Well,' she said thoughtfully. She drew the Well out. 'How would you do that?'

'I don't know yet. But I'll do it.'

'I would like out of it,' Chantal said.

'Okay. That's all I called about. Look. I'll talk to you later in the day. I've got to go somewhere. Try and keep your mouth shut about all this stuff. Try.'

'It would do me no good anywhere to talk about it, that I can see.'

'Fine. I'll call you later. Goodbye.'

'Goodbye, darling.'

I hung up. That Darling wasn't the sincerest Darling I'd ever had thrown at me. But then I remembered I had received no call from Pekouris in Athens, about the news of Chuck and his machete which I had planted with her, and with Kirk. That meant neither of them had called it in, to Kronitis. – Or did it? That Pekouris was such a slippery character.

I went back out on my porch and sat down. I wanted a drink. But I wouldn't let myself have it.

I killed another hour over lunch at the taverna. I didn't eat much. I trained on Scotches, but only a couple that I sipped, making them last a long time. Red wine was no good. It slowed up the reflexes. Scotch could heighten the reflexes, if you took only a little, and didn't take it too long before.

After lunch I figured it was time. I had a second coffee. Then I went and got Sonny.

I had told him to stay around, that I would be wanting him, and he was down by the boat, squatting in the dirt in the hot sun and talking to several of the old Greek men who sat all day in chairs out in front of the taverna playing with their Greek beads. Watch out for the beads, some Greek my own age I had met had warned me, laughing; when you buy the beads that means you are old. You sit in front of the taverna and play with the beads, you are old man.

Sonny and the old men were laughing. It was a sleepy, sun-lazy summer afternoon; people were still drinking their after-lunch wine at the taverna tables.

I took Sonny on board the *Daisy Mae*, and took him back to the stern where nobody could overhear us.

'I'm going over to that villa to pick up Jim Kirk,' I told him, very slowly. 'I'd like for you to go with me. We know he's there. I'm going to perform a citizen's arrest on him, or whatever they call it in Greece. But I'm going to need somebody to help me.'

The deep wrinkles around his eyes squinched up at me, and the thick Elliot Gould moustache twitched.

'Won't Kirk be on his guard, over there?'

'Well, I think I've done something that will help keep him occupied,' I said.

'There's two other men there, though,' Sonny said.

I nodded. 'I think I can get them locked up in that cellar. If it all works out like I'm hoping. But maybe it won't,' I said, very slowly. I didn't want to get him all excited. I didn't want to get myself excited. I looked at him.

Sonny only nodded, warily.

'I know you're a stupid ass,' I said slowly, 'and can hardly find your way out of a paper bag. I know you're supposed to hate violence. But I've no one else to turn to. And I want someone to cover me. I'll do all the dangerous work. At least, as much as I can.'

Sonny stared at me a long moment. 'You're taking him in for the heroin?'

I nodded.

'Or for the killing of Girgis?'

'That, too. I'm convinced he did it. I have been for quite a while. And now I've got proof that he did. I've been getting surer and surer that this kid Chuck didn't do it. Now, do you want to go, or don't you? If not, give me the goddamned keys and I'll go alone.'

I thought I had him figured right. He didn't even answer. For answer, he turned his back and went to the motor hatch and started the motor.

I went forward to cast us off.

After we rounded the little lighthouse, and passed the low roofs of Georgio's taverna on our right, I ordered Sonny to stop the boat along a deserted stretch of the coast. We were maybe a quarter of a mile out.

I went below and got the little satchel and brought it up and opened it, and handed him one of the guns.

'Now, do you know how to handle one of those things? I don't want you to shoot yourself in the belly or blow off your foot.' I stuck the other one in my belt.

He took it, and looked at it. It was a standard snub-nosed .38 Police Special, the twin of mine.

'Well, I learned how to use a gun in the ROTC in school, but in principle I am very much against the use of firearms,' Sonny said stiffly.

'Well, this may very well be a case of your ass or Kirk's,' I snarled. 'And using an Army rifle in the ROTC is a whole lot different from shooting a pistol.'

'I fired the .45.'

'Is that all?'

'Well, I've shot a few other pistols. For fun. On a range.'

I looked around. I grabbed up an empty five gallon gas can that was sitting by the motor hatch, and tossed it out over the side maybe six or seven yards. 'Don't worry. I'll buy you a new one,' I said. 'Here. Let's see you take a shot at that.'

Sonny looked at the little gun again, then levelled it and sighted a long moment, then fired. The slug hit the can at the water line, and there was a 'Plowww!' from the water. The gas can began to sink. Actually, it wasn't at all bad.

'All right,' I said, and nodded. 'That's not too bad. It'll have to do. Okay, let's get on with it. Here, give me the gun and I'll slip another round in it.' I took it while he started the motor and turned into the shade and slid another shell in it and gave it back to him.

'What about reloading?' Sonny said.

'Don't worry,' I grinned. 'If you get to where you have to do any reloading, it will already be far far too late.'

He stared at me.

'Don't get nervous,' I said. 'I'm hoping we won't have to use these things at all. It's only a precaution, really. Here, give me the helm. Let me run it the rest of the way in.'

CHAPTER FIFTY-SIX

In a while we rounded the last point before the villa and I started bringing us closer in. I came in as close as I dared. Only a few yards from us now, the sea swell heaved and dropped and smacked ponderously against the rocks. We were close in enough to catch some of the spray.

'I'm going to run her straight in,' I told Sonny as I jockeyed the boat. 'I'm counting on the fact that nobody will be down at the cove. The launch from *Agoraphobe* is at the harbour. The two guys are going to be working down in the lab in the cellar. Kirk wouldn't go down to the cove anyway.'

I was beginning to get my combative feeling. There was a battening-down process that came with any competitive physical event. It was the feeling a player got before a game. Or a fighter before a fight. Or a pianist before a recital. Wherever something important was at stake. All your sensories got screwed down tight and hard, into concentrated essences.

The feeling was more than mildly unpleasant. But the excitement vivified you more than the unpleasantness made you suffer. It could get to be like dope. Unless you had an iron will. I wanted to whistle.

Right then, I wouldn't have traded my profession for anybody else's on earth. I was going to get my killer. Sure as anything.

Where we were they could not possibly see us from the villa on the bluff. I was sure they couldn't hear us, either. And at this time of day the wind was blowing towards us from the northwest, in addition.

At the narrow entrance I made the sharp turn, and cut my motor immediately as soon as I was around. We glided in in silence.

There was nobody there. As I'd predicted. Silence surrounded us like cotton wool. Outside, the sea still hammered faintly at the rocks. Up the bluff a couple of birds sang. The *Polaris* lay moored at one of the docks. Her bumpers squeaked against her hull. The water lapped against her.

'Grab her rail,' I called in a low voice as we drifted to her. Sonny grabbed, and at the stern I grabbed. We made fast to her and then sneaked out over her to the concrete dock.

I motioned Sonny to come on to the long staircase up.

'Now don't shoot me in the ass with that thing,' I muttered.

Once we were on the long staircase, we went up it fast. We made no noise in the sneakers I'd had us wear. I paused at the top. Nothing moved. Nothing was visible. The villa seemed deserted, if anything. We crossed the patio at a slow run.

When we were safe against a wall, I told Sonny to wait there, and went around to the back where the outdoor cellar was. I listened down the slanting stairs. I could hear the two men working and talking. A faint odour of heat came up. Silently I closed and barred the double doors. I waited a moment to make sure they hadn't heard, then sneaked back around to Sonny.

Nothing had moved. Nothing had stirred. Inside, or out. The high french doors of the villa were not only unlocked. They were wide open to the afternoon breeze. I motioned Sonny to stand by the door.

'You cover me from behind,' I said in a low voice. 'I don't know where he'll be. But for God's sake don't shoot that thing in my direction. Don't shoot it at all unless you absolutely have to. If you have to shoot somebody, shoot them in the leg.'

I slid over to the open door and leaned against the wall beside the sill. While I gathered myself, I realised momentarily that I was enjoying myself immensely. I was loving every second.

I moved my head and winked at Sonny, and came out from behind the wall and put a foot over the sill. I went in in a crouch.

It was a lovely old villa, both outside and in, if a little run down. It was built like they built them at the turn of the century, when they still believed in things lasting. When planned obsolescence was not a concept. The big front room had tall french doors, and high windows above them, on the three sides that faced the sea. The old-looking curtains were blowing in the sea breeze like loose sails. The fourth wall, equally high, had a balcony that ran across it and gave access to some rooms, the bedrooms I guessed.

Around the corner of the main room was a pantry. I moved a step so I could see around the corner. Deep in the pantry Jim Kirk was standing before a refrigerator, concentratedly drinking a bottle of beer. The funny thing was he was in his underwear, and his socks.

The underwear was some kind of fancy flowered boxer shorts. The socks were ordinary sweat socks but they sagged badly. He had no shirt on. Also, his hair was rumpled. Beside him on a plastic tray were two more bottles fresh from the icebox with moisture beaded on them in the heat, and two glasses that looked like they'd been chilled in the icebox too. Kirk looked as if he had just gotten out of bed upstairs with Jane Duval, and had come down to get them some refreshment before going back.

Also on the tray was a large Smith & Wesson revolver. I guessed, because he had no place else on him to carry it.

I didn't know why, being an old sea captain, he was in his socks. You would have thought he'd be used to going barefoot on deck. But maybe he always went to bed with ladies in his socks. I didn't know very much about him, really.

He was so concentratedly drinking his beer he had no idea I was there. But then I could be pretty quiet, when I had to.

'Okay, Kirk,' I said. 'Finish your beer. But then turn this way and come out of there with your hands on your head. Whatever you do, don't touch that tray.'

He stopped swallowing and slowly untilted the bottle. He turned his head. He set the bottle on top of the refrigerator. 'What the hell?' he said. But he came out with his hands laced on his head.

'All right, Sonny,' I said. 'Come on in.'

I listened to his footsteps coming in. He certainly wasn't as quiet as me. 'Keep your gun on him,' I said.

'What the hell is this?' Kirk said.

'Where's Jane?' I said.

'She's upstairs. Now, what do you want?' He grinned. 'You didn't have to come with a gun. And what's he doing here?'

He was no panicker, Kirk. He was an old hand. He had probably had guns pulled on him a lot more than once. But this time he had a right to look puzzled. Because, this time at least, I knew he was innocent.

I didn't answer his question. 'You better call her down,' I said.

'Fine,' Kirk said. He bellowed. 'Jane!'

From upstairs there was no answer, no movement.

'I'm sorry about this part, Sonny,' I said. 'But I had to do something to keep him occupied. It was the only way I could think of.'

Sonny didn't say anything. 'You sent Jane over here?' he said after a minute.

'It was the only thing I could think of to do,' I said.

'You son of a bitch,' Sonny said.

'Sorry about that,' I said. 'But what the hell? You knew she was sleeping with Kirk ever since she got back from Athens. Didn't you? If you didn't, you're pretty dumb. I thought you condoned it.'

Sonny's ears turned slowly red.

'I put up with it,' he said. 'But that doesn't mean I liked it.'

'Well. I'm sorry. It can't be helped,' I said. 'We better get on with this. Jane!' I bellowed, myself. No answer from upstairs. She had to be hearing us. 'Here,' I said to Sonny, 'you've got your gun? You keep him covered while I collect that cannon of his.'

'Say, I want to know what the hell is going on here,' Kirk said, as I started past him. He still had his hands on his head. I picked up the gun. 'If you think you're moving in here to break up this operation we've got going, you better think about it. I warned you, Davies. You're messing around with things you don't know anything about. You've been lucky up to now. Because certain important people have protected you. If they hadn't, you'd be dead already. But they're going to take a very dim view of this.'

'Shut up,' I said. I took a look around the pantry, and in the kitchen. I didn't see any cellar stairs. I came back in front of Kirk. 'So certain people are protecting me, hunh? Who?'

'You'll find out. Soon enough,' Kirk said. 'After this mess.'

'Shut up,' I said again. 'All I want to know from you is if there's an inside cellar stairs in this place.'

He gave me a look. If he was hoping for help from the cellar, he knew now it wasn't coming. It showed on his face, and was the answer I wanted. I grinned. 'Yeah. They're all locked up nice and tight,' I said. 'Now, you want to know what's going on? I'll tell you what's going on. I'm taking you in for the murders of Girgis and the girl Marie. That's what's going on, old buddy.'

'You're *what*!' His big face expressed total disbelief.

'That's it. There's no question in my mind. You killed Girgis to have all this heroin trade to yourself, and then had to kill Marie because she knew you'd done it.'

'You must be off your rocker,' Kirk said disbelievingly.

'There's nothing personal in it,' I said, and grinned.

'We're not here because we dislike you. Are we, Sonny?' I looked over at him. Then back at Kirk. 'What's more, I'm taking Jane Duval in as an accomplice. Or at least, an accessory after the fact. Now call the broad down.' I leaned heavy on the Broad.

'You're crazy,' Kirk said with his mouth open. 'You're really crazy.'

'Go on,' I said. 'Call her down here. Or I'll go up there and drag her down.'

Behind me I heard Sonny curse.

'Oh, Christ,' Kirk said under his breath. Then he bellowed. 'Jane! Come down here! You better come down here, damn it!'

There was a kind of pause everywhere, it seemed, for a moment. It seemed to me even the breeze stopped blowing the curtains, but I was sure it didn't. Then a door creaked upstairs, and Jane Duval came out. All three of us looked up at her. She was clad only in a towel she had wrapped around her. It was a short towel and it didn't hide much except her nipples and her navel. And we were looking up at her. I felt like hollering 'Beaver!' but refrained. She came clear out to the balcony railing and she had a big broad sexy smile on her face. A fake one. I guessed for the first time since I'd met her anyway, she wasn't looking superior and self-confident. I was rather pleased.

'Sonny!' she said. 'What are you doing here?'

Behind me Sonny cursed again.

'You better step back, honey, you're exposing your secrets,' I said. I hardened my voice. 'Then you better put something on, it's breezy, and come down here. Because we've got something serious to talk about.'

Behind me Sonny began to curse again, steadily this time. I turned to look at him. I was holding the two guns carefully in my left hand, dangling, with my first finger through their two trigger guards. Sonny was dead white. His face was all squeezed up between his heavy brows and his Gould moustache like a pair of wrinkled pants between the two bars of a hairy pants-hanger, and his mouth was wide open and contorted with his cursing.

'I didn't do it!' Jane Duval cried from the balcony. 'I didn't have anything to do with it. Nothing to do at all. Okay, I screwed them. Girgis said he would take me away from here, to America. Marie was going to go back to New York with me together, at one point. Con Taylor said he would take me away to Rome. But I didn't kill them. I didn't. And I don't care. I don't care, and I'll shout it from every court in the land. I'll tell it to everybody. You take me to court and see! I'll go to court. I'm willing to go to court. I want to go to court! I can prove I didn't do it. I don't know who killed them. But I didn't!' She clutched her towel around her.

There was a long silence after she stopped. I turned to look at Sonny. So did Jim Kirk. So we both saw it when he moved the gun.

'Hold it!' Kirk said urgently. 'Hold on. Let's just talk about it a minute.'

'God damn you,' Sonny said. 'God damn both of you. Davies, turn around here. Put those guns on the floor. Keep your right hand away from them. Lay them down, with your left hand, and push them over here.'

I turned and put the two guns on the floor and slid them over to him meekly. Kirk watched me, hungrily. Sonny kicked the guns away from him into a corner viciously, a dangerous thing to do if you knew a hammer could bang up against a wall and ignite a cartridge.

'You thought you were a smart guy, huh?' Sonny said, in a contorted voice.

I didn't answer him.

He was breathing heavily. 'Thought you'd get me over here, and get me to expose myself, did you? Okay, I'll expose myself.

'I killed them. I killed them both. Me. Sonny Duval. And I'd have got Con Taylor too, if you hadn't stuck your damned nose in it. And this one, too.' He glared at Kirk. 'I'd of got him too. You think I give a damn? I don't give a damn. I don't give a *damn*.'

He sucked a breath. 'But it won't do you any good, all your smart shit, smart guy. Because you forgot one thing. You didn't think about it. You gave me a gun, you dumb bastard.' He grinned.

'I guess you've got the drop on me, Sonny,' I said. 'You outfoxed me.'

Beside me Kirk's eyes were getting bigger and bigger. He kept looking back and forth from Sonny to me.

'You're goddamned right I have. I've outfoxed everybody. Until you got into it, Davies. But it doesn't matter. This way's just as good as any other. I was going to cut out from here anyway, soon. As soon as I'd taken care of Con Taylor. But I'll get him some other time.' He stopped, and swallowed. He threw a quick glance upwards.

'Jane, come down here! Put your clothes on, honey, and come down. There's nothing to be afraid of. These tough guys aren't going to hurt you. They're not going to hurt anybody. Come on down, and we'll get out of here. For good.'

I looked up at the balcony. Jane Duval's eyes were getting bigger and bigger, too. Her hands, knuckle-white, were gripping the balcony railing. Her towel was slowly slipping off her. Now she was just about all exposed. Nobody seemed to care, at the moment. I certainly didn't.

Sonny swung his eyes on me. 'The money's been stashed away a long time. And I've got the boat. All I need is our passports. I've had it all ready a long time, actually. Nobody'll ever catch up with us. When you've got the money, nobody can touch you. All you need is enough money, Davies. And I've got it.' He grinned, and swallowed.

'They won't even know I killed you two. I can make it look like you shot each other.

'Honey, put your clothes on! Why are you standing there? Don't look so scared. There's nothing to be afraid of.'

Jane didn't move. Sonny didn't know it, but I could have told him. Jane wasn't about to get ready to go anywhere with him, ever. She'd rather have married me.

Sonny looked at Kirk. 'You none of you ever understood her. You thought she was an easy lay. I told you over and over you didn't understand her. Big tough he-man males. Every woman a notch on your gun. Knock them over like the ducks in a shooting gallery. Sure.'

He swung the gun on me. 'You think I didn't see her over there at that house of yours all morning? I saw it. I recorded it. Here.' He tapped his temple with his other hand.

Back to Kirk. 'But you. You fat slob. You're the worst of all. So I'm giving you the honour of being first.'

Covertly I looked over at Kirk, whose eyes were

bulging with disbelief. His whole face seemed to bulge outward with a mighty effort to stop what was happening to him. Here he was, his face screamed, about to die, really actually about to die, at the hands of a stupid madman, who was shooting him, who was in the act of shooting him, the whole thing was crazy, and nobody was doing anything to stop it, him, Jim Kirk.

In front of us Sonny pulled the trigger on the little gun, the hammer rising and falling with a kind of inexorable inevitability.

The gun crashed out, enormously loud in the room. Jim Kirk stood, blank-faced, waiting for something to hit him.

I had an enormous desire to laugh. Sonny was still firing, at Kirk and at me, the shots crashing out deafeningly in the room. Kirk and I stood and looked at him. On the balcony Jane was screaming to add her share to the racket. For once in my life I thought I could award myself first prize, for staging and set designing if not for anything else.

About the time he ran out of ammo and began firing clicks, it dawned on Sonny that neither of us had gone down. He looked down at the gun in his hand.

'That's it, Sonny,' I said, quietly. 'That's right. I put 'em in there for you myself.'

He looked down again at the gun, a moment longer. Then, 'You son of a bitch,' he screamed, and threw the gun at me and bolted out the door.

I ducked the gun, and jumped for the corner where the two honest guns were. It was about eight steps. But the duck had cost me the split second I needed to beat Kirk, and he was there ahead of me. He blocked me off with his big butt and fell on his knees and grabbed both of them. He was sobbing.

'I'll kill the son of a bitch! I'll kill him!'

'You dumb bastard,' I hollered. 'You'll kill nobody. Give me one. He's getting away.'

He simply glared at me. 'I'll kill the son of a bitch! I'll kill him! I'll kill him!'

He was on his feet now, and I slugged him on the jaw as hard as I could. He sat down, his eyes a little glazed, but still holding tight to both guns. Waveringly, he pointed one of them at me. I wasn't sure he knew I wasn't Sonny.

Anyway, I didn't have time to sit down and discuss it with him. I turned my back and ran for the door.

Up on the balcony Jane Duval was still screaming, monotonously, without an opera singer's inflections.

CHAPTER FIFTY-SEVEN

I hit the patio running, and went across it at a dead run for the boat stairs. I was sure he'd head down for the boat, and I wanted to catch him before he could get it moving. The thought that he might get away now was unbearable. Instead, I ran right into him, head-on, at the top of the stairs on the landing.

I didn't know why he had stopped. I didn't have time to think about it. Suddenly he just appeared in front of me. He had stopped just below the landing of the staircase down to the cove, and then run back up. I caught a momentary glimpse of deep confusion, and deep rage, on his face. He seemed undecided whether to commit himself to the boat, or take a chance on trying his luck in the hills. Nobody but a tinhorn would think of going for the hills on a tiny island like Tsatsos.

I was trying to slow up, and get my feet under me, and get my arm cocked for a punch.

Sonny jumped in the air, and took two steps towards me. I threw the punch in mid-stride and missed. Sonny, whining high in his throat like some animal, grabbed me just above the waist with both hands and lifted me, and threw me down on the stone patio on my back.

I weighed 195 pounds. It was an impossible physical feat. Even Kirk wasn't that strong. I knew Sonny wasn't.

I lit flat out, and the wind whooshed out of me. My bad side seemed to burst open like a melon. Pain knifed through my chest like a jolt of electric current. It was as if someone had thrust a red-hot sabre in, between my bad ribs and shoved it through me till it pushed against the skin on the other side.

He could have killed me then. All he had to do was stomp me. Or kick in my head. Instead, he turned and ran down the long staircase to the boats. As if I had made up his mind for him which way he wanted to go.

I rolled over and got to my feet like a crippled bird with a broken wing, cursing weakly. I had gone feeble all over. My left arm was clamped against my screaming side and felt paralyzed. I had to go after him. I had to get him. But what the hell. In this kind of shape, what the hell was I going to do with him when I got hold of him? I couldn't stand the thought he might get away, now.

I started down the steps one at a time. Even one at a time was an effort. They seemed about a mile down, down there. I couldn't go faster. I kept my left arm clamped against my side. I was still cursing. I could clench and unclench my fist, but I couldn't seem to lift the arm. I worked on flexing and unflexing my hand. Down below I could see Sonny scrambling out across *Polaris*, and untying the lines from the *Daisy Mae*. He ran to the helm.

For a long moment he looked up at me, his head thrust back, his neck corded, his mouth a black hole. The whites of his eyes seemed enormous in his face. I crimped on down, trying to run. There was no point in hollering anything at him. He knew what I was after.

From the stairs his face was a study in planes and angles. It wasn't even the same face. There were no curved surfaces or lines in it. Even his eye holes seemed squared off into rectangles.

He started the motor as I was just about down. I jumped the last three steps.

I was beginning to move a little better. But the jar of the jump hurt me. I started to run across the bottom of the U of the docks for the *Polaris*. I could move my left arm a little now. The motor's roar came across to me. Up on the bluff they wouldn't even be able to hear it, or just barely.

The thought that he might get away was intolerable.

There was one thing in my favour. He was going to have to turn the boat to get out. And it was going to take him a little time. The space was narrow. He was going to back right past and around *Polaris*'s higher stern. The only other choice was to back right out into the sea swell that was coming in at an angle and kicking up waves at the narrow angled entrance.

I didn't think anybody would back a boat out into that swell. In here, it packed an enormous wallop when it burst against the unmoving rocks at the entrance.

Daisy Mae's nose was already swinging wide of the Polaris when I got to her. Too wide to jump. I didn't bother to cross her deck. I ran aft along the starboard rail for the stern.

As I reached her stern, Sonny swept back past me in a stately way, his eyes glaring above his black hole of a mouth. There wasn't anything he could do to change her movement, now. He didn't say a word, I didn't either.

When his midships passed me, I jumped down on to her coach-roof and grabbed the awning.

That jump hurt me, too. Worse than the first. It was as though an exploding fireball went through my side. But my blood was up now. I started aft after him along the boom.

Sonny was having his troubles. He was trying to manoeuvre the boat, watch the rocks at his rear and me in his front, all at the same time. I was unhampered by any such concerns. I gave him a grin. With his strangely planed and angled face he gave me a snarling glare. Neither of us spoke. I jumped the gap from the coach-roof to the motor housing and went for him.

He had already put the engine in neutral, but momentum was still carrying *Daisy Mae* backwards towards the rocks. As I jumped he shoved the gear lever forward into forward gear and at the same time picked up a spanner wrench he must have kept in the motor well, for the engine. It was a heavy spanner.

I had no choice but to go in into the wrench. I figured the less time I gave him to get set the better. I wasn't going to let a spanner wrench stop me at this stage of the game. It was easy enough to see coming, as I dived. He drew it back and hit me with all his force. I hunched and took most of it on the pad of muscle on my left shoulder and rolled my head with it but it slid off upward and hit my cheekbone and the whole left side of my face went numb. But I managed to grab his sleeve with my left hand. It would have killed me if I had taken it straight.

The force of the blow was so great it knocked me sideways in mid-air. My feet hit the bulwark, and I scrambled them against it and dived in again, still holding on to the sleeve. Sonny went down under me, and I rolled my back into him and got my other hand on the arm and began working on the hand holding the wrench. Behind me Sonny was snarling and cursing and whining in his throat, and punching me in the side of the head as hard as he could with his left hand. Blood was pouring down the left side of my face past my mouth. His fist kept slipping in it. Then he bit me in the back as hard as he could bite.

But I'd found the tendon in his wrist, and shook the wrench loose and pushed it overboard. I tore my back loose from his teeth and rolled on around and hit him in the jaw with my right.

It was as hard as I could hit. It should have knocked him out. It hardly fazed him. He hit me with his right and left, from down under me, and made my head ring. I hit him back repeatedly with my right. My left wasn't much good, but I used that too, and hit him on both sides with all the punches I could throw.

But I couldn't put him out. He punched back and rolled and squirmed, and fought with what seemed to be four times his strength. He fought like a madman. Which, at least at that moment, I guessed he was. But I was turning into a crazy man myself. Then, by accident, he hit me under the arm on the left side in the ribs.

Everything went white in front of me. For a long moment, I thought I was going to faint. When I could see again, everything was blurry and milky. The pain was just about the worst I thought I had ever felt. If he had hit me there again, I was sure I would faint. But Sonny didn't notice, and kept hitting for my head.

But then I thought I wouldn't faint. If he hit me there again. If he hit me there a dozen times, I wouldn't faint. I seemed to swell up inside with some force in me that couldn't be licked. Not by him, anyway. And I was happy.

Anyway, to faint, here, in these circumstances, was to be dead. The thought of him getting away from me, even if I was dead, was still intolerable.

I got him by the throat with my good hand, and grabbed him by the hair with my weak one, and moved to let the blood still pouring off my face run down into his eyes, and began to choke him and bounce his long-haired head on the deck. If I couldn't choke with my weak hand, I could guide with it.

His punches got slower and feebler and stopped. I stopped banging his head. When I let go his throat, his right arm jerked up and tried to hit me. I banged his head again. That seemed to do it.

I got up shakily and looked around. Everything looked different. Everything looked washed, and strange and new and as if on a different planet. The boat was in no danger. The helm had been pushed hard over to starboard, and the *Daisy Mae* was turning in slow tight circles to port. The wind was blowing her slowly towards the far dock, but she wouldn't hit for a while. I stepped and got a hank of waxed seizing and tied him up before he could come around. I tied his hands behind him, and tied his feet, then ran a loop between them and cinched him up tight. He wouldn't be getting loose from that. Then I turned to take care of the boat.

Up on the bluff Kirk and Jane Duval were standing on the edge of the patio, watching. They had had centre box dress circle seats for the thing. I waved to them jauntily.

Sonny was still out when I tied up to *Polaris*. But his breathing was regular. I left him there.

I went below and got a handful of gauze compresses to stop the bleeding from my cheek. In the little mirror I saw it had been laid wide open. It was still numb. It would take eight or ten stitches to close it properly. I would have a nice scar, for about year.

Also, I had barked two knuckles and sprained one thumb. I couldn't see my back. But any kind of real assessment at the moment was ridiculous. I could hardly take a breath because of my side, which seemed to be burning with fever.

I left the boat pressing the compresses to my cheek.

It was a long, hard climb up those stairs again. I tried to make it look like it was easy for me.

CHAPTER FIFTY-EIGHT

'By God. That was some fight,' Kirk said, as I came up on to the patio.

There was a nice breeze blowing under the pine trees up there on the bluff. I sat down on a stone bench and let it blow me.

The dappled shade was pleasant. But my side was killing me. Kirk came over.

'I was all ready to shoot him,' he said. 'If he whipped you.' He held up his big Smith & Wesson. He seemed to be all over his big scare. He handed me my two .38s. He didn't seem to be mad at me over my little trick.

'Thanks.' I stuck the guns in my belt. 'You mean before he killed me? Or after?' My side was really ruining me.

'Well, I couldn't hardly shoot that close to you while he was killing you. I might have hit you.' He grinned.

Jane Duval followed him over, as if she did not want to get far away from him, and stood beside him not saying much. She was still shocked. She was back in her Mother Hubbard. It had not dawned on her yet that soon she would probably be in control of a good part of Sonny's money.

It was pretty plain she had never entertained any ideas about Sonny being the killer.

I found it pretty hard to work up any sympathy for her, anyway.

I turned my head and looked at her bleakly, but she didn't say anything to me. So I didn't speak either. She kept looking at Kirk. She was depending on him now. I wanted to boot her in the ass.

'I would have killed him,' Kirk said, 'if I could have. If you hadn't got in the way.'

I didn't say anything. I could have sat there on that bench and let that wind blow me just about forever.

'I'm getting too old for this business,' I said.

'You don't look too good. How do you feel?'

I made myself get up. 'How do you think I feel? I'm coming apart at the seams, that's how I feel.'

I turned to Jane. 'Go on inside the house and wait there,' I said with male chauvinist authority.

She went, without a word. But the look she left with me was not exactly loving.

'I want you to take her back to town,' I said. 'I don't want her on the boat with me and Sonny, trying to cut him loose, and then the two of them trying to kill me a second time.'

I couldn't stand the thought of her on the boat with me.

He leered. 'I'll take care of her. She's very docile. Right now. I know just what she needs. What are you going to do with him?'

'I'm turning him over to the local police chief, with a deposition. Then I'm calling Pekouris in Athens. I'm not at all sure Pekouris will be happy. It's liable to upset his tourist trade.'

Kirk grinned. I looked at him. I wanted just one thing from him. That was to get as far away from him as possible before he stole something from me. I allowed myself to sit down again.

'By the way,' I said. 'Your two crewmen from the *Agoraphobe* are still locked in the cellar. Don't you think you should let them out?'

He shrugged. 'To hell with them. I'll let them out after.'

'I'll be wanting depositions from you and the girl, too. So don't be going off on any honeymoon with her yet. I want her in town this afternoon.'

'I guess I'll have to sign one,' he said. 'Under the circumstances.'

'I guess you will. When the police come around and ask for it.'

'I guess you'll be leaving the island now,' Kirk said, in a sudden crafty way. 'Hunh? And leave us in peace? I hope so, anyway. Now you've found your killer.'

Something about the way he said it made me furious. I'd done a lot of pretty low things. In my checkered career. But fronting for a heroin factory hadn't been one of them, yet. I got a lot of my business because of people like Kirk. I spent about half my time picking up strayed dumb brats, and helping their dumb parents piece them together after they'd been shooting the H people like Kirk shipped into the Land of Promise. I would rather have not had the business.

But talking to Kirk wouldn't do me anything. Kirk was only the capo. I wanted to talk to the big boy. That meant Mr Leonid Kronitis. I still found it hard to believe old Kronitis could be the head of all this.

'You said something, before, about some powerful people protecting me,' I said.

'Did I say that? I don't remember saying that,' Kirk said. 'I must have been excited.'

'You must have been.' I got to my feet a second time. 'Well, I guess that about does it.' I was bored and I was tired. This was like a hundred thousand other valueless conversations I had had with a hundred thousand other crooks and con-men. I gave him a dirty look, and asked him where I could find a doctor for my face and he told me there was one in Glauros, who had an X-ray machine and fluoroscope and a regular surgery.

I thanked him. I didn't offer to shake hands. Kirk didn't seem to mind that at all.

'That was one hell of a fight you put up down there,' he called after me as I went to the landing.

I just moved my head. I was concentrating on getting down those stairs again. I started down. I looked just as long as it had coming up.

From the *Daisy Mae* I looked back up the bluff. Jane Duval had come back out of the villa, and was standing by Kirk on the edge of the patio. Kirk waved. I saw him urging Jane to wave, too. Finally, she did.

I figured I might as well wave back.

'Call Kronitis,' Kirk yelled down. 'Before you do anything.' They turned away.

I figured they'd be back in bed before we rounded the point.

CHAPTER FIFTY-NINE

Sonny was groaning a little bit when I climbed back on board. I left him alone. I suspected he was playing possum, and wasn't really unconscious now at all. I didn't really care.

It made me crazy mad every time I looked at him. But there wasn't anything to do about it. Just as there wasn't anything to do about Marie, now, either. He had done it and it was done.

I could no longer disguise that I was limping with my bad side. The pain just hurt me too much. I busied myself with getting us out of there. I took in the bow and stern lines, started the motor, backed into the slot Sonny had tried to use, and headed us out in the sunshine for the little white-water waves of the entrance.

Sonny lay without moving. He groaned every once in a while. I hoped they were genuine groans. I had no sympathy for him at all. I hated everything about him.

I had figured it out last night at Chantal's. I had known who it was since then. But after that I had been so preoccupied with figuring out how to trap him, and then doing it, that it had become an abstraction. A game.

Now, though, it was real enough. Looking at him lying there, alive and breathing and solid, just as if he still had the right to call himself a human being, it was plenty real.

It was what Chantal had said about Jane Duval having an affair with Marie that had switched on the lightbulb inside my head.

I had known about that, but I had never looked at it in that special light. Jane had had an affair with Marie. Jane had had an affair with Kirk. She had had an affair with Girgis. She had had an affair with Con Taylor. Two of them were dead. It was the juxtaposition.

I had been looking for Girgis's murderer in the area of his hashish and heroin smuggling. Marie, who had worked for him, had to be tied in. I hadn't looked in the area of his amatory exploits. Nor in Marie's.

Once I saw it, it became clear as daylight.

I couldn't even legitimately blame myself for not saving Marie. I could feel guilty, and regretful. But it wasn't rational; only personal. Sorry, Marie. Sorry I'm so stupid.

But who would believe that on an island as chic and sophisticated on the one side, and as orgiastic and free love preaching on the other, somebody would kill two people over a piece of ass?

Once I knew it, it was easy to piece it together. Girgis had been killed the first night I had visited Chantal. That was the same night Sonny returned from Athens with Jane. He had been hanging around the taverna before dinner. When I came back later and met Kirk for the first time, Sonny was gone and had disappeared.

Marie had been killed the day after my fight with the hippies outside the Cloud 79. It was Sonny who had found me. I had given him the next day off. He knew I was going to stay home. He had asked for the day off, in fact.

So he was available both times.

It was slim evidence. Slimmer than what Pekouris and I had against Chuck and his machete. But I didn't need any more evidence. I knew Chuck hadn't done it. And I knew Sonny was guilty; in exactly the same way I knew it was Marie's body I was going to find when I walked out on the beach at Georgio's.

Sonny, the hippie. Sonny, the pacifist. Sonny the free-love advocate. Sonny the anti-violence man. Sonny the millionaire, who only lived off what he earned. Sonny, the boatman. My Sonny. My *Today the university, tomorrow the world* Sonny. Who in the past week had with great craftiness devoted himself to trying to become my friend. He wasn't, I guessed, even worth being called despicable. But I sure didn't like him.

Every time I looked at him, I saw Sweet Marie – Marie in the water, her nearly cut off arm spouting blood, trying to avoid Sonny's speedboat, as it roared down to make its second pass. Marie trying to jerk her head away, and hold pressure on her spouting, ruined arm at the same time. I wondered again if she had known? Had she recognized the boat? Had she thought it was an accident, the first time? Had she seen Sonny?

He pretended to come out of it as we came out the other side of the rough chop at the entrance. He began to groan more and more. Then he raised his head. Then he tried to move his arms. He pretended surprise. But he spoke too soon. He'd been faking, all right.

'What happened?'

I didn't say anything.

'Please untie me. Please get this rope off me. It's killing me. I can't stand it.'

I didn't say anything. We were about rounding the point.

'I said, please untie me. At least let me sit up. This position is murdering me. I'm getting cramps.'

I said nothing. I went on running the boat. It didn't take much running, out here.

'Please, at least let me sit up. I'm dying like this. I'm so uncomfortable it's killing me, damn it!'

I put the two holding ropes on the helm bar. I didn't hurry. I untied the cord between his hands and feet and let him straighten out. I got him up on the bench and tied his hands to the stanchion behind him.

'Can't you untie my feet? My legs are cramping.'

'No.' I sat back down. I left the holding ropes on.

'Where are you taking me?'

'In to Tsatsos Port, to the police station.'

'It won't do you any good. I'll deny everything.'

'Go ahead,' I said.

'They won't testify against me. Jane can't, and I'll buy Kirk off. It will be your word against mine.'

'Fine.'

'You hate me, don't you?'

'What would make you happiest? If I said yes, or no?'

'If you said yes,' Sonny said.

'Then, no. I don't hate you.'

'Yes, you do. I know you do.'

'Stop playing games, Sonny,' I said. 'You've been playing games too long. You're the result of what we socio-criminologists call over-crystallized self-indulgence. I suppose you can't help it. But I don't give a shit.'

He didn't say anything to that, for a while.

'You know what they're going to do to you?' I said. 'They're going to take you out in the prison yard, and stand you up against the wall, and put a blindfold on you, and a squad of Greeks are going to shoot rifle bullets into your chest cavity. The trouble is they don't know anything about indulgence in Greece yet. They're not an affluent society. You should have waited till you got home to kill your wife's lovers.'

'Do you believe in the death penalty?' he said.

'No. I don't,' I said. 'But I'm not a Greek. I'd lock you up for life and make a guinea pig out of you, and study you to see what went wrong with you somewhere back down the line.'

'I believe in the death penalty,' he said. 'I didn't used to. But I've come around to it. Lately.'

'Well,' I said, 'you better. My advice to you is to think of it as a game, Sonny. Just a game. Like all the other games you play. Like when you ran down Marie in your speedboat. Or when you cut off Girgis's head and buried it. It's only a game. That way it'll keep you from crapping and peeing in your pants when they stand you up.'

'You're a pretty cruel son of a bitch,' he said.

'I guess that's what I am,' I said. I let him breathe a while. 'You want to talk about it?'

He turned his head at me and glared. 'I'll tell you nothing, you fascist pig son of a bitch.'

I let go the roped helm and stepped to him and all in one movement right-hooked him on the jaw. It slewed his head around until his tied hands brought him up short. It wasn't much of a punch. I was too weak, and hurt too much. It probably hurt me more than it hurt him. But it gave me a great deal of satisfaction.

'Mind your manners,' I said, and sat back down. I was trembling, but I didn't know whether from fury, or my side, or plain fatigue.

'That's what I mean,' Sonny said. 'You see what I mean? You're supposed to treat criminal prisoners with humanity. I know my rights. I don't have to talk.'

'Okay. Don't talk about it,' I said.

Then he started to cry.

'You don't know what it was like,' he said after a while. I didn't answer.

'I used to lay awake nights,' Sonny said. 'Night after night. Thinking about it. Thinking about her. And them. You didn't any of you understand her. I was the only one. I knew her needs.'

'Didn't you have other women of your own?'

'For a while. But I didn't want them. I wanted her. I knew it was wrong, to want one woman. I couldn't help it.'

'When did you first decide to kill Girgis?'

'Coming home on the plane from Athens. I was just sitting there. I decided to kill him first. He was such an evil bastard.'

'And then you just went down the line,' I said.

'No. I was going to take them chronologically. But it became too difficult. Then when you had that fight, I knew you wouldn't be able to go out or go diving. And I knew Marie was going. Actually, Kirk came before Marie, chronologically. But it became too difficult to adhere to a strict chronology. So I took Marie second.'

I bit my teeth together for a minute. 'Why did you cut off Girgis's head?'

'That was an idea of the moment. I hated his guts so much. But then I thought it might make it look like a gang killing, for the hashish. It's not as easy to do as you might think.'

'No,' I said. 'I guess not. Where did you bury it?'

'It's in that chapel yard, back from the head of the draw, in that grove of trees I put it under one of those ancient altar stones in the yard. The knife's with it.'

'Did you kill him first? Or was it the knife killed him?'

'I killed him first. I hit him with a rock, and then I choked him.'

'Did the throat pump when you cut it, or did it just flow out?'

'It pumped. But that doesn't matter. He was already dead. To all intents and purposes.'

'I guess you don't feel bad about any of it, do you?' I said.

'In a way I do. I hated to have to do it. You know, I never really minded the one-nighters, like Steve, and all the others. It was the ones like Girgis and Kirk and Marie, and Con Taylor, who tried to have real love affairs with her. And talk to her about love. And lie to her. Those were the ones who really didn't understand her.'

'Marie didn't talk about love to her,' I said. 'Maybe she talked to Marie about it.'

'Oh, yes she did. There's no question in my mind about that.'

I didn't argue. 'Just for the record, how many times did you have to hit Marie?' I said.

'I hit her twice. But I think the once would have been enough anyway.'

'Yes,' I said. 'Yes, I think it would.'

'I'm really a martyr, that's the truth,' he said, as if he were trying on a new suit for size. 'A martyr is what I am. Some day there will be freedom. Real freedom. Complete freedom.'

'Did she yell?' I said. I found I had this thing about her, that I hoped she hadn't panicked. That she had gone out cool and clean and thinking clearly.

'No,' Sonny said. 'Or if she did, I didn't hear her. Of course, it would be hard to hear, with the motor.'

What with all the pauses, we had passed Georgio's and rounded the lighthouse, and now we were approaching the Port jetty, jutting out whitely into the blue water. Lots of small boats were out, and lots of people dotted the swimming beaches.

'Well, this is where you get off, Sonny,' I said. I slacked off on the throttle.

'I guess you think I'm evil, hunh?' Sonny said. 'People always think that of martyrs.'

'I don't know, Sonny,' I said, 'I guess I do. I don't know.'

'You do. You people always do. Look at Savonarola. He was fighting the decadence of his time, too.'

'Yes,' I said. 'Savonarola was the one who made fanatic believers out of all the kids and got them to turn in their parents.'

'Will you shake hands with me before I go in?'

'Yes,' I said. 'I'll shake hands with you. But not until I untie you.'

I pulled around the jetty and cut the throttle again, to enter the Port.

CHAPTER SIXTY

We created quite a stir in the Port. Both of us were covered with splotches of my blood, and I was limping, and Sonny was tied. I had to walk him across the crowded quayside to the police post from the boat and before we got there there was a mob around us. Tourists, and hippies, and freaks, and Greeks.

I was beginning to feel chipper again. I guessed getting rid of Sonny helped. I felt I was once again my inimitable, indestructible, bent but unbreakable self.

I got out of there as fast as I could. I dictated my deposition to a Greek girl from one of the shops who spoke English, and signed it. I told the chief I was taking the Daisy Mae. He was pleased and delighted to let me. I wanted to go to Glauros and get my face sewed up.

But when I got Daisy Mae outside the jetty, I brought her around to starboard and headed for the yacht harbour. I wanted to call Chantal. I wasn't going to cover up for her heroin ring. And I wanted to tell her.

Also I wanted to call Pekouris in Athens. The fat chief was calling him right now, from the town. But I hadn't put anything about the heroin ring in my deposition, and I wanted to tell him what I'd discovered about it. Then we would see what he did.

When I got upstairs to my trusty little bathroom mirror, and began the same old daily repair job, I saw my cheek was laid open from the point of the cheekbone back along the bone almost to my ear. You could see the white bone at the bottom, between the labia of the cut. This one was going to take a lot more than a year to fade.

I washed myself, and put on clean clothes and put the bloody ones to soak in cold water, and put a fresh compress bandage on the gash, and went to call Chantal.

It was five o'clock and she should have just gotten home from her afternoon bridge game with the Greek Chorus ladies.

She had.

She wasn't going to be very happy when she heard

what I had to tell her.

'I've had an interesting afternoon,' I said. 'How was yours?'

'Fine. I won a few drachmas.'

'Well, I caught my murderer,' I said. 'He's all tied and taped and delivered to the local police.'

There was a frightened sounding pause from her end. 'You did?'

'Aren't you going to ask who it was?'

'Who was it?'

'Sonny Duval. He's already confessed. He killed them both, because they had affairs with his wife. And he intended also to kill Con Taylor and Jim Kirk. How about that?'

'Oh, no!' Chantal said, in a kind of helpless wail. 'Oh, no!'

'You don't sound very pleased,' I said grimly.

'Oh, I am. I am. I really am. I just wish that I'd known, is all.'

'You thought all along it was Kirk, didn't you?'

'Well, it looked that way. Didn't it?' she said. 'Well, damn!' In that wail again.

'That wasn't why I called you, though.'

There was that frightened sounding pause again. I cleared my throat. 'I'm calling Pekouris in a little while about the murders, and I'm telling him all I know about your heroin ring. I'm telling you so you can leave and get out of town for a while.'

'So you're turning me in,' she said.

'I'm turning in the operation. Not you,' I said. 'I'm sorry you're mixed up in it. But the operation I am turning in, yes.'

'Turning *us* in, then,' Chantal said bitterly.

'If that's the way you want it. If you'd seen what heroin has done to too many people in my town, too many dumb-ass kids, you'd know why I can't do anything else.'

I took a breath. 'I'm sorry about you. But I don't give a damn what happens to Kronitis and the others. Kronitis will probably buy his way out of it, anyway. But I'd like to see Kirk and the rest of them go to jail for a good long time.'

'Well,' she said, slowly. 'I suppose there's nothing I can

do to dissuade you. You're just ruining my life, is all.'

'Go away for six months or a year,' I said. 'That's why I'm calling you. When you come back, it will be blown over. They probably won't even book you then.'

'But my life will still be ruined among my friends, and everywhere I'm known. Paris. Rome.'

'Maybe not. You may even become a minor hero. A celebrity. That's the way things work nowadays. Get yourself on a New York TV programme.'

She didn't say anything for a little bit. I listened to her thinking. Then she said, 'Well, I guess I've got something to tell you, too, then. In this connection. If that's the way you're going to handle it.'

'What do you mean?'

'Has Leonid – Has Kronitis called you yet?'

'No. But you promised me you wouldn't call him today.'

'I didn't call him! He called me.'

'So?'

'He will certainly be calling you. He may have already. While you were out solving murders.' She laid a heavy bitterness on the Murders. Then she paused and took a breath. 'Freddy Tarkoff is here.'

'Tarkoff?' I said.

'Yes, Tarkoff. And he'll almost certainly be wanting to see you. He flew in from New York this morning, and flew down in a private plane. He's at Leonid's villa.'

'Tarkoff,' I said, and another lightbulb flashed on somewhere. 'Well, I'll be damned.'

'Yes! Yes, Tarkoff! Who did you think has been running this whole thing and masterminding it? Surely you didn't think it was poor old Leonid? It was Freddy's idea. And he's been running it from the beginning.'

'Tarkoff?' I said. 'Well, I will be damned. My Freddy Tarkoff.'

'It was Freddy who got me to be his runner for him. It was Freddy who organized everything. That was how I lied to you last night. I let you think it was Leonid. I'd sworn not to tell you.'

'That was what Kirk meant when he said powerful people had been protecting me,' I said.

'When things began to go *really* bad yesterday, and we thought it was Kirk, and thought you were going to take him in, Leonid called Freddy in New York. He took the first plane he could get.'

'Freddy Tarkoff,' I said inanely.

'Maybe you will think twice before you call Pekouris. I suggest you talk to Freddy before you do.'

'I'm putting the call in anyway,' I said, shortly. 'Also, I'm leaving tonight on the seven o'clock ferry.'

'You mean because Freddy came?' Chantal said. 'He wants to see you.'

'I was planning it, anyway,' I said abruptly. 'But now I'm certain.'

I could hear her voice still coming out of the instrument, as I hung up on her.

I went over to my bar and made myself a big, stiff Scotch which I only wetted with soda. I had already made one big one when I first came in. This one tasted better. I looked around the place with it in my hand. There wasn't much around to mark that I had ever stopped there. I was not caring. I raised the glass and toasted the portrait of one of Georgina's stuffy English burgher 19th-century ancestors over the fireplace, but I was really toasting Freddy Tarkoff.

Then I went over and placed my call to Pekouris. A secretary's voice, in excellent English, told me the Inspector had already left his office for Tsatsos and would be there within two hours. He had moved faster than I expected. A lot faster. Well, I would catch him here, later. I was even willing to miss my ferry to see him.

I had not hung up the phone very long, before it rang again the long distance ring, and Kronitis came on. I went through the whole rigmarole of politeness with him. I listened respectfully to what he had to say. I said I would be delighted to come over to his place, right away, to see my old and dear friend Freddy Tarkoff.

Then, and only then, I told him I had just returned from capturing my murderer. Or rather, Girgis's and Marie's murderer. I had just delivered said murderer to the local police chief. There was a long silence on the phone. The murderer was Sonny Duval, an American millionaire who lived on an old boat here in the harbour. I thanked Mr Kronitis for calling me and I hung up the phone.

Then I made myself another drink and shouldered into

my clean shirt, not without some wincing, and unlocked my closet and took Mr Kronitis's $4,000 retainer out of my briefcase and put it in my wallet. I tried to avoid thinking how wafer-thin the wallet was going to feel later. Screw his lousy blood money. I went out and fired up the *Daisy Mae* to go to Glauros.

But before I did I had one more quick drink.

CHAPTER SIXTY-ONE

I realized as I ran her out into the freshening breeze and sparkling sea toward the mainland, that it was the first time I had ever had *Daisy Mae* out alone. Always before there was somebody with me, Sonny, or Chantal, or Marie. I loved being alone on her.

I would have loved to take her up along the coast exploring by myself.

Instead, I ran her to Glauros.

The chauffeur and the big black Rolls were waiting on the dock. It was going to be the same routine, with me the football again. Well, I had had some practice being a football lately. I told the chauffeur he was going to have to wait a bit for kick-off time.

'Very good, sir,' he said, with English unruffleability. He was still sporting his big .357 Magnum in his armpit.

The doctor was down the single street of Western storefronts. He had a snazzy waiting room. His receptionist took me ahead of several poor-looking Greek women with haggard faces, when she saw my face. It took him about ten minutes to sew me up. Nine stitches.

But it was when he looked at the X-ray of my ribs that he got excited.

Unfortunately, he spoke English. He also had that over-developed sense of his own importance the medical profession gives a man who gets used to being vastly overpaid for helping humanity.

'When did this happen?' Sternly.

'Four days ago,' I said.

'My dear sir, you have been walking around for four

days with two broken ribs. Your physical activity, whatever it has been, has aggravated them considerably. You should be in bed. Instead, it appears you have been in some kind of a fight. You have this strange abrasion on your back that looks like a human bite.'

'Doc,' I said. 'What can you do for the ribs?'

He shrugged. 'Tape them up. Then go to bed. Take care of yourself until they can knit.'

'I'll do that, Doc, as soon as I can,' I said.

'You must do it now,' he said brusquely. 'By the way, that was an excellent bandage, that you had there. Who did it?'

'I did it myself.'

He stared at me.

'Well, I instructed a friend how to do it. She actually did the taping.'

He gave me a sort of Don Juanish look. So I gave him back one of my merry winks.

'And now, Doc, if you will just tell me what I owe you for all this humanitarian aid and advice. I'll pay you and let you get back to fleecing your regular customers.'

His eyes turned to black flint. He grabbed a piece of letterhead paper that must have cost a dollar a sheet and wrote on it and handed it to his girl. Outside, as if all this part was too lowbrow for the doctor's sensibilities, she read me what was on it. I paid, but bitterly.

It was pretty high, for nine stitches, an X-ray, and a lecture.

Kronitis's chauffeur was still waiting patiently by his big Rolls. He opened the door for me and I got in and we started the routine. We went up and over the same dry, sere hills. The same peon was at the gate, or anyway he had the same face.

When I came into the big deep-carpeted office, there were two men in it now, instead of one. Kronitis was behind the desk.

The other man turned to me, as the male secretary shut the door. He had a rueful, sorrowful smile on his face.

Tarkoff was tanned, slim and muscular. But he was always tanned, slim and muscular. His New York suit pants and white shirt and tie stuck out like a sore thumb here. He had taken the suit coat off.

'Hallo, Freddy,' I said.

'Hallo, Lobo,' he said, warmly, and stepped toward me with his hand out.

I put my hands in my pockets.

'Let's do this fast,' I said. 'There're only a couple of things. I'm returning Mr Kronitis here his $4,000 retainer, because he fired me before I finished the case. I've made out a bill for my daily fees and expenses up to the time he fired me. He can send a cheque to my New York account.'

I took Kronitis's bills out of my old wallet. It collapsed. I put it away.

'The other thing is that I'm turning over to Pekouris all the information I've turned up on this little heroin operation of yours. I don't honestly know what Pekouris will do with it. Or whether he'll do anything. You guys can take it from there.'

They both started to talk at once. Freddy held up a lean, tanned hand. 'First, the money.'

'I told him he should keep it, Freddy,' old Kronitis said. He came out from behind the desk. Between us two he looked elderly.

'Then you should keep it,' Freddy said, and looked at me.

'I don't figure I earned it,' I said. I stepped to the desk and laid out the forty $100 bills in a leafed row. They were only a little more wrinkled than when Kronitis gave them to me brand new. 'Anyway, it's pretty dirty money,' I said. It didn't look dirty.

'As for Pekouris,' Freddy said, 'we don't have any special dealings with him.'

It was not as if a look passed between them. It didn't. It was more that they seemed to particularly avoid movement that might even be construed as a look passing between them. At the moment, that seemed enough evidence to me.

'So we don't know either, what he will do with your information,' Freddy said. 'We assume he'll have to put it on into the grinding machine. If it's laid in front of him baldly.'

'I'll believe that,' I said, 'because two such honest upright gentlemen like yourselves tell it to me.'

'That's a bit harsh,' Kronitis said.

I gave him a stony look. 'Is it?' I said. I shook my

head at him. 'You had me fooled, Mr Kronitis. You fooled me completely. That hurts my vanity a little. I just couldn't believe an upstanding decent old gentleman like you could be an international heroin trafficker. I believed you were being honest with me. That's my fault.'

'The reason you believed him,' Tarkoff said, 'was just because he was being honest. He didn't know anything about Kirk and Girgis Stourkos being involved in a stupid local hashish racket. He told you the truth.'

'He didn't tell me the truth about anything else,' I said.

'He wasn't asked,' Freddy said.

'That's true. And that's my fault.' I turned to Freddy. 'Naturally, I didn't make any connection between Mr Tarkoff here and the heroin ring. My fault again.'

'I'm sorry as hell this had to happen, Lobo,' Tarkoff said.

I gestured at the money, and then at Kronitis. 'I'm out of it. You gentlemen have to take it from here.' I started to turn to the door.

'Hold on,' Kronitis said. 'We would like to talk to you just a little bit about this whole thing.'

'I'm out of it,' I said. 'You talk to Pekouris.'

'Have you told him yet?' Kronitis asked.

'Not yet,' I said. 'But it's only because I missed him in Athens. He should be arriving here any time.' They were a good team. They worked well together. It was like the Russian cop routine. If Tarkoff had asked me that, I would have told him to go to hell.

'Will you just listen to us for five minutes?' Kronitis said, in his cool mathematician's voice.

I didn't answer. Behind me Freddy stepped to me and put his hand on my shoulder. 'Lobo.'

'Don't do that,' I said sharply. His hand went away.

'We would only like for you to listen,' Kronitis said levelly. 'I think that's reasonable.'

I turned back. 'I'll listen,' I said. 'But nothing is going to change my opinion.'

'We don't want to change your opinions,' Kronitis said patiently.

'My opinion is that you are a couple of low, sneaking, lying, conniving, criminal bastards,' I said.

'We still wouldn't want to change your opinions,'

341

Kronitis said. 'But we'd like for you to listen just a little to some factual aspects of this whole situation.'

'Go ahead,' I said. 'Tell me some factual aspects.'

'First,' Kronitis said, 'we have talked to Kirk.'

I stared at him. 'How the hell could you have talked to Kirk?'

'He came here,' Kronitis said in his dry matter-of-fact way. 'As soon as you left the villa with Duval in the *Daisy Mae*, he came here in the *Polaris*. He went around the other way. He brought the girl, the uh woman, Jane Duval, with him. We have also talked to her.'

I just looked at him.

Freddy Tarkoff, who knew my facial expressions pretty well, said, 'That's the God's truth, Lobo.'

'Oh, it's the truth,' Kronitis said hastily. 'They're still here. If you'll look out the window, you'll see *Polaris* down at my dock.'

I went to the window. I could see the top half of her at the man-made cove below the house. She sat there rocking quietly. Nobody was visible on her. Her cabin windows stared back blindly.

'He's a shrewd son of a bitch,' I said grudgingly.

'They're waiting on board,' Kronitis said.

'I don't want to see them,' I said quickly. 'I might punch both of them in the head. And I'm not up to it.'

'You don't have to see them,' Freddy said.

'The point is,' Kronitis said patiently, 'we have talked to both of them. Kirk can keep the girl quiet. It will cost us something.'

'Kirk is not famous for his generosity or honesty,' I said.

'As I've learned,' Kronitis said patiently. I suddenly had the feeling I was talking to a well-programmed, well-oiled computer system, walking around posing as a man. 'But we'll have to pay the girl, too. In any case, the girl is willing to keep her mouth shut about the villa and our business affairs there. She will keep it out of her deposition, to protect Kirk, and she'll keep it out of her testimony at the trial.'

'I see,' I said. 'But what about Sonny?'

'I think I might be able to arrange a trade with Duval,' Kronitis said. 'I'm not without influence in Athens, and I think I can arrange to guarantee him that he will not get a death sentence. In return, of course, he will have to keep his mouth shut about our business interests. The girl assures me that he will co-operate on such deal.'

'So that leaves only me,' I said.

'That is right,' he said, and smiled his thin dry smile.

'I don't expect to be here for the trial,' I said. 'Sonny's confessed, anyway. But I would fly back for it if it meant the difference in getting a conviction.'

'You're a hard man, when you set your mind to something, aren't you,' Kronitis said. It was not a question.

'Are you going back to New York, Lobo?' Freddy Tarkoff said.

'I don't know,' I said shortly.

'The girl is very shrewd,' Kronitis said. 'If there is no deal, if you give your information to Inspector Pekouris or the other law enforcement people, and implicate Kirk, she will tell everything she knows at the trial. She expressly mentioned Chantal von Anders. She seems to know about your feelings for Chantal.'

'Who told her that?' I said.

Kronitis raised his shoulders. 'I can only assume that Kirk told her, when he briefed her, on their way here.'

I didn't believe him. I didn't believe him at all. But it didn't make much difference.

'Is Jane Duval trying to get Sonny released entirely?' I asked.

'I think,' Kronitis said, 'I uh think if she had her choice, if she could pick the ending she wanted, she would have Duval committed somewhere to an institution for the criminally insane. Preferably in the United States.'

I shook my head. You had to admire it.

'I think there is some reason for thinking him perhaps slightly deranged,' Kronitis said softly.

'Yes. There's reason,' I said. 'And is she ever happy there is.'

Kronitis raised his shoulders again, and spread his hands. He didn't speak.

'So,' I said. 'That lays it all in my lap.'

'Exactly,' Kronitis said.

I didn't have to think about it. I had been thinking about it already. Ever since he first mentioned Chantal.

They had me up the back. Unless I wanted to just say screw it.

'This is the way they do it when the big shots and money get involved,' I said, and grinned at them. It hurt my cheek. 'Everybody saves a little something. I keep forgetting that, when I'm picking up pieces in my dirty little job down in the East Village. That's the way we used to do it in Chicago. Horse trading, my dad would call it.'

I guessed I didn't really mind it.

'It's one of the reasons I left Chicago,' I added.

It wasn't really such a bad solution. I didn't really want to see Sonny executed. And I didn't want to see Chantal ruined. The one I really wanted, the one who had really murdered both Girgis and Marie, was untouchable. Jane Duval. There was no way I could touch her.

'Okay,' I said. 'You've got yourselves a deal. Except that I'm a pretty good horse trader myself. And I've got a couple of conditions of my own.'

'What are they?' Freddy Tarkoff said.

'First, I want Chantal out of your racket, and your influence. She told me she wanted out. And I told her I'd get her out. I want a promise that you'll never try to use her as a carrier again, under any circumstances.'

Tarkoff smiled. 'What if she changes her mind, and comes and asks us some day?'

'Even then.'

Freddy shrugged.

'Second, I want this thing broken up. Here on Tsatsos. Totally. Dismantled, dismembered, shut down.'

'There's not much question of that,' Freddy said ruefully. 'You've already successfully accomplished that. Inadvertently, maybe. But nonetheless completely. When Kirk goes back, he's taking everything out and dumping it way off shore in the sea. I think we can guarantee you both of those, Lobo.'

'For this week,' I said. 'I'm thinking about next month. I'll keep an ear to the ground, Freddy. If I ever hear about you starting up again, here or anywhere, I'll come back around and blow you sky-high, by God. I'll go to Washington, even. I've got some contacts there. You guys didn't know it but you had a Narcotics Bureau man working undercover right under your noses. You very nearly hired him to work on the *Polaris*.'

They looked at each other. Freddy gave Kronitis a hard look.

'God,' Kronitis said. 'That man Gruner? Was a Narcotics fellow.'

'I can't prove it,' I said. 'He denied it. But I'd bet my bottom dollar on it.

'The truth,' I said, 'the truth is, you're a couple of rank amateurs. You may be good at figures,' I said to Kronitis, 'but you don't know anything about handling the creatures of the lower depths like Kirk. He's robbed and cheated you all around the horn.'

'You're absolutely right,' the old man said. 'I had no idea about anything.'

'But you're the one I really don't understand,' I said to Tarkoff. 'You're on the City Anti-Drug Commission. You make trips to Washington to help fight the drug traffic. You make speeches at the universities against drugs. I don't understand you.'

'They are two different things,' he said, and smiled. 'This was business. The other was a social duty.'

'So you're the angry citizen, fighting the criminal drug traffickers. Who turn out to be yourself,' I said. 'Do you ever catch you? You must be some kind of a schizophrenic.'

'Maybe I am,' Freddy said. 'But it was business. And a damned good business. And if I didn't do it, somebody else would. The other,' he shrugged. 'Well, I'm against the heroin traffic, in principle.'

'You're a wheeler-dealer,' I said contemptuously. 'You may blow yourself all apart some day.'

'Actually, it was you who gave me the idea,' Freddy said and gave me a rueful smile. 'Running around with you on your cases showed me what a really great market it was, in America. I had the rest of it, the contacts and the geographical position, all just waiting for me here, by accident. As they get tougher and tougher on the French labs in Marseille, it's beginning to spread out to other quieter areas.' He shrugged. 'It was a natural.'

'Was any of that money I helped you recover in Athens part of this?'

He gave me an unreadable look. 'A little. But only a

very small part of it. That's the truth, Lobo.'

'You must be nuts, sending me down here for a vacation,' I said.

He shrugged again, sorrowfully. 'Who knew some nut was going to start killing people, and blow it open? Normally you would have come and gone, and never noticed a thing.'

'I'm not trying to understand it,' I said. 'Or you. I don't even want to try. But if I ever hear of you starting anything else up down here, or getting Chantal von Anders involved in anything, I'll hound you all the way to the moon. I mean that.'

'I know you do. And I know what you're like when you get your teeth in something.' He gave me a sad smile. 'I'm just sorry all this happened. But there's not much chance of that, now,' he said. 'We're getting out of it. Entirely. Like you said, I'm afraid we're amateurs.

'Will you shake hands with me?' he asked.

'No,' I said. 'I shook hands with Sonny Duval, but I wouldn't shake hands with you. You've done me a lot of harm that you don't even know about. As far as I'm concerned you're not my friend. I never knew you. Maybe ten years from now I might be able to think about it. Shaking hands with you. Think about it, not do it.

'Well, I guess that winds it up, gentlemen,' I said. I hit the Gentlemen hard. I looked both of them in the face for a long moment. They both looked like sheep-killing dogs, as my old grandad would have said.

'Oh, there's one more thing,' I said. I stepped to the desk and picked up the still crisp sheaf of $100 bills. 'I'm taking this.'

'But, please,' Kronitis offered.

'No. Don't "Please" me,' I said. 'I'm taking it. You're not giving it. You've got nothing to do with it. You couldn't even stop me. Try to think of it like that. Think of it as though I've got a pistol at your head, and I'm taking it, and there's nothing at all you can do about it.'

'If you like,' Kronitis said. 'If that's how you prefer to think of it.'

'That's how,' I said. 'I prefer to think of it as I'm holding you up and robbing you.'

I put the sheaf of bills back into my wallet, and felt it grow fat again. I put it back in my pocket.

'You've still got my bill,' I said to Kronitis. 'Send the cheque to New York. Goodbye, Gentlemen,' I said, and went across the long room over their thick carpet to the door. There wasn't a sound behind me.

I went out the door and turned myself back into a football for delivery at Glauros and the *Daisy Mae*.

CHAPTER SIXTY-TWO

There wasn't much left to do. Just pack my bag.

I thought of calling Chantal. But then thought Oh, to hell with it. She had lied to me enough times. In fact, she was batting just about .1000. Why give her a chance to ruin that by being honest once?

I enjoyed the lone run back across the channel. At the last minute I veered off from the harbour, and took her out around the lighthouse point and back. When I tied up at the taverna and put the fenders over and stepped on shore and gave the keys to Dmitrios to hold, I felt like a grounded flier.

I started the dusty walk up to the house, then stopped and looked back once at the stocky little caique.

I half-hoped Pekouris would be waiting for me in my living-room. But he wasn't. He was much too smart for anything like that. There wasn't anything he wanted from me now. I was sure he had been on the phone with Kronitis.

I left 2000 drachs under a plate on the kitchen table for the old woman. More tip than she'd earned.

Then I got myself a big drink and went out and sat on my porch.

It wasn't such a bad finale really. It was not such a bad arrangement really, either. I supposed some years back I would have been incensed at the bald indecency of it. At least Chantal was all right, with this arrangement. Anyway, it was the best I could do for her.

I had a last minute thought, and went in and called Tarkoff at Kronitis's and told him I wanted him and Kronitis to pay Chantal $6000. Call it a separation pay, I said. He agreed. He was too guilty not to, and I used that on him. I didn't know why I chose the arbitrary figure of $6000. Instead of $5000, say, or $7000.

I still had my bag to pack. But when I got upstairs I found the upper floor was full of some kind of smoke. It smelled like garbage smoke. When I looked out the window, I saw that they were burning trash in an oil drum out behind Dmitri's. The freshening breeze was carrying the great clouds of acrid evil-smelling smoke straight across the vacant lot into my house. I stood at the window looking at it. I thought it was a fitting farewell, along with all the rest.

I finished the suitcase and strapped it down and took it down and set it in the living-room.

I got my briefcase out of the locked closet to put with the suitcase and saw Chuck's machete sitting there. I took it and took it downstairs and gave it to Georgina to give to Steve and Chuck. When she asked me if I wanted to leave any message with it, I thought a minute, then then said no. What the hell was I going to tell those two? I didn't like them any better now than I had when I'd saved their ass from a bum murder rap.

'They're really good boys, you know,' Georgina said.

I just looked at her. 'You don't know your ass from a bull fiddle, Georgina. That's the truth,' I said. 'They're a couple of bums. The percentage of phonies among hippies is no higher and no lower than any other given group. In other words, about 89.9%. That's what we insurance adjusters call a continuing statistic.'

'Isn't this smoke terrible?' she said.

'You ought to do something about that,' I said. 'But don't do it on my account.'

I shook hands with her, and escaped back upstairs.

I was content to sit on my porch with my drink till time for the ferry. Smoke or no smoke.

I didn't hear the door open, but I heard the steps on the little stairs.

'I couldn't let you go like that,' she said coming out through the living-room. 'Don't you even want to kiss me goodbye?'

'Sure,' I said. I put down my drink and put my arms around her, and gave her a medium-light, passionless kiss.

'Is there any chance I might see you in Paris?'

'I don't see how,' I said. 'We don't run in the same

circles.' I stepped back, and looked at her a minute. Her lower lip was trembling. 'Anyway, you're out of your thing,' I said. 'They may even give you a little severance pay.'

'I don't know whether I'm glad or not,' she said. 'What will I do now?' She worked up a smile. 'I guess I can sell my hot body to a rich old Greek. But I'm getting a little too old even for that.'

'There must be some around,' I said. I slugged back the rest of my drink. 'I've got a horsecab waiting, honey. You go down and have a drink with Georgina.'

I went past her and got the suitcase and my briefcase.

'Tell me something, will you?' I said from the door.

'Yes. If I can, I will.'

'Why did you come to me with that phony made-up story about Girgis blackmailing you?'

She stood and looked at me. 'I made it up on the moment. Because I wanted to get close to you. I had a little thing for you. And I wanted to interest you.'

I nodded. I went out and shut the door.

At the ferry dock in the Port I went on board and put my suitcase down on deck and went to the rail. Nobody had come to say goodbye, just as nobody had come to say hallo when I arrived.

Above my head the big horn hooted twice. I remembered my next alimony payment was due in two weeks.

James Jones

The Thin Red Line
His novel of the Marines on Guadalcanal—a gory, appallingly accurate description of men at war. 'Raw, violent, powerful and terrible, the most convincing account of battle experience I have ever read.' *Richard Lister, Evening Standard*

From Here to Eternity
The world famous novel of the men of the U.S. Army stationed at Pearl Harbour in the months immediately before America's entry into World War II. 'One reads every page persuaded that it is a remarkable, a very remarkable book indeed.' *Listener*

The Merry Month of May
Paris in the Spring of 1968: students on the rampage and their effect on a wealthy American family living in Paris. 'Very gripping . . . a novel of our time which takes the reader into the heart of the Revolution. The atmosphere is splendidly conveyed.' *Financial Times*

 Fontana Books

Ross Macdonald

'Classify him how you will, he is one of the best American novelists now operating . . . all he does is keep on getting better.' *New York Times Book Review*. 'Ross Macdonald must be ranked high among American thriller-writers. His evocations of scenes and people are as sharp as those of Raymond Chandler.' *Times Literary Supplement*. 'Lew Archer is, by a long chalk, the best private eye in the business.' *Sunday Times*

Sleeping Beauty

The Instant Enemy

The Moving Target

The Underground Man

The Way Some People Die

The Galton Case

Black Money

Find a Victim

The Barbarous Coast

The Goodbye Look

 Fontana Books

Fontana Books

Fontana is best known as one of the leading paperback publishers of popular fiction and non-fiction. It also includes an outstanding, and expanding, section of books on history, natural history, religion and social sciences.

Most of the fiction authors need no introduction. They include Agatha Christie, Hammond Innes, Alistair MacLean, Catherine Gaskin, Victoria Holt and Lucy Walker. Desmond Bagley and Maureen Peters are among the relative newcomers.

The non-fiction list features a superb collection of animal books by such favourites as Gerald Durrell and Joy Adamson.

All Fontana books are available at your bookshop or news-agent; or can be ordered direct. Just fill in the form below and list the titles you want.

_____

FONTANA BOOKS, Cash Sales Department, G.P.O. Box 29, Douglas, Isle of Man, British Isles. Please send purchase price, plus 8p per book. Customers outside the U.K. send purchase price, plus 10p per book. Cheque, postal or money order. No currency.

NAME (Block letters)
_____

ADDRESS
_____

_____

_____

While every effort is made to keep prices low, it is sometimes necessary to increase prices on short notice. Fontana Books reserve the right to show new retail prices on covers which may differ from those previously advertised in the text or elsewhere.